A
Letter
From
Pearl
Harbor

BOOKS BY ANNA STUART

The Berlin Zookeeper
The Secret Diary

A
Letter
From
Pearl
Harbor

ANNA STUART

bookouture

Published by Bookouture in 2021

An imprint of Storyfire Ltd.
Carmelite House
50 Victoria Embankment
London EC4Y 0DZ

www.bookouture.com

ISBN: 978-1-80019-846-3
eBook ISBN: 978-1-80019-845-6

This book is a work of fiction. Whilst some characters and
circumstances portrayed by the author are based on real people
and historical fact, references to real people, events, establishments,
organizations or locales are intended only to provide a sense of
authenticity and are used fictitiously. All other characters and all
incidents and dialogue are drawn from the author's imagination
and are not to be construed as real.

For my Auntie Barbie – an alpha amongst beta readers.
Thank you for all your help and support.

Prologue

Ginny laughed out loud as a smiling sailor spun her across the crowded dance floor, sending her silky red skirts swirling around her legs. With four of the biggest destroyers back in Pearl Harbor this afternoon, Honolulu was packed with men in crisp white uniforms, eager to dance, and Ginny hadn't sat down all night. Her feet were aching but she didn't care. It was the first Saturday in December, the Christmas decorations were up in the Royal Hawaiian Hotel and, despite the many soldiers and sailors all around, it was almost impossible to believe there was a war going on somewhere over the balmy Hawaiian horizon.

The song ended and Ginny thanked her dancing partner, relieved when her friend Lilinoe grabbed her hand and pulled her off the floor.

'I have to get a drink, Ginny,' the petite Hawaiian girl gasped. 'I'm parched.'

'Me too,' she agreed. 'Let's find Jack.'

Her older brother was sitting with their friends at a table out on the Ocean Lawn, and as the girls headed gladly into the relative cool of the night, Ginny paused to take in the golden sands of Waikiki and the great stretch of the Pacific beyond, sparkling in the moonlight. Even in December the Hawaiian air was soft and warm. As the palm trees waved gently over the myriad fairy lights illuminating the terrace, she put a hand to her heart, unable to quite believe she was truly here.

'You all right, sis?'

Ginny turned her attention back into the buzzing bar and her brother. He was sitting with his girl, Penny, pulled tight up against him, tenderly stroking her blonde hair. That boy was so in love! Ginny wasn't convinced about the whole happy-ever-after thing herself, but it certainly seemed to be working for Jack.

'I'm very well, thank you. Just drinking in the beauty of the island.'

Jack smiled and stood up to join her at the edge of the lawn, pulling her in for a quick hug. Ginny was tall but Jack even more so and she fitted easily under his arm, their hair a matching shade of chestnut as he dipped his head to touch hers.

'I'm so glad we came out here, Gin.'

She threw her arms round him, hugging him tight.

'Me too, Jack, me too. It's so pretty, so peaceful.' At that moment, a roar of raucous laughter rang out from the group at the next table and Ginny lifted a wry eyebrow. 'OK, not *that* peaceful!'

She stepped back to the table to pick up her Mai Tai and took a deep drink. It was zingy with the pineapples that grew on the slopes just above Honolulu and was the freshest thing she'd ever tasted. You didn't get this back in Tennessee, and Ginny intended to make the very most of all that Oahu had to offer this festive season. She looked to the model Santa on the beach, driving his wooden sleigh up into the stars above the Pacific, and, hooking her arm through her brother's, raised her glass to her friends.

'Happy Christmas!'

'Happy Christmas,' they chorused, but then, somewhere inside the hotel, midnight chimed out. Lilinoe groaned.

'It's late, Ginny. We should really head home. We're flying tomorrow, remember?'

Ginny did remember. She'd been teaching flying lessons at the John Rodgers airfield for five happy months, and bookings had never been so tight as more and more people scrambled to learn to fly. She was taking her friend Will up at dawn for his last lesson before his pilot's test – but dawn was still ages away.

'Just a couple more dances, doll,' she pleaded. 'The weather's set fair and they'll be easy flights.'

Lilinoe smiled. 'Just a couple more dances then.'

Ginny beamed, grabbed her friend's hand, and made a dive for the ballroom where the great and the good of the Pearl Harbor command were happily dancing the night away. She did not look back to the ocean. She did not see the moonlight shining a silver path across the water, or the waves plashing on the soft shore. And she most certainly did not see six Japanese aircraft carriers sliding into position behind a set of rocky islands four hundred miles away and readying their planes for first light on 7 December 1941.

Chapter One

Sunday 17 February 2019

Robyn Harris stared up at the big old house, tears tangling in her throat in much the same way that the ivy tangled in the brickwork before her. *Ridiculous*, she told herself crossly. She was twenty-four years old, this was her happy childhood home, and inside was her beloved Granny Ginny, so there was nothing to fear. But she still found herself lingering at the bottom of the drive, shivering as the February chill crept into her bones. She'd forgotten how bleak it could be in England. Two years of Hawaiian sun had spoiled her and she tugged her woefully inadequate denim jacket tighter across her chest. *Get a move on*, she urged herself, but the thought of her poor grandmother lying in bed, pale and helpless, was too much to bear.

Suddenly the front door flew open, scraping across the tiled porch and making her feel instantly like a teenager again. With Granny Ginny's razor-sharp hearing, the noise of that door had been a nightmare if you'd wanted to sneak in late.

'Are you going to stand there like an idiot all day, or what?'

Her older sister, Ashleigh, swung out into the porch in her wheelchair and glared at her. Robyn sighed.

'Nice to see you too, sis,' she said, uprooting her feet and moving towards the door.

Ashleigh tossed her chestnut hair.

'Well, it's not exactly "nice", is it? None of this is nice, as you'd know if you'd got here sooner. Poor Granny has been lying in her bed waiting for you.'

Robyn gulped. She'd forgotten how direct her big sister could be. 'I'm sorry, Ash. It wasn't easy getting flights.'

'Or tearing yourself away from all those beaches and cocktail bars?'

'Hardly! I've been in Honolulu for two years. I can't even remember the last time I actually went onto the sand at Waikiki.'

'Boo hoo for you.'

Robyn bit her lip and prayed for patience. She'd missed her sister but looking down at her, bristling with bitterness, she had to admit that she mainly missed the Ashleigh she'd grown up with rather than the spiky woman she'd become. Not that she blamed her. The horrible accident that had landed her in the hated wheelchair would have been enough to make anyone spiky, and especially her hot-headed big sister.

'Please, Ash. I'm here now, aren't I?'

She leaned down, reaching out her arms for a hug. Ashleigh moved stiffly forward in her wheelchair, but then her arms closed around Robyn's back with surprising fierceness.

'At least you beat Mum and Dad back,' she mumbled into her shoulder. 'No surprise there.'

Robyn squeezed harder. Their parents were wonderful people, but devoted to their work as humanitarian engineers and forever off on projects to improve the lot of the poor around the world. Robyn and Ashleigh were very proud of them but throughout their lives they'd been little more than a fleeting presence, home for a month and then gone again. It had been Granny Ginny who had given them stability, a home – a childhood. And now she was dying. Robyn pulled back and sat on the bench to one side of the porch to avoid standing over Ashleigh.

'How is she?' Tears pooled in her sister's hazel eyes and Robyn's heart sank. Even in the terrible weeks after her accident, Robyn had rarely seen Ashleigh cry. Shout, yes; rage, even scream; but not cry. 'That bad?'

'She's just so weak, Rob, and so grey. Fighting this is taking all her strength and I don't think she can do it for much longer.'

Tears tangled in Robyn's throat again. Their grandmother was only two years off her hundredth birthday so it was little wonder that she'd fallen ill, but she'd been such a robust character all her life that it was still a shock. She glanced through the front door to the wide staircase beyond.

'I'd better go up and see her.'

'You'd better. She's been waiting for you – holding on, you know.'

Robyn's stomach churned; this all felt horribly real now.

'I really did come as soon as I could, Ash. Work's been so busy and finding flights wasn't easy.'

'Robyn, you work at an airport.'

'I know that, but it doesn't mean I can just rejig the schedule. I design planes, Ash, not fly them.'

'Even so, you—' The tinkle of a bell from inside the house cut her off. 'That's Granny. She's heard you, you'd better get up there.'

Robyn nodded and looked again to the stairs. She told her feet to move but they were pathetically reluctant. Granny Ginny had been such a force of nature all her life – a vibrant, go-getting American dame who never took no for an answer and loved an adventure. Robyn didn't want to see her lying ill on her deathbed.

'Chicken,' Ashleigh teased.

Robyn looked at her, grateful that her sister was trying to lighten the mood.

'Chicken,' she admitted.

Ashleigh reached out and, to her surprise, squeezed her knee.

'I don't blame you, sis. It's horrid. But there's no point in flying halfway around the world to sit in this frigging porch with grumpy old me, so get your arse up there.'

Robyn had to laugh at the sheer Britishness of the instruction. She'd missed that living in the States and so, giving her sister a weak smile, she stood up and made her way inside, dropping her

bag by the door as she'd done every day as a kid. She headed up
the stairs, taking the right side, away from the stairlift, and heard
the mechanism whir into life as her sister prepared to follow her.
Now that she was actually on the move, her feet picked up speed
of their own volition, and she scrambled upwards and flung herself
into her grandmother's beautiful, big bedroom.

'Granny!'

'Robyn, doll – you made it.'

Granny Ginny was, as Ashleigh had said, grey. Minus the full
make-up she'd worn every day of her life and the bright, elegant
wardrobe she'd always insisted on, she looked drained of colour.
Her voice quavered too but the emotion was strong within it and
her eyes, as they fixed on Robyn, burned with all her familiar
fervour. Robyn ran to her, clasping her outstretched hand and
bending to kiss her.

'Are you OK? Oh God, stupid thing to say. Obviously you're
not OK, but…'

'But I'm all the better for seeing you. Sit down, let me look at
you properly.' Robyn perched on the chair at the bedside, leaning
in to her grandmother who smiled at her. 'You're glowing, doll.
Hawaii suits you. But then, why wouldn't it? Gorgeous place. I
loved it there. Well, I did until…'

'The Japanese bombed Pearl Harbor?'

Ginny frowned.

'That wasn't the only reason.'

'Granny?' Robyn looked at her grandmother in alarm. 'What
do you mean? Did something else happen?'

In reply, Ginny simply said, 'I kept meaning to come and visit
you out there, Rob, but it's so far away, you know.'

'I know,' Robyn agreed, staring at her grandmother, sure there
was more to it.

'There are things I should have told you about my time in
Hawaii,' Ginny said. 'Things I should have… confessed.'

'Confessed?' Robyn looked over to Ashleigh as her sister wheeled herself into the room. 'Do you know about this?'

'Don't worry,' Ginny said. 'I haven't told Ash either. Always so damned competitive, you pair.'

Her voice was as sharp as it had ever been, though again Robyn caught a tremor in it which turned her heart upside down.

'Sorry. Oh, Granny, I'm so sorry. I came here to see you, not to argue with Ashleigh.'

Ginny rolled her eyes.

'You've always been the same, you two – at each other hammer and tongs one minute, then curled up like kittens the next.'

Robyn glanced at her sister, thinking about this. It was true that, back in the day, she and Ashleigh had spent many happy hours sprawled in each other's bedrooms, looking at magazines, watching telly, gossiping. There hadn't been so much of that after Ashleigh's accident, though, and then, of course, Robyn had gone to university in America and secured a job as an aeronautical engineer in Hawaii. These days, she FaceTimed Ashleigh whenever she could, but it was easier to bicker than to gossip via a screen and Ashleigh seemed to prefer bickering anyway. Not that that mattered right now. Robyn turned her eyes firmly back to her grandmother.

'We'll grow out of it, Granny,' she said.

'I doubt it, doll, but it would be good if the pair of you could at least learn to manage it. You'll need each other, you know, when…' Words failed her and she just gestured at the oxygen tank and drip set up either side of her oak bed. Both girls leaned in contritely as she composed herself, but then Ginny suddenly said, 'Remember the treasure hunts?'

Robyn glanced to Ashleigh, then back to their grandmother.

'Of course – you did the best treasure hunts in the world.'

Ginny smiled.

'They'd take me ages to set up but they kept you pair busy for hours so it was well worth it.'

Robyn looked out of the bay window to the sprawling garden beyond. A big, classically English lawn was flanked by tangles of rhododendrons and led down to an apple orchard, complete with potting shed, treehouse and tyre swing. It had been paradise for kids and they'd spent long summers happily playing in it. If they'd ever got bored, Ginny had set out a treasure hunt – a proper one, with silly riddles taking them from secret box to secret box until they'd finally track down the last one and unlock the coveted chocolate coins.

As they'd got into their teens, the hunts had widened out across the neighbourhood, taking them all day to reach the treasure which had also been upgraded to lipsticks, mascaras and cinema vouchers. One Comic Relief, Ginny had set up a hunt for the whole town, making it so hard that it had taken a week for someone to crack it. It had made the local news and Ginny had been dubbed Queen of the Hunt for ages afterwards. She'd loved it.

'Remember the hunt where the last box was in the river,' Ashleigh said now.

Robyn laughed.

'God, yes, in a special watertight box tied to the underside of one of the fishermen's platforms. I had to dig out a snorkel to dive down and release it.'

Granny Ginny smiled.

'I was very proud of that one.'

'Until I got an ear infection.'

She shrugged.

'What are antibiotics for, doll?'

Robyn laughed again and Ashleigh nudged her.

'What about the one with the box at the top of that oak tree on the green.'

'Cost me a bit to pay that Tommy Mills to climb up and put it there, as I recall,' Ginny chuckled.

'And me a broken arm to retrieve it,' Ashleigh said drily. 'I couldn't cycle for weeks. And I missed the under-fifteen champs.'

Her grandmother grimaced.

'You weren't very happy about that. Taught you to hold on tight, though.'

'True, and it's not like it mattered in the long run anyway, is it?'

Ashleigh hit at the wheels of her chair and silence fell. Robyn looked up at the support equipment standing sentinel either side of the bed and bit back tears.

'I'm sorry I wasn't here sooner,' she said.

Ginny reached out for her hand, clasping it with surprising strength.

'I'm sorry I won't be able to hang on longer, Robyn, but I've had a full life, you know.'

'A *good* life, Granny.'

'Mainly. Not always.'

'A few reckless treasure hunts are hardly going to keep you out of heaven!'

But at that the old lady shook her head, her expression serious. 'It's more than that. When I was younger I was an arrogant, foolish idiot. In the war…'

'Granny, the war's a long time ago. You—'

'Please, Rob, let me finish. You know that I flew?'

'Of course.'

It was a point of pride for both girls that their beloved grandmother had been one of America's first female pilots, helping ferry planes around the country in the Second World War to release their male counterparts for combat. She'd even come to Britain for a while to fly Spitfires with the ATA, leading to her eventually moving across the Atlantic for good.

'You were a brilliant pilot,' Robyn said to her now.

'I was. Too brilliant sometimes – or, at least, too dazzled by my own brilliance.'

'What do you mean?'

Robyn's stomach turned again. It was hard enough seeing her ever-active grandmother stuck in bed, but hearing her talk of herself like this was worse. She'd always had an all-American belief in her own abilities and had brought both girls up the same way. It was in part down to her fiery competitiveness and optimism that Ashleigh had gained her cycling scholarship to Indiana and Robyn a hurdling one to the University of Michigan. She'd taught her granddaughters to dream big, reach for the stars, want the world – all the clichés!

And OK, it hadn't exactly worked out for either of them as they'd imagined, but it had still driven them on. Even when Ashleigh had been lying in hospital after her accident, Ginny had refused to let her give up. 'You're good with wheels,' she'd said to her, over and over. Others had thought it harsh, cruel even, but her granddaughters had understood – Harris girls didn't give up. So what was Granny Ginny saying now?

The old lady had closed her eyes and for a dreadful moment, looking at her gaunt face on the pillow, Robyn thought she'd gone, but then they flew open again and she fixed them both with a familiar determined stare.

'I've done you a treasure hunt.'

'What?!'

It was the last thing Robyn expected her to say. She glanced to the window, confused, and Ginny chuckled.

'Oh, not here, doll. You know every nook and cranny here.'

Robyn looked to Ashleigh, who wheeled herself as close to the bed as she could get.

'Then where?'

Ginny smiled.

'Hawaii.'

'What?!' they chorused.

'How?' Robyn added.

Ginny gave her a slow wink.

'I have my ways and means. And if I can lay out the hunt from this pathetic old sickbed, then you two can definitely complete it.'

'Us *two*?' Ashleigh asked. 'You want me to go to Hawaii?'

'I do.'

'In this?!' She rapped her hands on the arms of her chair.

'Yes, Ash, in that, unless you've grown wings?'

'Granny!'

'Well, really. People do it, Ash. People fly without legs.'

Ashleigh winced and Robyn felt her pain. Her sister had stubbornly resisted all attempts to offer her the sort of amazing aids that could help her get back to something approaching normal life, but this was brutal, even for their frank grandmother. She felt a rush of guilt and a familiar urge to do more for her sister, but surely taking her to Hawaii was a huge leap? She pictured her flat in downtown Honolulu – it was barely big enough to fit basic furniture with room to squeeze between on foot, let alone manoeuvre a wheelchair. And it was five floors up in a block with a lift that could best be described as dodgy. She took her grandmother's hand again.

'How about you just talk to us now, Granny? Whatever it is, it can't have been that bad and we'd far rather hear it from you, wouldn't we, Ash?'

Ashleigh nodded eagerly; clearly she was no keener on coming to stay with Robyn than Robyn was on having her. Ginny, however, shook her head.

'I can't.'

'Why not?'

'You wouldn't understand, not unless you see it all for yourselves.' Her eyes misted and she smiled softly. 'It's been fun, these last weeks, working out how to set it all up. It's taken me back down memory lane and, let me tell you, it's been a helluva ride. The things we got up to back then, when Pearl Harbor was at the centre of the Pacific world and *we* were at the centre of Pearl Harbor.'

'We…?' Robyn asked.

'Me, my brother Jack, Penny, Eddie, Dagne, Joe, Lilinoe…' The names reeled off her tongue, faster and faster, and then died in a sudden fit of coughing that almost jack-knifed her wasted body. Robyn leaped back in alarm but Ashleigh was there straight away, grabbing the oxygen mask and placing it firmly over Ginny's mouth. The machine gave a little pop and hissed out air, soothing the rattle in her lungs, and slowly her coughing subsided.

Ginny lay back on the pillows, greyer than ever, and Robyn fumbled for Ashleigh's hand, finding it as shaky as her own. The tears that had been stuck in her throat from the moment she'd stepped onto the drive of her childhood home fell from her eyes.

'This is it, isn't it?' she whispered to her sister.

Ashleigh's fingers stroked her own.

'Not yet,' she whispered back. 'Not today. But yes, soon.'

'Very soon,' Ginny's voice rasped through the mask, making them both jump as it had always done when she'd somehow overheard them as kids. Her eyes opened, though the effort was clear. 'I don't want you to remember me like this, girls. I want you to remember me as the Queen of the Hunt. And I want you to know me as I was at your age – young and free and desperate to live life to the full, as you should be. Just don't make the mistakes I made.'

'Granny…' Robyn could feel her heart physically cracking apart. 'Granny, we love you, nothing will change that.'

Ginny gave a small nod of her head.

'Thank you. But if you love me, do this for me. Please. Go to Hawaii together. Drink Mai Tais in my memory. And do my last, foolish treasure hunt. Will you, girls? Will you do that for me?'

There was only one thing they could say. This glorious, buoyant livewire of a woman had been their rock and inspiration all their lives. She'd given so much to them and asked so little.

'We'll drink Mai Tais to you,' Ashleigh said.

'And we'll do the hunt,' Robyn added.

'All the way to the end?' Ginny pushed, her voice fading as she slipped into sleep. Robyn watched her, tears flowing.

'All the way to the end,' she promised.

Chapter Two

Sunday 3 March

The first thing Robyn saw when she finally let herself back into her Honolulu flat two weeks later was the letter on the mat, addressed in her grandmother's distinctive sloping hand. She'd meant it then; the treasure hunt was really happening. It was probably a good job after all the effort of getting Ashleigh to Hawaii, but even so her heart squeezed at the sight of the letter.

She already felt weakened from so many tears, so many memories shared, so much love poured out from family and friends as they'd said goodbye to their amazing grandmother. The funeral had only been two days ago, and she was raw with the sorrow of it and exhausted from the subsequent travel to a home that now felt so far away. A double-leg flight from London to LA and then on to Honolulu would have taken it out of anyone, but doing it with a wheelchair and an occupant who hated having any attention drawn to her had been testing to say the least.

A particular highlight had been Ashleigh telling the poor air hostess loudly that if the plane were to go down, she should leave her to go down with it.

'At least that accident would finish me off,' she'd said when a red-faced Robyn had shushed her. 'And at least it wouldn't be my fault.'

'The other one wasn't your fault either, Ash.'

Ashleigh had given a bitter laugh.

'Of course it was. I cycled into the blasted car, didn't I?'

'In driving rain and hideous fog. Your coach should never have taken you out. If it was anyone's fault, it was his.'

Ashleigh had shrugged.

'It was the British trials the next day. We had to get the miles in.'

There had been little more to say, and the two girls had sat in near silence half the way across the Atlantic. The day of the accident, Ashleigh had been just three months off heading to Marian University in Indiana on a cycling scholarship, and almost certainly about to make selection for the British team. In foul conditions, she'd smashed into the back of a stationary car, injuring her legs so badly that they'd never work again. It had been a dark, dark time for everyone, and only Ginny's indomitable cheer and determination had got them through. Now she was gone and Robyn wasn't sure she had the strength to replace her, though at least she was finally home.

'This it?' Ashleigh bashed her way into the flat, wheels scraping against the narrow walls of the corridor. 'It's not exactly a penthouse!'

'I never said it was.'

'I thought aeronautical engineers were well paid?'

'I've been saving for my own place – it seemed silly to throw money away on rent when I'm not even here much.'

'Because of your rampant social life?'

'Because I'm usually either at work or at training or, yes, out with friends.'

'Training?' Ashleigh's eyes narrowed. 'I thought you jacked in your hurdling scholarship.'

'I did,' Robyn said through gritted teeth, 'but that doesn't mean I don't still like hurdling. I train two or three times a week with a great group.'

'Do you compete?'

'Yes.'

'But not at the top level?'

'No, Ash, because—'

'Because you couldn't hack it.'

Robyn dug her nails into her palms. Receiving the scholarship to the University of Michigan, also renowned for the aeronautical engineering that so fascinated her, had been one of the best moments of her life and she'd flown off across the Atlantic with high hopes. At first things had gone well, but over time it had become clear to Robyn that, although she was good, she wasn't excellent, and as the stress had started impacting on her degree, she'd made the decision to prioritise her studies.

'Because I wasn't quite good enough to make either the US or British team, and I didn't want to give all my time up to a lost cause when I had a degree to earn,' she explained.

For her it had been simple pragmatism; for Ashleigh it had been cowardice, weakness, even cruelty to turn her back on her talent. No wonder they'd struggled to get on since. Now, Ashleigh snorted and turned her attention to shoving Robyn's dining table aside to allow herself the space to get into the main room.

'We can put that table away while you're here,' Robyn suggested with forced patience. 'And, look, you can have my bedroom. It's bigger. I'll go in the spare.'

'Spare' was pushing it as a description. 'Broom cupboard' was closer, and Robyn wasn't even sure she'd fit her long legs on the camp bed, but she'd figure it out somehow. It wouldn't be for long. Ashleigh's return flight was booked for two weeks' time, so they just had to crack on with this crazy treasure hunt and it would all be fine. She held the letter up to show her sister but Ashleigh had made it over to the window and was staring out, rapt.

'Nice view, hey?' Robyn said proudly, going to stand next to her and look between the roofs of the city to the golden strip of Waikiki Beach in the distance and the glittering bay beyond.

'Not bad, I guess. Do you know where Granny Ginny lived when she was here?'

'I asked her a few times but she always just said "downtown". Uncle Jack was at Hickham Field, just across the harbour entrance from the airport we flew into today, but Granny wasn't in the forces before Pearl Harbor so I think she was renting rooms. She was always weirdly coy about it.'

'And now we have to do this ridiculous treasure hunt to find out the truth.'

'Not ridiculous, Ash, and look...' She held out the envelope.

Ashleigh snatched it from her, her eyes gleaming, despite herself. 'The first clue?'

'Seems that way.'

'Bit weird, isn't it? Like a letter from beyond the grave.'

'Ashleigh!'

'Well, it is. Only Granny Ginny would have managed to set treasure chests around Honolulu from a sickbed in rural Oxford-shire. It's creepy.'

'It's clever.'

'It's hard work.'

'Don't be pathetic, Ash.'

'Pathetic?!' Ashleigh spun round to face Robyn so fast that she caught her knee. She was flushed and her eyes were burning dangerously brightly. 'I've just travelled halfway around the world. My medication is all over the place, my back feels as if someone has stuck fifty needles into it, and I'm sweating like a pig in this damned heat because I can't get up and change my stupid clothes.

'And now I'm here, in your poncy apartment, with your frigging beautiful view of your frigging beautiful life, and all it's doing, Robyn, all it's blinking well doing, is showing me just exactly how rubbish my own is in comparison. If that's pathetic then I apologise. And if I'm not in the mood for some half-baked treasure hunt then I apologise for that too, but if you don't mind, I think I'd like to lie on a bed and see if I can get just a minuscule amount of the pain to subside.'

Ashleigh glared at her, panting from the effort of her tirade, and Robyn swallowed.

'Sorry,' she managed. 'I didn't think.'

'No, well, you're lucky not to have to.'

'I am. I'm so lucky, Ash, and I so wish it hadn't happened. Every single day I wish that.'

'Yeah? You and me both, babe. I was meant to be getting a degree and a fistful of medals, instead of which I'm a lowly lab technician who, until two weeks ago, lived with her grandmother. Now – that bed?'

'Of course.'

Robyn took hold of the chair and carefully manoeuvred her sister through to the bedroom. Ashleigh stretched out on the bed, grimacing in pain, and Robyn fetched her case, grabbing the bag of medicines and finding water.

'Thanks,' Ashleigh said, when she'd finally sorted what she needed and settled herself against the pillows. 'It's a pain in the arse, I know.'

'It's OK,' Robyn dared to tease. 'You were always a pain in the arse.'

'Oi!' Ashleigh objected, but half-heartedly. Whatever pills she had taken were clearly having an effect and she looked very sleepy.

'I'll let you rest.' Robyn started to back out of the room, but to her surprise Ashleigh patted the bed.

'Soon,' she said. 'First, let's read this damned letter. Annoyed as I may be about this treasure hunt, I have to confess I'm bloody curious too, aren't you?'

Robyn smiled and nodded.

'Never more so.'

'Then, here, sis…' Ashleigh took the letter and slit it open. A tiny brass key fell out and she lifted it up so that it glinted in the late sun slanting in through the window. 'Let the treasure hunt commence!'

Chapter Three

Ashleigh and Robyn,

You've made it then? Thank you. I know this must all seem very strange but humour your old granny, will you? I hope, once you get started, you'll enjoy the trip through my past as much as I did. I want to show you what life was like when your Uncle Jack and I landed in Honolulu Harbor. It felt like the holiday of a lifetime those first few days, but I'd accompanied Jack all the way to Hawaii in the hope of getting a job, not just swanning around the cocktail bars. Pearl Harbor was where it was all happening back in 1941 and there was an extensive Civilian Pilot Training programme. I was determined to be a part of it and prepared to fight until they let me in.

1 July 1941

Ginny Martin stepped onto the John Rodgers airfield and looked around, impressed. The set-up here on the beautiful island of Oahu was far larger and more professional than she'd expected. She'd assumed that the civilian airfield would be playing second fiddle to the vast military installations at Pearl Harbor, but she supposed the two were interlinked these days. Certainly, several of the gleaming hangars looked new and Ginny eyed them up carefully, deciding where to start her job hunt.

She was ready for a fight. The American public loved female flyers but, in her experience, those in the industry weren't always so welcoming. She'd learned to fly in their hometown in Tennessee with her brother Jack. Her parents had been more than wealthy enough to afford lessons for them both and enlightened enough to encourage it, but the treatment Jack had received at the airfield had been frustratingly different from hers. They'd been happy to have Ginny learn to fly and proud of her when she did so, calling her their 'Little Earhart' after the famous aviatrix and letting the press take photos of her in the air. Once she'd got her instructor's licence, however, it had been a different matter. Apparently, it was fine to have women flying glamorously around in the skies, but not to have them teaching men to do the same.

Despite being desperate for instructors as more and more well-off Americans clamoured to fly, they'd refused to take her on. It wasn't until several of her parents' high-profile friends had insisted on learning with her that the airfield had begrudgingly backed down. Ginny had resented having to have her daddy step in but had bitten back her pride, taken the job and soon proved herself worthy. Now, with over three hundred flying hours under her belt, she was ready to fight for a job again here in Hawaii.

She sized up the airfield. It sat almost on the sea edge and, with the summer sun beating down, the little planes taking off and landing on the long runway were sparkling as much as the blue sea beyond. Ginny smiled, looking across to the harbour where she and Jack had landed four days ago on the *Lurline*. It had been such a party, with the Hawaiian band playing lively tunes and the hula girls dancing to welcome them in. Delicious food had been for sale at stands all along the harbour, and everywhere they went lei sellers had rushed forward to throw flower garlands around their necks for a dime. Ginny had ended up with six by the time she and Jack had found a taxi, and the hotel room had smelled beautiful with them draped over every mirror and hook.

She'd had a lovely few days getting to know Honolulu. The officers Jack would be stationed with on the naval airfield had been very welcoming, as had their wives, and Ginny already had a few invitations to dinner and cocktail parties. It had all been great fun but, dearly as she loved a party, she was here on Oahu to do a job and this morning she was determined to find it.

The biggest building on the field was a white hangar with 'Inter-Island Airlines' written across the front. Passengers flowed in and out and it was good to see such a lively service in action, but Ginny was here to teach so this wasn't the place for her. Thankfully, she noted the words 'Flying Service' painted brightly on the two hangars at the far side of the airfield and headed that way. A guard gave her a sideways glance and, feeling very glad she'd decided to wear her flying jacket despite the heat, she gave him a cheery wave and walked determinedly on. He didn't stop her and she happily patted the fur-lined leather of the precious jacket Jack had given her for Christmas.

She stopped before the two hangars. The right one had 'Andrews Flying Service' written across it and was filled with little Interstate planes, all bright blue with yellow trim along the wings and body. The left hangar was emblazoned with 'K-T Flying Service' and to her delight she spotted a clutch of canary-yellow Piper Cubs sitting inside. She and Jack joint-owned a Cub and she loved the little planes. Mind made up, she headed for the second hangar, though she did feel as if she was going against the flow as a number of men came rushing out in the opposite direction.

'Excuse me…' she tried. 'One moment, sir, could I…'

They surged past and Ginny stopped, hands on hips. This was going to be harder than she'd thought if they wouldn't even stop and talk to her. She stepped firmly in front of the next man.

'I'd like to speak to someone about flying,' she said loudly.

He paused.

'Well, you've certainly come to the right place, dearie – but it's a poor time. Come back later.'

'Why? Where are you…'

But he was gone, off after the rest. They all seemed to be heading for the Inter-Island terminal and, bemused, Ginny looked at her watch. It was almost midday. Was lunch such a set ritual here on the island? Looking around the emptying hangar, she spotted two engineers at the back, working away on the engine of one of the Cubs, and headed over.

'Excuse me.'

The first of the engineers looked up. He was a Hawaiian man, small and neat with a leathery face that broke into a kindly smile as soon as he saw her.

'Can I help you?'

'I hope so. I'm a pilot, an instructor, and I'm here looking for a job.'

'That's good,' he said, with another smile and a bobbing nod.

'So – can you help me?'

'With that? No. Sorry. I'm just a humble engineer. You need to talk to the boss man – to Mr Tyce.'

'I've tried but everyone seems to be running away.'

She gestured to the empty hangar and the figures heading off across the field. The man's eyes widened and he nudged at his companion, still bent over the engine.

'It's time, Lili!'

'Lili?' Ginny questioned, but even as she did so, the second engineer turned and she saw that she was a young woman, also Hawaiian. Petite and pretty with glossy dark hair pulled up under a cap, she was drowned by her overalls, which she'd hitched up with a tight belt. She looked around the hangar and panic crossed her eyes.

'Let's go, Papa!'

Tossing a spanner into a big toolbox at her feet and wiping her hands down her overalls, she, too, made for the exit.

'Go where?' Ginny asked, scuttling after her.

'To the Inter-Island building, of course. It's nearly midday.'

'But what happens at midday?' Ginny almost wailed.

The girl stopped and looked at her curiously.

'I thought you said you were a pilot?'

'I am. A good one. I've got over three hundred hours of—'

'So you should know what's happening.' The girl shook her head as Ginny frowned, confused. 'Jacqueline Cochran! She's on the television at midday and the Inter-Island building is the only place around here with a set.'

'Of course!'

Ginny couldn't believe she'd forgotten. Jacqueline Cochran was her heroine. A daring aviatrix, she'd won the Bendix race three years ago and broken every record going – speed, distance, height. She was one of the best pilots of their generation, and yesterday she'd returned to America after flying a Hudson bomber across the Atlantic to Britain – the first woman ever to do so. Ginny had met her once, at a dinner in the Long Island Aviation Country Club, and had been very impressed with the bold, glamorous blonde. She'd followed her progress closely ever since and it was only the excitement of arriving on Oahu that had let this important date slip out of her mind.

'I've met her, you know,' she said to the young engineer as she hurried after her.

'Jacqueline Cochran?' Her dark eyes widened. 'Wow – you're so lucky. She's amazing.'

'She is. I'm Ginny Martin, by the way.'

She stuck out a hand and, without breaking stride, the girl took it and gave it a firm shake.

'Lilinoe Kamaka. And this is my father, Kalani.'

The little man shook Ginny's hand too, bobbing his head again, still smiling away.

'Welcome to Oahu, Miss Martin.'

'Ginny, please.'

Lilinoe was moving fast, and Ginny had to focus to keep up as they joined the other people making for the white hangar she'd not long passed.

'Do you fly?' Ginny asked her as they slowed a little at last.

Lilinoe looked away.

'No.'

'You should,' Ginny urged. She'd seen, first hand, how talented women could be at flying planes and was determined to enable more of them to discover the joys of the air. Why not start with her new friend? 'I could teach you,' she offered, but Lili shook her head.

'No. That is, no thank you very much.'

'But—'

'I'm needed to mend the engines. K-T is very busy. We cannot afford to have planes stuck on the ground so, you see, I have no time to fly.'

'No, no, I see that. But surely you have days off?'

Lilinoe swallowed and looked to her father, scuttling along behind them.

'No flying,' she said firmly, and Ginny bit her lip and followed her into the Inter-Island terminal without another word.

The place was packed. Every pilot and engineer on the field seemed to be gathered around a tiny television set on the main desk. Ginny pushed her way into the crowd after Lili and Kalani and felt the thrill of the group's interest. She wasn't tall enough to see over the men, but a cry for hush was rippling around the jostling group, and they all fell obligingly silent as someone turned the volume to maximum and the interviewer announced Jacqueline Cochran. A cheer went up but was hastily stifled as they all strained towards the set.

The interviewer asked Jacqueline about her flight across the Atlantic and she laughingly described how easy the bomber was to fly. She'd not been allowed to either take off or land the plane, on the spurious grounds that she wasn't strong enough to handle it on land – grounds cooked up, Ginny knew, by jealous male pilots – but she'd taken the controls all the way across the Atlantic and the press, at least, fully understood the achievement.

'So tell us, Mrs Cochran,' the interviewer said, after another laughing report of her rough twenty-hour return trip in the bomb bay of a big Liberator AM261, 'what's next?'

Jacqueline's voice rang out around the terminal, clear as a bell: 'I believe it's time for women to serve their country. I've been talking to the amazing female pilots of the Air Transport Auxiliary in Britain who are ferrying new planes to military bases around the country, to free up their men for combat. We should be preparing our own women to do the same job in the States if it comes to war for us too.'

The interviewer audibly sucked in his breath.

'You want women to fly for the military?'

'Yes. Not to take over from men, you understand, but to release them for combat. America has many talented female pilots and I believe Uncle Sam is going to need them.'

There was a clamour of questions on the TV and the little crowd in the sunny terminal out on Oahu also began chattering away, but Ginny didn't need to hear any more. She looked around and saw Lilinoe still at her side.

'That's what I want to do,' she told her. 'I'm sure I could fly any plane with a bit of training, and wouldn't it be better for me to be doing it rather than male pilots who could be attacking the enemy?'

'It would,' the girl agreed. 'I think it's a great idea, although we're not at war yet, are we?'

'No,' Ginny agreed, looking around her, 'and until we are, there are pilots needing training. Who do I speak to about a job?'

Lilinoe shrugged and pointed across the terminal.

'I'd say Marguerite Gambo would be your best bet.'

Ginny stared. Coming towards her was a smart older woman with a flight jacket flung over her shoulder.

'Can I help you?' Marguerite asked.

'This lady would like a job,' Lilinoe supplied.

Ginny cleared her throat and stuck out her hand.

'Virginia Martin at your service, ma'am. I've got my instructor's licence and over three hundred hours of flight time.' She fumbled for her licence and flight book in her jacket pocket and handed them over. Marguerite Gambo gave them a cursory glance and smiled.

'Great. Why don't you come and have a look around?'

She waved for Ginny to join her as she sauntered out of the building and made for the next-door hangar. Ginny glanced at Lilinoe – was it really going to be this easy? She'd come prepared to fight to be recognised as a female pilot, but here on Oahu it seemed women were already not just flying but running their own training schools.

She hurried after Marguerite, who was stepping into a hangar marked 'Gambo Flying Service'. It was filled with little orange planes, Aeroncas, and her heart dropped slightly. She'd only flown an Aeronca a few times and she didn't like it as much as the Piper Cub, but she reminded herself that if she was ever going to join Jacqueline Cochran's ferrying service, she'd have to get used to flying all sorts. At that moment, however, a man came running into the hangar after them.

'Oi, Marguerite – hands off her!' Ginny jumped and looked at the new arrival. He was tall and dark with a dapper moustache and a wicked twinkle in his eyes. 'Begging your pardon, ma'am,' he said, doffing his cap with an exaggerated flourish, 'but did I hear you say you're a pilot?'

'A pilot and an instructor, sir, yes.'

'Perfect! I'll take you.'

Ginny turned to Marguerite, confused. She was shaking her head at the newcomer, a wry smile on her glossy lips.

'I got her first, Bob.'

'But you've got a woman already, Rita.'

'You've got the only female engineer.'

'And Lili is a total gem but I need an aviatrix. You've got you and Andrews have got Cornelia. K-T is the only service without a bit of glam, so surely I should get first dibs on this little gem. You got much experience, young lady?'

'Over three hundred flight hours,' Ginny offered.

He clapped his hands.

'Perfect! Let me offer you a job. I'm Robert Tyce, head honcho at K-T Flying Service over there.'

He gestured back to the first hangar Ginny had visited and she felt a spark of excitement.

'The Piper Cubs?'

'Those babies are mine, yep. You know them?'

'I own one.'

'Even better! Oh, come on, Rita, this girl is made for K-T and you know it.'

Marguerite rolled her eyes at him.

'I'd say it's very much up to the "girl", wouldn't you? Miss Martin?'

But before Ginny could say anything, Robert Tyce had dropped onto a knee before her and grabbed her hand. 'Miss Martin, Queen of the Skies, make me the happiest man in the world today and tell me you'll join K-T as our first female pilot.'

Ginny blinked down at the flamboyant man before her and looked uncertainly to Marguerite, who laughed.

'You might as well, girl, if you know the Cubs best. Bob's an idiot, of course, but he runs a pretty decent service and, to be fair, it would be good to have a woman flying out of all three hangars here at John Rodgers. Women make the best instructors so I suppose we should spread ourselves evenly.'

She winked broadly at Robert, still on one knee, and he laughed. 'You are the best, you really are. So, Miss Martin?'

Ginny laughed. This was totally the opposite of what she'd expected to find on the airfield this morning, but it was wonderful. These people actively wanted female pilots – surely she'd found her home from home?

'It would be my pleasure to fly for you, Mr Tyce,' she said. 'But don't you want to see what I can do first?'

'Robert, please. I'm sure you're brilliant but, yes, let's grab a Cub and head up, shall we?'

'Now?'

'No time like the present.'

With that, Ginny had to agree, and as she thanked Marguerite and headed back to the K-T hangar with Robert Tyce, she looked to the calm blue skies above, eager to get up. Flying had been in her blood since her parents had taken her and Jack to an air show when she was just ten years old, and now, another ten years later, it seemed she was finally at a point in history when her skills would be properly recognised.

'Did you see Jacqueline Cochran speak?' she asked Robert as he strode out across the field.

'Sure did. Quite a dame!'

'Do you think she'll make it happen – women flying for the military?'

'It won't be easy, but if anyone can, Jacqueline can. Now – how about we take this little honey up.' He paused by a Cub parked near the entrance of the K-T hangar, nose out in the sunshine as if it was as eager to get up into the skies as Ginny. 'Lili – is she ready?'

Lilinoe came across.

'Good as new, boss.' She looked to Ginny. 'Are you joining K-T?'

'Looks that way.'

The girl smiled.

'Guess we'll be working together then. It'll be good to have another woman around.'

'Exactly what I said,' Robert crowed. 'All yours, girl.'

He held out a hand to help Ginny into the cockpit and, with a grin, she grabbed it and swung herself up. This was where she truly belonged, and as she taxied the little plane out onto the runway and headed up into the skies above Hawaii, she glanced across to the Hickham Field naval base where Jack was stationed. It seemed they were both going to be flying out here on Oahu and maybe even both serving their country. She didn't want war, of course, but fascism had to be stopped. And, with the sun shining over the beautiful islands of Hawaii, it was hard to see how it could really touch them out here in the middle of paradise.

Chapter Four

Robyn jumped off the bus and almost ran into the Clarence T. C. Ching Athletics Complex. She was guiltily aware that Ashleigh had been on her own all day but she really didn't want to miss her hurdling session. The first meet of the season was in just two weeks and she needed time on the track.

'Robyn!'

'Hey, Zak!'

Robyn smiled as her training partner came bounding over and gave her a hug.

'How are you?' Robyn fell gratefully against her friend as he opened his arms to hug her. Zak was part Hawaiian, part Afro-Caribbean, with caring almond eyes and long lean limbs that gave the very best hugs. Robyn sank against him, feeling the most relaxed she had since the terrible moment she'd stepped onto her childhood drive to face her beloved granny dying.

'It's so good to see you, Zak.'

'It's so good to have you back.'

He hugged her a little longer until she forced herself to pull away, wiping hastily at the tears that still spilled out of her eyes ridiculously often.

'Tough couple of weeks?' Zak asked gently.

'You could say that.'

'Get any training in?'

'Not much.'

'Then it's about to get a whole lot tougher. Coach is on a mission.'

He gestured to the far side of the track where Coach Tyler, a wiry ex-pro, was setting up hurdles and already barking at the other athletes as they started their warm-up.

'Good,' Robyn said, setting her jaw. 'I need it.'

'Race ya!' Zak cried, and set off across the track at speed.

Robyn groaned but chased after him, glad to feel her limbs stretching out in the warm evening air. Zak always made her feel better. He was such a kind, fun guy. Sexy too, if you liked your men tall and dark – which to be fair she did – but they'd established over a year ago that they were best as just friends. They'd been set up on a date by mutual mates but, both quite shy with strangers, they'd had little to say to each other and the whole thing had been an embarrassment they'd been glad to put behind them. Today, though, as Robyn watched Zak's fluid body leap a warm-up hurdle, she had to confess that it sent funny tingles around her stomach. How stupid. It must just be tiredness or something. They'd tried dating; it hadn't worked. End of.

She set her mind to her training, glad to be back with her group again, even when Cody, an earnest seventeen-year-old local, was bawled out for arriving late. She poured her pent-up grief into her limbs and hurdled well enough to gain a 'not bad' from Coach Tyler – praise indeed.

'Can I buy you a drink to celebrate your triumphant return?' Zak asked afterwards.

Robyn grimaced.

'I'd love that, Zak, but I better not leave my sister any longer.'

His eyes widened.

'Your sister? She's here?'

'Yep.'

'And how's that going?'

Over the last year Robyn had bored Zak on far too many occasions about her spiky phone calls with Ashleigh, and she rolled her eyes at him as they strolled together to the bus stop.

'So far, so strained. I think the journey really took it out of her and my flat isn't exactly made for wheelchair access. Granny Ginny has set us up this mad treasure hunt around Oahu and Ashleigh wants to get on with it, but I'm so busy with work and training that it's hard.'

'I'll help,' Zak offered. 'I love treasure hunts.'

'Really?'

'Totally. I have a pirate's costume and everything.'

He struck a silly pose and Robyn laughed.

'Perfect. It still doesn't solve what I do with Ashleigh the rest of the time though.'

Zak considered this.

'I have a mate who runs a wheelchair basketball club if you think she might like that?'

'I dunno, Zak. Granny tried to get her into some wheelchair sports a couple of years ago and it didn't go well.' Robyn grimaced to herself at the memory. Ginny had been determined to get Ashleigh out again and had taken her down to a handcycling taster day. Ashleigh's stinging opinion of 'lying down sport' had embarrassed them all and even Ginny had given up at that point. Ashleigh, it seemed, would take nothing less than her old self and as that was impossible, she was left with nothing. 'I think the contrast between what she used to be able to do and what she can now was too much to bear,' she went on. 'And she hated people seeing her as "weak" – her word, not mine.'

Zak nodded.

'I can imagine, but maybe out here, where she doesn't know anyone, it would be easier?'

Robyn's bus was coming and she stood up on tiptoe to drop a kiss on Zak's cheek.

'Maybe. It's a nice idea. I'll suggest it to her when I get home. Fancy a run tomorrow morning?'

'I'll be there. And Robyn…' The bus had pulled up and she was already jumping on but she swung round. 'Good to have you back.'

'Good to *be* back,' she cried as the bus pulled away, smiling as Zak waved madly, almost knocking two girls aside. Not that they seemed to mind.

The last thing she saw as the bus turned the corner was them simpering up at him. She reminded herself that he could flirt with whoever he wanted to but, even so, her stomach squirmed and she wasn't in the best of moods by the time she got home.

'Well, look who's here at last,' Ashleigh snapped.

'Sorry, Ash. It's been a long day. There was loads to catch up on at work after being away for two weeks. And then I had to train. The season starts in two weeks.'

'The super-dooper lower league season.'

'Yes,' Robyn said, refusing to be drawn. Her stomach rumbled. 'Don't suppose you've made dinner?'

'In this chair?'

Robyn could think of various answers to that but she bit her lip and forced herself into the kitchen.

'Pasta OK?'

'I guess.'

Ashleigh followed her, bumping pointedly off the walls.

'Have you had a look at the first clue?' Robyn asked, as she found pasta and gratefully dug a jar of sauce out of the cupboard. It wouldn't be cordon bleu but it would keep body and soul together.

'I have. Wanna hear it?'

'Please.'

Ashleigh pulled the envelope out of the pocket on the side of her wheelchair and unfolded it. Tossing back her hair, she declaimed:

Some might say he's in the lion's den,

But he has wings to escape and lead all men.'

Robyn frowned. 'The lion's den?'

'I'm thinking Daniel. You know, from the Bible – got thrown into the ring by some evil king but tamed the lions before they could kill him.'

'Figures. But this Daniel has wings.'

'True. Was there an Angel Daniel?'

'I don't think so. Anyway, angels don't lead men.'

'They led the shepherds to Baby Jesus.'

Robyn laughed.

'True, I suppose. All those hours in Sunday school did you good, Ash.'

Ashleigh groaned.

'God, I hated Sunday school. Remember the tricks we used to get up to, to bunk off?'

'Amazing how many tummy aches we had on a Sunday. You even claimed to have appendicitis once.'

'I was very convincing.'

'I know! Three hours in A&E made Sunday school look like paradise.'

They smiled at each other and, with the pasta boiling, Robyn sank gratefully onto a stool next to her sister and considered the clue.

'Why would Daniel fly?' she asked.

'No idea. Any famous Daniels around here?' Robyn stared at her. 'What?'

'OMG, Ashleigh, I've been so stupid.'

'Nothing new there, sis.'

'Watch it! I'll have you know I'm very smart, but not this time. There's a *very* famous Daniel around here – so famous that the airport is named after him!'

'The airport? Where you work?'

'The very same. The Daniel K. Inouye Airport, where we both landed the other day.'

'Yeah, well, I wasn't looking at what the wretched place was called, was I? That explains the wings bit, then. Who is he?'

'He was an amazing senator here in Hawaii for fifty years. He did loads to improve life for the islanders.'

'A leader of men then?'

'Definitely a leader of men. I'm ashamed I didn't think of him the minute I read Granny's riddle. The question is, though, where has she hidden a treasure chest in the airport? And how on earth did she do it?' The only answer was the merry ping of the cooker timer. Robyn shrugged. 'Fancy coming to work with me tomorrow, Ash?'

'Why not. It's about time I found out a bit more about the amazing job that cost you an Olympic hurdles medal.'

'Ash, it wasn't—'

'Like that. I know. You've said. But…'

'You'd have done better. I know. *You've* said.'

They glared at each other and Robyn leaped up to drain the pasta, fighting to control her anger as she ran the water through the colander. Ashleigh didn't understand anything about what she'd gone through and how hard the decision had been to make. She'd have loved to compete at a top level but she hadn't been prepared to sacrifice everything for it and that, frankly, was nothing to do with her sister.

'How d'you fancy basketball?' she shot at Ashleigh, tipping sauce onto the pasta.

'Basketball?'

'Yes, Ashleigh – wheelchair basketball.'

'Not at all, frankly.'

'Who's the quitter now?'

'It can't be quitting if you never even start.'

'I think you'll find it can.' Ashleigh sucked in a wounded breath and Robyn cursed herself for her insensitivity. Why on earth did they always end up arguing? Placing bowls of pasta on the tiny table against the kitchen window, she sat down across from her sister. 'I'm sorry, Ash, that sounded harsh, but you're still really athletic, you know. There are plenty of things you could do; you just have to want to.'

Ashleigh picked up her fork and toyed with her food.

'I know that, Rob,' she said, her voice low. 'But how *do you* want to if you don't, you know, want to?'

It was a good question and one for which Robyn wasn't sure she had the answer.

'I guess there's more than just Granny Ginny's boxes to hunt for,' she said eventually, 'but at least we can do it together.'

Ashleigh opened her mouth to contradict her, but then shovelled pasta into it instead, and they finished their dinner in almost companionable silence.

Robyn woke early the next morning, dreading the fuss of getting Ashleigh up and out in time for work, but to her surprise she heard her sister already clattering around the kitchen. To her even greater surprise, Ashleigh pushed her way into the tiny box room, proffering a cup of tea. Most of it had sloshed out of the cup, but Robyn sat up gingerly in the camp bed and took it. If Ashleigh was prepared to make an effort, then so was she.

An hour later and they were pulling into the airport car park. Usually Robyn preferred to cross busy Honolulu on the bus, or at a jog, but she kept a battered old Mini Clubman for driving out into the hills at the weekends and was glad of it now. Ashleigh's chair just fitted in the boot and it was a hell of a lot easier than trying to manoeuvre their way onto the bus. She got out, unloaded the chair and helped her sister into it, then they both faced the huge terminal.

'It's not the most pinpoint clue, is it?' Ashleigh said.

'Nope,' Robyn agreed, 'but we're just going to have to ask around. I'm hoping Mikala will know something.'

'Mikala?'

'Security guard, receptionist and all-round busybody. He knows most things going on in the airport so I've got my fingers crossed he'll be our man.'

She pushed Ashleigh into the terminal, heading past the check-in counters to a big desk with 'Information' written over it. It was manned by a tiny Polynesian man who was chuckling away with a pair of old ladies in a deep voice that seemed far too large for his body.

'Don't you worry, my gorgeous girls,' Robyn heard him saying. 'Micky here will make sure you get all the assistance you need with those adorable little doggies.'

The doggies in question peeped happily out of the ladies' giant handbags as their owners twittered their thanks. Mikala waved them to nearby seats and got straight onto his radio, presumably to call in the dog-sitters. Ashleigh eyed up the Chihuahuas in their matching pink bows but thankfully said nothing, and now Mikala was turning to them and flinging open his arms in welcome.

'Robyn Harris! Lovely to see you in my little part of the airport. What the devil can I do for you?'

Robyn eyed him.

'I think you know exactly what, Micky.'

'No idea what you're talking about.'

'You don't know anything about a treasure hunt then?'

His dark eyes twinkled.

'Well, that would be saying, wouldn't it?'

'It would,' Robyn agreed, waiting.

He rolled his eyes. 'You're no fun, girl. Not like your grand-mammy. Quite a woman she seemed, when I spoke to her.'

'You spoke to Granny Ginny?'

'Sure did. We had a lovely few chats over the phone. You know she flew Piper Cubs out of this very airfield back when it was plain old John Rodgers? Hell, she was here when Pearl Harbor was attacked.'

'I know, Micky. That's what this treasure hunt is all about.'

'Cool. Sounds like she had some stories to tell.'

Ashleigh tutted impatiently.

'So,' she asked, 'do you have it?'

Mikala peered over the counter at her.

'Maybe.'

'Micky…' Robyn pleaded, and he threw his big hands up.

'OK, OK. Wait a minute.'

He bent down beneath the counter and fumbled with the keys to the lost-property cupboard. Robyn had seen him magic a few amazing finds out of there in her two years at the airport, including an enormous diamond earring, a teddy bear the size of a child, and even, once, a goldfish in a Tupperware, but what he drew out now was better than any of those.

It was a wooden box, beautifully carved and about the size of a well-packed gym bag. Trimmed in brass, with two curved handles at either end, it had a beautiful lock holding the lid on. As Mikala placed it on the counter, Ashleigh held up the little brass key that had come in Granny Ginny's letter and he rubbed his hands.

'Exciting!' he pronounced.

The two old ladies shuffled over, Chihuahuas barking, and it was to that peculiar chorus that Robyn took the key, inserted it in the lock and turned. It gave a smart little click and when she put her hands to the lid, she felt it loosen immediately. She hesitated, strangely nervous, but, feeling Ashleigh nudge her on, she lifted it and peered inside. Mikala, the old ladies and even the Chihuahuas leaned over to see, and Robyn heard Ashleigh tut in frustration below them.

'You're not missing much,' she said to her, pulling out the sole object inside the beautiful box – a slim, white envelope.

'No gold coins?' Ashleigh asked with a weak smile.

'Not yet.'

'Not even a peacock-blue mascara?'

Robyn smiled, remembering how she and Ash had fought over that particular treat.

'Just another letter.'

Mikala gave a low chuckle.

'If that's got your grandmammy's stories in it, then I'd say it's treasure enough.'

Robyn nodded.

'You're right. Thanks, Micky.'

'Pleasure. Oh and, when you do get your hands on that peacock-blue mascara – it's mine!'

He winked at her, and she laughed and took down the treasure chest. It could just about sit on Ashleigh's knees and she looked at it uncertainly. If all the boxes were this size, she had no idea how she was going to fit them in her flat; it was tight enough in there already.

'Shall we take it to your office, sis?' Ashleigh asked and Robyn nodded.

She had fifteen minutes before she was due to start work and she prayed it was enough time to read Granny Ginny's words. She still felt her absence from the world like a deep pain in her heart and hoped that, as Micky had suggested, the stories of her past would keep her alive. Clasping the handles of Ashleigh's chair, she blew a kiss to Micky and wheeled her sister through the terminal, out to the big hangars beyond. This was where she spent her working days and also where, some eighty years ago, Granny Ginny had started out on her own flying journey. Quite where it had taken her, it seemed they were about to find out.

Chapter Five

So, girls, you've found my first box. Beautiful, isn't it? I had them made specially by a lovely craftsman on the outskirts of Honolulu. An amazing thing, the internet. You can have anything delivered anywhere! An extravagance, of course, for one tiny letter, but as my own dear grandmother used to say, 'You never regret your extravagances.' Remember that, girls, and don't forget to treat yourselves as you make your way through life.

But enough advice, you're here for my story. Reluctantly perhaps. I bet you moaned on the plane, didn't you, Ash? And I bet you're grumbling about having to share your flat, Rob? But you're here all the same. Thank you.

I told you, I think, Robyn doll, that I started out flying right where you've ended up working. I probably didn't tell you how much you getting that job meant to me. It felt as if fate had taken the Harris women full circle and I loved that, I really did, but it scared me too. It was a circle that, for me, became more of an inward spiral, and I didn't talk to you about it enough. I'm sorry.

I hope you love your job there as much as I did. Hell, I hope you love Hawaii as much as I did, and that you've found friends as good as mine. I was a lucky, lucky girl and, for now, let me introduce you both to the people who made life on Oahu so special for me.

6 July 1941

'Jack!'

Ginny waved madly at her brother as he came into the bar of the Royal Hawaiian Hotel with a small group of other officers.

It had only been three days since they'd parted, but so much had happened and she found herself ridiculously pleased to see him. Clearly life on the island was already suiting him. His chestnut hair, so like her own, was now army-short, making his brown eyes look bigger than ever, and they were full of smiles as he came across, swooping her into his arms and hugging her tight.

'Ginny! How's things? Did you get the job?'

'Certainly did.'

'That's my girl – bet you told them what's what.'

She gave him a sheepish grin.

'To be honest, Jack, I didn't have to. There's already a woman running her own flying school on the airfield and the others were falling over themselves to recruit female flyers. Seems it's not quite like home out here.'

One of the other men laughed.

'Hawaii's its own little world. Anything goes. And besides, we know how badly we're going to need pilots when it comes to war.'

Ginny looked curiously at the man. He was a few years older than her, but very handsome with straw-blond hair and sharp blue eyes.

'This is Eddie Layton,' Jack said. 'Naval intelligence liaison officer to Admiral Kimmel himself.'

'Should I curtsey?' Ginny asked cheekily.

'I wouldn't recommend it,' a glamorous woman said, coming up at Eddie's side. 'His head's big enough already.'

Eddie protested but with a laugh.

'My wife, Dagne,' he introduced her.

Ginny shook hands with both of them.

'Pleased to meet you. I'm Ginny, Jack's—'

'Smart little aviatrix of a sister,' Eddie supplied. 'We know. He's been boasting about your skills all around the barracks.'

Ginny felt a warm glow spread through her and took Jack's arm gratefully. He was only eighteen months older than her and they'd grown up pretty close. Oh, they'd fought, yes, but she adored him, and when he'd signed up and been stationed to Hawaii, she'd been eager to go along. Her parents had been unsure about it at first, but they'd talked them into buying her ticket. The island of Oahu, they'd insisted, was about the safest place in the world – unless the volcano chose to erupt for the first time in about a million years – and at least with Ginny out here, Jack wouldn't be lonely. Not that Jack looked lonely.

Ginny fought to take in the names of the other friends that he introduced her to. There was Joe Rocheford, who worked with Eddie in naval intelligence. He was a skinny, serious man with smart glasses that made him look a little like an intellectual Glenn Miller. Eddie told them that he'd been the brains behind some seriously clever codebreaking in the last year and that, thanks to him and his fellows, the US navy were able to understand at least part of the myriad enemy communications flying around the Pacific. Joe and Eddie were clearly close, and Ginny watched them chatting away as their group were shown to a table down on the beachfront and tried not to feel jealous.

She'd moved out of the hotel she'd shared with Jack when he'd gone to his barracks and found herself a room to rent with an older couple. They'd seemed very friendly when she'd gone to look around but the moment they'd got her deposit, they'd cooled off. The place wasn't too bad and they provided reasonable meals, but it was clear they resented having to rent out part of their home and she spent most of her time hiding in her room or walking the island.

Watching Jack's new friends laughing easily with each other, she felt the contrast, but she reminded herself that she'd only been on Oahu just over a week. Besides, she was here with these lovely people now and should make the most of it. As Jack pulled her into a chair at his side and a round of Mai Tais arrived, Ginny gladly joined in a 'Cheers' and turned to chat to Dagne.

'Are you really a pilot?' Dagne asked, looking curiously at her.

'I am,' Ginny agreed with a smile. 'I love it.'

'Isn't flying scary, though?'

'Oh no, it's wonderful. Take-off does make your stomach go a bit until you get used to it, but once you're in the air, it's the best feeling in the world. You know that sort of lightness that you get swimming?' Dagne nodded her perfectly coiffed head. 'It's like that times ten. You feel so free, so light…'

'So powerful,' Jack put in.

Ginny grimaced.

'Not powerful, Jack, but I suppose you do feel in control. Up there, it's just you and the plane – you can go where you want and do what you like.'

'Did you see Jacqueline Cochran on the television the other day?' Dagne asked.

'Oh yes!' Ginny agreed eagerly. 'Amazing, wasn't she?'

'I love her hair. And her cosmetics are wonderful.'

Ginny nodded. Jacqueline Cochran's 'Wings to Beauty' range of foundations and powders was perfect for girls like her who found it hard to sit still for long. But they weren't why she admired the woman.

'If she gets this ferrying corps going, I want to be part of it,' she said.

'Flying bombers?' Dagne asked, wide-eyed.

'Maybe one day, if I had the training. But definitely the smaller planes. Why not?'

'Don't they go terribly fast?'

Ginny grinned.

'I really hope so. I love going fast.'

Dagne shook her head.

'I'm not sure Eddie would like me doing that.'

'What's it got to do with Eddie?' Ginny demanded.

Dagne looked shocked. 'He's my husband.'

'So? Does that mean he can tell you what to do?'

'Well, no. I mean, not when it comes to most things, but flying off around the country in military planes – that's a bit different to choosing which beauty parlour to go to, right?'

Ginny felt Jack press a warning hand on her knee under the table and bit back the many responses she could have offered. Dagne seemed a lovely woman and it wouldn't do to offend her on their first night out together.

'Right,' she agreed, taking a sip of her Mai Tai and letting the fruity flavours tickle away her frustration at the other woman's attitude.

When it came to marriage, the truth was that she just couldn't see what was in it for a woman, and glamorous Dagne's comments underlined all her objections. Why on earth would she want to tie herself to some man who could then make decisions about her life? She'd had this conversation time and again with friends back home. They talked about security and comfort, which Ginny thought was ridiculous – she was perfectly secure and comfortable without a man cluttering up her life. And then they talked about love. That one was harder to argue against because people seemed to imbue it with strange, magical properties, as if it made everything else worthwhile. Ginny was unconvinced. She liked men a lot. They were funny and interesting and good company, but they weren't worth giving up your own hopes and dreams for.

'You just haven't met the right one yet,' her friends would tell her, misty-eyed.

'Good,' Ginny would retort, but they'd look smug and insist that her time would come. Frankly, she very much hoped it did not.

'I'm sure if it comes to war, Jacqueline Cochran would love to have you in her service,' Jack was saying soothingly.

'*When* it comes to war,' Eddie put in from across the table.

Ginny looked at the handsome blond man. He'd said something similar when they'd first been introduced and she was intrigued.

'You think it's a sure thing?'

'I do.'

'Surely Hitler won't invade America?' she gasped.

Eddie gave a little bark of a laugh.

'Not Hitler. I do think we should commit to helping poor old Britain defeat him, but he's not our main concern right now.'

'Then who is?'

'Japan, of course. They may not want to rule the whole world, like Hitler does, but they sure as hell want to rule Asia. They hate the sanctions we're imposing on them – especially those on oil. They're invading deeper into China all the time and heading down into Indochina so that they can establish their own supply. If they take that, they'll be on to Thailand and Malaya and eventually…'

He waved a hand out across the beach, which was turning a soft peach colour as the sun began to sink beneath the rippling ocean before them.

'Hawaii?' Ginny breathed.

Jack threw an arm around her shoulders.

'Not yet, sis. Not *ever* if we have anything to do with it. The US has the best navy on the seas – the Japs won't get this far, especially not once we get our planes up in the air.'

'They have planes too,' Eddie said.

Ginny looked at him curiously. 'I heard they aren't very good at flying.'

He shook his head. 'That's not true, I'm afraid. Joe and I were out in Tokyo together a few years back and I can tell you that Admiral Isoroku Yamamoto is a sharp operator. His men are capable of anything they put their minds to and afraid of nothing, including death. We underestimate the Japanese at our peril.'

Ginny shifted uncomfortably and Dagne batted at her husband's arm.

'Eddie! This is hardly nice conversation for cocktails.'

Eddie looked at her.

'Sorry, baby. You're right. Why spoil such a beautiful evening with talk of war?' He kissed her and smiled around the table. 'How about another round of Mai Tais!'

The moment passed but Ginny could see that he'd been in earnest, and suddenly this Pacific paradise didn't feel quite as idyllic. She sipped at the last of her Mai Tai, watching the sun drop behind the dark shape of a giant aircraft carrier making slow progress across the bay, presumably heading into Pearl Harbor. She could make out the silhouettes of the fighters on the decks and was aware, for the first time, of the deadly capacity of her beloved airplanes. Shivering, she pulled her eyes back to the beach and that's when she spotted a familiar figure.

'Lili!' The engineer looked around but clearly hadn't spotted her. Ginny excused herself from her group, and rushed across the hotel patio and out of the little wooden gate onto the boardwalk beyond. 'Lili!' she cried again, and this time Lili spotted her and waved. She was with her father, who gave Ginny a little bow hello before heading across to a small group of men playing Kōnane – a form of chequers – at the top of the beach.

'Come and have a drink,' Ginny suggested, waving at the bar. 'My treat.'

Lili looked awkward.

'It's very kind of you but really, no – I'm not dressed right.'

Ginny looked at the floral dress she was wearing.

'You look lovely, doll.'

'It's just a handmade thing.'

'Then you're as talented with a needle as you are with an engine. Your father's happy, so why not join us for one?'

Lili looked longingly to the bar and that was enough for Ginny. Gently taking the girl's elbow, she guided her through the gate and to their table. Joe Rocheford jumped up straight away, offering her his chair and heading off to find another, and Lili, flushed with pleasure, lowered herself into it.

'Mai Tai?' Ginny asked, signalling for the waiter.

'I really shouldn't.'

'You really *should* – they're delicious. Here.'

She handed Lili her own drink, happy to wait for the next one to arrive, and was pleased to see the young engineer's look of pleasure as she took her first sip. She introduced her to the group and when Eddie asked her what had got her into planes, Lili lost her shyness and came alive.

'I just think they're wonderful. Imagine – we've made something that can take off into the skies and swoop across them like a bird. I love the way the pieces of the engines all fit together to make that happen, and I want to be a part of making planes bigger and faster and better.'

'Good on you,' Joe said. 'It's that sort of spirit that's going to win us this war.'

Jack leaned in.

'It's a wonderful job you're doing,' he agreed, 'but don't you want to fly?'

'No,' Lili said, but she didn't sound as certain as she had when Ginny had asked her the other day.

She buried herself in her cocktail and the conversation moved on, but Ginny kept a close eye on her new friend and when the moment arose, she leaned in to her.

'I meant it when I said I'd happily teach you to fly,' she said softly.

Lili had almost finished her drink and her cheeks were flushed with it. She looked at Ginny and shook her head.

'Don't you see, Ginny? It's not that I don't want to fly – it's that I can't afford it.'

Ginny cursed her own stupid arrogance at not even considering this.

'So don't pay me,' she said impulsively.

Lili flushed even deeper.

'Oh no,' she said. 'That wouldn't be right.'

'I'd be happy to cover it, really. I get a great rate on the planes from Bob so it wouldn't cost me much at all, and...' But Lili was standing up now, her chin held high.

'It wouldn't be right,' she said firmly.

Ginny stood up with her, aware that she was handling this all wrong. A little yellow Piper Cub flew across the bay in the dying light, and she saw Lili's eyes follow it and brim with tears.

'I'm sorry, Lili,' she said. 'I just thought...'

'I'd love to fly,' Lili said, eyes still on the plane. 'It would be my greatest dream. But I pay my way, always, and I can't pay for that. I should go now, Ginny – my father is finishing his game.' She waved a hand towards Kalani who, as far as Ginny could see, was still deep in the Kōnane. 'Thank you so much for the drink. In return, you must come for dinner at our house one night.'

'I'd love that,' Ginny agreed, but already Lili was saying her goodbyes and edging anxiously out of the smart bar, and she was left feeling that she'd done more harm than good by inviting her in for a drink.

'I'm an idiot,' she said, sinking down next to Jack and watching Lilinoe slide away through the crowd.

'You were just being kind.'

'I thought I was,' she agreed, 'but, in the end, it felt more like cruelty.'

She liked Lili a lot and already she was sure that the girl would make a good pilot. Anyone with that sort of love for planes was bound to handle them well and it would be such a good way to get to know each other better. It was lovely being part of Jack's set of smart, happy friends, but something about Lilinoe spoke to her like the little sister she'd never had and she treasured their time together. It would take patience and tact – neither of them strengths of hers – but as she watched the Cub turn back towards the airfield, a proud shape against the burning sunset, she made a vow to find a way to talk her new friend into taking flying lessons.

Chapter Six

'There's something fascinating about keys, isn't there?' Ashleigh said, twirling the second of the treasure hunt ones around in her fingers.

'There certainly is, especially when they're the key to your granny's past.' Robyn collected up cereal bowls, enjoying the fact it was her day off and she didn't have to rush out and leave Ashleigh. 'How many clues do you think there'll be?'

'Eight,' Ashleigh said promptly, and Robyn nodded. There had always been eight clues; it had been Granny Ginny's favourite number. A woman's number, she'd called it – curved, self-contained and proud.

'We'll need a key ring,' Ashleigh added. 'Do you have any spare?'

''Fraid not but, don't worry, I'm heading out for a run in a minute so I'll pop into a shop and get one.' Ashleigh froze and the key fell from her hand, pinging off the table and onto the tiled floor. Robyn looked at it nervously. 'Ash? Are you OK?'

'Oh, I'm fine,' Ashleigh said, her voice frighteningly controlled. 'I'm absolutely fine. I'll just sit here and look at the sliver of a view from your fancy window whilst you "head out for a run" and "pop into a shop".'

'Ashleigh…'

'If I get bored, I can do some thrilling arm exercises. Oh, and I've got a plethora of pills to choke down so that'll be fun too.'

Robyn bit her lip.

'I don't have to go.'

'No, no, no – why curb your life just cos mine is totally and utterly wrecked?' Robyn went across to her sister but she flung her hands up to ward her off. 'Don't, Robyn. Don't pity me.'

Robyn sighed, hating what the accident had done to her once-sparky sister but feeling out of her depth about how to respond.

'Why not? It's awful what happened to you. It's a huge pity, a shame – a tragedy.'

'That's me, a walking tragedy. Sorry, a non-walking tragedy.' Ashleigh spun her chair away from the breakfast table. 'This was a mistake. I don't know what Granny Ginny thought she was doing, making me take more time off from the lab and sending me halfway across the world on some childish treasure hunt. You do it, Robyn – it'll be far quicker without me.'

'But not as much fun,' Robyn protested, though her sister was already battering her way down the corridor.

Her bedroom door slammed and Robyn was left alone. So much for it being nice to have the day together…

'What do you want me to do with her, Granny Ginny?' she asked sadly as she washed up the bowls, but there was no answer and when the doorbell rang to tell her Zak was downstairs, she gratefully headed out. His welcoming smile lifted her spirits instantly.

'You OK, Rob? You look… flustered.'

'Ashleigh,' she said darkly.

'Ah. The sisterly bonding not going so well?'

He picked up his pace and she fell into step alongside him.

'She's just so unpredictable. One minute we're having a lovely chat and the next she explodes.' She looked up to the hills above the city. 'She's like the volcano, Zak, with all this anger simmering away inside her. It's not good.'

'Her accident sounds awful.'

'It was, but it was eight years ago and she still seems as angry as in those first few months. There was so much more to Ashleigh than just being a cyclist. She's got a great brain and she was always so funny, so daring, so up for an adventure. It's such a shame that all of that seems to have gone out of the window too. I wish I could help her.'

Zak reached over and took her hand.

'All you can do is be there for her, Rob.'

She nodded, intensely aware of his hand around hers as they ran. 'Would you like to meet her?'

'Love to,' he agreed easily.

'This morning?'

'Why not! I'm meant to be writing up a report but it can wait.'

'Anything interesting?'

'Of course! All my work is interesting.' He grinned at her. Zak was a marine biologist, doing a PhD at the university, and was almost as much of a nerd about sea creatures as Robyn was about engine parts. 'But not as interesting as meeting your legendary sister. I'll come up when we get back.'

'Brilliant!'

Already Robyn felt lighter. Zak's hand was still in hers, but as they turned onto the busy streets of Waikiki he dropped it to wave to someone and she saw Cody coming towards them in an ill-fitting McDonald's uniform.

'Hey, guys,' the lad said, looking self-consciously around.

'Hey, Cody. No school today?'

'Not till later. Twelfth grade is flexible. Good for my job.' He gestured awkwardly to the uniform.

'Suits you,' Zak joked.

Cody grimaced. 'It's horrible, but we need the cash.'

'We?'

'The family.'

'Right.' Robyn looked at his tight shoulders and shaded eyes. 'Are things hard at home, Cody?'

He shrugged.

'No harder than most. Dad doesn't get as many hours at work as he'd like so, you know, every little helps.'

'And your mum?'

'Mum's dead,' he mumbled, then: 'Better go. They kill you if you're late. See ya.'

He shot off, leaving them staring after him.

'Poor kid,' Zak said.

'There must be something we can do to help,' Robyn agreed, her mind racing as they ran on.

She pushed herself hard, as if that might help, but could come up with nothing much. Worn out, she was relieved when she spotted one of Waikiki's tourist shops and could distract herself with finding a key ring.

Not that the choice was great. She didn't want to carry Granny Ginny's pretty keys on the inevitable hula girls and palm trees, but then Zak spotted a Pearl Harbor section and she gratefully grabbed a little Peashooter monoplane. She took it to the counter to pay, admiring its elegant lines. Had her grandmother flown one of these? Suddenly she was keen to get on with the treasure hunt and she picked up the pace again as they headed back along Oahu's famous beach.

'Wow, Robyn – you're on fire,' Zak gasped, as they eased to a stop outside her door.

'I've got a treasure hunt to get on with.'

'Of course. Shall we go up?'

'Let's.'

Robyn led the way, feeling distinctly nervous as she opened the door of the flat, but Ashleigh came wheeling towards her as if nothing had happened at all.

'Hey, Rob. Good run?'

'Great, thanks. I found a key ring.'

She held out the little plane and Ashleigh took it with a nod of approval, then spotted Zak.

'Oh,' she said, 'and it looks like you found a man too. Hello.'

Robyn flushed.

'This is Zak, a friend from training.'

'A *friend*, lovely.'

Was it Robyn's imagination or was her sister sitting up straighter in her chair and running her fingers through her glossy chestnut hair? Robyn tugged at her own sweaty ponytail and stepped a little closer to Zak.

'Water?'

'Great, thanks.' Zak followed her through to the living area, pouncing on the letter on the coffee table. 'Is that part of this famous treasure hunt you've been telling me about?'

Robyn turned to answer but Ashleigh was wheeling up next to him. 'Sure is. This is Granny Ginny's second letter and the clue for the third.'

'A clue, great.'

Zak rubbed his hands together and leaned in to read. Looking at the pair of them, close up together, Robyn's hand slipped on the glass she was taking down from the cupboard and she only just caught it in time to stop it smashing across the tiles.

'*This dark, rich taste is very fine, old bean,*' Zak read, then again in an exaggerated English accent that had Ashleigh giggling away:

'*This dark, rich taste is very fine, old bean,*

And we can dine on bonnets and be seen.'

'You could be the King of England himself,' Ashleigh simpered.

'We don't have a king,' Robyn snapped, thrown by her sister's unpredictable behaviour.

'Well, I can hardly call Zak a queen, can I?' Ashleigh said, darting her eyes to his muscled thighs.

Robyn did not deign to reply and thankfully Zak seemed focused on the clue.

'Coffee beans, I assume?' he said.

'I thought that,' Ashleigh agreed. 'Is there a coffee plantation around here?'

'Several, but mainly on the Big Island – Hawaii itself. There's Green World Farm here on Oahu but I can't see what that has to do with bonnets. Why would anyone dine on a bonnet anyway? That's a hat, right?'

'Or a part of a car,' Ashleigh said. 'The, you know, lid bit.'

'Lid bit?' Robyn laughed, but Zak gave Ashleigh a wide smile. 'The hood! Right. So it could be a drive-in?'

Ashleigh wrinkled up her nose.

'Like McDonald's? Surely Granny Ginny was classier than that?'

Zak shook his head.

'A drive-*in*, not a drive-through. You show up with your best wheels, park, wait for the chicks to flock around.' He coloured. 'I mean, *I* don't do that. Some people do. Cool people with, you know, cool wheels.'

Robyn smiled to see how pink he'd gone but before she could tease him, Ashleigh, who'd been tapping away into her fancy phone, cried, 'Bingo!'

'What have you got?' Zak asked eagerly. Ashleigh showed him. 'Ooh yes! I know this place. My first-year lecturer used to go on about going there when he was young.'

'What place?' Robyn asked, straining to see as Ashleigh and Zak pored over what looked like black-and-white pictures on her big screen. 'Can *I* see, please?!'

They jumped.

'God, sorry, Rob.' Zak leaned back. 'Look – it was a funky drive-in restaurant and coffee shop called Kau Kau Korner.'

'And now?'

'Now it's the Honolulu Coffee Experience Center. Doesn't sound quite as romantic but at least it's there to visit.'

'We don't need romantic,' Robyn said reprovingly, and then felt stupid. 'Let's go!'

*

The Honolulu Coffee Experience Center was a bright, friendly place, on the junction of two big roads not far from Robyn's flat. She must have walked past it often without paying any attention but now she scanned it, curious for remnants of its past incarnation. To their delight, they found several black-and-white photos tucked discreetly in the entrance lobby.

'One of those could be Granny Ginny,' Ashleigh said, stretching up to point at an atmospheric photo of a group of youngsters gathered around a smart little sports car. Behind them a waitress was carrying a tray piled high with fried chicken, and other groups filled the big parking lot.

Robyn peered at it intently, trying to step back into 1941 when life out here was still lived in the sunshine of peace – even if the shadow of war was creeping closer than any of them knew. She shivered at the thought that Granny Ginny could so easily have been killed on that terrible day in December 1941 when the Japanese bombers had swooped in.

'Any sign of a treasure chest?'

'I think we'd better ask behind the counter,' Ashleigh said.

Robyn nodded and went to wheel her sister into the thankfully open café, but Zak got there first.

'Allow me.'

'You're too kind,' Ashleigh said, sweet as pie, and didn't even grumble when he clipped the wheel on a table leg.

Robyn told herself sternly that it was nice to see her sister content for once and, leaving Zak to grab them a table, she made for the counter.

'What can I get for you?' the barista asked with a cheery smile.

Robyn ordered coffees and three of the delicious-looking cakes. She probably shouldn't with less than two weeks to go to her first race, but she'd run hard this morning.

'Anything else?' the girl asked.

Robyn cleared her throat self-consciously.

'This is probably going to sound insane, but you don't happen to have a treasure chest, do you?'

It *did* sound insane, but the girl just clapped her hands and cried: 'You're here! Maria, they're here for the chest!' Several people looked over and Robyn felt herself flush. The girl had run into the back and now she came out again, grinning widely, and said, 'Do take a seat – we'll be over with your order shortly.'

Robyn headed to the others, very aware of all eyes upon her.

'You've gone very pink, Rob,' Zak said, reaching out to touch her cheek and only making her flush more deeply.

'The barista certainly knew about the hunt,' she said, sitting hastily down.

'That's great. Ooh, carob loaf – my favourite.'

The girl was bringing their order across already but there was no sign of a chest. Robyn looked at her quizzically.

'Someone will be over shortly with your, er, other order.'

'Thank you,' Ashleigh said, reaching for the chocolate brownie and taking a big bite. 'Wow – they really do make good brownies in the States.'

'You're from England?' the waitress asked, clearly intrigued.

'That's right,' Ashleigh agreed, 'but our grandmother was American. She flew planes out here back in 1941.'

'1941?' the waitress asked, wide-eyed. Everyone on the island knew the significance of that particular year.

'She was a pilot,' Ashleigh confided easily.

Robyn looked curiously at her sister. She hadn't seen Ashleigh this relaxed or expansive for years and, whatever her reservations about the cause of her sudden good humour, it was lovely to see. When they'd been young, Ashleigh had always been the outgoing one. She'd got Robyn into endless scrapes in their early teens, dragging her off to picnics and pubs and parties until, of course, it had all been cut away one dark, rainy day not long after her eighteenth birthday.

'You must be sooo proud of her,' the waitress was gushing.

'We are,' Ashleigh agreed. 'And now she's set us up this treasure hunt to find out all about her life.'

'It's sooo exciting.'

The waitress all but skipped, and Robyn sipped at her excellent coffee to hide her smile and took a bite of her cake. It was delicious and she was very happy sitting down after her punishing run, but she was desperate to find the treasure chest and was relieved when, finally, an older lady came out from behind the counter carrying a box. It was identical to the one Mikala had handed them at the airport, if perhaps slightly smaller, and as Robyn felt in her pocket for the aeroplane key ring, she felt like a kid again, chasing clues around their back garden. She reached for Ashleigh's hand as the lady approached and placed the box down on the table.

'Thank you,' Zak said.

'Yes, thank you so much,' Robyn echoed hastily. 'I'm Robyn Harris and this is my sister Ashleigh. Somehow, my grandmother arranged for this box to be in your café.'

'She did,' the lady agreed with an enigmatic smile.

'How?' Ashleigh asked.

She tapped her finger to her nose.

'That would be telling. Let's just say that Virginia Martin – sorry, Harris – still has friends on this island.'

'You knew Granny Ginny?'

'Only a little. I was quite young at the time but Virginia wasn't someone you forgot in a hurry. Now, I'll leave you to your coffees – and your treasure.'

She gave them another smile and melted away. The people at the next table were looking over, openly curious, and Robyn fumbled the keys at Ashleigh.

'You open it, Ash.'

'Shall I?'

'Please,' Zak moaned. 'The suspense is killing me.'

Ashleigh looked at him with a cheeky smile, lifted up the second key and slotted it into the lock.

Chapter Seven

You made it to Kau Kau's then – not that it's called that any more. The manager tells me it's more of a museum these days which seems a shame, but I guess there's no room for a drive-in restaurant in the middle of Honolulu any more. Let me tell you though, it was fun back when Jack and I were first there. Oh, the nights we had in that autumn of 1941 when Pearl still seemed like paradise on earth!

12 September 1941

'*Hipa hipa!*'

Lilinoe lifted her cola glass to Ginny's with the local toast and Ginny clinked hers against it.

'*Hipa hipa*, Lili!'

She looked around the big lot of the Kau Kau Korner carhop, loving the relaxed party atmosphere of this late summer evening. It was still wonderfully balmy out in the middle of the Pacific and Ginny, used to the cold winters of Tennessee, was looking forward to the tropical warmth continuing all the way to Christmas. She'd miss snow, she supposed, but she and Jack were due to sail home mid-December for a festive month with their folks, so they'd get a bit of the white stuff then. In the meantime, she was loving being in a summer frock in late September and so, it seemed, was everyone else at the busy drive-in restaurant.

'*Hipa hipa*, Will,' she said, turning to their other companion.

William Dauth was one of Ginny's pupils at K-T. He'd been posted out to Pearl Harbor as a naval lieutenant but was keen to fly, and had told her that his uncle-in-law was paying for him to learn privately with the hope of transferring into the naval air force when he got his licence. He'd been cagey about who his uncle-in-law was, mind you, and no wonder, as earlier today Ginny had found out that he was married to the niece of none other than Admiral Husband Kimmel himself.

'Why didn't you tell me your uncle was the main man in these parts?' she teased him now.

'I didn't want any favours.'

'Don't worry, you wouldn't have got any from me. You have to be safe to fly whoever you're related to.'

'Good. But I didn't want it to even look like I was name dropping, you know.'

Ginny did know. Hadn't she resented having her own father help her get her first instructor job?

'Your secret is safe with me,' she promised him. 'And you're flying really well. A few more lessons and we'll get you up solo. You'll be a fully fledged pilot before Christmas, I promise.'

In truth, Ginny wasn't entirely sure of that. Nervy Will was far from a natural. He seemed to be too scared of what he might do wrong to truly give himself to flying, but saying so would only make him worse.

'I hope so,' he said. 'Helen's just booked tickets for her and the little ones to sail out on the *Lurline* when school term finishes, and she'll be so excited if I can take her up in a plane.'

His eyes shone and Lili placed a hand on his arm.

'You must miss her.'

'Oh, I do. Every moment.' He thought about this. 'Well, not every moment – I'm busy a lot of the time – but at least fifty times a day.'

'Fifty?' Ginny squinted at him. 'Fifty times a day you stop what you're doing to think, "I wish Helen were here"?'

Will nodded easily. 'What's wrong with that?'

Lili laughed. 'Ginny doesn't believe in love, do you, Ginny?'

Ginny shrugged. Lili was as hopelessly romantic as the rest of the world, convinced she'd soon be swept off her tiny feet by someone and pleased about it too. It seemed like madness to Ginny; she was quite content to be squarely on her feet, thank you very much.

'Nothing's happened to convince me of it yet,' she said to Will.

He grinned that knowing, sideways grin that so many people seemed to feel was an appropriate response to her perfectly logical statement.

'You will,' he said. 'One day you will.'

'I hope not,' she retorted tartly. 'Ooh, look – there's Jack. Jack, over here!'

She waved as her brother pulled into the parking lot in an army jeep, blond Eddie and dark Joe hanging out of the back. Dagne was on Eddie's lap and Joe was laughing with another man Ginny hadn't met before. Jack pulled up and they all leaped out.

'Billy,' Jack said, grabbing the young man, 'this is Ginny, my sister.'

'Evening, Ginny.' Billy gave her a lopsided grin. 'You look just like Jack here, only pretty.'

'Oi!' Jack protested, pretending to flick back his short chestnut hair.

'My apologies, Jacky-boy, you're quite the prettiest one at Kau Kau's.'

'Not that,' Jack shot back. 'Penny's definitely the prettiest. Ginny, meet Penny.'

He turned to help a petite blonde woman down from the passenger seat and Ginny stepped keenly forward. Jack had mentioned he'd been dating a nurse from the Queen's Hospital; clearly it had been going well.

'Lovely to meet you, Penny.'

'You too, Ginny. You brother says you're a pilot. That's amazing.'

'Not as amazing as your job,' Jack said promptly, looking devotedly down at her as if she were Princess Kawānanakoa, last of the deposed Hawaiian monarchy.

'Far too good for you then, Jack,' Ginny teased.

'Far too good,' her brother agreed happily.

Ginny groaned but Billy gave him a hearty pat on the back. 'You make the most of being together, buddy. My wife's at home in San Diego with our three lads and I miss her something rotten.'

'Fifty times a day?' Ginny suggested jokily, glancing at Will.

'At least,' Billy agreed, unabashed. 'Your lady back home too, buddy?'

''Fraid so,' Will agreed, 'but she's coming out for Christmas.'

'Bet you can't wait!'

The two of them were off then, chattering away about their families. Ginny shook her head crossly. Why had everyone around here got the damned love bug?

'Shall we order?' she asked sharply. 'I'm starving.'

There were general murmurs of assent and Ginny waved to a waitress who came bouncing over, order pad at the ready. Music was blaring out of the big white restaurant and in between the cars people were starting to dance as the sun went down, leaving only streetlamps and car headlights to illuminate the party. Ginny laughingly accepted as Billy pulled her into a jive. He was a good dancer – light and neat on his feet – and she happily let him spin her around as Jack pulled Penny out to join them. Eddie and Dagne were hot on their heels and even Lili was talked into it by Will.

'You should learn to fly, Billy,' Ginny said, as they came together.

'Fly? Why?'

'My instructor used to tell me that good dancers make good pilots – something to do with lightness of touch.'

Billy gave her a little skip of a bow.

'Well, I'm glad you think I'm a good dancer, but I'll stick with ships if it's all the same with you. I'm due a command any time now and I cannot wait.' He spun her round and back in against him. 'My captain's a miserable old geezer and I'm desperate to get away and onto my own vessel. Problem is, of course, that he's the one who'll recommend me for promotion. I can't decide if I'm better to impress his socks off or just annoy the hell out of him so he wants rid of me.'

Ginny laughed.

'Surely if you annoy him, he'll just have you scrubbing decks, or whatever it is you naval lot do.'

'True, true. Guess I'll just keep my head down and hope for the best. But, I tell you now, if we go to war, I want to go in on my own ship.'

Despite the lively swing music and the laughter all around, Ginny shivered. Her landlord and landlady were always chuntering away about the news, poring over the papers and muttering about the 'evil Japs'. Given that almost half the island's population were of Japanese descent, Ginny found it offensive and was desperately looking for somewhere else to stay.

They were right, mind you, that the situation in the Pacific was volatile. President Roosevelt was supposedly in talks with the Japanese government, trying to persuade them to pull out of China in exchange for dropping oil sanctions, but they didn't seem to be going well. Then there was the Atlantic. Every so often they caught tales of German submarines blowing up US ships carrying supplies to Britain, and Ginny hated the thought of them getting as far as the sparkling waters around Hawaii. As a child, she'd been scared of swimming in the lakes back home, convinced the fish were lurking to gobble up little girls, and the thought of hidden war machines patrolling beneath ships holding bright young men like Billy gave her the same chills. There could be little worse than an unseen attacker.

'Maybe Churchill will defeat Hitler,' she said, as the music slowed and their dancing with it. 'Then we can put all our efforts into the Pacific.'

'That would help,' Billy agreed, 'but I can't see it happening any time soon. The Germans are dug in across Europe and now they're making headway in Russia too.'

'Surely though, Billy, the Nazis won't ever make it to America?'

Billy shrugged.

'I can't see it myself, but if the world turns Nazi in the West and commie in the East then one way or another they'll do for us. Have you seen the sign?'

'What sign?'

'You don't know?' He dragged her across the parking lot and there, on the far side of the Kau Kau carhop, was a sign far taller than any man and emblazoned with the words 'Crossroads of the Pacific'. Ginny stared up at it, scanning the arrows that pointed in all directions with the names of cities and the distance in miles. 2,090 miles to San Francisco, 3,450 to Tokyo. They were all so far away. Even Midway, the closest destination and itself just a tiny island, was 1,150 miles from Oahu, and London, where the war was raging, was separated from them by 9,490 miles. It was an almost unimaginable distance, so surely they were safe?

She'd written to Jacqueline Cochran, listing her qualifications and asking to be considered for a ferrying corps if the great flyer ever managed to get one going. Jacqueline had been kind enough to write back, thanking her for her interest and assuring her that she had noted down her name. If it came to war, Ginny was all set to do her bit, but right now she had to admit that keeping the peace beneath these tropical skies looked a far more attractive option.

'Chicken's here!' Jack called, and gratefully she turned from the daunting sign and ran back across to her friends.

Later, she walked home with Lilinoe, arm in arm. The house her friend shared with Kalani was on Ginny's way back and she was glad of the company. Her head was buzzing with all the great tunes that had played the night away, and it was nice to wander along to little more than the buzz of the crickets and the chirp of the nightjars.

'Would you like a drink of something?' Lili asked her when they reached her gate. 'Or maybe some cake? Papa made his special chocolate cake earlier – you'll love it.'

'Kalani bakes?'

'Oh yes. Mama left a recipe book full of cakes and Papa works his way through them in strict rotation. I think it's his way of keeping her close.'

She looked sadly at the little house and Ginny squeezed her arm.

'I'd love some, thank you.'

Lili smiled shyly and fished out her key.

'It's not very smart,' she warned. 'Not like you're used to, I'm sure.'

Ginny shook her head.

'Compared to where I'm lodging, it will be a palace.'

Sure enough, although Lili and Kalani's home was basic, it was spotlessly clean and decorated with love. The fabric of the chairs, curtains and cushions was brightly patterned and cheerful; there were fresh flowers on the side and photos all over the whitewashed wooden walls. Lili led Ginny into the kitchen, poured glasses of milk and lifted a bamboo cover to reveal the most delicious-looking chocolate cake. Ginny's mouth watered and she sank gratefully into a wooden chair, worn beautifully smooth from years of use.

'You have a lovely home, Lili.'

Lili flushed.

'Thank you. Papa and I are kicking around in it since my sisters married and moved out, but we can't bear to leave.'

Ginny's ears pricked up.

'You've got spare rooms?'

'One, yes.'

Ginny looked longingly around her.

'Would you ever consider renting it out?'

'Our spare room? Who on earth to?' Ginny held her gaze and Lili's dark eyes widened. 'To you? Oh, it wouldn't be nearly good enough.'

'Can't I be the judge of that?'

'You must be used to far more luxury than this, Ginny.'

'Luxury is someone who smiles when you walk through the door, a place you can sit and feel comfortable, somewhere that feels like home.'

Lili picked uncertainly at her cake.

'I'd have to talk to Papa, but you'd be very welcome, I'm sure. We couldn't charge rent though – you're a friend.'

Ginny smiled. A brilliant idea had just occurred to her.

'Not rent,' she agreed. 'Flying lessons.'

Lili gasped. 'No?!'

'Yes! Oh, go on, doll, please. You'll be a wonderful pilot, I know you will, and I'd so love to teach you.'

Lili let out a little squeal.

'Really? Really, Ginny?'

'Really, really!'

Ginny laughed as Lili pulled her up and danced her around the cosy kitchen. A sleepy-eyed Kalani appeared, looking sweeter than ever in flannelette pyjamas.

'What's going on?' he asked.

'Ginny's going to come and live with us, Papa,' Lili said, letting go of one of Ginny's hands to pull her bemused father into the dance. 'She's going to come and live with us and in return she's going to give me wings.'

'Wings?'

Kalani clearly suspected that he was still asleep and dreaming his daughter's laughing words.

'Piper Cub wings, Papa – I'm going to be a pilot!'

'Truly?' Kalani looked as if he might cry. He turned to Ginny. 'It is what my daughter has dreamed of for many years, Miss

Martin. Always she looks at the birds and the ladybugs in the skies, always she reads of fairies and dragons and other creatures of the air. And always she loves the planes. Will you really teach her?' It was the most Ginny had ever heard the shy engineer say and she beamed at him.

'It will be my pleasure, Kalani. Lili and I will fly together.'

They both hugged her over and over, and it was with some relief that Ginny extricated herself and made for the bleak room that need not be her home any longer. Tomorrow she would move her stuff in with Lili and Kalani, and the day after she would start Lili's lessons.

She climbed up the little hill to her lodgings and paused to look out across the island. The ships were all lit up in Pearl Harbor, big and brash and beautiful beneath the stars. Beyond the oyster-shaped harbour she could see stragglers heading home from the hotels and bars of Waikiki, and she smiled as she stretched out her own feet, aching from a happy night of dancing. This lovely place was truly starting to feel like home.

Chapter Eight

Wednesday 6 March

'Yes!'

The two mechanics looked up from the turbofan jet engine as it roared into life and high-fived Robyn delightedly. She smiled. It had been a battle to unblock the stators but they'd done it at last, and she left the hangar feeling quietly satisfied with her afternoon's work – until, that is, she saw the sun dropping down behind a big Airbus. She was late! Ashleigh would kill her.

After devouring the last letter introducing all of Granny's fascinating friends on Oahu they were meant to be cracking the third clue today, but after having two weeks off to be with Granny Ginny in her last days, Robyn didn't dare take any more holiday. She hurried into her office and quickly changed her work shoes for the trainers she kept in her bottom drawer. It would be faster to jog home than wait for buses and, despite feeling ridiculous in her work clothes, she headed out of the airport, picked up her feet and ran.

By the time she got back to her flat twenty minutes later, she was hot and sweaty. The lift, of course, was playing up and she had to pant on up the stairs to her door. There, however, she froze. She could hear voices inside, and was that… laughter? Yes, that was definitely the tinkle of Ashleigh's laugh, like a bell from her child-hood, and there was a deeper voice too. Had her sister somehow got herself a date? She shot inside and stared.

'Zak!'

'Rob, hi! Are you OK?'

'You look like you've been dragged through a hedge backwards,' Ashleigh added helpfully. She, Robyn noticed, was looking very fresh and pretty in a deep red maxi dress.

'I ran home.'

'In those clothes?' Zak asked. 'Is that wise?'

Robyn felt she might cry.

'Of course it's not wise, but I was late. I thought Ashleigh would be upset.'

Ashleigh gave that alien tinkle of a laugh again.

'I'd have understood, sis. Work's work, and Zak and I have been having a lovely chat. He's told me about this wheelchair basketball club his mate runs – sounds good, doesn't it?'

Robyn gaped at Ashleigh.

'Sounds great,' she spluttered.

'So, you see, you needn't have rushed.'

'I see,' Robyn agreed fiercely. 'You could have let me know that. I thought you were desperate to get on with the treasure hunt.'

'Yes – and I have done. With Zak's help.'

She reached out and patted him. Robyn stared. She'd barely seen Ashleigh touch anyone since the accident but now here she was, running her fingertips down Zak's arm. She felt an alarming rush of jealousy. Why was that? It was lovely to see her sister interested in someone at last, but why did she have to pick Zak? *Her* Zak?

'He's not yours at all,' she muttered to herself.

'Sorry, Rob?'

'Nothing. I'd just, er, better get a drink. Excuse me.'

She ducked through to the kitchen to grab some water and, catching sight of herself in the window, saw the sweaty, dishevelled mess she was presenting. *Fantastic.*

'Rob?' Ashleigh was calling. 'The clue.'

'Coming.'

She turned reluctantly back, but just then Zak came through and she bumped straight into him.

'Oh God, sorry,' she spluttered.

'No, my fault. I startled you.' Zak had caught her arms to stop her falling and she looked up to find herself very close to his handsome face. 'Are you OK with me here, Robyn? I didn't mean to intrude.'

His eyes were so full of concern that she melted.

'You're not intruding. It was lovely of you to come and see Ash.'

'Oh, I didn't… That is, I came to bring you a copy of the coaching programme.'

'Doesn't that come by email?'

Now it was Zak who blushed.

'It does, yeah, but I always like a paper copy to, you know, stick on my wall, so I printed it out in the lab and, well, I must have pressed the wrong button because I got two copies so I thought that you might, you know, like the other one. Save wasting paper.'

'Right.'

He was looking very shifty and as he handed her the sheet, it was pretty clear that it had just been an excuse. *Well, good*, Robyn told herself, looking at her sister glowing with life. After years of battling, she deserved a bit of happiness.

'I've been telling Zak all about Granny Ginny lodging with Lilinoe,' Ashleigh said cheerily, 'and d'you know what, I think I remember the name.'

'You do?'

'You know that picture of Granny in her aeroplane on the wall at home?'

'Of course.'

'Well, there's another woman in it with her, right? I think that's Lilinoe. I'm sure I remember Granny telling me her name when I was younger – I thought it sounded like an eastern princess.'

'It sort of does,' Robyn conceded. 'Damn, I wish we had it with us.'

'I'll text Mrs Deans next door and see if she can take a photo of it when she's watering the plants, but for now, we'd better crack on with the next clue.'

'Right,' Robyn agreed. 'Read it to me again.'

Ashleigh did so, in a triumphant voice:

'A regal building this, for the finest guests.

If you want a Mai Tai, you must wear your best.

'It's not one of Granny Ginny's finest. Zak got it straight away, didn't you, Zak?'

'I'd say it's the Royal Hawaiian Hotel, wouldn't you, Rob?'

Robyn forced herself to think about it. Regal was certainly another word for royal and everyone said they did the best Mai Tais – and the most expensive.

'Remember what Granny Ginny told us,' Ashleigh was saying. '"Drink Mai Tais in my memory."'

Robyn closed her eyes as the words echoed to her in Ginny's voice, fading but still rich with all the assurance with which she'd brought them both up. She felt grief, held at bay over these last few hectic days, suddenly hit her again and battled to fight back tears. This treasure hunt made it feel as if Granny Ginny was still sitting at home waiting for them to come running back when they'd tracked down all the clues, but she wasn't at home any more and she never would be again.

'OK, Rob?' Ashleigh asked, her voice unusually hesitant.

'Fine,' Robyn managed, but it came out ridiculously squeaky.

Zak jumped up. 'I'll leave you two to get on with the hunt.'

She shook herself.

'No, no, you don't need to go. Sorry if I've been a bit weird. I was just startled and, you know, tired.'

'I'm not surprised. You've had a hard time of it.' His kindness almost made her cry again and she looked hastily down. 'Best if I leave you to it. I'll see you at training tomorrow, yeah?'

'Right. Yeah. Thanks for the programme.'

'No problem.'

Zak fumbled at the latch and was gone, and suddenly the flat felt horribly empty. An awkward silence fell, then Ashleigh cleared her throat noisily.

'Guess we're free to go out now, then. Hope you're not coming dressed like that?' She screwed up her nose at Robyn's sweaty work clothes.

'No,' Robyn bit back. 'I'll change.'

'Something nice. Or they won't let us into the Royal Hawaiian.'

Robyn groaned. A fancy cocktail was the last thing she needed right now, but then Granny Ginny's voice came back to her – 'Drink Mai Tais in my memory, girls' – and again the tears swirled. With a resigned sigh, she made for the shower. Cocktails it was.

'Oh goodness, Ashleigh, it's very posh.'

Robyn looked nervously up at the Royal Hawaiian. She'd often admired this beautiful building with its curving, Moorish roofline and coral-pink walls, but she'd never before dared to go in.

'Looks great to me,' Ashleigh said, rubbing her hands together. 'And besides, these are Granny Ginny's orders!' She suddenly reached out and squeezed Robyn's hand. 'I know this is weird for you, Rob, but we belong in this hotel just as much as anyone else and don't you forget it.'

With that, she wheeled herself confidently up to the grand entrance, leaving Robyn with no choice but to follow. She needn't have worried. The doorman swept the doors wide with a gracious smile and, once inside, they could hear the chatter of happy people enjoying an evening drink, much like in any bar around town.

'That way,' Ashleigh said, gesturing to a big white archway across the vast marbled lobby. Through it the moonlit sea was framed like a perfect picture and tables with bright umbrellas filled the foreground, lit from subtle lights in the flowerbeds. Despite her nerves, Robyn's spirits rose. So what if the drinks cost a fortune? Granny Ginny had left them a fortune in her will and now was the time to honour her.

'A table on the Ocean Lawn, ladies?' a smart young waiter asked, and when they nodded, he showed them to a lovely one near the sea, sweeping away a chair to make room for Ashleigh. 'What can I get you?'

'Mai Tais, please,' Ashleigh said without hesitation.

'An excellent choice.'

He bowed away and Robyn sat down, feeling her whole body relax as she looked around the happy lawn. For a moment she wished Zak were here to see this, and then she looked at her sister and was glad it was just the two of them.

'You seem to like Zak,' she said casually.

'Zak?' Ashleigh met her gaze. 'Yes, he's very nice.'

'I haven't heard you chatting to anyone like that for ages.'

'He's easy to chat to.'

'Good-looking too.'

Ashleigh looked archly at her across the pretty arrangement of hibiscus flowers in the centre of their table. 'You think so, sis?'

'No! I mean, objectively, yes, but I don't, you know, fancy him.'

'No?'

'No!'

Ashleigh shrugged.

'Fair enough. I'd say you must be blind though.'

'So you *do* think he's good-looking!'

'He *is*. Objectively.'

Robyn ground her teeth in frustration. She'd forgotten how good her sister was at this game.

'He's a very good hurdler,' she said, seeking safer ground.

'Can't be that good if he trains with a loser like you.'

Robyn looked crossly up but Ashleigh's eyes were twinkling and she told herself not to rise.

'Our group are all pretty good actually. There's this great lad, Cody, who might really have what it takes, but he has to work to support his family.'

'He's got kids?'

'He *is* a kid. Only seventeen, but it seems his mum died, leaving his dad and four boys, and he's doing his best to help out.'

Ashleigh sighed.

'We were lucky on that front, weren't we? Money's never really been a worry for us.'

'And it certainly isn't now that Granny's left us her house.'

That was something they really had to discuss, but there was no time to dwell on it now for the waiter was reappearing with their cocktails, beautifully presented in curved glasses, deep orange at the base, fading to bright yellow at the top, with a cherry and a curved slice of pineapple wedged on one side.

'Enjoy, ladies.'

'Oh, we will,' Ashleigh said, reaching keenly for hers, then pausing. 'Can I ask you something?'

'Of course, madam.'

'Do you know anything about a treasure chest?'

The young man blinked but kept his composure admirably.

'Treasure chest, madam? Here at the Royal?'

'We're told one has been left here for us.'

'Right. I'll, er, go and find out for you.'

'That would be very kind.' He scuttled off and Ashleigh burst out laughing. 'Poor man – he thought I was crackers.'

'You are! We should have asked at the desk.'

'Why bother when he can do it for us? Now, my lovely sister, I believe We have a toast to drink.'

Robyn swallowed, the waiter instantly forgotten, and lifted her Mai Tai. 'To Granny Ginny.'

'To Granny Ginny!' Ashleigh echoed, tipping the glass gently against hers before they both took a sip. It was delicious – soft and fruity with the spiced kick of the alcohol beneath.

'Did Granny really drink here back in the forties, do you think?' she asked.

'I guess that's what the letter will tell us, but it seems likely. She and Uncle Jack were quite the society pair.' Robyn looked around, imagining their grandmother here back when the grand old hotel was still quite new. 'I miss her, Ash.'

'Me too. She was an amazing woman. She got me through after, you know…'

'The accident?'

Ashleigh nodded and looked down. 'I might not have made it without her.'

'What?' Robyn looked at her sister, aghast. 'You would have…'

'Killed myself. Maybe. I mean, I hope I'd never have gone through with it – Harris girls don't give up and all that – but some days when I first came home, I admit that I was close. Everything just felt so pointless. You were off at uni and I was stuck at home in a frigging wheeled chair, like I was a toddler again. Mum and Dad were always hovering around, wanting to hug me but having no idea how to actually help. And then there was Granny Ginny. She was the only one who didn't treat me as if I'd changed, who still talked to me like a normal human being, who wouldn't let me wallow in self-pity.'

'"You're good with wheels, Ashleigh",' Robyn quoted, and Ashleigh gave a rueful smile.

'She said that all the time. Mum and Dad used to try and shush her but I liked it. I mean, I grumbled about it, shouted even, but I liked it underneath and Granny knew that.'

She sipped at her Mai Tai, her eyes misty, and Robyn felt a lump form in her throat.

'I'm sorry, Ash, I didn't realise.'

'Good. I didn't want you to. No point both of us being miserable, was there?'

'Even so…'

'Even so nothing.' She leaned in. 'Do you know what I regret, Rob?'

Robyn shook her head, scared to speak in case she cried into her Mai Tai.

'I regret not getting out sooner. I wish I'd been brave enough to do this sort of thing before Granny… I wish I'd shown her that she was right to have faith in me, that I could get on and live my life properly and not just skulk around in the house.'

'She knew you could, Ash. She bought you tickets to Hawaii after all.'

Ashleigh gave her a sad smile.

'Bit drastic though, right? I mean, I should really have started with my own high street.'

Robyn squinted at her.

'You didn't go out at home at all?'

'Not other than work, no.'

'I don't believe that. I've just seen you being all sassy with that waiter.'

Ashleigh grimaced.

'I know! It's come back to me pretty fast, which is what makes it even more of a shame. I could have been bossing it in pubs for years. I could have gone with Granny Ginny. She'd have liked that; she'd have been proud of me.'

'She *was* proud of you.'

'Not as proud as I'd have liked her to be.'

Ashleigh blinked fiercely, and Robyn reached out and took her hand.

'Well, you're doing it now, and if there's any sort of heaven then I reckon she's up there, sitting on a shiny barstool, toasting us both. *Hipa hipa*, Granny Ginny!'

'Hipa what?' Ashleigh spluttered.

'*Hipa hipa*. It's Hawaiian for cheers.'

'Fantastic. *Hipa hipa*, Granny!' Ashleigh lifted her glass high but she still looked fragile and Robyn was relieved when the waiter came rushing back, his careful composure askew.

'There *is* a treasure chest,' he blurted excitedly.

'Fantastic,' Robyn said. 'Where?'

He coughed, trying to claw back his dignity.

'Someone will bring it over shortly.'

'Right. Wonderful. Thank you very much.'

'Is it really treasure?'

'It is to us.'

She smiled as the waiter turned reluctantly back to his duties, wondering if he'd been hoping for a gold doubloon as a tip. She tried to relax and enjoy her drink but they were both on tenterhooks, and she was relieved when Ashleigh finally pointed into the hotel with a small squeal. A woman was coming out, carrying a chest. Dressed in a very smart suit, with her hair in a tight bun, she tapped across to them on heels that were surely too high for a hotel manager, and Robyn had the strangest feeling she'd seen her before.

'Ashleigh and Robyn Harris?' she asked. They nodded. 'Then this is for you, with the compliments of the Royal Hawaiian Hotel.'

She placed it on the table and Robyn was glad to see that it was smaller, again, than the first two. It seemed that Granny Ginny had cleverly designed Russian Doll treasure chests for her tiny flat.

'How did…?' she started to ask the woman but, to her surprise, she'd melted away into the curious crowd, with only the echoing tap-tap of her heels to mark her exit. 'Weird!'

Her sister laughed.

'This whole thing is weird, Rob. I've no idea how Granny managed it but, hey, it beats scaling trees for clues.'

'Or diving into murky rivers,' Robyn agreed, taking out the aeroplane key ring and placing it on the table between the chest and their two jaunty cocktails.

Her sweaty run home already felt as if it had been yesterday, and she blessed her grandmother for sending her to places on the island that she'd never dared visit before. This was truly turning out to be the ultimate treasure hunt, and she couldn't wait to read the next instalment of Granny Ginny's tantalising story.

Chapter Nine

I hope you have Mai Tais in your hands, girls, and hipa hipa *to you both! I bet you haven't been in the Royal Hawaiian before, Robyn – you were always so shy about whether you were entitled to go into smart places. It's a ridiculously British approach that you need to shake off. You girls, both of you, are worth more than most, and I want you to hold your heads high always. My dear friend Lilinoe used to fret about her place in the world, and let me tell you she had no reason. She was the best pilot I knew and the day she gained her licence will always be a fond one in my memory.*

3 November 1941

'Champagne, please,' Ginny called to the waiter as she swept Lilinoe into the Royal Hawaiian Hotel, Kalani scuttling in their wake.

'Ginny…' Lili protested, but Ginny pressed a gentle finger over her friend's lips.

'My treat, Lili. We have to celebrate. You were amazing today.'

After only two months of lessons, Lili had taken her test this afternoon and passed with, literally, flying colours. Ginny had been certain she would. She'd rarely had a more natural pupil. Lili already knew all there was to know about the Piper Cubs from working on them all day long, but her feel for them in the air had been instinctual. She'd gone solo after only five lessons and Ginny had had no hesitation about putting her up for her test. Even so, she had paced on the side of the runway with Kalani like a nervous mother hen as Lili had coasted out with the tester, and had leaped for joy when she'd watched her execute a perfect landing at the end.

'Nice job,' Robert Tyce had said, coming out at the sound of her whoops. 'We'll have her instructing with you before long.'

'Do you really think so?' Kalani had asked excitedly.

'Don't see why not. That girl really knows how to fly – well spotted, Ginny. How about a drink to celebrate?'

Robert was often suggesting a drink to Ginny. He was very kind to her and very charming but she wasn't sure she trusted his intentions, or his claims to be widowed. She loved him dearly as a boss, but there was no way she was risking her job for a dalliance with someone who'd clearly had his fair share of women. It just wasn't worth it.

'Lovely idea,' she'd said smoothly. 'I'm sure Lili would be really grateful. And you must come too, Kalani, of course.'

Robert's face had fallen and the promised drink had, in the end, been a rather swift soda in the Inter-Island terminal. Lili had been delighted to be treated by the K-T boss, however, and at least now the celebrations could properly begin. Ginny had sent word to Jack and was hoping he'd be able to join them with anyone he could find to bring along. President Roosevelt's negotiations with the Japanese had not been going well and they'd all been working hard building the force up to full strength, making fun nights out rather thin on the ground.

Will Dauth had told them that his uncle-in-law, Admiral Kimmel, was repeatedly asking Washington for more ships and, in particular, more planes, but although production had been stepped up across the United States, all available hardware was going east. Hitler was making worrying advances into Russia, encircling some vital city called Kiev, and if he took the country, the eastern border of the Nazi Fatherland would hit Japanese-controlled China, potentially bringing the war full circle back across the Pacific to America. Tonight though, with a new pilot in their midst, Ginny was praying her friends would be able to get leave to come out and she scanned the room hopefully.

She spotted her brother at the bar and was about to call out to him when she noticed that he was with Penny, and paused to watch them together. Her brother was leaning solicitously towards his sweetheart, and Ginny saw him reach out to tuck a curl of her blonde hair behind her ear and drop a tender kiss onto her lips. She put a hand to her own mouth to hide her gasp. It was apparent, even to her, that she was no longer the first woman in Jack's life.

'He looks happy,' Lili said at her shoulder.

Ginny shook herself.

'You're right, doll, he looks very happy.' That, after all, was what counted, and Penny seemed a lovely girl, so why the hell not? 'Jack!' she called, heading over. He jumped up and came to hug her.

'Hey, Ginny. Hey, Lili – how did it go?' He looked down at the Hawaiian girl and his brown eyes sparkled. 'You passed, didn't you? I can tell that you passed – and no wonder. Let's get some champagne!'

Ginny stopped him.

'Already ordered, thanks, Jack. Can we join you?'

'Of course. Let's grab a table.'

They sank happily into a nearby booth. A few hardy folk were drinking out on the Ocean Lawn, but with a wind coming in off the sea it was a little chilly and they were happy to stay inside.

'I don't think we've met,' Jack said, offering Kalani his hand.

'Of course.' Ginny flushed. 'Sorry. Jack, this is Kalani Kamaka, Lilinoe's father and my wonderful landlord.'

'The cake chef!' Jack cried. 'Ginny's told me all about your wonderful cooking, Mr Kamaka. Lovely to meet you at last and thank you for taking care of my sister.'

Kalani flushed darkest red and bowed over Jack's proffered hand. Jack, unfazed, bowed back and ushered him into a seat at his side.

Ginny slid in next to Penny and watched with pride as Jack asked the little Hawaiian all about his work with the planes, putting him at his ease with his natural charm.

Perhaps one of the reasons why she was so sceptical about love was that it was hard to see how she'd ever find a man as lovely as her brother. She looked at Penny, adoringly watching him talk to the old Hawaiian, and hoped the girl knew how lucky she was.

'All well, Ginny?' Lili asked and she turned to her, shaking her self-centred thoughts away.

'Very well. Oh, and look, here's the champagne. Marvellous.' She beamed at Lili as the waiter popped the cork with a discreet flourish and poured out glasses for them all. 'Looks like Robert wants you piloting for him as soon as we can get you your instructor's licence. What do you reckon?'

'Wouldn't that mean more lessons?'

'Many more,' Ginny agreed. 'Which is a good job as it means I can keep staying in your wonderful home.'

'It's your home too, for as long as you want it. We can never repay you for this.'

'Nonsense. Let's get you that instructor's licence and plenty of hours in the air and then, if Jacqueline Cochran gets her ferrying service up and running, we can both join.'

Kalani looked alarmed and Lili smiled at him.

'He worries about losing me, Ginny. With Mama dying and then my sisters leaving to set up home on their own, I'm all he's got.'

'And we'll keep you safe. Our planes have the best engineers on the field, right? And what other harm can come to you here? You've got half the US navy in Pearl Harbor to keep the war away.'

'Pray God,' Kalani said, crossing himself and looking to the ornate ceiling.

But now the champagne was poured and, as everyone lifted their glasses, Ginny stood up to propose the toast: 'To Lilinoe Kamaka – ace engineer, ace friend and now ace pilot!'

'Ace pilot,' the others echoed, and Lili blushed furiously as they clinked glasses.

Their party were making rather a lot of noise and Ginny flinched as a man in a very smart dress uniform came striding across.

'Oh no,' Jack muttered, leaping up. 'That's Admiral Bellinger.'

'Bellinger? *The* Bellinger?'

Ginny's legs quaked. Admiral Patrick Bellinger was a hero of the Great War and a renowned pilot. He'd been put in charge of Naval Operations in 1919 and throughout the interwar period had battled to establish a permanent aviation branch. Not only was he a brilliant pilot himself, but he was one of the men pushing the airplane as the key instrument of modern warfare and Ginny had read every article she could find about him. To have him storming towards her noisy table was, therefore, mortifying.

'I'm terribly sorry for the racket, sir,' she said, hastening forward, but to her surprise, Bellinger was smiling.

'Did I hear you toasting a new pilot?'

She blinked.

'You did, yes. My good friend Lilinoe Kamaka here.'

Little Lili looked as if she would happily sink through the floor as Bellinger turned his eager gaze upon her.

'A girl, hey? Great work.'

'And taught by another girl, sir,' Jack put in. 'Meet my sister, Virginia Martin, instructor at K-T Flying Service.'

Bellinger turned back to Ginny, leaving Lili almost fainting with relief.

'You're an instructor? Good on you.'

'You don't object to women flying then?'

'Don't see why I should. We have a great tradition of aviatrixes in this country. Not that I'd send you lovelies to war, of course. No one wants wives and mothers shot at by Krauts. Wouldn't be right, would it? End of civilisation as we know it. But I believe what the redoubtable Ms Cochran is proposing is that women take over the ferrying of planes from factory to field in order to release the men to fight – right, Virginia?'

'Exactly right, sir. I've written to her and she's assured me that if the top brass give us the nod, she'll be straight in touch.'

'Good on you, girl.'

Ginny flushed.

'That means a lot, sir. I've read all about you; you're an amazing pilot.'

'Was,' Bellinger corrected her sadly. 'I'm too old and beat to be allowed up these days – just stuck controlling others.'

'But you think planes are the future, don't you?'

'Of course. Any fool can see that. Don't get me wrong, I love a great big destroyer but, Lord, they're slow. Aircraft carriers – that's what we need. Get the little mosquitos into position and let them sting the enemy hard and fast.'

Penny whimpered and Jack put a protective arm around her shoulders.

'*If* it comes to war, sir,' he said.

'Oh, it'll come to war,' Bellinger retorted darkly. 'Everyone knows that. Enjoy this Christmas, folks, because come 1942 we'll be fighting. Now – how about another bottle of champagne on me? Waiter!'

He sat down on a bench, the others hastily moving up to make room, Lili and Kalani crushing themselves as far into the corner as they could. Ginny felt bad for taking the spotlight off her friend but she seemed far happier out of it, and it wasn't every day a girl was toasted by a hero of the skies.

'Truth be told,' Bellinger was saying, 'I reckon we're going to need all the pilots we can get. The lads in intelligence have been picking up Jap talk of something they say translates as a "First Air Fleet".'

'That's right,' Jack agreed. 'Eddie was telling me as much the other day.'

'Eddie Layton? Good man that. Knows his stuff. Reckons Admiral Yamamoto is building up their air force, so we need to make sure ours is twice as big before they hit us with it.'

'I'm ready to fly for my country, sir,' Jack said eagerly.

'And you are?'

'Lieutenant Jack Martin, sir.'

'Course you are – brother to this firecracker of a pilot, right? Well, Jack Martin, get practising your gunnery skills. You're going to need them. Ah, champagne, marvellous!'

He made way for the waiter, and Ginny watched as the bottle was popped and the beautiful creamy liquid frothed into their glasses anew, but her throat was suddenly too tight to drink. Like a fool she'd been eager to fly her way into her country's service, but until this moment she hadn't really thought about what it might mean.

She might only have to ferry planes around, but her beloved brother would be facing enemy bullets with only their flimsy fuselage for protection. Suddenly Penny's whimper didn't seem so pathetic, and for the first time since she'd come to beautiful Hawaii, Ginny prayed with all her heart that America would not, by some miracle, have to enter the war after all.

Chapter Ten

Thursday 7 March

'Robyn? Robyn, wake up!' Robyn fought her way to the surface of a deliciously deep sleep to find herself on the sofa. She remembered coming in from work and sitting down for a rest, but then nothing. She must have nodded off. 'Robyn! Come on, I need you.'

Her heart skidded and she sat bolt upright, the world lurching. 'Ash? Are you OK?'

'Fine,' her sister said crisply. 'But if we're going to make basketball you need to wake up.'

'Basket…' Robyn collapsed back onto the sofa with a groan and glanced at her watch. 'It's only six thirty.'

'So? It starts at eight and who knows how long it will take us to get there. What if your stupid lift isn't working?'

Robyn groaned again. When they'd got in from the Royal Hawaiian last night, the lift had refused to function and Robyn had ended up carrying first Ashleigh and then her chair up five flights of stairs. It had taken a lot of energy on her part and a lot of indignity on her sister's, and they'd both been worn out by the time they'd finally got in. It would seem, however, that Ashleigh had bounced back better than Robyn, probably because she got to sleep in her lovely, comfy double bed instead of a bit of canvas strung between two poles.

'The basketball *was* your idea,' Ashleigh wheedled.

Robyn nodded wearily.

'Give me five minutes, Ash, and I'll be right there.'

The lift had thankfully been fixed, probably due to her furious messages to maintenance, and they got into Robyn's car with the minimum of fuss and set off for the sports centre. The minute they were on the road, however, Ashleigh's mood dipped.

'It'll probably be rubbish,' she muttered. 'Oh God, Robyn, I think this was a mistake.'

'Let's just try it.'

'What's the point? I'm hardly going to win, am I?'

'No one's asking you to win, Ash, just to give it a try.'

Ashleigh gave a little grunt and Robyn suppressed another groan. She had to confess that a tiny bit of her was looking forward to her sister going home next week, though they still hadn't addressed what she was going to do without Granny Ginny. She swallowed.

'Where are you going to live, Ash?'

'What?!'

'When you go back to England, are you going to live in Granny's house?'

'Why? Are you going to stop me? Do you want your share?'

'No! I mean, eventually maybe, but not yet, not if you want to live there. Can you?'

'Live there? Why would I not?'

'I mean, you know, alone.'

'You mean with me being totally useless?'

Robyn chose not to point out that it had been Ashleigh ducking domestic duties all week rather than her assuming she was incapable.

'I just wondered if you'd want help? Or if you'd be better in a different sort of house, a, a…'

'Bungalow?' Ashleigh spat, as bitterly as she might say 'slum', or even 'gutter'.

Robyn sighed. Why had she even got into this?

'I want you to be happy, Ash, that's all.'

'Then get me some new legs.'

Robyn supposed she'd asked for that. She sought for a change of topic – and found it.

'Did you bring the latest letter along? We could maybe have a think about the fourth clue?'

'Coward,' Ashleigh muttered, but with an exaggerated sigh, she pulled the letter out of her bag and unfolded it. 'It's a weird one. Listen:

A desert island, some might say, but see,
You wipe your feet on the mat, son, just for me.'

'A desert island?' Robyn said. 'Is Granny Ginny sending us out to sea?'

'Is there an obvious island?'

'Not that I know of. What was the second bit? Wipe your feet on the mat? I don't get it at all.'

'And why "son"? We're daughters, clearly – well, granddaughters.' Ashleigh twisted the paper as if it might make more sense upside down. 'I can't even think what to put into Google with this one.'

'Well, it will have to wait for now. We're here.'

Robyn indicated the smart sports centre and Ashleigh fidgeted in her seat.

'Perhaps we should give it a miss, Rob. It's pointless really. I'm only here another week so we'd be better off focusing on this clue, right?'

Robyn looked at her and smiled.

'Wrong. There'll be time for the clue later. And look, there's Zak!'

He was standing in the entranceway looking out for them and Robyn's spirits rose instantly. She leaped out of the car, feeling the night air still warm on her face.

'Hey, Zak!'

He came loping over.

'Evening, Robyn. All set, Ashleigh?'

'All set, but I'll be rubbish at it.'

Zak glanced uncertainly to Robyn, who gave him an apologetic grimace as they helped Ashleigh out of the car and through into a big sports hall, where several people were already zipping around in very funky-looking wheelchairs.

'That's my friend Chad who runs the club,' Zak said, before calling out: 'Chad! This is Ashleigh, who I was telling you about.'

A young man spun an impressive 360 and shot across to them. He had a huge grin, a buzz cut, and the most enormous shoulders Robyn thought she'd ever seen.

'Welcome to the crew! Who needs legs when you got wheels, hey?'

Ashleigh sent a fierce look Robyn's way, but Chad was beckoning them all over to the other sporty chairs lined up at the far side and they had little choice but to follow. Getting Ashleigh into one was a bit of a struggle, but once she was strapped in, she moved it cautiously, then with more style.

'This thing's actually quite cool. It's so light and so manoeuvrable. Look!' She spun it right round with a grin and then rolled her eyes at herself. 'Help, Robyn,' she hissed, 'I'm turning into Chad!'

Robyn laughed.

'Never, sis.'

The hall was filling up with other players and Robyn sat down on a bench to one side, delighted when Zak joined her.

'Ashleigh seems OK?' he said.

'She does,' Robyn agreed cautiously, as her sister lined up with the others for a warm-up length of the hall, then shot off at speed, her eyes alight as she accelerated out in front. 'She's a little competitive.'

'You don't say!'

They watched as Ashleigh almost crashed herself into the far wall in an effort to stop Chad catching her.

'Nice work, girl!' Chad cried, unabashed. 'Let's go again.'

'How do you know Chad?' Robyn asked Zak.

'He's a pilot on one of our research boats. Used to be in the navy but got taken out by a bomb in Beirut harbour. Lost both his legs. Says he was in a dark place for ages, though it's hard to imagine as I've never met anyone more relentlessly cheerful. Then he got the job on the boats and started playing basketball, and he's never looked back.'

'That's nice to know.'

'I guess your sister just needs to realise there are still things to look forward to, right?'

His eyes were following Ashleigh around the hall.

'What sort of things?' Robyn asked.

'You know, normal things – a job, friends, a partner. Chad says life really turned around for him when he met his wife, Jane. She gave him the incentive to get on and do something with his life.'

'You're saying Ashleigh needs love?'

'Don't we all?'

Zak looked at her and the vast hall felt suddenly very small, and rather short of oxygen. What was he saying? Was he falling for Ashleigh? Robyn's thoughts raced. On the one hand, it would do her sister the world of good to have someone to care about her. On the other... She didn't even want to think about the other, but somehow seeing Zak through Ashleigh's eyes was making him more attractive by the minute. Why hadn't she realised this before?

'Robyn? Are you OK?'

She shook herself.

'Sorry, yes. Just thinking.' She dared herself to look him in the eyes. 'Ashleigh's only got another week here.'

'Right. Shame. She looks like she's enjoying herself and I wanted—'

'Zak!' Chad called. 'Sorry, buddy, but do you think you could help referee?'

'Sure thing.'

Zak bounded up, leaving Robyn sitting on the bench alone. He took the whistle and she watched as he dodged around the court, avoiding the chairs as the teams battled it out. The speed and agility of the players was breath-taking. Chad was especially brilliant and his team were soon two goals up. Ashleigh was, thankfully, on his side, though she was, unsurprisingly, struggling to keep up.

Robyn watched Zak closely as he gave her smiles of encouragement and the odd helping hand. It was kind of him, and she saw Ashleigh smiling back with something that looked almost like gratitude – rare from her proud sister – though as the game went on, she drew back and was clearly relieved when it was finally over. Ashleigh's team had won 26–22 and Chad celebrated volubly.

'Hot chocolate for my top new defender?' he shouted to her, wheeling over at speed.

Ashleigh signalled Robyn a desperate appeal for help.

'That's very kind of you, Chad,' Robyn said smoothly, 'but I'm afraid I've got work early in the morning and really need to get to bed.'

Zak was quick on the uptake.

'Yes, thanks anyway, Chad, but we'd better get this old thing her beauty sleep.'

'No problem. See you next week, Ashleigh?'

'Great,' Ashleigh managed faintly and made for the door at pace. Once outside, she let out a groan. 'I've never met anyone so sickeningly keen in my life!'

'He was a nice guy, Ash.'

'Lovely. But so bloody positive. Is it an American thing?'

She turned to Zak who shrugged. 'Maybe, but Chad is an extreme example for sure.'

'He was good at basketball,' Robyn said.

Ashleigh huffed.

'He was. Far better than I'd ever be.'

'You've had *one* go.'

'And I was useless. I was a – what do Americans call it? – klutz. I was a total klutz. Can we go now? Please.'

'Course.'

Ashleigh managed a relatively pleasant goodbye to Zak but maintained a stony silence with Robyn as they set off for home. Robyn turned to drive along the harbour, winding down her window and looking out to sea. It was a beautiful evening and she so wanted her sister to enjoy it.

'Perhaps there's another sport you'd prefer,' she tried.

'No.'

'Just no?'

'OK – no way.' The hard tone grated at Robyn's tired brain.

'What about everything you said about getting out more?' she demanded. 'What about making Granny proud?'

Ashleigh sucked in a sharp breath.

'That's low, Robyn. You try it. You try having to rely on someone else to get anywhere. You try everything being twice as hard as it is for other people. You try being pushed into playing frigging basketball just because some other people are doing it in a wheelchair, as if that's all that counts about you now.'

Robyn prayed for patience.

'*You* wanted to go to the basketball, Ash.'

'Yes, and I was a stupid idiot, suckered by this relentlessly bright home of yours into thinking it might be possible to do something fun for once. I was wrong. It's not possible, not here, not now, not ever again.'

'Oh, Ashleigh, don't be like that.'

'Why not? Did you see me in there? I was useless.'

'It was your first time. And you weren't useless. You were so fast.'

'I couldn't throw. It's kind of a vital skill in basketball, being able to throw, and I couldn't do it. Or catch. I kept fumbling the wretched ball into my own stupid face. I looked like an idiot and I felt like an idiot and I, I hated it. I hated all of it.'

Her voice had risen alarmingly and now she burst into tears. Robyn looked over, aghast, and, spotting a handy layby up ahead, pulled over and turned to her sister. She was crumpled in on herself and her shaking shoulders looked so fragile that Robyn's heart broke. She reached out a tentative hand and suddenly Ashleigh was turning and flinging herself into her arms. Wrapping them tightly around her, Robyn let her sister cry against her chest.

'I'm sorry, Ash. I'm so, so sorry.'

'I so wanted to cycle,' she wept. 'I loved it. I really, really loved it. And I was good at it. I had my life all mapped out – university, the circuit, the Olympics, medals. I was prepared to work too. I mean, really work. I wasn't afraid of that. I wasn't afraid of the long hours, or the sacrifices, or even the pain.' She lifted her tear-stained face to Robyn.

'That was one of my skills, you know – being able to push through the pain barrier. Coach said he'd never seen anyone more able to put themselves through hell. Stupid, isn't it? Turned out, hell was going to be a battle with the worst pain I'd ever known and all for nothing. Nothing! Before, pain got me records and medals and places on the top teams. Now it just spirals in and in until the pain itself seems to be the only goal left to me. I hate that, Robyn. I *hate* it.'

She was crying again, her breath rasping out of her like chalk on a blackboard. It went through Robyn like a knife, but all she could do was hold her close until finally her sobs subsided into small sighs. Finally, she pulled back, but her eyes were curiously glazed, fixed on something over Robyn's shoulder.

'Ash? Are you OK?'

'Wipe your feet on the mat, son,' she said, still staring.

Robyn gawped at her. 'Are you actually going mad?'

'No! Look, Robyn – over there.' She turned Robyn inland to a large white tower of a building. Lit up across the top in big red letters were the words 'Matson Liners'. Robyn squinted at it.

'The clue, idiot!' Ashleigh fumbled for the letter, tears apparently forgotten as fast as they'd come. 'Listen:

A desert island, some might say, but see,
You wipe your feet on the mat, son, just for me.'

Robyn's eyes widened.

'You're right. Look!' She pointed to a road sign just across from their layby that read 'Sand Island Parkway'. 'Desert island! You really think Granny Ginny has somehow stashed a treasure box in there?'

Ashleigh shrugged.

'Only one way to find out.'

'Are you sure you're up to it?'

She yanked down the sun visor to wipe mascara from under her eyes.

'I'm up to it, honest. Sorry for the emotional outpouring. Must be America rubbing off on me.'

'Must be having to cope with more than most of us will ever have to, more like.'

'Yeah, well, it does get to me a bit sometimes, but what can you do? Chin up and crack on and all that.' She gave Robyn a sad smile. 'I am OK, really. I'm not often in pain these days and I can manage most things. I'm just permanently sort of pissed off!'

'No change there then,' Robyn said lightly, and Ashleigh gave her a grateful look and reached for the door handle.

Robyn forced herself to get out and go round to help her, but although the storm had passed, she could still feel its after-effects raging. Somehow, she had to do more to help Ashleigh whilst she was still here. Perhaps she could invite Zak over for dinner and find a reason to make herself scarce. The thought of it tore at her heart but not as much as holding her sobbing sister had done. Besides, she'd had her chance with Zak and chosen not to go for it. If he and Ashleigh liked each other, who was she to stand in their way?

'Come on,' she said, wheeling the chair around. 'Let's go and wipe your feet on the mat, son.'

Shaking their heads at Granny Ginny's poor wit, they made for the Matson Liners building, glad to see a young security guard sitting behind a big desk just inside the glass doors. Robyn waved, feeling slightly foolish, but he buzzed them through and came out to be sure that they could wheel the chair in.

'Can I help you, ladies?'

Robyn looked at Ashleigh. They'd asked three complete strangers for a treasure box now but it still felt ridiculous.

'I don't suppose,' Ashleigh said, 'that you know anything at all about a treasure chest?'

The man's eyes lit up. He was pretty good-looking actually, in a chiselled sort of way, and as he beamed on them Robyn couldn't help feeling slightly dazzled.

'Gee, I never truly thought anyone would come for that. And especially not anyone as lovely as you two.'

Robyn laughed.

'You have it then?'

'Sure do. Boss asked me to keep it under the counter weeks back, but I thought it must be a joke. Who has treasure chests these days?'

'Our grandmother,' Robyn said.

'You're English! Gee, I love the English. Talk to me.' Robyn had had this a few times when she'd first come to Hawaii but still had no idea what to say. He chuckled. 'Tell me about this grandmother of yours, maybe?'

That Robyn could do.

'She was American, from Tennessee. She came out here to Hawaii with her brother Jack when he was posted to Hickham Field as a naval pilot and, as she could fly too, she got a job instructing pilots.'

'When?'

'Nineteen forty-one.'

'No! Was she here for the attack?'

'She was. And she's set up this treasure hunt to tell us all about it.'

'Can't she just talk to you?'

Robyn's breath caught.

'She's dead.'

It was the first time she'd said it since coming home and it dug into her heart; today was turning out to be a toughie.

'I'm so sorry for your loss.' The man caught at her hands, looking intently at her. 'But at least she's speaking to you now through this treasure hunt. Come on, you must have the chest. I'm Connor, by the way, Connor Lee. I'm not really a security guard. I'm an artist but not, you know, a very well paid one – yet – so I do this to make ends meet.'

'How sweet,' Ashleigh said drily. 'The chest…?'

'Of course. Coming right up.' Blushing, Connor ducked behind his desk and drew out another of Granny Ginny's chests, now getting to an almost manageable size. 'It's locked,' he warned.

'We have the key.'

Robyn dug in her bag for the key ring and, with Connor leaning in as if she was unlocking Tutankhamun's tomb itself, she clicked it open.

'It will only be a letter,' she warned.

'A letter from your grandmother? Priceless, surely.' Robyn smiled at him and reached in to lift it out, but as she did so Connor pounced excitedly. 'Not just a letter – look!'

He pointed at a second white square and Robyn picked it up, turning it over to reveal a photograph of a group of people huddled together, smiling broadly as a huge liner came in to dock behind them.

'That's a Matson liner,' he cried, adding self-consciously, 'I guess that's why you're here. Which one's your grandma?'

Robyn lifted it to the light, very aware of handsome Connor at her side. She spotted Ginny straight away – younger and slimmer but still with the same twinkle in her eye. She was right in the middle of the group, her arm around someone very similar-looking, who must be Uncle Jack. On the white border, written in Granny Ginny's distinctive scrawl, was a date: November 27th 1941. Robyn gasped.

'This was taken about a week before Pearl Harbor.'

'Look at them,' Connor said. 'Poor dudes have got no idea what's about to hit them.'

'They look so happy,' Ashleigh agreed. 'Let's get home and read the letter, Rob.'

'You're not going to read it here?' Connor objected.

Robyn looked around the shiny lobby.

'No, Connor.'

'Shame. I'd love to know more.' He brightened. 'Tell you what, why don't you give me your number… Rob?'

'Robyn,' she supplied, very aware of Ashleigh sniggering behind her.

'What a lovely name. So, could I have your number, lovely Robyn? Perhaps I could take you out to dinner and you could fill me in on your grandma's adventures?'

Robyn looked at him. He was very smiley and kind and really very handsome, so what had she got to lose? It wasn't as if she was seeing anyone, was it?

'Sure,' she agreed, and tapped her number into his phone.

'I'll call you,' he said, then darted round to hold the door open for them. 'Happy reading, ladies.'

Robyn pushed Ashleigh down the path, trying to keep her back straight and her head high and ignore her sister's childish chanting of 'Connor and Robyn sitting up a tree, K-I-S-S-I-N-G.' She was glad Ashleigh couldn't see her because, despite herself, she was smiling. It was a while since a man had shown an interest in her and she had to admit it was flattering. For now, though, there was another letter to read and, with the Pearl Harbor date fast approaching in Granny Ginny's timeline, she couldn't wait to learn more.

Chapter Eleven

So, you pair aren't stupid. You can see the date on the photograph and you'll know what's coming, which is more than we did! We were so naively ignorant out there on Oahu, so innocently happy. Sure, those at the top knew that there were tensions bubbling, and when the officials looked pompously back at the whole affair afterwards there were many signs that were missed, but hindsight, as we all know, is a marvellous thing.

Aren't there many moments we'd all change if we had the chance to do them again? And no, Ashleigh, not just that one – there are things you could have done differently other than riding into a car in the rain. That time when you snuck out of the house to go to that older lad's party and ended up nearly falling out of a window because you couldn't take your cider, for one. I'm not being horrible, just frank. You always said you liked that in me; I hope you meant it. By the end of this you will know why I understand, why I always understood.

Life pivots on critical moments. We wobble through a series of near-misses and then get surprised when something finally hits. I certainly did. This isn't just a jaunt through my life during the war, you see – it's an admission, a confession if you like. I'm sorry I had to do it this way but there you go, maybe I'm more of a coward than I thought. But more of that later. For now, let's go back to what was looking set to be such a happy Christmas for all out at Pearl Harbor.

27 November 1941

'Say cheese!'

Ginny smiled broadly at the camera as Eddie snapped the shot with Jack's camera. Her brother was frantically taking photos that he could have developed when they sailed back home in two weeks so they could show their parents a little of what island life was like, not to mention all the lovely friends they'd made. Ginny looked around at their group – glamorous Eddie and Dagne, serious Joe, Billy, Will, Penny and her own dear Lili. Even Pat Bellinger and his curvy wife Miriam were leaning in for the photo as Eddie snapped away and then released them to enjoy the party atmosphere around the docks. Honolulu always turned out to celebrate the bi-weekly liners but today felt like something special. With December just around the corner, many families were coming out to join servicemen for the festive season and the docks were abuzz with excitement. Will Dauth could hardly contain himself.

'This one, do you think?' he asked Ginny, pulling her across to a grass-skirted lei seller. 'Or this one? I think pink for Lois, definitely – she's five – but what about Helen? Do you think Helen would like the red one, Ginny, or the blue and yellow? Or this white one? Is white classier, do you think?'

Ginny laughed as Will fretted over the garlands on display.

'None of them are classy, Will, and she'll love whatever you choose. It's you she's come to see, after all.'

'But I want her to know I care.'

'So tell her. It will mean far more than some cheap flowers.'

Will shook his head.

'I don't even know why I'm asking your opinion. You haven't got a romantic bone in your body. Hey, Penny, which lei do you think Helen would like best?'

Penny came bouncing across, hand in hand with Jack.

'Definitely the white one. It's more delicate, less obvious.'

'See,' Will said to Ginny, 'Penny understands.' He bought a pink and a white lei from the girl and looked out at sea, putting his hand up to shade his eyes from the low winter sun. 'It's still so far away!'

Ginny looked at the *Lurline*, which had to be within fifty feet of the dock.

'You've waited six months to see her, Will, what's another half-hour?'

'Agony!'

Ginny rolled her eyes. Will's excitement seemed to be infecting everyone. Jack had bought Penny a single flower and was tucking it behind her ear with a tender kiss. Penny, in return, was gazing up at Jack as if he were a god and, looking at them gazing into each other's eyes, Ginny had to admit to a sudden stab of envy. What must it feel like to love someone that much?

'Vulnerable,' she tutted to herself. Look at Will running up and down the dock as if his pants were on fire because he was so eager to see his wife and daughter; look at Eddie and Dagne fawning over each other. It was all so… so self-involved.

'What are you frowning about?' Lili asked, coming up to her, beautiful in a simple floral dress.

'All these couples simpering away at each other,' Ginny said. 'It's as if Noah's ark is coming in to dock, not the *Lurline*.'

Lili laughed.

'You're such a grump, Ginny. Don't you want to date?'

'Date, yes – dating is fun. Marry, no. A husband would want me at home cooking and cleaning and waiting to soothe his brow when he came in from a hard day's work, and I can't think of anything more tedious. He might even stop me flying and I *definitely* couldn't have that.'

'I think, Virginia Martin, that any man foolhardy enough to propose to you would already know you well enough not to dare do any of those things.'

Ginny considered this.

'You're probably right, doll, which means that no one ever *will* propose, so the issue will never arise.'

'Or you might meet your perfect match and live happily ever after.'

'No such thing.'

'We'll see.'

'What about you then, my romantic friend? I saw that handsome officer asking you to dance several times at Kau Kau's the other night. Are you going to see him again?'

Lili flushed instantly.

'Maybe. I don't know. I don't want anything to distract me from getting my instructor's licence.'

Ginny clapped delightedly.

'Quite right! You're doing so well, Lili.' She leaned in and added in a low voice, 'Far better than Will.'

Will, bless him, was still scared of flying and that made him tentative and over-reactive. A plane needed a firm, confident hand. Any jitters on the stick were magnified across the wings, and Ginny still had to frequently take the controls when she was up in the air with him. It would be a miracle if he got his licence.

Lili, meanwhile, was acing every move Ginny taught her. She was a calm, happy pilot with a feel for air currents and a natural sense of direction that meant she could always find her way back to base. Will, in contrast, would flounder over Oahu, apparently unsure which way was land and which sea. If he actually got his licence and was allowed up alone, Ginny was not at all convinced he would ever find his way back to base.

'He'll get there,' Lili said kindly. 'It's just a shame he didn't manage it in time to take his wife up.'

'I'm not sure he'd impress her much anyway. Although actually… Lilinoe – you're a genius!'

'I am?'

Lili looked puzzled but Ginny gave her a quick hug and ran off after Will, who was now eyeing up miniature grass skirts, presumably for his daughter.

'Will – I've had a great idea. Far, far more impressive than a lei, whatever the colour.'

'Great. What is it?'

'You may not be able to take Helen up in a plane, but she can certainly watch you fly.'

'Solo?'

'Better than that. If I come up with you, we can do some tricks.'

'Tricks?' Will paled slightly. 'I can't do tricks, Ginny.'

'No, but *I* can.' He gaped at her. 'And how will Helen know which of us is at the controls?'

'You're suggesting I lie to her?'

'Not lie, Will, just create a lovely illusion.'

'The lovely illusion that I can fly far better than I actually can?'

'Exactly.'

'Brilliant!' He grabbed Ginny and planted a kiss on each cheek. 'You're dead right – it's a great idea.' Behind them the *Lurline* hooted loudly, as if in approval, and Will swung round, jumping up and down. 'There she is! Look, Ginny, there's Helen and little Lois with her. Can you see?'

Ginny was about to point out that she had no idea what his family looked like, and had little chance of distinguishing them from the myriad people on the giant boat even if she did, but he looked so excited that she hadn't the heart.

'Wonderful, Will. Any minute now, she'll be in your arms.'

She went back to Jack and the others as the vast ship came alongside the dock and men ran to catch the ropes being flung from her side. People around the railings were tossing coins into the sea for the agile local boys to dive for, and now the Royal Hawaiian band struck up a jaunty tune. Ginny was reminded of her and Jack's own arrival here just a few months back. Already Hawaii felt like home and a little part of her was sad to be leaving for Christmas. Still, that was two weeks away yet and a lot could happen in two weeks. For a start, she had at least five parties scheduled; she really ought to get a new dress.

She watched, amused, as Will bounced around at the bottom of the gangplank, but just then a slim woman dragging a wide-eyed girl came swooping down and into his arms.

'She must love him too,' she said curiously.

'That's kind of why people get married,' Jack said. 'All that meeting someone you can't bear to be without and wanting to spend the rest of your life with them stuff doesn't just go away after a year or two – well, not if you find the right person.'

He turned his brown eyes fondly on Penny, who snuggled in even closer against him. Ginny groaned, then noticed something amusing.

'Look, Jack – poor old Will is having to share his grand reunion.'

Jack followed her pointed finger to where a stately man in a very fine uniform was stepping between Will and his wife.

'That's Admiral Kimmel,' he gasped. 'Of course – isn't he Helen's uncle?'

Sure enough, she was kissing him and reaching up to tweak his smart hat as if he were a kid with a new toy. He didn't seem too abashed, and offered her his arm to escort her from the docks as people parted before them like the Red Sea for Moses. Poor Will was left to scurry behind, though he did at least have his daughter on his hip. As they came close, Will tried to stop Helen to introduce them, but her uncle was dominating her and he gave them a helpless shrug.

'Airfield,' Ginny said to him. 'Four o'clock tomorrow?'

He nodded eagerly and ran after his wife.

'What the hell are you planning, Gin?' Jack asked.

She grinned up at him.

'If you want to know that, brother dear, you'll have to come along and see.'

'It'd better not be anything stupid.'

'Come on, Jack, you know me.'

'Which is precisely why I said that.'

Ginny just shook her head and tripped away. It was an excellent plan, as they'd all see tomorrow.

'Ready?'

'As I'll ever be.'

Will looked terrified as he and Ginny coasted onto the runway in their little yellow Cub, but he managed a wave from the front cockpit and got an excited one back from Helen and Lois, standing by the hangar with Jack, Penny, Lili, Kalani and the formidable Admiral Husband Kimmel himself. The plane was dual control, with the dominant position from the rear, where the instructor could keep an eye on their pupil, but Helen wasn't to know that.

'Nice time last night?' Ginny asked, trying to keep Will relaxed as they turned the plane to take up position for take-off.

'Once I finally got them to myself, yes. "Uncle Hubbie" insisted on having us to dinner. I couldn't believe it. I'd got in all sorts of goodies but you can't say no to the blinking head of Pearl Harbor itself, so we had to get penguin-suited up and trip off to his house to be served by starchy waiters. Honestly, Ginny, he's got this enormous place up in the new development on Makalapa Drive and it's just him kicking around in it. Such a waste! Not that I'd dare say as much or he'd have us up there with him like a shot. I reckon he's lonely. His wife's back home in California and he says it's better that way as he can't afford the distraction of family with the whole navy to run, but we couldn't stop him talking so I'm not sure he's got that quite right. I was just grateful we had Lois with us as an excuse to get home, or he might have had us sit up with him till dawn.'

'Not what you wanted for your first night with Helen, hey?'

'Not at all! That is…' Will broke off, flustered, and Ginny laughed.

'Wait until she sees you flying stunts in this little baby, Will – you'll never get out of the bedroom.'

'Ginny!'

She chuckled.

'Come on, I may not be a wife, but I'm not stupid. Now, let's get this baby in the air and show Helen what a stud she's married to.'

Will looked forward and gulped.

'Are you sure this is a good idea?'

'Course I am. Now, look like you're flying this thing. Ready… Here we go!'

Ginny pulled back the throttle and sent the little Cub speeding down the runway and up into the blue skies. There were a few gusty winds this afternoon but nothing that she couldn't handle, and she pressed on the left rudder pedal to tip them out and round the bay to fly back in across the airfield, low and fast. She saw Helen put her hands to her mouth and little Lois jump up and down.

'They're loving it, Will. Even the Admiral looks impressed.'

'Really?' It was the first word Will had spoken since they'd got into the air and now he risked a glance down, if only for a moment. 'I'd like to impress him,' he admitted. 'Helen thinks the world of him – the whole family does – and of course he's got quite a lot of influence around here.'

'You can say that again. You get this display right and you'll be heading up a bomber command next year.'

Will shuddered.

'Only if I can take you with me to do the actual flying.'

Ginny laughed.

'I wish. Now, how about a little barrel roll?'

'What? Ginny, I don't think that's a very good— Aaaaah! Oh God, no. I don't want to— Ooh. Oooh, Ginny, we did it. We actually did it.'

'*You* did it, Will, remember?'

'I remember. What else can I do then?'

The roll seemed to have emboldened him, and the adrenaline of it was coursing through Ginny's veins. With a tight schedule of pre-programmed lessons, she rarely got to do tricks like this and she'd forgotten how much she loved it. The Piper Cub was such a responsive little plane, straining to loop and spin, and today she could give it its head.

'How about an inside loop?' she called to Will.

'An inside…?'

But Ginny was already dropping the plane fast towards the earth and then, as Will gasped in horror, wrenching back on the stick to send it up and around in a full circle before settling back into a steady path.

'That was amazing!' Will cried.

'You can do it yourself if you want to?'

'God, no. I might mess it up.'

'You won't. Try it. You just have to push down on the stick to drop the plane and then, as it picks up pace, pull it back and steadily round. Ready? Controls to you.'

'Ginny, no, I—'

'Go on, Will – now!'

She saw him push forward and felt the plane tip, but just then a gust caught the left wing and the plane wobbled precariously.

'Pull back,' Ginny commanded.

'I can't. It's going too fast.'

'Pull back!'

But Will seemed fixated on the fast-approaching ground, and Ginny had to grab control and yank on the stick with all her might to scoop the little Cub back up into the air, right over the heads of the watching crowd.

'Oh my God, Ginny – we almost killed them.'

'Rubbish. We were miles off. I bet it looked really impressive.'

Will swallowed audibly.

'Good. Can we go down now?'

'Already? Nah. Come on, let's just fly around a little, do a lazy eight or two, and then we'll head in.'

'Promise?'

'Promise. You fly her.'

Will nervously took the controls again, running the plane out to sea and turning her competently to head back across the runway.

'Good, Will. You'll be flying solo any time now.'

'Not upside down though.'

'No? Not even a little roll?'

'Ginny…'

'I'll do it, Will – relax.'

She took back control, performing a lazy eight and then turning to show off with a sharper roll and spin combo. God, it felt amazing. Up here, just her and the Cub, she felt in control of the whole world. If she had to fall in love, she reflected, then she hoped it felt like this – wild and free and happy right to her very core. She checked the fuel gauge.

'We need to go in shortly, Will.'

'OK,' he agreed without hesitation.

'Just time for one more trick.'

'Must we?'

'A grand finale – no show is complete without it.'

'What are you going to do?' he asked, as she checked the skies – all clear.

'An outside loop. Like an inside one but a tad more complex.'

'In what way?'

'In this way. Hold on…'

'Ginny, please, I don't think—'

Will's words were cut off by the G-force as Ginny rolled the little plane over and sent it dropping to the ground, cockpit facing down. It was harder to pull the plane up and over this way but it looked amazing from the ground.

'Ginny!'

She ignored Will's yelps, focused on getting just the right point to start the loop.

'Ginny, there's a—'

She spotted the second plane coming in to land out of the corner of her eye and her heart leaped against her ribcage. It was going very fast and wobbling precariously in the winds. If she completed the loop she would cut straight across its path and they'd both be goners. There was only one option so, gritting her teeth, she pulled back on the stick, battling to roll the plane at the same time so that, instead of heading back up in a circle, she shot it forward, barely twenty feet off the ground, running alongside the landing plane for a few heart-stopping seconds before soaring into the skies once more as it screeched to a stop in front of the hangar. Ginny felt a rush of pure elation and patted the side of the cockpit.

'Nice one, girl,' she purred to the plane. 'Nice one.'

'We made it!' Will was shrieking in front of her, and she pulled herself back into the moment and looked down at the airfield with a shake of her head.

'Where the hell did that come from?'

'It dropped in over the mountains whilst we were upside down. The pilot was coming in very fast.'

'Too fast. I'll kill him.'

'You nearly did.'

'Nearly,' Ginny agreed cheerily as she turned the Cub and lined her up for landing, checking the skies with exaggerated care before starting her descent. She could see Will shaking and didn't entirely blame him. It had been a close call and she had to admit to feeling pretty relieved herself when the wheels touched down safely on the packed coral of the runway. The others came running.

'Will!' Helen flung herself into her arms. 'Oh, Will, I thought I'd lost you.'

'He had it all under control,' Ginny said, clinging gratefully on to Jack as he hugged her. 'That rookie came out of nowhere.'

'We've reported him already,' Jack told her. 'Though I warn you, he's shooting his mouth off about "idiot acrobatics" so it's probably best just to let it blow over. Amazing skill to pull out of that loop in time.'

'Wasn't it?' she agreed. 'Nice one, Will.'

Jack squeezed her tight and she leaned gratefully in to him as they watched Will's fearsome uncle-in-law pump his hand whilst his wife and daughter hung on to him like a hero.

'I told you not to do anything stupid,' Jack whispered to Ginny. 'I thought I'd lost you for a minute there and I almost died myself. I couldn't bear to be without my little sister, truly I couldn't.'

'I'm sorry, Jack.' She reached up to give him an apologetic kiss, then, remembering the rush as she'd turned the Cub out of trouble, added, 'I tell you what, though, it felt amazing!'

Chapter Twelve

Friday 8 March

'This is a really bad idea, Ashleigh,' Robyn objected.

Ashleigh chuckled and dived into Robyn's wardrobe.

'Why is it?'

'Because I don't want to go out on a date when you're here.'

'Because you don't want to go out on a date full-stop. Ooh – what about this?'

Ashleigh tugged a dress out of the wardrobe, clattering the hangers as she struggled from her chair. Robyn looked at it with a jolt of longing. That was the dress she'd bought for her date with Zak last year and she hadn't worn it since. It was a dark green maxi dress in simple jersey cotton, but with a scooping back and criss-cross straps that made it that little bit special. She loved it.

That didn't mean she wanted to wear it out tonight though.

'Ashleigh, stop! You're only here for one more week and we've got a treasure hunt to complete. You heard what Granny said in her letter.' She grabbed the sheets of paper and fumbled for the right place. 'Here: *This isn't just a jaunt through my life during the war, you see – it's an admission, a confession if you like.* What does she mean by that, Ash? What did she do wrong?'

Ashleigh sighed.

'I don't know, Rob, but I'm guessing that's what this elaborate damned treasure hunt is going to tell us.'

'So we should get on with it!'

'You're probably right, but I'm afraid that right now I'm totally knackered and ready for my bed. If you stay here you'll be getting on with it alone, so you'd be much better off going out to eat with this lovely man.'

Robyn groaned. Connor had texted her just as she was getting home from work to ask if she fancied 'a bite to eat in the hills tonight'. Robyn had laughingly shown it to Ashleigh, who'd promptly taken the phone off her and replied with 'Lovely. 7 p.m.?' The 'great' had taken seconds to come back, and now it was six thirty and Robyn felt very much backed into a corner.

'Why are you so tired?' she asked Ashleigh suspiciously. 'What have you been up to?'

'Wouldn't you like to know?' Ashleigh teased.

'Yes, I would. And I'm not going on this damned date unless you tell me.'

'Oh, OK. I had an email from my boss this morning, all excited because she's realised that there's a lab at the University of Honolulu that specialises in XPS.'

'XPS?'

'X-ray photoelectron spectroscopy. It would really help us with a big project we're running on hydrogels. She asked if I'd go down to meet them.'

'You went to a lab? Today? On your own?'

'Sure did.'

Robyn's stomach lurched.

'Were you OK? How did you manage?'

'Pretty much the same way I manage to get to my lab at home, Robyn.'

'Right. Yes. It's just harder in a strange city.'

'True, but luckily you've taken me out and about a bit, and Google Maps did the rest. Plus, America has such lovely wide pavements – sorry, sidewalks! – that it's actually easier than in England.'

'Right.' Robyn was struggling to take this in. 'And did you find them?'

'Found them, met a lovely professor-chap who showed me their spectroscopes and offered to let me use them next week. My boss has put our samples in the post already.'

'Wow.'

'Yep. It was good actually, being useful again. Gave me less time to, you know, dwell.'

Robyn nodded. That she did know. When she was up to her eyes in work, she could just get on; it was only in breaks that grief crept up and bit her.

'I'm sorry I've had to leave you in the flat all day.'

'God, Rob, don't be. I get it. You've got a job, and now I have too, and it's knackered me, which is why I have to get to bed and you have to shift your arse into that dress before Connor rings your intercom.'

Robyn glanced at her watch: six forty. There really was no getting out of this now.

'I haven't been on a date for a year, Ash.'

'Then it's time you did. And you're off work tomorrow, so there's really no excuse. Get into that dress and get a bit of slap on – quick!'

She wheeled herself away and Robyn was left with little choice but to do as she said. She was just slicking on some lippy when, bang on seven, she heard the intercom and Ashleigh's voice cheerily calling out, 'Come on up.'

She shot through to the living area.

'Ashleigh! He can't come in here, it's a tip.'

'It's cosy. Oh, and he can – because here he is.' She wheeled herself to the door as the bell rang. Robyn frantically tried to straighten the mess, but it was a forlorn hope and Ashleigh showed Connor in just as she was shoving Granny Ginny's letters back into the smallest treasure chest.

'Good evening, Robyn. You look lovely.'

Robyn took the flowers he held out to her, touched.

'Thank you, Connor, they're beautiful.'

'No problem. Oh, and are these the other treasure chests? Gee – the boxes fit together. That's very clever. And lovely craftsmanship. Look at how the handles are inset so they can be neatly stacked.'

Robyn glanced at Ashleigh as Connor examined the chests. No one in their relentlessly sporty family had ever been artistic and she was intrigued. He looked very smart in chinos and a crisp white shirt, but she noticed paint under his fingernails and a fleck on the back of his neck and felt a curious urge to touch it. Maybe this date wouldn't be so bad after all.

'We're stuck on the next clue,' Ashleigh was telling him happily, 'and Robyn is fretting about it.'

'Well, we can't have that,' Connor said, beaming at her. 'Can I hear it?'

Robyn gave Ashleigh a surreptitious glare but lifted the letter back out of the chest and read it out:

'*With two fine palms, you're my clapper when you drive, dolly.*
Or perhaps more like when you serve and volley.'

Connor stared at her. 'That's weird. Presumably it means palm trees, but they're everywhere so that doesn't help much.'

'No,' Robyn agreed ruefully.

'My clapper when you drive?' He rolled it over his tongue. 'My clapper, my clapper.' He suddenly beamed. 'Of course – clever!'

Robyn and Ashleigh looked at each other.

'What?'

'My clapper – Makalapa.'

'That makes sense to you?'

'Sure does. Makalapa Drive is a smart street halfway up the hill. The houses were built for the officers when half the US navy was suddenly stationed on Oahu.'

'Granny Ginny knew all the smart set,' Robyn told him. 'She was hanging out with admirals and generals.'

'Then she certainly knew Makalapa Drive.' His eyes lit up. 'Tell you what, we have to pretty much go past there to get to the restaurant, so we could drive along it once we've eaten and see if we can unravel what the rest of this means.'

'Great idea,' Ashleigh agreed. 'Are you ready, Robyn?'

Robyn was not at all sure that she was, but with both her sister and her date looking keenly at her she had little choice. She gave Ashleigh a hug goodbye.

'Have fun!' she sang out, adding in a whisper: 'Keep your location on.'

'What?'

'Just to be sure. Modern dating, sis.'

And on that encouraging note, she hustled Robyn out of the door.

'This is Makalapa Drive?'

Robyn leaned out of the window of Connor's car and looked in awe along the elegant road. To the left it stood open to the hills, offering a stunning view down into Pearl Harbor, bathed in moonlight. To the right were the houses, though all that could be seen of them were glimpses of high roofs behind big gates. Robyn, stuffed full of beautiful food served fresh from a grill on a fairy-lit terrace in the hills, felt as if she might have stepped into some sort of fantasy land.

'Nice, hey?' Connor said. 'No idea how we're going to find the one you're looking for though. What does the clue say again?'

Robyn read it out:

'With two fine palms, you're my clapper when you drive, dolly.
Or perhaps more like when you serve and volley.'

Connor laughed.

'I guess we're looking for a tennis court then. Oh, and...'

He gestured to where, just up ahead of them, a court stood to the right, glowing in the streetlamps. Connor pulled up alongside and they both got out.

'Shall we hunt for treasure chests?' he suggested, and when Robyn nodded, he took her hand and led her onto the court.

His fingers were warm in hers and she appreciated the way he seemed to genuinely be looking, as if finding the chest mattered to him too. He was a lovely man. The food at the restaurant he'd taken her to had been fantastic and they'd chatted away all night. He'd told her more about his art and how much it mattered to him, and she'd talked to him of her hurdling, her work and Ashleigh's accident.

'Poor girl,' he'd said softly. 'I can't imagine how I'd feel if I couldn't paint. It would be like I just wasn't myself any longer.'

It had been a rather clever way of putting it and now Robyn paused at the far edge of the court, trying desperately to think of a way that Ashleigh could find herself again. Wheelchair sport clearly wasn't the solution, and she couldn't see her impatient sister going for anything arty. Confused, she looked down into Pearl Harbor, taking in its strange shape – almost like a flower with different petals of water.

She'd researched its history in her lunch hour the other day and found out that the locals had called it Pearl because it looked like an oyster shell; and, of course, because their divers had found many of the precious pearls back when the waters had been free of naval ships. For the first time, Robyn thought about what the Hawaiians must have made of the influx of military in the first part of the twentieth century – especially when it brought the Japanese screeching into their skies.

'Robyn? Are you OK?'

Connor squeezed her fingers and she looked at him.

'Sorry, yes. Just thinking about what life must have been like for the islanders in the build-up to the war.'

'Thrilling? Annoying? Crazy? I believe the population of the island doubled in the 1930s. If nothing else, it must have been exciting.'

'It certainly was for Granny.'

Connor stepped a little closer.

'Tell me about her. She must have been quite a woman to set up this hunt in her last months.'

'She was. My parents worked abroad a lot so she more or less brought Ashleigh and me up and she was brilliant. She had a few rules – mainly about letting her know where we were – but other than that she let us do anything, encouraged it even. "Life is for living, girls," she used to say. She was so bold, so daring – she taught us that anything was possible.'

'She sounds amazing.'

'She was,' she muttered.

Out of nowhere, Robyn felt tears well up. She thought again of the latest letter and her amazing granny's suggestion that she'd been a coward. That just couldn't be true.

'You miss her,' Connor said softly.

'I do. I really do, Connor, and although this treasure hunt is, as you say, kind of cool, it also hurts that she felt she had to do it. There seems to be a secret at the heart of it – something she didn't want to tell us to our faces – and I hate that she didn't feel she could do that.'

Connor considered this.

'Maybe she just felt that she had to be strong for you?'

'Well, I wish she hadn't. Everyone deserves someone to lean on, don't you think?'

'I do,' he agreed, pulling her hand gently to tug her in against his chest.

She looked up to see him gazing intently down at her. Oh God, he was going to kiss her. Did she want that? Was she ready for it? He was very good-looking, and very kind and—

Over his shoulder, her eye was caught by a big, wrought-iron gate across the road from the tennis court. Through the gaps she could see a beautifully manicured lawn and a driveway curving tantalisingly between hibiscus bushes. Either side of it stood two big palm trees.

'Two fine palms!' she cried.

'Sorry?' Connor blinked and pulled back.

'The clue,' she said, stringing her arm around his waist to lead him across the empty road to the gate. 'This must be the house. Who do you think lives here?'

'No idea. Did your grandma have friends on Oahu?'

'Loads, but most of them were navy and army officers and their wives. Oh, and… of course – Lilinoe!'

'Lilinoe?'

Robyn nodded eagerly. Earlier Mrs Deans had sent through a snap of the picture of Ginny and her flying partner. It had been taken at a slightly strange angle, with the sun glinting off the glass and the focus on the frame, but it had filled in the gaps in both her and Ashleigh's memories and they'd pored eagerly over it.

The picture was of the full plane – a Brewster Buccaneer, if Robyn remembered rightly from her degree – and you could just see the two women waving merrily from the dual cockpit. Behind was Ginny and in front was another woman who might, if you looked closely enough, have Hawaiian features. It had to be the friend who had filled the letters so far.

'Lilinoe Kamaka was an engineer here on the island,' she told Connor. 'Granny lived with her and her father, and taught her to fly in return for board. She's in all the letters, but I don't remember Granny talking about her to us, which seems odd.'

She put her free hand to one of the iron bars of the gate, feeling like a little kid trying to peek into a toyshop. Did Lilinoe Kamaka live here? Or her family? Hadn't Granny Ginny described her as poor? Maybe learning to fly had opened up wonderful new job prospects? She was dying to know, but the house looked so smart and inaccessible, and she could hardly press on the intercom to ask for a treasure chest at this time of night. They'd call the police. She turned away.

'I'll come back with Ash tomorrow.'

Connor checked his watch.

'Sadly for me, that might be best. Now, where were we…?'

He cupped a hand gently beneath her chin and she felt a too-long-forgotten thrill ripple through her. Closing her eyes, she stepped a little closer, her body tingling in anticipation of his lips against her own, but then a parakeet cried out and, opening her eyes, she jolted back, her heart pounding. For it was not Connor she'd been picturing but another man, from another date, almost a year ago.

'Robyn? Are you OK?'

'Sorry, Connor. I'm just… not quite myself. It's a funny time with all this…'

She waved a hand at the mystery house beyond the gates, and he nodded and gave her a gentle peck on the cheek. 'I get it. No rush.'

'You're very kind.'

'And you're very lovely. Come on, I'll take you home.'

As his car drove away down Makalapa Drive, Robyn looked back at the house. It had been an unsettling night in many ways and it was clear she had some serious thinking to do, but one thing, at least, she was sure of – she couldn't wait to come back and find the next chest.

The next day, standing outside the house with Ashleigh in the glaring sunlight, Robyn felt rather less certain.

'Posh, isn't it?' she said to her sister.

Ashleigh shrugged.

'You could say the same of Granny Ginny's house – sorry, *our* house.'

Robyn swallowed. What they were going to do about the beautiful Oxfordshire house they'd inherited was something they'd still not discussed properly. In fact, Robyn was beginning to realise that there was rather a lot they'd not discussed and time was running out on Ashleigh's visit. They were only on clue five, so she supposed that now they were here, they'd better get on with it. Taking a deep breath, she pressed the intercom and braced herself for whoever might reply.

There was a crackle of static, then a beep. Robyn's breathing caught but instead of a voice, the gates simply began to open before them.

'Looks like we're expected,' Ashleigh said. She pointed to a camera, set discreetly between the leaves of the right-hand palm tree, and Robyn flushed.

'They must have seen me here last night with Connor.'

'Oh yes?' Ashleigh grinned. 'And what were you doing?'

'Nothing! Just trying to peer through the gates.'

'And after that…?'

'Nothing then either. Connor was a complete gentleman.'

'Shame.'

Robyn rolled her eyes but Ashleigh was already off up the drive and she had little choice but to run and catch up with her. Together, they stopped before the entrance of a sprawling villa.

'Look!'

Ashleigh pointed to where, sitting on the tiled step between two exuberant gardenias, was the next treasure chest. Robyn stared. Could it really be this easy? The house had seemed so mysterious last night, so off-limits, but here they were, surrounded by flowers and sunlight and with the next letter right there waiting for them. She looked self-consciously around but there was no one to be seen, so, reaching into her bag, she drew out the key and sat down on the step alongside Ashleigh to open it up.

Chapter Thirteen

Honestly girls, we didn't see the Japanese coming, not once.
The signs were there, even amongst our little set. Eddie and
Joe, in particular, had often warned us not to underestimate
them, but no one ever thought they'd manage to transport
353 planes 4000 miles in secret. America was poised for an
attack that weekend, yes, but all eyes were on the Philippines.
Out there, they were on high alert, stood by their guns with
their eyes peeling the skies, but in Oahu, we were still looking
happily down into our brightly coloured cocktails with no
idea of the tragedy that was lurking.

6 December 1941

Ginny adjusted her cardigan over her shoulders and looked down
into Pearl Harbor, sparking into life as the sun went down like
the grandest Christmas lights show ever. She couldn't believe
that it was warm enough to still be having drinks on the lawn
and looked gratefully around at her friends, gathered in front of
Admiral Bellinger's beautiful house on Makalapa Drive. It was
almost six months since she'd arrived on Oahu but felt ten times
more. She sometimes thought she'd left home a girl and was now
a woman – not in a foolish, romantic way but because she was
doing the things she wanted to do with her life.

Every morning she got up with a sense of purpose and made for
the airfield excited about the day ahead. Even tomorrow, despite
it being Sunday, she would be heading into the hangar at 7 a.m.
Will's test was next week and, although he had greatly improved

recently, he needed all the lessons he could get to be sure of passing, so she'd agreed to take him up in the Cub at dawn. She looked ruefully into the pretty colours of her cocktail and reminded herself this should be her last. She hated flying on a hangover.

'Grand sight, isn't it?' Pat Bellinger said, gesturing to Pearl Harbor before them.

'Amazing,' she agreed. Bellinger's lawn, like those of all the top naval brass, looked right out across the length of the harbour, and she could see every military building, ship and seaplane laid out clearly before her. As could, she thought uneasily, anyone wandering down the road. It wasn't exactly a secure location, but then, with every battleship bristling with guns, it probably didn't need to be. 'There are so many ships.'

'Not as many as we'd like but, yes, a fine showing. The carriers aren't here, of course – off out to—' He caught himself and finished with a vague wave of his hand to the ocean.

'I saw the *Lexington* heading out this morning when I was up flying,' Ginny said. 'She looked magnificent with all those planes on deck.'

'She *is* magnificent – they're the future, the carriers. I keep telling everyone that, but they do love their battleships, bless 'em.'

He gestured disparagingly to the harbour where the big destroyers were lined up. Ginny had also seen the *Arizona*, *Nevada* and *Oklahoma* coming back into port earlier, and had no doubt their sailors would be flooding the bars of Waikiki after a week's training out at sea. She, Jack and the others were heading down there for a dinner dance shortly and it would be a lively one, she was sure.

'Are you feeling better, sir?' she asked. Miriam Bellinger had said that her husband had been laid up in bed for most of the week with laryngitis, but he looked as hearty as ever.

'Fully recovered, thank the Lord. I hate being ill. Such a waste of damned time. I read all the papers, mind you – full of the peace talks with the Japs collapsing. Messages have been flying out from Washington all across the Pacific. The poor old Philippines are on high alert.'

'But we're not?'

'Goodness, no – far too far from Japan. We've got eyes on them in China and they're moving thousands of troops south. They must be getting ready to hit Indochina and try to take the islands. Kimmel's champing at the bit to go on the attack the moment the Japs hit American territory. He's just waiting for the nod.'

'And Japan hitting the Philippines will give him that?'

'Yep. Act of aggression, see – an effective declaration of war.'

'Right.' Ginny swallowed nervously, her throat suddenly as tight and sore as if she, too, had had laryngitis. 'And will the Japanese attack here?'

Bellinger gave a low sigh.

'Who knows. They could. I did a bit of theoretical modelling back in March and our little group concluded they could sail carriers to somewhere in range, attack at dawn, and bomb out the harbour before anyone knew what was happening.' Ginny pulled her cardigan tighter around herself, suddenly feeling the cold, and Bellinger gave her a hearty pat on the back. 'But please don't worry yourself, Virginia. It won't happen. Or, if it does, we'll be ready for them. I'm gathering planes for reconnaissance and once we're on a war-footing I'll have my pilots buzzing all around the Pacific day and night. No one will get through on my watch.'

'We're not doing that already?'

Bellinger huffed.

'It's not really our job. Naval planes are here to fly in combat over the seas. When we're in port, we're resting, and it's up to the army pilots to protect our positions around Pearl Harbor. Problem is, they're an incompetent lot. Got no idea how to conduct them-selves out in the islands. Not bad guys on land, you understand, perfectly fine taking enemy lines and cities and all that, but hopeless surrounded by sea. Bloody Major General Short's got no idea. He spends most of his life fretting about sabotage. Sabotage, I tell you! You might get that over in occupied Europe where there are organised guerrilla groups, but not on Oahu.'

'There are a lot of Japanese living here though, aren't there?' Ginny asked.

'Oh yes. Been here years. Most of them are on the coffee and pineapple plantations, doing the backbreaking stuff no one else fancies. But they left Japan for a reason and that reason is that they like being American. Who can blame them? Land of the free, right?'

'Right, sir.'

'So why, having bothered to come all this way to escape Japan, would they turn on us to invite it onto our shores? Doesn't make sense. Or only to halfwits like Short. D'you know, he's ordered all of his army planes into the middle of the runway out at Wheeler Field so that any saboteurs can't get to them without being spotted. Right in the middle – perfect targets.'

'Except that no one is targeting them, right?' Miriam said, joining them.

Bellinger shook himself.

'Right, dear. For now.'

Miriam gave Ginny an apologetic smile. 'A week in bed has done him no good at all,' she said. 'I think perhaps it's supper time. Come on, Pat, let's go and check what's happening in the kitchens.'

Pat grimaced but went docilely enough. Ginny looked for Jack and went over to where he was chatting to Eddie, Joe and Will.

'Will we be able to get home if we go to war?' she asked, sliding an arm through her brother's.

'Of course we will, Gin. This is probably all just political games. It'll settle down.'

'Will it though? The Admiral says we're expecting a Japanese attack in the Pacific.'

Eddie nodded grimly, running nervous fingers through his immaculate blond hair.

'Their messaging system has been going wild. And Admiral Yamamoto changed their codes last week.'

'Is that unusual?'

'No. He does it every six months, like clockwork.'

Ginny heard the reserve in his voice. 'But…?'

'But it's only a month since the last time.'

'You've cracked them though, right?'

Eddie nudged Joe, grinning.

'See what faith she has in your intelligence, Joe.'

Joe nudged his glasses uncomfortably up his nose.

'Please don't, Ginny. We barely crack 10 per cent of the Jap codes and far less when they change them.'

'So, we don't know where they are?'

'Oh, we have ways and means of telling that even without actual messages. The very fact that ships are transmitting a signal tells us plenty.'

'So you *do* know where they are?'

Joe shifted and looked out across the harbour.

'Most of them. We're missing an aircraft carrier or two, but they're most likely just in port where they don't transmit a strong enough signal for us to pick up. More importantly – have you seen Billy's ship?'

He pointed towards the dark ocean and Ginny squinted but could see little beyond the lights of the harbour.

'What ship?'

Jack chuckled.

'I didn't tell you, sis. Billy Outerbridge got a promotion yesterday, out of the blue – command of the *Ward*.'

'His own ship? He'll be over the moon.'

'He was. It's only a little destroyer but he's already out on active duty, patrolling the harbour mouth for subs.'

'Enemy subs?'

Ginny thought of all those scary sea creatures she'd pictured beneath her as a child and fought to remind herself that had just been her imagination.

'Standard practice, sis. Billy's made up, so be glad for him.'

'I am,' she agreed, shaking herself. 'To Billy!'

'To Billy!' the others agreed, clinking glasses.

'And to Christmas,' Joe said. 'I hear Santa's going to be in the offices of the *Honolulu Advertiser* tomorrow morning.'

Little Lois Dauth, playing with the Bellingers' dog at their feet, leaped up at the magical word.

'Santa? Here?'

'Of course,' Joe agreed, bending down to her. 'Santa gets everywhere.'

'And *you'd* better get to bed,' Helen said, coming across with the other women and taking her daughter's hand, 'so you're awake in time to see him.'

Lois jumped up and down.

'Do you hear that, Daddy? Santa! Will you come? Will you come and see him with me?'

'After my lesson,' Will agreed, winking at Ginny. 'Still on for a dawn flight, teach?'

'Still on,' Ginny agreed. 'And we'll be back in plenty of time for Santa. Now, are we going into town or what?'

The others nodded eagerly but Jack put a hand on her arm.

'Not quite yet, Gin.'

Something in his voice made Ginny's heart lurch. She looked up into his dear face and saw it was unusually serious.

'What is it, Jack? Do you know something?'

'I do,' he agreed solemnly. 'And I think it's something we should all hear.'

'What? Jack, what is it?'

Ginny tugged on his arm, but he just gave her a little pat and cleared his throat noisily as the Admiral and his wife came back out to join their party on the lawn.

'Could I, er, say something?' he asked their host, unusually hesitant.

Ginny's heart battered against her ribs. It was one thing the Admiral talking about Japanese attacks, or Joe muttering about missing ships, but what did Jack know? He was her big brother, the person she'd always looked up to for guidance. If he had a warning, she'd obey it straight away. But then Jack was beckoning Penny to his side and a shy smile was splitting across his face, and joy flooded through Ginny as she realised this was nothing to do with war and everything to do with love.

'You lot have become such great friends in this last half-year,' Jack said, still a little awkward, though everyone else was nudging each other and grinning. 'So I wanted you to be the first to hear my news, *our* news.' He beamed at Penny. 'Earlier today this caring, kind, beautiful girl agreed to be my wife.'

Their cheers echoed out across Makalapa Drive and into the night skies above Pearl Harbor. Ginny ran forward, hugging first Jack and then Penny.

'That's wonderful news! Welcome to the family.'

Penny hugged her back.

'Thank you. I'm so happy, Ginny. Jack's wonderful, just wonderful.'

'He is,' Ginny agreed, feeling a foolish tear prick at the corner of her eye. 'See you look after him, yes?'

'Of course.' Penny hugged her tighter. 'Of course I will, Ginny. I'll keep him safe and happy and...'

Penny was in danger of crying too now, and Ginny was relieved when Admiral Bellinger produced champagne and poured it exuberantly into glasses. She took hers gratefully. So much for her vow to make that cocktail her last drink of the night, but it wasn't every day that your only brother got engaged, and if she had to fly with a bit of a headache tomorrow morning, so what? Will was a capable enough pilot now, the weather was set fair, and it was time to celebrate.

Chapter Fourteen

Saturday 9 March

Robyn paused at the bottom of the third page of Granny Ginny's letter and looked at Ashleigh. There were another three pages to go in this, by far the longest letter yet, and, given the date, they both knew what was coming – though not, perhaps, Ginny's personal part in it. A shadow fell across them and Robyn jumped, but when she looked up, it was just a stray cloud crossing the sun. All the same, it drew her out of the spell of the story and back into the grounds of the beautiful house on whose doorstep they were blithely sitting.

'Is this a bit weird?' she asked Ashleigh.

'I'm sure Granny Ginny wouldn't send us somewhere dangerous.'

'Into a river, up to the top of the tree…'

'Those were just physical challenges, not actual safety risks.'

Robyn nodded, but stood up to scan the area all the same. It was a normal, gloriously sunny Hawaiian day, and the green lawns and blossoming flowers in the manicured garden whispered benignly in the spring breeze. Even so, the absence of people was disturbing. Someone had known they were coming, left the chest out and then hidden themselves away. Why?

'Do you think they're watching us?'

'Who?'

'Whoever lives here.'

'Maybe, though I doubt it's very interesting for them. Why don't we just ring the doorbell and ask?'

'We can't!'

Ashleigh laughed.

'So we can walk through their high-security gates and up their drive, then sit on their porch to open our treasure chest, but we can't ring the bell…?'

Put like that, it did sound a bit foolish but Robyn still felt nervous.

'Surely if they wanted to meet us, they'd have come out already?'

'Maybe they're just giving us a chance to open the chest in peace. Ring the bell, Robyn.'

'No, I—'

'Oh, for God's sake, out the way.'

Ashleigh turned her chair awkwardly on the porch, knocking the treasure chest aside and sending it clattering off the tiled step. Robyn cringed.

'OK, OK, I'll do it.'

Ashleigh's smile was distinctly smug as Robyn stepped past and put her finger to the neat bell by the honeyed oak door. A ring echoed somewhere inside the house and she stepped hurriedly back, wiping her clammy palms on her shorts. No one came.

'They must be out. Fine. Let's take the chest and get…'

She froze as she heard footsteps rapping neatly towards them from the inside.

'They're not out,' Ashleigh said with a grin.

'No.'

Robyn swallowed as the door swung open, but the figure who stepped out couldn't have been less scary. She was a neat older woman with a dark bun, smiling eyes and a very familiar face.

'You're the manager of the Royal Hawaiian!' Robyn burst out, then clamped an embarrassed hand over her mouth. 'I mean, hello.'

The woman smiled.

'Hello, Robyn, Ashleigh. I'm not actually the manager. He just happens to be a good friend of mine.'

'You're the woman from the Coffee Experience, too,' Ashleigh said.

'Guilty as charged,' she agreed easily, putting her hands up. 'Maria is also a friend.'

'You know a lot of people.'

'Honolulu is a small place, at least when it comes to the locals. I'm Malie Garcia, daughter of Frank and Lilinoe Palakiko.'

Robyn gasped.

'I knew it! Granny Ginny and your mother flew together.'

'That's right. Virginia taught my mother to fly and they were partners throughout the war. Friends too, though that wasn't always easy.'

Robyn's heart spiked. Was this the secret at the heart of Granny Ginny's treasure hunt?

'What happened?'

Malie, however, just gave her a quiet smile.

'I'm under firm instruction to let you girls find that out for yourselves. Your grandmother was most insistent. Now, would you like to come in?'

'That would be lovely,' Robyn agreed, all nerves forgotten in the thrill of meeting this direct link to a past that had been so vividly unfolding to them over the last week.

Malie ushered them into a wide corridor and on through to a beautiful open-plan kitchen. Bi-fold doors stretched across the back of the building, leading out into another pretty garden. It was dominated by a table and chairs, enough to seat at least ten, and Robyn spotted a wooden playhouse nestling in the banana trees and a well-worn tennis court beyond. This was definitely a family home.

'You knew Granny Ginny then?' she asked as Malie made for the fridge.

'A little. She used to come and stay sometimes when I was younger.' Robyn tried to do the calculations in her head but it was impossible to judge quite how old this lively woman might be. 'That was back in the sixties, when I was a teen,' Malie supplied

helpfully. 'Way before either of you two were born. She was like
an auntie to me for a time, but then I guess I grew up, left home,
made my own life. The last time I saw your grandmother was at
Mum's funeral.'

'I'm so sorry,' Robyn said. 'When was that?'

'Nineteen-ninety-five. She was seventy-four and got cancer,
sadly. My father was devastated. We all were.'

'I'm so sorry,' Robyn repeated, feeling useless.

Malie smiled again.

'It was a long time ago. We lost my father ten years later. Virginia
must have been in amazing health to make it this far.'

'She was amazing full-stop,' Ashleigh said.

'She certainly seemed it when I talked to her about this treasure
hunt of hers. You can't imagine how surprised I was when she
contacted me a few months ago through Facebook. I think she'd
set up an account just to find me, as she only had a profile picture.
It made me jump when I saw it though – it was as if Mum had
come back to life right in front of me.'

Robyn turned to Ashleigh, but she looked blank.

'I didn't know Granny Ginny even had an account, so I've
never seen it.'

'She called herself Silver Wings – that was the badge the women
pilots got when they passed their military training. The picture was
one of Mum and Virginia. She must have known I would recognise
it and hoped I would get back to her message.'

'Was it this one?' Ashleigh asked, fumbling for her phone and
showing Malie Mrs Deans's squint photo of the picture from back
home.

Malie shook her head.

'Not that one, though I know it too. Here…'

She led them over to a cosy area at the far side of the lovely
room. Squashy floral sofas were grouped around a rag rug and
against the wall was a small log-burner that made Robyn want to

smile. It rarely got cold enough for a fire in Hawaii, at least if you were used to English weather. To either side of the burner were elegant bookcases and sitting on the middle shelves of both were clusters of family photos. Malie reached out and lifted one down, passing it to Ashleigh.

'This is the one you have there, right?'

'Right,' Ashleigh agreed. The faces were far clearer in the original photo, and as Robyn leaned over her sister to see, she could make out the pretty Hawaiian features of the girl who must be Lilinoe, Malie's mother. She was beaming broadly and waving so fast that her hand had blurred in the old lens.

'Your mother looks lovely,' she said.

'She was. Always so full of life and fun. Even after...' Malie stopped, then grabbed a second picture and handed it over. 'This is the one your grandmother used.'

Ashleigh took it from Malie, looked at it and then turned a strange shade of green. The picture shook in her hands and she looked fiercely up at Malie.

'Is this some sort of a joke?'

'What? No, I—'

'Because if it is, I don't find it funny, not funny at all. How did you do this?'

'Ashleigh!' Robyn cried, horrified.

Their hostess looked very upset and no wonder, as Ashleigh was advancing on her in her chair, waving the picture like a weapon. Robyn stepped hastily in front of her and snatched it out of her shaking hand. She lifted the picture to the light flooding in from Malie's garden and her breath caught. In this one the two women were in front of their plane. Granny Ginny was standing tall and proud, every inch the woman Robyn recognised and loved. Lilinoe was next to her, but much lower down. Robyn peered at it, unable to quite believe her eyes, and already wanting to read more of the letter.

Lilinoe Kamaka was sitting in a wheelchair.

Chapter Fifteen

7 December 1941

'Honestly, Will – did you arrange that blasted sunrise just for me?'

Ginny squinted into the orange sky, feeling it pulse in her eyeballs. Her head was throbbing and she cursed under her breath as she realised she'd forgotten her sunglasses. It was going to be even worse up in the sky as the sun rose. It had a way of refracting against the cockpit cover that would do her no good at all.

'Feeling a bit rough, Ginny?' Will laughed. 'Whose fault's that?'

'Oh, come on, Will – my brother got engaged. I couldn't exactly go to bed with a cocoa, could I?'

He gave her a sympathetic pat on the back.

'Course not. Jack and Penny looked very happy.'

'Sickeningly so.' She grinned. 'It's lovely. I can't wait to see my parents' faces when Jack tells them that he's found himself a wife.'

She smiled, feeling better already, though that sun was getting brighter by the minute and for once she wasn't looking forward to flying with unalloyed pleasure.

'All right there, my Queen of the Skies?'

She jumped as Robert Tyce came out of his office and looked curiously at her.

'She was out partying too late,' Will told him.

'Lucky you. Take me along next time, hey?'

Ginny laughed.

'Come on, Bob, I'm sure you've got far better parties of your own to go to.'

'You'd be surprised.' Robert looked momentarily lost then shook himself, smoothed out his moustache and, with a little bow, proffered her his sunglasses. 'Can I offer you these, madam?'

Ginny stared at them.

'Really? They're yours.'

'Well, for this morning they're yours, if you want them.'

'Yes, please!'

'And how about a quick coffee before you hit the skies?'

'Ooh yes!' Ginny agreed eagerly, but Will tugged at her sleeve.

'I can't be too long, Ginny – I've got to get to Santa, remember?'

'Course.' Ginny grimaced at Robert. 'Maybe when we come back down, Bob?'

'It'll be waiting for you, my lady.'

She gave him a grateful smile and slid his sunglasses on. They were a little large but of excellent quality and cut the glare magically.

'Thank you,' she called to him, as he turned to head back into his office.

He gave a little wave of acknowledgement and was gone.

'He's a nice man,' she said to Will as they clambered into their cockpits, 'but a terrible flirt.'

'Do you think?' Will started the engine. 'I think he's rather lonely.'

'What?' Ginny shouted over the noise.

'Lonely! I've heard that since his wife died last year, he doesn't go out much. K-T is his life.'

Ginny craned round to look back at her dapper boss, astonished.

'Which is why he's here at this ridiculous hour on a Sunday?'

'Exactly. Now – are you ready?'

'Sure am,' Ginny agreed. 'Rudders moving freely?'

'Check.'

'Oil pressure normal?'

'Check.'

'Then, chocks away!'

Will leaned out of the cockpit to wave the ground crewman to spin the propeller and remove the chocks. As she watched, Ginny thought of all the planes she'd seen heading out of Pearl Harbor on the *Lexington* earlier this week, chocks firmly in place, and wondered if they'd be seeing action before Christmas. God, she hoped not. The thought of all those elegant aircraft being shot down in flames was unbearable – and that's before you even thought about the brave men piloting them. She shuddered.

'OK, Ginny? We don't have to do this if you're really feeling unwell.'

'It's not that, Will. I'm fine, let's go.'

She waved him on and he turned the Cub onto the runway. Behind them a second plane was coming out with Lili at the controls. Despite dancing with Ginny until 2 a.m., she looked sickeningly bright this morning. She'd probably stopped at the second drink like a sensible girl; when on earth would Ginny ever master that?

Reaching for her water bottle, she took a deep drink and waved to her friend, who gave her a cheery wave back and turned her Cub out behind theirs. The sky was a near perfect blue now, the sun rosy through Robert's glasses, and Ginny sat back as Will applied the throttle and enjoyed his flawless take-off. Something about having his wife with him had made him more relaxed and confident, and, as a result, his flying had improved immeasurably. Once he was out at sea, she'd talk him through all the manoeuvres one last time, but for now she could take the chance to look down at the pretty island, laid out like a postcard.

Will was skimming west along the coastline over Ewa Beach, thankfully away from the sun, and she could look over the oyster shell of Pearl Harbor. A few men were moving slowly on the decks of their ships, but it was Sunday morning and most were seizing the chance for a rare lie-in. A small destroyer was patrolling up and down outside the harbour entrance and Ginny craned to see if it was the *Ward*, Billy Outerbridge's new command. It looked busy, with a lot of men standing along the railings peering into the sea, and for a moment Ginny thought perhaps they'd caught a sub, then told herself not to let her imagination get away with her. There was nothing in Hawaii's crystal waters but coral and fish.

Will reached Barbers Point and banked left, turning the Cub out to sea. For a minute, all Ginny saw was blue, then Will banked again and Oahu was before her once more, the rich forest green of the volcano's ancient slopes lush against the acidic sky. She spotted Hickham Field, the naval airbase just inland from the civilian airfield, and wondered how Jack was feeling this morning. Did love soothe sore heads? She hoped so, for his sake.

Out of the corner of her eye she spotted a plane.

'Craft to the left,' she warned Will.

'Got it,' he shouted back. 'It's Lili.'

Of course it was. Ginny watched her friend fondly as she executed a perfect castle turn, then reminded herself that she was here to instruct, not just to enjoy the views, and straightened up.

'Right, Will, let's get ready to...'

She squinted. Behind them and coming up fast was another plane. It couldn't be Lili because she'd just seen her go east.

'Ginny?'

'Sorry, Will.' She shook herself. Another plane in the skies over Oahu wasn't exactly unusual, and it was a beautiful morning for flying so others were bound to be taking advantage. It didn't look like one of Marguerite's Aeroncas, though, or one of Andrews's Interstates. It was too big and dark – and, oh Lord, there were several of them, all heading straight for their little plane.

'Back to the field, Will,' she rapped.

'What? Why? I haven't—'

'Back to the field, now!' The first of the planes shot past above them and as Ginny looked up, she saw, painted bright as the morning sun on both wings, the red circle of Japan. 'It can't be,' she breathed.

The Japanese were in the Philippines, everyone knew that. Hadn't Pat Bellinger told her so just last night as she'd stood on his lawn, cocktail in hand? Yet here was another plane, and another, all with the ominous red circle painted defiantly on them, and, now she looked more closely, she recognised the shape of the Japanese Zero. It was a new, much talked about airplane, previously believed only to be of any use over defenceless Chinese paddy fields, but now apparently swarming over Hawaii.

A new sound filled the still air – the ack-ack-ack of machine-gun fire. Will yelped in fear and the Cub wobbled precariously as two more planes came past, so close that Ginny could see their pilots, eyes set on the land dead ahead. A bullet pinged off their tail and the plane wobbled again.

'They're shooting at us!' Will cried, his voice shrill. 'Why are they shooting at us?'

'It's the Japanese, Will. I'm taking the controls.'

Ginny's mind was spinning but she forced herself to focus on the one thing she knew well – flying. Dropping the plane low to let the enemy planes go over the top, she made for John Rodgers at full throttle. Another bullet hit their tail, then another.

'Duck!' she shouted to Will.

'They're everywhere.'

'We're not their target.'

'Then what is?'

They both knew the answer to that. Even with her eyes on the little civilian runway, Ginny could see Pearl Harbor up ahead and, to her horror, she spotted one of the lead Japanese planes open its hatch and let a silver bomb drop. It caught the sunlight, flashing out a warning for the brief seconds it took to drop, and then it hit its target with a boom, sending bits of ship flying. Dark smoke filled the air and Ginny had to drag her eyes away from the horrific sight as the runway, thank God, came close.

She fought to keep the plane steady. More bullets were cutting across their flight path and her left wing tore, sending the poor plane listing sideways so that it took all her strength to keep it level as she headed in to land. Her thoughts flew to Lili, and she scanned the skies in all directions but could see only the buzzing Japanese Zeros, like a swarm of mosquitos darkening the air.

The wheels touched down on the runway and she let out a breath she hadn't even realised she'd been holding, but the danger wasn't over yet. Still the Japanese planes were coming, and even whilst the pilots were focused on dropping their bombs, they seemed to have time to spray bullets in all directions. Panting, Ginny brought the Cub to a halt as close to the hangar as she dared, and watched two other pilots dashing from their plane, arms over their heads as bullets rained down on them.

'Are you ready, Will?'

'To do what?'

'To run, of course. They'll hit us easily if we sit here. Come on – we've got to get to the hangar. Ready, set, go!'

She flung back the cockpit, heart pounding faster than she'd ever known it could, and leaped down, making for the hangar at a run. She heard Will's footsteps behind her but daren't turn to see. A plane swept down, hard and low, and a bullet pinged off the tarmac just behind her feet.

'Run!' she screamed.

'Ginny!'

Robert Tyce came rushing forward, holding his hands out to pull her into the safety of the hangar. Ten more steps and she'd be there. She reached for her boss, but at that moment a bullet whizzed past her, so close she felt it whistle through her hair. She gasped as Robert's outstretched hands went to his chest, his eyes widened in shocked horror, and he fell to the ground.

'Bob, no!'

She grabbed at his shoulders, tugging him back into the hangar. Will, thank God, came up at her side and together they dragged him deep into the big metal building. Bullets were pinging off the roof like the darkest of hailstorms as she dropped to her knees next to her flamboyant boss.

'Bob, stay with me. We'll get help. We'll get you sorted.'

He gave her a slow, sad smile.

'I'm glad you got down, Queen of the Skies,' he muttered. 'Not sure there's time for that coffee though.'

He tried to smile but his body creased up in a racking cough, and as Ginny clutched him close against her, blood spewed up over his immaculate suit and he went horribly still. Ginny looked at Will. She could feel herself shaking all over and had no idea how to stop it, save to cling on to Robert's broken body.

'Goodbye, Bob,' she whispered. 'Fly high.'

She stroked his hair back off his poor, still face, but there was little time for mourning with the Japanese death machines still roaring across the skies. The noises from Pearl Harbor were deafening now – the blast of bombs, the crackle of flames and, worst of all, the screams of men.

'Jack!' Ginny gasped, finally looking up as the terrible thought hit her. Her brother was on Hickham Field, just alongside the harbour at the heart of the attack. 'We have to do something, Will. We have to help.'

She looked around for her pupil but he'd ducked into the office, and she could see him through the window frantically talking into the telephone. Two men prised Robert's body from her and moved him gently across to the side of the hangar, but now someone else came rushing towards her – someone small and neat, in dark overalls, his usually smiling eyes full of fear.

'Where's Lili?' Kalani asked, grabbing Ginny's arm. 'Where's my Lili?'

Ginny swallowed and looked to the skies as another wave of Japanese Zeros droned past with no sign of a little yellow Cub amongst them.

'I don't know.'

Kalani dropped down onto his knees to stare at her.

'You taught her to fly, Virginia. You sent her up there into the skies – what if she never comes back?'

Ginny stared at him in horror as, over the harbour, another bomb exploded with an air-splintering boom. Kalani was right. She'd wanted to teach Lili to fly so that they could be buddies in the air together, but that might now have cost the gentle, clever girl her life.

Her thoughts clouded as black as the smoke from America's finest ships, and all she could do was pace the hangar entrance, desperately scanning the skies for Lilinoe's plane.

There was still no sign of her, and the world seemed to be nothing but smoke and fire, as if hell itself had come to Oahu. K-T pointed straight towards Pearl Harbor, and with the land flat between them, they could see far too much of the horror show being played out like some sick movie.

Most of the naval planes had been bombed in the first passes by the enemy aircraft, but a handful of US planes had taken off and were bravely battling to take out the Japanese Zeros. Ginny watched, heart in mouth, wondering if one of them was Jack. It would be just like him to get up and out there first, and she could only pray that his hangover had made his reactions slower than usual. Not that it looked much safer on the ground. Many of the barracks buildings were alight and they watched, sickened, as men came running out of them like ants, screaming in pain and fear.

In the harbour, the scenes were even worse. A bomb had hit one of the big battleships, and within moments its proud stacks had listed to one side and disappeared in a cloud of the blackest smoke Ginny had ever seen. The smell was disgusting – acrid and metallic, with a stomach-churning undertone of cooking meat – and already flakes of burning material were floating in on those huddled in the hangar, choking in their lungs.

Some of the men must have managed to get to their gun stations because the sound of anti-aircraft fire rang out across the other carnage, and those bits of the Hawaiian sky still clear of smoke were pitted with strange black puffs where the shells exploded. For the moment, there seemed to be a lull in the relentless wave of Japanese fighters, but they were bound to be back and fear hung in the air, as tangible as the fuel-thick smoke and the cries of the wounded.

'I can't bear it,' Ginny cried. 'I have to do something to help.' She turned and grabbed Kalani's arms. 'Lili's fuel would have run out by now so she must have landed somewhere else – and very wise too. Why come back here, where the bombs are falling? There are loads of fields she could have landed the Cub on and she's more than skilful enough to do that. She'll be fine, Kalani, I'm sure of it. She'll be back to us, later – you have to believe that.'

He nodded bleakly and Ginny had a feeling it was more herself she was talking to. She could feel her skin itching with fear and frustration and knew she couldn't just stand in here, watching as Pearl Harbor burned, possibly taking her friends with it. She turned to Will.

'I'm going to head over there. Try to get to the hospital. They must need all the help they can get.'

'I'll come with you.'

Will had got through to Helen on the phone. She and Lois were fine and had promised to hide in their basement until it was all over – whenever that would be – so that was one less worry for him, but they both had so many friends on the naval base and who knew what trouble they must be in right now.

'Let's go,' Ginny said.

'No!' Kalani cried. 'Not you too.' But all she could do was to throw him an apologetic wave and run after Will as he made for the airfield entrance, keeping tight to the buildings in case the planes returned. None darkened the skies, and they made it out and down the road towards the imposing white-walled entrance to the Hickham Field naval base. There were no sentries on guard and they ran straight in.

Ginny felt bile rise in her throat, and pulled her shirt up over her mouth to try and block out the smell of blood and oil that seemed to permeate every speck of air this close to the water. If she'd thought it looked like hell from the hangar, it was ten times worse now she was actually diving into its mouth. Everywhere men lay on the ground crying out for help, some with fellows holding them, others alone, writhing in miserable agony. One man, young enough to surely only just be out of school, wept for his mother, and Ginny dropped to her knees at his side.

'I've got you. I've got you safe.'

He turned delirious eyes up to hers.

'Mom?'

'I've got you,' she said again, gently brushing his blood-soaked hair back off his face.

He smiled a moment, then, with a deep inward breath, went still. Tears filled Ginny's eyes. This was the second man to die in her arms, and her only consolation was that he had gone to God believing himself cradled by the mother he'd yearned for.

Turning her eyes to the skies, she saw, not angels coming for the poor lad's soul, but a second wave of Japanese planes. She crushed herself in against the wall of a barrack building as the sound of death filled the air once more. It couldn't be more than an hour since Robert Tyce had laughingly offered her his sunglasses to protect her from the minor inconvenience of a head made sore from too much fun. Now he lay dead and hundreds of others with him. Ginny ran through a list of all her friends. Somewhere out there amidst the carnage were Eddie and Joe, Dagne, Penny, Lili and her dear brother Jack.

There were still a few brave American planes in the air, chasing the Zeros like lone kids harassing a gang of bullies. Ginny couldn't take her eyes off the horrific dogfights. She heard Will, next to her, give a hoarse cheer as someone took out a Zero, sending it spinning to the ground, but the next minute a US plane was also hit. Right engine on fire, it dived downwards and went into an uncontrollable spin. It was so close that she could just make out the silhouette of the pilot battling to steer it away from the heavily populated harbour before it crashed, with a sickening shriek, into a field just beyond.

'Jack,' Ginny choked out.

Will put an arm around her.

'It wasn't him. I'm sure it wasn't him.'

Ginny didn't question him; she needed this assurance, however contrived, if she was to stay sane. An ambulance skidded up and two men jumped out, a stretcher between them. Grateful for something to focus on, Ginny ran to them.

'Can we help?'

Their eyes were already weary.

'God, yes. There's another stretcher in the van – get anyone who looks like they might be saveable.'

It was a stark, cold statement but Ginny could see the sense of it. There were far, far too many wounded here to waste hospital space taking in those who had only as long to live as the young man she'd just held. How on earth she could make those sorts of decisions, though, she had no idea.

'Come on,' Will said, already jumping into the van and grabbing the stretcher. 'Any one we can save is one more than without us.'

He was right, and Ginny ran to help him as another young man cried out. He had a horrible wound to his lower leg but looked otherwise whole, and swiftly she and Will gathered him up and transported him back to the ambulance, eyes half closed against the bullets that might strike them at any moment. The medical crew had already loaded four men into the van – two more than it ought really to take – but they added their own and three more besides before the driver nodded grimly and closed the doors.

'You coming?'

He held open the door of the cab, and Ginny and Will crushed inside with the two medics, squeezing the door shut as they screamed off towards the naval hospital. The Japanese planes seemed to be thinning out but they had wreaked black havoc. To Ginny's horror, she saw that the big, white hospital was sitting right at the entrance to Pearl Harbor, but it was too late to back out now and, as they pulled through the gates, she could see the full devastation of the US fleet right before her.

All the great battleships were going down. The *Arizona* was half submerged and lost in a bluish-purple smoke that rose high into the sky as if it were coming from the volcano itself. The *California's* side was ripped open, the *West Virginia* tipped sharply to port, and the *Oklahoma* was upside down, its underbelly to the skies and men scrambling all over it, desperately trying to cut holes in the thick metal to release those trapped beneath.

The smaller cruisers were also ripped apart by torpedoes, and even in the dry dock three big ships listed drunkenly against each other. Far worse than the jagged remains of the beautiful ships, though, were the men caught between them. The water all across the oyster-shaped bay was slicked with oil, much of it on fire, and men jumping for safety from sinking ships only found themselves in worse trouble. Ginny could see them waving burning arms and screaming for mercy through the haze of smoke that blocked even the Hawaiian sun, turning the whole scene into a Dante-esque horror.

'Get 'em into the hospital – now!'

The bark of the ambulance men brought Ginny back from the nightmare before her and, shaking herself, she leaped out and ran round to the back. The men inside were listing against each other, much as the poor ships were doing beyond, and she focused on helping them into the hospital.

It was chaos inside as well. Bodies filled the wards and lay along the sides of the white corridors, smearing them with blood. The wounded wept and cried out for help and doctors and nurses scurried between them, trying to sort them into priority and offering merciful shots of morphine to detach them from their pain. Ginny helped unload their patients and looked around for a nurse.

'Penny!'

Her sister-in-law-to-be's pretty face was drained but determined. She held a syringe and ampules of morphine and was working efficiently down a line of suffering men, pausing to speak soothing words to each one in turn as she administered the magic drug. Now, though, she ran across.

'Ginny! Oh Ginny, thank God you're safe. Have you seen Jack?'

Ginny clasped Penny tight and shook her head.

'I've seen no one but Will, sorry, but Jack will be OK. I know he will. Jack's always OK.'

Penny nodded her head fiercely against Ginny's chest and then pulled back.

'Come on,' she said, jaw set, 'there's work to do.'

Looking round the broken, wailing, burning men, Ginny thought it might be the biggest understatement she'd ever heard. How had their happy Sunday morning been so callously and ruthlessly ripped apart? She wanted it to end. She wanted to close her eyes and have it all just go away, but that wasn't going to happen so, swallowing down bitter tears, she rolled up her sleeves and did the best she could.

Chapter Sixteen

Saturday 9 March

Robyn had to fight tears from her own eyes as she got to the end of this terrible section of Granny Ginny's letter. She'd heard of the Pearl Harbor attack, of course, but only as the event that brought America into the war. At home in Britain, it had been taught in passing as almost a lucky blow – the thing that pushed the States into joining the Allies and set them on the path to victory. Reading Ginny's account now she felt shocked and ashamed.

'I didn't know,' she said, her voice shaky.

'Me neither,' Ashleigh agreed. She'd eased herself onto the sofa at Robyn's side, and it felt nice to have her close without the wheels of her chair between them. 'Poor Granny. Poor everyone. It must have been such a terrible shock.'

Malie nodded.

'That's what Mum always said.'

'She survived then?' Robyn asked.

Malie smiled.

'I wouldn't be here if not. I was born in 1947.'

'Right. But her plane must have gone down if she…'

'You should read on for that. I'm sure the treasure hunt will reveal all.'

Ashleigh let out an impatient sigh.

'I'm sure it will, but it's such a protracted way to do it. Why couldn't she just have sat us down on one of the many, many days and nights we spent together throughout our lives and explained it all?'

Malie smiled again.

'I can't help you there, but I don't think that generation were brought up to talk about themselves much, and certainly not about the war. It took years and years for there to be any information at all on Pearl Harbor even right here, where it happened. There were memorials up in the cemetery, with all the dead honoured as they deserved, but no actual information. Even when I was growing up in the sixties it was a ghost story, only to be half believed – and yet nearly two and a half thousand people died that morning, and you shouldn't bury their memories.'

Robyn nodded slowly.

'There's plenty of information here now.'

Malie grimaced.

'I sometimes think we've gone too far the other way. I'm a bit uncomfortable with war tourism, but, yes, it's better than sweeping it all under the carpet.'

Robyn looked down at the letter, smoothing her hands across it and desperately wishing she could talk to Granny Ginny. She wanted to make hot chocolate and crawl up against her on their battered old sofa and ask her how that morning had felt, how she'd coped, what it had done to her afterwards. But she couldn't ask her and she couldn't crawl up against her grandmother ever again. A tear fell out of her eye and dropped onto the letter, and she dabbed it hastily away.

'I'll get you both a drink,' Malie said, tactfully moving away. 'And perhaps you'd stay for some lunch?'

'Oh, we couldn't impose.'

'Not at all. I'd love to have you. Trey, my husband, is out at golf so the company would be very welcome. Think about it.'

She gave them a kindly smile and moved to the smart kitchen area, leaving Robyn and Ashleigh alone on the sofa. They looked at each other.

'This time last week we were on a plane,' Ashleigh said eventually.

'Is that all it was?'

That trip back to Hawaii after the funeral seemed forever ago. Robyn felt as if she'd travelled through so much time and space since that she was giddy with it. Granny Ginny wrote so eloquently about her friends that she almost felt as if she knew them, and picturing their grandmother in the hospital with Penny, battling to save lives as she longed for information on those closest to her, turned a screw in her heart.

'Are you glad you came?' she asked her sister.

'Of course. I mean, I'm not going to say it's easy.'

'The flat's a nightmare, I know, I'm sorry.'

'Not the flat, you idiot – all this, Granny's past. What's one little wheelchair in comparison to men burning alive in an oily harbour? It kind of puts things in perspective.'

Malie came back bearing a jug of something cloudy and fresh-smelling, chinking with ice cubes. She set it and two glasses down.

'Lemonade OK?'

'Delicious.' Robyn reached eagerly for the jug, pouring them both a glass. 'Are you not joining us?'

'I'll put lunch together whilst you finish reading that, and then perhaps we can talk about it more.'

'You're very kind,' Robyn said. 'And you have a beautiful house.'

'I'm lucky. Mom and Dad bought this after the war when so many of the senior officers went back to the mainland and houses in Makalapa were going for a bargain. I grew up here, and when Dad got frail, Trey and I moved back in to help him – and stayed.'

'I don't blame you,' Ashleigh said. 'It's a great place. You've even got a tennis court. I love tennis. Loved...' she corrected herself hastily. Malie coughed and she looked defiantly up at her. 'I wasn't always this... useless.'

Malie met her glare.

'You don't seem useless to me, Ashleigh Harris.'

'I don't?'

'Quite the reverse. A wheelchair is there to push you forward, you know, not to hold you back.'

'How dare—' For once Ashleigh cut herself off, but Malie gave her a wry smile.

'How dare I? Because I grew up with a mother in a chair. I saw her battles. I saw her struggles and I saw her victories. I saw the way a disability can expose you and the way it can give you something to hide behind. I saw her hate it and I saw her love it. At the end of the day for me, it was just something that got my glorious, funny, brave, exciting mum around.' Ashleigh gaped at her and she flushed. 'I'm sorry – it's really not my place to say any of that. If my grandkids were here now, they'd be horrified. They're always telling me that I open my mouth without engaging my brain.'

Despite herself Ashleigh laughed.

'No. No, it's fine. It's good to talk to someone who understands.'

'Yeah, well, it's a horrible thing to have happen to you, but you seem like the sort of girl who'll make the most of it.'

'I'm really not.'

Malie reached over and gave her shoulder a tiny squeeze.

'But you will be. Now, I must get on with lunch. It's just cold stuff, so there's no rush.'

She slid away and Robyn sat awkwardly as Ashleigh watched her go with a curious look on her face, half fury, half admiration.

'You OK, Ash?' she asked tentatively.

Ashleigh turned to her.

'Me? Fine. Really. Shall we do as Malie suggests?' She pointed to the remaining portion of the letter, then leaned in and added, 'Do you think this is going to tell us that Lilinoe was taken out by the Japanese?'

'If she was, why wouldn't Granny Ginny have told us about it herself?'

'Good point. There must be more to it than just the Pearl Harbor attack.' Ashleigh gasped suddenly and grabbed for the letter. 'Uncle Jack,' she cried. 'Oh Robyn, this is going to be about Uncle Jack.'

Robyn's heart squeezed in a way she was getting horribly familiar with. Granny Ginny had talked often of her beloved brother, Jack, and his picture had had pride of place on the wall throughout their childhood. He'd been something of a legend in the family – the brave pilot who'd risked all to try and keep Pearl Harbor safe.

'He'd just got engaged,' Robyn said, looking at the remaining pages of the letter and over to Ashleigh. 'Must we read on?'

Ashleigh took her hand.

'We must.'

Chapter Seventeen

7 December 1941

'No!' The limp form being wheeled into the hospital had to be at least the hundredth one Ginny had seen today, but if she'd thought her heartstrings had been stretched before, now they snapped in two. 'Jack, no!'

She ran to him, flinging herself onto his chest and pulling him in tight against her.

'Careful, miss – you'll hurt him.'

'Hurt?' Ginny pulled back. 'He's not dead?'

The man swallowed.

'Not yet.'

Ginny didn't even want to think about what that meant. Jack was here, in her arms, and she wouldn't let him die.

'Jack. Jack, darling, wake up. It's Ginny, I'm here. I'll make you well, I promise.' Miraculously his eyelids fluttered and Ginny stroked his cheek, willing him to wake up properly and look at her. 'Jack!'

'Ooh, Gin, don't shout.'

'Jack! You're all right.'

'Dunno about that,' he said, his words slurring. 'Helluva headache.' He half sat up on the trolley, putting a hand to the back of his head, and when he brought it away, it was slick with blood. Ginny gasped but her brother just looked at it with curious detachment. 'Red, isn't it?'

His normally deep brown eyes were hazed to the colour of dirty straw, and now they rolled back in his head.

'Jack! Oh God, Jack, stay with me. I'll get you help.' She looked desperately around the packed hospital, but every doctor and nurse she could see was already tending to people. 'Penny!' she shouted frantically. 'Penny, it's Jack!'

Several people frowned in her direction but she didn't care. Penny had to be here; she had to see him. She clutched at Jack's hand, ignoring the blood that stuck instantly to her own skin.

'Jack,' she said urgently. 'Stay with me. Penny's coming. Penny – your fiancée…' She thought she saw the ghost of a smile cross his face and pushed on. 'Penny's a nurse, remember. She'll help you. She'll save you.'

'Penny,' he murmured. He blinked furiously, clearly trying to focus on Ginny's face. 'What happened?'

'The Japanese came,' she told him, fighting back tears.

'Oh yes! I got one, Ginny. Got two actually. But they kept coming. They kept on bloody coming.' His hand tightened suddenly round hers. 'I don't want to die.'

'You won't,' Ginny insisted. 'Penny will be here. She'll know what to do.'

And then suddenly Penny was at her side. The skin around her eyes was stained blue with tiredness and her shoulders were hunched, but Ginny saw her battle to stay professional for the man she loved, and admired her more than she ever had before.

'Where does it hurt, Jack darling?'

'It's his head,' Ginny told her. 'The back of his head.'

Penny cradled Jack gently, lifting him up as if embracing him, but her eyes scanned the wound and, to Ginny's horror, she saw the nurse's legs buckle. She put out a hand to steady her and Penny looked gratefully her way.

'It's not good, is it?' Ginny whispered.

Penny shook her head.

'Bullet. Right in the middle of his cranium. Ginny – you, you need to say goodbye.'

'No!'

'We both do.'

Ginny looked at the nurse, holding her fiancé of less than twenty-four hours tight against her slender frame, and nodded bleakly. Together they laid Jack back down on the trolley. His body was limp now and his hand flopped sideways but his eyes fought to stay open.

'Jack,' Ginny said. She sought for words but could find only the simplest ones. 'I love you, Jack.'

His mouth flickered, and she leaned over and pressed a soft kiss on his forehead.

'Love you too, Gin. And the olds. Tell the olds for me. Tell them I love them. Tell them I… I'm sorry.'

'There's nothing to be sorry for, Jack. You're a hero.'

He gave a little shake of his head.

'There are no heroes today. I'm still sorry though, Gin – I don't think I'll be able to look after you any more.' His breath caught in his throat and he battled to find it again. 'Good job,' he spluttered, 'that you're so damned good at looking after yourself.'

Ginny kissed him again, tears filling her throat too much to say more, then forced herself to step back and make room for Penny. The other girl took her brother's poor broken head in both her hands, leaned over and kissed him tenderly on his lips.

'Sleep well, darling man,' she murmured. 'Sleep well.'

Jack smiled, then his eyes slowly closed and he was gone. Ginny fell to her knees, clutching at the trolley as if it might somehow hold her together. Her brother was dead. Her beloved older brother, who she'd followed here to this paradise of an island, was dead. Just last night she'd hugged him as he'd proudly told the world he was getting married, and now here was his fiancée, weeping over his still body. It was too much. For nearly twelve hours she'd battled to save men in the hellhole that had once been Pearl Harbor, but this was one man too many. As Penny sank to the floor next to her, Ginny wrapped her arms around her and let the tears flow until they blurred the horrific images of death all around them.

'Ginny? Ginny, is that you?'

The voice, soft and kind, penetrated Ginny's grief and she looked slowly upward. The fog cleared and she stared in amazement.

'Lili? God be praised, Lili!'

She leaped up and flung her arms around her friend before pulling back to check that it was truly her. Sure enough, Lilinoe Kamaka stood there, apparently unhurt, her dark eyes looking into Ginny's own with unbearable kindness.

'I'm so sorry, Ginny. I'm so, so sorry.'

Ginny looked to Jack. Someone, with the ruthless efficiency of need, had laid his body on the floor so they could take the trolley for others, and Penny was sitting against the wall, cradling him as if he'd simply gone to sleep after a hard flight. Ginny thought, with a new wave of grief, of their parents. She would have to tell them when she got home that Jack was gone. But swift on the back of that thought was the sickening realisation that there would be no going home now. America was at war and Christmas was already over.

She watched as two orderlies bent down to take Jack away. They spoke kindly to Penny but she seemed incapable of taking her arms from around him, and Lili and Ginny had to bend down and prise her off to let them take him to the morgue.

'Name?' one of them asked Ginny apologetically.

'Jack,' she told him, watching him write it on a little card. 'Jack Martin. Naval pilot.'

She looked away as the orderly tied the label to Jack's wrist. She, too, wanted to cling to Jack and keep him here at her side, but Jack wasn't in that broken body any more, and instead she held on to Penny and Lili as tightly as she could manage as he was borne away. Another nurse came running up, crying Penny's name, and she turned to her, weeping.

'I'll look after her,' the new girl said. 'I'll see she's safe.'

Ginny nodded and gave Penny a gentle kiss.

'We'll bury him with all honour, Penny,' she assured her, her voice catching. It wasn't much of a promise but it was all she had, and as Penny was led away by her friend, Ginny turned back to Lilinoe. 'It's all so, so awful, Lili.'

'I can't believe Jack's gone. I'm so sorry, Ginny. You must feel—'

'Sad,' Ginny said shortly, pain grinding through her at the woeful inadequacy of the word. She fought for a distraction from her teeming feelings. 'What about you, Lili? What happened to you?'

Lili looked uncertainly at her but thankfully saw that her grief was too raw to probe and, taking Ginny's hand tight in her own, gave a little shake of her dark hair.

'I'm still not sure. One minute I was throwing lazy eights in the bluest of skies and the next they were dark with planes. There were so many of them, Ginny.'

'I know. They shot at us. All I could think of was getting down to the hangar.'

'I saw you go. It was awful. I was convinced one of the bullets was going to take you out and I was praying like I've never prayed before.'

'Did they not get you?'

'I was too far east. A couple of them veered towards me, but they were clearly under orders to make straight for Pearl so they left me alone, thank God. I flew straight up over the hills, hoping to get across to the naval air station at Kaneohe Bay, but as I rose over the top another wave of Japanese planes came in, dropping bombs right on it. I panicked then. The naval station is the only decent place to land around there but I wasn't going straight into the bombing.'

Ginny clutched at Lili anew.

'You poor thing. What did you do?'

She shrugged.

'What could I do? I took her down on the lower slopes.'

'Among all the trees?'

'I found a flattish bit where they'd been cutting them back. It was just about long enough.'

'Just about?'

Lili grimaced.

'I glanced off a tree or two at the end. The plane's not looking great, I'm afraid.'

'Damn the plane – as long as you're all right.'

Her friend spread her hands wide.

'As you see.'

'So why are you here?'

'Ah. Well, I did bump myself slightly. Hit my head on the dash and may have been out for a little time.'

'How long?'

'Some locals found me around midday.'

'Lili! You were unconscious in the plane all morning?'

'It would seem so. Bless them, these two men pulled me out and took me back to their house, and their mother looked after me. Then they drove me themselves, through all this, to get checked up. I must go back with gifts when, when…' She looked around the scenes of carnage in the hospital and shuddered. 'Will they come again, do you think? Will they come again tomorrow?'

Ginny stared at her in horror. Why would they not? Pearl Harbor was defenceless. Most of the ships were heading to the bottom of the still flaming harbour and almost all the planes were out of action. She'd heard someone say the dry docks were still functioning and the vast fuel tanks were intact, so what was to stop the Japanese coming back for a second attack?

'What can we do?'

Lili shook her head.

'I've no idea but I do know one thing, Ginny – I must get home. The docs say I'm fine and, Lord knows, they've got much, much worse to deal with. I need to see Papa. He must be worried sick about me.'

Ginny remembered Kalani's dark words to her at the hangar: *You taught her to fly, Virginia. You sent her up there into the skies – what if she never comes back?* Had that really been just this morning? It felt like forever ago and the poor man would have been pacing all this time, thinking his precious daughter was dead.

'Yes,' she agreed, glad of something positive to focus on amidst all this horror. 'We have to get you back. Come on.'

She felt a little guilty leaving the hospital with men still being brought in, but she wasn't a nurse and she was exhausted. For now, the best thing she could do was to get Lili back to her father. She needed a rest herself, and a little time to face up to the grief that was threatening to overwhelm her. Tomorrow she could return – if the Japanese didn't do so first.

Arm in arm, the two girls left the hospital and made for the town. It was gone nine and the sun had long since set on 7 December, but the burning battleships made it as light as day. Figures scurried around on the decks of those still upright enough to man the guns and nervous shots flew into the air, making them both jump. Ambulances buzzed around but all civilians were hiding indoors, and the only people out on the streets were the wounded and soldiers armed with guns.

'Who goes there?' someone rapped at them, making them both squeal. 'Ooh, sorry, miss. Misses. Er, ladies.' The soldier stepped forward, revealing himself to be as nervy as he was young. 'You shouldn't be out,' he told them.

'Just coming back from the hospital,' Ginny told him, too weary for politeness.

'Understood. Where are you going? Can I escort you back?'

'That would be very kind,' Lili said, but at that moment a jeep pulled up and someone jumped out.

'Lili? Ginny?!'

Ginny looked up into blissfully familiar eyes.

'Eddie!' His blond hair was dark with ash and his blue eyes hazy with tiredness, but he was whole. 'You're OK. The others?'

Eddie gestured to the jeep where an exhausted-looking Joe waved weakly from the passenger seat. 'All fine. I mean, devastated obviously, but fine. You?' Ginny nodded, but couldn't bring herself to look him in the eye. 'Jack?' he asked nervously. It was all Ginny could do to shake her head. 'No? Oh Ginny, no?'

'He made it up in the air,' she heard Lili tell them. 'Took at least one Zero out before they got him.'

'He's a hero,' Eddie breathed.

'He's dead,' Ginny told him dully.

She still couldn't conceive of a world without her bold, amiable, loving big brother in it; still didn't want to. *There are no heroes today*, Jack had said, and she knew what he meant. He'd been uncommonly brave but he'd been able to do little to stop the wave of destruction. There were no heroes; only villains.

'I'm so, so sorry,' Eddie said. 'Jack was a good man. The best.' He held out his arms and Ginny stepped gratefully into them. For a moment, she closed her eyes and imagined this was Jack hugging her as tight as he'd done for so many years, but then a gun fired somewhere nearby and she jumped back. The past was cut away, and if they weren't careful the present could yet be too.

'We need to get home,' she choked out.

'Of course. Jump in. We'll give you a ride.'

'Really?'

Ginny felt herself wilt with relief. Her legs had had enough of supporting her today and she almost fell into the jeep. Lili climbed in too, and they sank back onto the seats together as Eddie got into the driving seat and roared the engine.

'Terrible day,' Joe said, turning to press Ginny's knee as best he could through the seat backs. 'I'm so sorry, Ginny. It's all my fault.'

'What?' Ginny stared at him, her mind fuzzy with tiredness and grief. 'How can it be your fault, Joe?'

He took off his glasses and ran a hand over his shadowed eyes.

'I should have known. I should have warned people. What's the bloody point in naval intelligence if we don't provide any actual information?'

'You weren't to know about this. They changed the codes. You said so yourself.'

'Exactly! That alone should have been enough for me to go shouting warnings from the rooftops but no, we all just beavered away in our little dungeon offices, playing code-cracking and doing nothing of any actual use. We knew there were aircraft carriers unaccounted for. We knew it and we did nothing about it.'

'I told Kimmel,' Eddie said to him. 'I told Kimmel and he wasn't worried. No one at the top was worried. You heard Pat Bellinger last night, Ginny – was he worried?'

Ginny looked up at Makalapa Drive, above the main route they were now tracing into downtown Honolulu, and couldn't believe that it was just last night she'd stood there chatting with Bellinger about the Philippines.

'He wasn't worried,' she said, her voice breaking as she remembered them all toasting Jack and Penny as if there wasn't a care in the world. All that time Japanese aircraft carriers had been lurking just around the nearest island ready to attack.

'He was wrong,' Lilinoe said, her voice unusually bitter.

'He was,' Eddie agreed. 'Which way, Lili?'

Lili leaned forward to direct him and Joe looked sadly at Ginny.

'It's been a catalogue of disasters all day. D'you know, Billy Outerbridge's ship caught a sub at around 6.30 a.m. Torpedoed it out of the water. He called it in but no one saw fit to do anything about it.' Ginny's breath caught. She'd seen him. As she and Will had coasted blithely up into the sky she'd looked down and seen the activity on board. Her stomach churned.

'Not only that,' Eddie said, 'but two young lads up on the radar unit saw the planes when they were still miles away. Called them in to command who told them it was a shipment of B-25s coming in from California, and to turn off the radar and go and get their breakfast. Imagine! If that had gone straight to high command, every man could have been at his gun in time to at least take more of the bastards out.'

Ginny stared at him, unable to believe what she was hearing. Jack might not have died. Then again, more likely Jack would just have been up in the air that bit sooner and would still have died. They'd have needed far more than half an hour's warning to save many lives. She remembered Bellinger saying blithely that he was gathering patrol planes to scour the Pacific 'once we're on a war-footing'. Well, that had been too late, it turned out. Too complacently, arrogantly, stupidly late. Anger surged up inside her, and she had to lean over the edge of the jeep to retch up the contents of her stomach.

Thankfully they were pulling up outside Lili's house. Hastily she wiped her mouth on her shirt – any stain would go unnoticed amidst the blood already coating it – and pulled herself together. Now was the time for care not for blame, and she let Lili past and leaned on the jeep for support as her friend ran inside, calling her father's name. They, at least, would be happy tonight.

'It wasn't your fault, Joe,' she said, squeezing his hand. 'You said what you could – they just didn't listen.'

'They will from now on,' he told her, mouth set in a grim line. 'I'm going to do everything I can to track those bastards – track them and destroy them.'

Ginny swallowed.

'Will they come back? Tomorrow?'

Eddie hugged her again.

'We don't think so. There's no way they can have enough fuel to mount a second attack and get back to Tokyo.'

'We underestimate the Japanese at our peril,' she said, quoting his own words from way back when she'd first come to the island.

He gave her a small nod and dropped a kiss on her head.

'I'm sorry, Ginny,' he said again. 'I hope you can sleep.'

Ginny stepped away as the jeep pulled off, the two exhausted men sitting rigidly inside. Through the window of the house she could see Lili and Kalani hugging each other as if they'd never let go, and her heart filled with sorrow as she pictured, again, Jack's bloodied head and his eyes as they'd looked into hers.

I don't think I'll be able to look after you any more, he'd said. Then: *Good job that you're so damned good at looking after yourself.*

Well, it seemed she had little choice now. Her parents were four thousand miles away in Tennessee and Jack, her dear Jack, was gone. Tears threatened again but it seemed she was drained dry and they didn't fall. She stood on Lili's porch, her heart aching inside her weary body, listening to the sound of cicadas and nervous gunfire punctuating the peace of Hawaii that had today been ripped away, possibly forever. So much sorrow, anger and hurt swirled inside her and she had to have something to do with it.

Out of the smoke of Pearl Harbor came a memory: Jacqueline Cochran, standing before the press on 1 July, the very day she'd first strode onto the John Rodgers airfield here on Oahu. The great aviatrix had faced the cameras and said: *America has many talented female pilots and I believe Uncle Sam is going to need them.* Well, now Uncle Sam did, and Ginny, for one, was ready. On this dark, cruel, shocking day, the war had taken her brother from her; it would not take her freedom as well.

'I'll do it for you, Jack,' she whispered to the smoke-thick skies, as a tear slid down her cheek once more. 'I'll do it for you.'

Chapter Eighteen

Saturday 9 March

'It sounds so awful,' Robyn said eventually.

Her words dropped inadequately into the quiet of Malie's beautiful house. That shock dawn attack on this beautiful island in the middle of nowhere had clearly been devastating for so many, not just in terms of the lives lost but the security and confidence of all the islanders too. How on earth had they slept again after that terrible awakening on 7 December? How many funerals must there have been? And what sort of dark Christmas must they have had?

'The islanders surely hated the US for bringing all that to their doors?' she murmured.

Malie came over.

'Very few locals died. I think it was sixty-eight, which is a horrible number obviously, but nothing like the naval casualties which were over two thousand. In some ways, it actually brought them together. The locals mucked in with cars and trucks and even boats to bring the wounded to the hospitals – like the two men who brought Mum in.'

'It's good to hear she got home safely, but I guess that means she must have been hurt another time?' Ashleigh said, looking coyly at her.

Malie shook her head.

'You won't get me that way. She was hurt later.'

'When...?'

'When you've found the rest of the letters, you'll know.'

Both girls groaned.

'You're as mean as Granny Ginny,' Ashleigh told her.

'I'll take that as a compliment. Now, would you like some lunch?'

Robyn looked over to the table laden with beautiful salads, and suddenly felt as ravenous as if she'd been through that long, hard day with Ginny herself.

'I'd love some, Malie. Thank you.'

'This way. Help yourselves. And why don't you give us the next clue while we eat?'

Robyn nodded and, once she'd served herself, she turned to the last page of the letter, reading clue six out loud:

'*This Garden Isle has Hawaii's finest cuisine,*

But why Cook when you can find the best ice cream?'

'What?!' Ashleigh spluttered.

Robyn read it again; it didn't help much.

'Where's the Garden Isle?' she asked.

Ashleigh was swiftly onto Google.

'It says Kauai. Is that around here?'

Robyn nodded. 'It's the island at the top of the Hawaiian archipelago. I've never been but it's meant to be beautiful. Very green.'

'Hence Garden Isle, I guess. But why cook?'

'It has a capital letter,' Robyn supplied. 'I assume that's deliberate. Is there a man called...'

'Captain Cook!' they said together.

Ashleigh tapped away again.

'It seems that Captain Cook landed on Kauai when he first discovered Hawaii. Well, not discovered it, obviously, because the natives already knew it was there, but decided he'd discovered it, due to being an arrogant Westerner who believed that places only existed if they were marked on a European map.'

Malie snorted. 'Well said, Ashleigh.'

Ashleigh grinned at her.

'It's true – and it sounds like he got his just deserts here as well.' Her eyes flickered across her screen. 'It seems things went swimmingly when he first landed. The natives were very keen on metal, which they hadn't seen before, and Cook's sailors traded iron nails for sex. Lovely.'

'I suppose if both sides benefited...' Robyn said awkwardly.

Ashleigh gave her a scathing look.

'You know as well as I do that the men benefited from the nails and the women had to put up with the sex.'

Robyn sighed; Ashleigh was dead right.

'But listen,' her sister went on. 'Cook's lot really messed up. They went back via the Big Island and were worshipped as gods for a while. Clearly, they made the most of that – more sex, I imagine! – but then one of their crew died, proving them distinctly mortal, and they were hounded off. They got away, but the seas around Hawaii chucked them a storm that sent them back into the bay where the locals stoned them.'

'They died?'

'A lot of them, yes – until they resorted to their Western trick of shooting everyone with great big guns. Cook went in the first wave and is buried there in dishonour.' She smirked. 'Serves him right.'

'A bit harsh, Ash. Without him we wouldn't have known about these wonderful Pacific islands.'

'And these wonderful Pacific islands would have been far better off. What did the West bring Hawaii? Three hundred and fifty-three Japanese fighter planes!'

Robyn pushed her salad around her plate, her appetite eroded by her sister's justifiable cynicism.

'You really think Granny Ginny wanted us to go to another island?' she said eventually, focusing on the practicalities. 'How will we get there?'

Malie cleared her throat.

'I could take you.'

'How?'

'In my plane.' They both gaped at her and she smiled shyly. 'I was so inspired by Mum's stories of flying that I followed in her footsteps and got my pilot's licence. It's been pretty useful around here, especially when I was working on the Big Island.'

'You flew to work?' Robyn gasped. 'That's so cool.'

'It was rather,' Malie agreed. 'But mainly I use it for fun – trips up with the kids and grandkids, with visitors, just for my own enjoyment. Being up in the skies seems to sort of recharge my soul, if that doesn't sound too mad?'

Ashleigh made a choking noise and Robyn jumped swiftly in. 'It sounds wonderful, Malie. A few people on my course learned to fly but I confess I never found time for it. Maybe I should have done.'

'What did you study?'

Robyn swallowed. 'Aeronautical engineering.'

Malie raised an eyebrow but confined herself to a mild, 'It wouldn't hurt then. I reckon the best way to understand a plane is to take it into the skies. So – how about a trip with me?'

'When were you thinking?'

Malie rubbed her hands together.

'No time like the present.'

'Now?!'

'If I can get a runway slot then, yes, why not?'

'Why not?' Ashleigh demanded. 'Because it's mad, that's why not. It's one thing following clues across Honolulu, but flying around the islands is a bit extreme. What if we're not right about where to go?'

'You are right,' Malie said.

Ashleigh glared at her, flushing pink.

'You know that? Granny Ginny told you?'

'I helped her with the whole thing, I told you that.'

Ashleigh shook her head.

'This is ridiculous! Robyn, please, this is ridiculous. Insulting even. Why was Granny Ginny happy to discuss this convoluted farce of a treasure hunt with a total stranger and not us? Why was she happy to tell Malie her secret and not her own granddaughters, the girls she brought up?'

Robyn swallowed. It was a fair point.

'I don't know, Ash,' she said. 'But we're here now – clue six. There's only two more to go after this and, I don't know about you, but I want to get to the end.'

'For what? What does it matter if we never find out? Maybe we're better off not knowing whatever dark secret Granny Ginny was too ashamed to tell us.'

Robyn thought about it. Ashleigh was right but doing this treasure hunt had been the last thing she'd asked of them – how could they deny her that?

'She wanted us to know, Ash.'

'So why the hell didn't she just tell us?' Ashleigh's voice caught and she rubbed an angry hand over her face. Robyn reached out and, to her surprise, Ashleigh clutched at her. 'She saw me at my absolute worst, Rob. She saw me broken and in pain. She saw me angry and miserable and absolutely bloody horrible. She saw me rage at the world and hate myself. She saw me at total rock bottom – every dark bit of me as exposed as the horrible scars on my legs. And still, still she couldn't tell me this one little thing about herself. Did she not think it would have helped me, when I was about as wrecked as possible, to see that she wasn't so bloody, damned perfect?'

Robyn stood up and put her other arm around Ashleigh's shaking shoulders.

'I get that, Ash. I really get that, but maybe she felt she had to be strong for you.'

Ashleigh looked up.

'Then she was stupid, Rob. I didn't want strength; I wanted to know other people could be every bit as weak as me.'

Robyn crouched down and reached for her sister's chin, forcing it up so that she had to look at her.

'That, Ash, is why we need to finish this hunt. So we can find out what made Granny Ginny so much less than perfect, so we can see her scars and put them to rest with all the other wonderful memories of her. She wanted us to know what happened in the war – hence…'

She gestured around the beautiful house of a woman who had been a total stranger until an hour ago and was now offering to fly them to Kauai. It was bizarre and bonkers and, yes, totally unnecessary, but it was all they had.

'I don't believe her scars could have been that bad,' Ashleigh murmured. 'Whatever she said, Granny was no coward.'

Robyn squeezed her hand.

'Only one way to find out.'

'I have to go up in this plane?'

'I'd say so.'

She gave a big sigh then looked to Malie.

'In which case, I'd like to come, please – if you'll still have me.'

Malie smiled at her.

'Of course I will, Ashleigh. I'll go and call the airport now.'

An hour later and Robyn looked down at Oahu from five hundred feet in the air. It was stunning and Malie's aircraft was so light.

'It's like being an actual bird,' she gasped.

Ashleigh gave a snort from behind but, at her side, Malie nodded.

'Isn't it? Fancy a go at the controls?'

'Me?'

'Why not.' Malie indicated the stick between Robyn's legs, identical to the one she was currently using to fly the plane. 'Take hold and keep it steady. Switching over to you – now!'

Robyn felt the stick judder as the control of the aeroplane fed into it and held it carefully level. Her pulse picked up dramatically but when the little plane didn't suddenly plummet, or turn, or do anything scary, she dared to pull back on it a little. The nose went up and she was climbing. She hastily returned it to level, but the very fact of making the craft move to her command sent a thrill right through her.

'It's amazing.'

Malie laughed.

'I'll let you into a secret – it's not actually that difficult. Far easier than a car.'

'But more drastic if it breaks,' Ashleigh grunted.

'Not if you know what to do. There are far fewer aviation accidents than road ones. Cars are lethal.'

'Even when stationary,' Ashleigh growled.

Robyn was grateful to be concentrating too closely on flying the plane to rise to her sister's griping. Malie talked her through a few simple manoeuvres and before she knew it, she was turning down towards the beautiful island of Kauai. It was, indeed, lush and green on this 'Garden Isle' and a trace of a rainbow curving over the centre told of rain not long gone. Silver-grey clouds were gathered over the top of Mount Waialeale, the long-dormant volcano at the centre, and for a moment Robyn imagined her grandmother sitting atop them. In her mind's eye Ginny was reclining in the rainbow light, elegant legs crossed at the ankles and a Mai Tai in her hand, and she half raised her own to toast her.

'OK, Robyn?'

Malie's voice brought her straight back to the here and now. Goodness, when did she get so fantastical?

'Absolutely fine. Amazing. Love it,' she gabbled.

Malie shook her head, amused, then took back the controls and landed the little craft with only the lightest of bumps. Robyn glanced back to Ashleigh.

'Good, hey?' she prompted.

Ashleigh grunted.

'Not bad. You were a bit shaky though. I'd be better. Can I have a go on the return flight, Malie?'

Robyn grinned. That was the active, competitive Ashleigh she loved, and it was great to see her back. They unloaded the chair and made it easily out of Lihue Airport. Malie haggled ruthlessly at the car rental desk, and soon they were heading down a stunning road along the lower slopes of the volcano.

'Here we are,' Malie said shortly, 'Hofgaard Park.'

'What's here?' Robyn asked, as they drove in through unassuming gates.

'Cook's statue. It's a replica of one erected in England.'

'Lovely,' Ashleigh muttered.

It wasn't busy, but there was still a handful of tourists gathered around the statue which showed the explorer standing on a plinth, his legs confidently splayed. A rotund guide was standing before an attentive group of older people, holding forth in a nasal voice: 'As Captain Cook and his crew sailed into view, hundreds of Hawaiians crowded to the shore, waiting to greet the great man with offerings of bananas, pigs and *kapa* fabric.'

'And then,' Ashleigh said in her loudest voice, 'he nicked all their resources and had sex with all their women.'

The group spun round and their guide went puce.

'They welcomed him on their knees, like a god,' he countered, battling for his script.

'And he stuck his—'

'Ashleigh!' Robyn rapped, jerking the chair away. 'Stop it.'

The group were staring at her wide-eyed and now one of them asked the guide, '*Did* he have sex with them?'

'Of course not,' the poor man spluttered. 'At least, there was some bartering but not till later.'

'Not till they'd eaten the bananas and the pigs,' Ashleigh threw over her shoulder as Robyn wheeled her frantically out of range. Her only consolation was that Malie was convulsing with laughter.

'That told them,' she said, as they reached a shady spot to one side of the park and Robyn deemed it safe to stop again. 'There's nothing wrong with history, but we should definitely tell all of it, not just the bits that suit us.'

'Perhaps I should move out here and get a job as a tourist guide?' Ashleigh suggested. 'I'm sure there's a market for "alternative tours" these days. I'll dye my hair pink, wear harem pants and put bunting round the chair. People will love it.'

'They probably would,' Malie agreed. 'Are you thinking of that then, Ashleigh?'

'Becoming a tour guide?'

'No. Well, not unless you want to. I meant moving out here.'

'What?' Robyn gasped.

Ashleigh stared at her.

'Would you not like that, sis? Would I get in your way? Would it be a pain for you having to look after me?'

'No! Of course not. It would be great to have you closer. I'd love that.' She swallowed. '*Are* you thinking about it?'

Ashleigh gave a coarse laugh.

'Relax, Robyn. Why would I?'

'To become a tour guide?'

'Yeah, right. There's only so much cynicism even "alternative" tourists can take. You're quite safe. Now, I don't know about you but I'm starving, and over there I spy…'

She pointed a finger past Cook's statue to a clutch of shops beyond. In the middle a bright pink frontage shouted out: 'JoJo's Shave Ice. The best ices in Hawaii'. Robyn gulped. What had the riddle said? *But why Cook when you can find the best ice cream?* Well, apparently here it was.

Her head spun. Was it really only this morning that she and Ashleigh had crept up Malie's beautiful drive to find clue six? Now they were on a different island altogether, about to ask yet another curious waiter for a treasure chest. Still, she would kill for an ice cream and, if this was the right place, they were on to the penultimate clue. Surely Granny Ginny's secret must be coming out soon? She drew in a deep breath, reached for the handles of the wheelchair, and headed to the parlour.

The jaunty pink shop was made even brighter by a striped awning and multicoloured tables and chairs set on a veranda outside. A dreadlocked seller beamed at them from behind a long counter bulging with every flavour under the sun. Ashleigh insisted on plain vanilla, but after much dwelling over the extensive menu, Robyn and Malie chose more exotic options, and Robyn ordered them all with nuts and home-made vanilla cream. As the man prepared their treats, she steeled herself.

'I, er, don't suppose you have a treasure chest, do you?'

It didn't sound any less ridiculous at the sixth time of asking but, as with all the others before him, the seller gave them a big grin.

'*You're* the treasure hunters?'

'Do we look unlikely?'

'You're not very piratical.'

Robyn suddenly remembered Zak offering to help. *I have a pirate costume and everything*, he'd said. She'd love to see him in it and made a mental note to ask him about it at training tomorrow morning. For now, though, there was a chest to secure.

'Sorry,' she said, 'but we do have a magic key.'

She pulled the key ring out of her bag and held it up.

'Well, in that case...'

He finished drizzling their delicious-looking ice creams with chocolate sauce, then bent to reach under the counter, pulling out their sixth chest.

'Here you go, ladies. If you've come all the way from England for this, I hope there's some good treasure at the end.'

'I'm beginning to doubt it,' Ashleigh muttered darkly, and wheeled herself out to the veranda.

'I'm sure there is, thank you,' Robyn said loudly, cursing her grumpy sister.

She smiled gratefully at Malie as she took the ice creams, leaving her free to carry the chest out to one of the colourful tables. Inside it, as they had come to expect, was another letter addressed in Granny Ginny's sloping hand and, with Ashleigh refusing to show an interest, Robyn drew it out herself.

'*So, girls – you made it to the Garden Isle,*' she read out loud. '*My apologies for taking you so far, but I very much hope this means that you've met Malie and had a ride in her plane. She's a wonderful woman, daughter of another wonderful woman who, as you might have gathered by now, was hugely important to me. And who I let down badly.*'

Robyn paused and swallowed. She looked to Malie, who nodded her on. Even Ashleigh glanced up from her ice cream, though her face was still dark.

'*Anyway, more of that later. For now, sorry about the convoluted clue but Captain Cook was the only link I could think of to England and, despite having sent you all the way around the world from the country of your birth, I have to send you back there. It's time to tell you about my fantastic time flying fighter planes around the airbases of England.*'

'Oh, for heaven's sake!' Ashleigh spat.

Robyn stopped reading and looked at her. 'What's wrong now?'

'What's wrong? Can't you see, Rob? This isn't some apology for a dark secret in Granny's past, it's just her showing off. "Look what marvellous things I did when I was young! How on earth can you pair ever match up!" Well I, for one, have had enough of it. Enjoy the story, I'll be over there.'

And with that, she stuck her ice cream in her lap and wheeled herself down the ramp and away at speed. Robyn watched her make for another unsuspecting group of tourists and glanced apologetically at Malie.

'Don't mind me,' she said, waving her phone. 'I'm quite happy on Facebook.'

'But Ashleigh—'

'Needs a little time to herself, I'd say. Relax, Robyn. You're not her keeper. We've got...' She glanced at her phone. 'About fifteen minutes before we have to head back to the airport for our runway slot, so enjoy your ice cream and your letter.'

'Right. Thanks.'

Robyn cast another anxious look at her sister, but she was busy baiting Captain Cook fans and was probably best left to it. She, for one, was keen – if a little nervous – to find out what was in the next instalment of their manic treasure hunt.

Chapter Nineteen

15 April 1942

'There it is – England!'

Ginny looked sideways at the eager young woman jumping up and down on the ship's deck and pointing into the grey mist ahead of them, then across to where she assumed the horizon must be. There was a possibility that a section of the grey was slightly more solid than the rest, and as she strained her eyes, she did begin to see what might be the outline of some buildings.

'How does anyone fly in this?' she asked.

'It's not always this bad,' the young woman told her cheerily.

'Only about half the time,' her companion added with a merry laugh.

Ginny squinted at them. 'You know England then?'

'Oh yes. Our dad fought with the Brits in the Great War and fell in love with our mom when she nursed him back to health after a shrapnel wound. Bit unoriginal, but sweet. We went to visit a few times when we were little, didn't we, Louise?'

Louise nodded.

'And we were always glad to get home.' She leaned in to Ginny. 'It rains a lot here! Still, at least they let girls fly, right, Susie?'

'Right,' Susie agreed firmly. 'And that's what counts.'

Ginny sighed at the truth of that. Despite huge demand for pilots, the US government were stubbornly resisting using their highly qualified female flyers. The country, it seemed, just wasn't ready to send its mothers and daughters to work and, after a frustrating battle with the authorities, Jacqueline Cochran had decided to take her pilots' undervalued services elsewhere. England already had a full military branch of female pilots – the Air Transport Auxiliary – and when Ginny had received a telegram inviting her to join the elite group, she'd snatched at it. Right now, though, staring into the forbidding grey mist, she wished with all her heart that she could have served her country from Tennessee. The only time she'd been away from home before had been in Hawaii and there she'd had Jack to support her. Without him, this long trip to England felt doubly hard.

Ginny peered into the grey mist and did her best not to picture the coastline she'd left behind two months ago – the exuberant stripes of yellow sand, turquoise sea and deep blue sky that were Hawaii. Mind you, her memories of Oahu were clouded as grey as this strange country ahead. The weeks after the Japanese attack had been dark ones, with bodies being pulled daily out of the harbour, people continually in fear of further attack, and funeral processions clogging the once-merry streets. Someone had had the sense to send soldiers out to pull down those festive decorations not burned on 7 December, and even the poor children on the island had not raised an objection. Santa Claus, they had already known, would not be coming to Oahu that Christmas.

Ginny had held a funeral for Jack, a quietly dignified interment in a pretty corner of Oahu cemetery. Many of the men from Jack's regiment had turned out to pay their respects, but many had also been missing – lined up around them in simple graves of their own. Her parents had, obviously, been unable to make it, and she'd stood alone before the coffin. Poor Penny had been a mess, only really able to stand with the help of the kind friend who had rescued her back in the hospital, and Ginny had pitied her the loss of all her quiet dreams of a happy future.

One of Jack's fellow officers had taken her aside afterwards and spoken to her of his bravery. 'Jack was out of bed like lightning that morning and pulling on his flying gear straight away,' he'd told her, his voice choked. 'He went charging around the barracks as if this was something we'd been drilling for all along. "Come on," he urged us. "We've got to get out there before they shoot all our planes off the runway. We've got to get them in the air where they can fight as they're intended." Then he was off, sprinting out of the barracks and round to the hangar, calling all the engineers out as he went. He was first up the runway. Only five others made it before the Japs did exactly what he'd said they would and shot the rest of the planes into flames. He was a brave man and a quick-thinking one and, and...'

'And it cost him his life,' Ginny had supplied sadly.

'But saved many others.'

It had been meant to be a consolation but Ginny knew, guiltily, that she would have taken twenty dead strangers if she could have kept her brother alive, and could only admire Jack for his greater goodness. Sometimes, in the darkest parts of the night, she would picture that US plane she'd seen shot out of the sky and wonder if it had been him – if she'd actually watched her own brother go down. She told herself that the poor pilot in that plane would never have made it to hospital alive, but the picture was still too vivid to ignore.

Ginny gripped the railings tighter and fought not to fall into the grief that churned inside her as violently as the grey froth beneath the boat. Christmas had been heartbreaking. She'd shared a quiet meal with Lili and Kalani and then they'd gone to take flowers to Jack and Robert's graves. The cemetery had been packed with mourners and, as the sun had gone down on the worst Christmas in American history, they'd all come together to quietly sing carols to their beloved dead.

'I'll fight, Jack,' she'd promised him as she'd placed red bougainvillea on his grave. 'I'll fight for you.' But she hadn't known then how far her vow would take her from home.

She'd finally got to her parents just before heading to Washington to meet Jacqueline Cochran and it had been wonderful to see them, if very sad. She'd told them about Penny, and they'd wept over the daughter-in-law they'd never known and now never would. Ginny had done her best to describe the lovely young nurse to them, but already Penny was fading from her memory and it seemed so strange to think this should have been a woman with whom she'd have grown old. Most mornings Ginny woke in a half-sweat, reliving those awful moments when she and Penny had cradled Jack and watched the life drain from the vicious wound in his head. It was an image she feared would never leave her. *I don't think I'll be able to look after you any more*, he'd gasped out, and she felt the absence of his precious care every single day.

She'd shown her parents the pictures they'd taken of Jack's grave, then the happier ones of them all laughing on the docks waiting for the *Lurline* to come in just ten days before his life had been cruelly snatched away. Her parents had cried with her and held her and told her how precious she was to them – and then she'd told them she was going to England. To their credit, they'd been very supportive. They'd always been an active, purposeful sort of family, and they'd understood her need to help win this war against the forces of evil that had torn her world apart at dawn on 7 December. She'd seen the fear in their eyes that they might lose her too, though, and had nearly changed her mind.

Nearly.

Ginny fought back tears and focused on the buildings that were now definitely coming into shape ahead of their great ship. The sight of land was reassuring. The four days and nights of the trip had been one long round of nerves, forever waiting for the alarm that would tell them a sub was hunting them down. So many American ships had been lost to the German wolf pack beneath the seas, and it had been all Ginny could do not to just curl up in a ball and scream with the creeping fear of it. Now, though, they were arriving in Liverpool unharmed and that, at least, was cause for celebration.

'Golly!' She stared incredulously at the city that was emerging from the fog, jolted out of her grief by the sight of some of the grandest buildings she'd ever seen. She pointed. 'That one's got birds on it!'

Susie and Louise laughed.

'Liver birds.'

'What?'

'They guard the city and keep it from harm.'

Ginny eyed the huge birds atop the magnificent building dead ahead and prayed they were up to the job. Still, a city that was protected by winged creatures was a pretty good one in her book, and was that a glimmer of sun creeping through the clouds? It was hard to believe it was the same bold, orange beauty that sent its warmth down on Hawaii all year round, but she was glad to see a hint of it all the same.

'Ginny?'

'Lili!' She swung round and hugged her friend, delighted to see her out on deck.

Instantly her mood lifted a little; Lili wasn't family like Jack, but she'd looked after Ginny as if she were and Ginny loved her for it. Mind you, the poor girl had been suffering with terrible seasickness on this scary four-day trip and had spent it huddled in her bunk, hardly even daring to sip water. Looking at her hunched-up form, Ginny had questioned her own wisdom in talking Jacqueline into letting the Hawaiian girl onto the programme, but now she looked at least close to her usual bouncy self.

'We're here,' Lili said, gazing at the docks ahead. They were busy, with all sorts of ships moored up and men scurrying everywhere, loading and unloading goods. 'It's quite… dirty, isn't it?'

Ginny laughed.

'We won't be here long, doll. Just one night, Jackie says, then we've got a bus to take us to the airfield somewhere near London.'

'Will that take long?'

'No idea. Jackie says it's in the south and this Liverpool place is in the north, so I'd have thought it's bound to be a day or two.'

Lili sighed.

'I feel like I've been travelling forever. Up until a month ago, the furthest I'd been was the Big Island, and that was only once a year when my uncle took us on his boat. I had no idea the world was so wide.'

Ginny hugged her close.

'Exciting, right?'

'Exciting,' Lili agreed determinedly, but Ginny heard the quaver in her voice and worried.

Kalani had not been as understanding about Lili joining Jacqueline's squad as Ginny's parents.

'First you send her into the skies to be shot at by the Japanese,' he'd raged to Ginny, 'and now you want to take her to Europe to be got by Hitler?'

She'd tried to explain that they would not be in the actual warzones, but Kalani had not bought it.

'Hawaii was not a warzone and that didn't stop the enemy planes from coming. What about when this Hitler maniac invades Britain? What then?'

'Then they'll stop women flying,' Ginny had said, more certainly than she'd felt. She had no idea what the British felt about women in combat. Perhaps they were already sending them to the front?

'Well, I think it's madness,' Kalani had said, arms folded.

Ginny would have backed down then and gone to England alone, but Lili had had different ideas.

'I'm sorry, Papa, but if I get a place, I have to go. I saw those Japanese pilots. I looked into their eyes and they were the eyes of evil. They want to annihilate us and our way of life. They want to conquer us and force us to obey them, and we can't have it. War is a terrible, terrible thing – but it's even worse if you lose.'

Put like that, in Lili's bright, determined voice, there had been little arguing. Kalani had wept and raged but ultimately given them his blessing. On the final day, however, as Lili had been packing her bag, he'd taken Ginny by the arm and led her out into their little patch of vegetable garden.

'Look after her, Virginia,' he'd said solemnly. 'Look after her for me. I know she's a woman now and able to make her own choices, but she's more naive than she knows so please, look after her.'

'Of course,' she'd promised him. 'I hold Lili as dear as a sister, Kalani, and with Jack gone she's extra precious. I'm not risking losing another person I love.'

He'd hugged her then, stroking her hair and dropping a kiss on her forehead.

'Look after yourself too, Virginia. You're precious as well.'

She'd been so choked at his unexpected emotion that she'd been unable to offer any more than a tight hug in answer, and now she held on to Lili and thanked God, again, that they'd made it across the Atlantic in one piece. The ship was coming in to the dockside and men were running along, catching the huge ropes that were cast down to secure her to land – to England. They spoke in strange, nasal accents and although Ginny strained to hear their words, she couldn't make out a single one of them.

'They speak the same language as us, right?' she asked Susie.

'So they say,' she laughed. 'But sometimes it's hard to tell. Come on, we'd better get our bags. Jackie won't want us keeping her waiting.'

Sure enough, Jacqueline Cochran was standing in the corridor by their cabins, tapping her foot, her own designer luggage at her side and her face immaculately made up. Ginny self-consciously brushed her windswept hair out of her eyes and dived into her cabin to throw the last bits and pieces into her suitcase. She dragged a brush through her chestnut locks, and quickly dusted on some powder and a slick of lippy. Jacqueline liked her women well-presented and would not be pleased if they let her down at this moment of arrival in their host country.

'I'm nervous,' Lili said, fumbling her own lipstick so that it slipped across her cheek.

Ginny took her pretty Hawaiian face in her hands and looked into her eyes.

'Don't be nervous, Lilinoe. You look beautiful – and you fly like a dream. It will all be fine, I promise. Now, hold still.'

She wiped the dark pink stain off Lili's cheek and drew it carefully onto her lips instead, and they were ready. They joined the other girls in the corridor, grateful not to be last out, and all twenty-four of them followed Jacqueline, like well-groomed chicks, up to the gangplank and out into the city of Liverpool.

No one was there to greet them.

Jacqueline stood, smart heels tapping increasingly irately on the rough dockside, as the rest of the passengers dispersed into the city, but no one came. Eventually, with a furious tut, she collared a dockworker and demanded he find them taxis.

'Where to, miss?' he asked.

'The Adelphi Hotel.'

'But—'

'Now, please.'

He looked very bewildered but few people ever said no to Jacqueline Cochran and, somehow, he summoned up four cars. They all crammed in and the little procession set off, but barely two minutes later, they pulled up outside a very pretty white building.

'We're here?' Ginny asked their driver incredulously.

'The Adelphi, miss? That's right. Could have walked it in five minutes, mind.'

Embarrassed, Ginny clambered out and paid him in the strange English money they'd been issued on the ship. She looked around her and gasped. Although the hotel itself stood strong and attractive before them, a brief turn revealed a broken city. Looking back towards the docks, Ginny could see that almost half the houses, shops and office blocks in between were obliterated. Piles of rubble sat bleakly along the main streets, and Ginny saw bedsteads and tables and even a forlorn-looking teddy sticking out of them.

'Bombs?' she whispered, unable to believe it.

She'd thought Pearl Harbor had been a horrific sight, but that had been just a two-hour attack. Here was evidence of day after day – or maybe night after night – of sustained bombing, and not just on military targets but on ordinary homes.

'The poor, poor people,' Lili said, clutching her arm.

But even as they stood there taking it in, they could see the 'poor, poor people' going about their everyday business as if nothing had happened. A tram came down the street, its bell jangling, and people ran to jump on. A group of boys scrambled over the nearest rubble heap, laughing as they played a precarious game of tag. A couple wandered past, wrapped up in each other, the picture of romance, save that the man was in full uniform and the woman carried a gas-mask over her shoulder like a grotesque joke of a handbag.

'War,' Ginny said, understanding what it truly meant for perhaps the first time – not just guns and dogfights and battle plans, but the day-to-day grind of life under siege. She'd thought coming to England would be an adventure, a chance to fly planes and 'do her bit'; she hadn't known it would be so gruesome.

'Come on, girls,' Jacqueline said crisply. 'Let's get some rest. Long journey south tomorrow.'

Ginny swallowed, picked up her bag and followed her across the scarred street towards the hotel. They were here, in the midst of a European theatre of war that suddenly seemed so horribly real, and as she went she cast a look up to the grey skies.

'Watch over me, Jack,' she whispered. 'Please, watch over me.'

Chapter Twenty

Sunday 10 March

Robyn got up for training on Sunday morning, thinking about her grandmother's dismal introduction to her own homeland. She'd read the first section of the letter out to Malie and Ashleigh as they'd flown back from Kauai at dusk yesterday. Ashleigh had pretended not to listen but Malie had been fascinated, and Robyn had enjoyed talking to her about England nearly as much as she had her considerable flying skills.

She'd ended up telling her all about their home in Oxfordshire and the original treasure hunts of their youth, and hadn't got round to the rest of Ginny's account before they'd landed. The letters seemed to be getting longer as the events in the past got more significant, and she was starting to dread whatever was to come. She thought of her granny in her sickbed, pouring her heart out about all that had happened to her, and a tear came to her eye.

Goodness, what was this final treasure hunt doing to her? She wasn't usually the crying sort but it was all, frankly, exhausting – and not helped by Ashleigh, who'd been withdrawn and sulky all last night. She'd refused to take her turn in the front of Malie's plane, shaking her head crossly when reminded about her previous request to have a go at flying, and had sat in Robyn's flat like a stone all night. Robyn, who'd turned down the chance to go out with friends, had not appreciated the surliness and they'd gone to bed in simmering silence.

Robyn had toyed with reading the rest of Granny Ginny's letter, but she had to confess that she was starting to worry more and more about what she'd find out and hadn't felt strong enough to face it alone. She'd eventually fallen asleep, worn out by the busy day, but had woken with the dawn, Ashleigh's unhappiness swirling uncomfortably in her stomach. Malie was right that she wasn't her sister's keeper, but she was horribly aware that since the accident she'd barely even seen her for more than two weeks of any year. Perhaps now was the time she had to step up and help her. But how? Ashleigh was almost impossible to help, especially in this mood.

She fixed her watch onto her wrist, looking at the hands with a groan. She was far too early for training. Perhaps she'd take a jog out, see the beach in the early light, grab some pastries for breakfast. She could leave one for Ashleigh to sweeten her up for when she got back from the track. Decision made, she slid out of her tiny room, made for the kitchen to fill up her water bottle, and almost jumped out her skin. Ashleigh was sitting in the doorway, staring at her.

'Ashleigh! You gave me a fright.'

'Sorry.'

'Are you OK?'

'Yes,' she said, but she was squirming uncomfortably and Robyn worried that something was wrong.

'Is it your legs? Or your back, or—?'

'Shut up, Robyn. Please. It's none of those things. I just wanted to, er...' She closed her eyes a moment, then opened them again and blurted out, 'To apologise.'

Robyn fought to hide the smile that leaped to her lips. Was it really a simple apology that was causing her spiky sister all this pain?

'Right,' she managed. 'What for?'

'For being a grumpy pain in the arse,' came the succinct reply. Now Robyn did laugh.

'Apology accepted.'

'Just like that?'

'Course. Do you want some breakfast? I was going to head out and buy some pastries but it would be nicer to eat out if you fancy it?'

Ashleigh blinked but then nodded. 'Sounds great.'

Robyn grabbed her keys and purse and held the door open for her sister, then stopped dead at the lift.

'No way!'

A sign dangled jauntily from it: *Out of Order*. She groaned.

'It's top class, this building of yours,' Ashleigh said lightly.

'It's infuriating! I pay a fortune in maintenance. I'm going to find them and make them mend it – now!'

'It's Sunday morning, Rob.'

'So?! It's their job. And it's my Sunday morning, *your* Sunday morning too. I work really hard, and at the weekend I want to relax and take my sister out for a pastry. Is that really too much to ask?'

'Robyn, shh.' Ashleigh's eyes had widened and she was looking nervously down the hallway but Robyn didn't care. She'd had enough.

'Let them all hear. They should be angry too. What sort of building is so lax in its disabled access? I've a good mind to go to the *Honolulu Advertiser*. I bet they'd be interested, I bet—'

'Robyn, stop.' Ashleigh grabbed Robyn's hand and tugged her down to her level. 'Really. It's very sweet of you to get so worked up on my behalf, but it's not necessary. This sort of thing happens all the time. You get used to it.'

'Well, you shouldn't have to. If I pay for a building with a lift, I should *get* a building with a lift. I'm calling them now.'

She grabbed her phone and pulled up the maintenance number, ringing it over and over until eventually a sleepy voice answered.

'Wha'?'

'The lift isn't working and it's unacceptable. I have a sick girl in a wheelchair stuck on floor five and I can't get her down. What if she dies up here?'

'Robyn!' Ashleigh protested, but Robyn shushed her.

'No, it wouldn't be very good publicity, would it?' she agreed with the now snivelling man on the other end. 'So get your arse out of bed and up here right now!' She clicked off the call, feeling a rush of triumph. 'That told him. He said he'd be here pronto.'

'Should be fun,' Ashleigh said drily. 'How ill do I need to look, would you say? A bit sickly or full-on close to death?'

Robyn glared at her.

'The latter can be arranged if you like.'

Ashleigh laughed.

'I'll just look sort of pale and unhappy, shall I? I'm good at that.'

Robyn shook her head, a smile threatening to break through her anger, but after ten minutes of pacing the landing all amusement was gone, and when the maintenance engineer finally came panting up the stairs, she was very frosty with him. Not that it was needed; one look at Ashleigh doing her Jane-Austen-vapours act and he was straight into the mechanism with his tools. Eventually the old lift cranked back into action and Robyn was able to wheel Ashleigh triumphantly into it and glide – well, judder – to the ground floor.

The problem, of course, was that they were no longer early for breakfast and all the nicest cafés were full. They eventually found a space in one but at the back, tucked away from the view Robyn had wanted to share with her sister.

'Sorry, Ash, this didn't quite go to plan.'

'As I said, it happens a lot. It's one of the frustrations of these' – she banged her legs – 'that any problems are fifty times harder to deal with. But we're here now, so let's enjoy it.'

Robyn shook her head at her.

'Listen to us – total role reversal from yesterday with you trying to chivvy me along.'

Ashleigh grunted.

'I'm not usually made for the positive role, but I'm doing my best.' Above their heads a little clock struck the hour and she glanced up. 'Aren't you meant to be training?'

Robyn looked up too and swore. Somehow, she'd gone from ridiculously early to late.

'I am! In half an hour. God, Ashleigh, Coach will kill me. He's huge on punctuality.'

'So, let's get going.'

'Now? What about breakfast?'

'Aren't Americans big on the whole "to-go" thing?'

'Well, yes, but—'

'So, two croissants to go and let's eat them on the way.'

'You're going to come?'

She shrugged.

'Why not? You took me to basketball last week so the least I can do is come to athletics. Besides, Zak said it's a nice atmosphere at the track.'

Robyn's stomach turned over again. So that's what this morning was all about. Ashleigh wanted to see Zak. No wonder she was up early and being so sunny. But, so what? Ashleigh was only here for another week, so why shouldn't she have some fun before she went?

'Great,' she forced out. 'Let's go.'

Two hours later and Robyn was bent double, fighting to suck breath into her lungs. With the first meet less than a week away, Coach had worked them hard and she was worn out, but pleased. He'd timed them over a full set of hurdles and, if the stopwatch was right, she might stand a chance of beating her PB this season. Of course, hurdling was a precarious business. It only took one missed step and you could clip a barrier, or even go crashing into it. If you got it right, it felt amazing. If you didn't... Well, Robyn had the scars to stand testimony to the hurt, not just to your body but to your pride.

'Good work, Rob.' Coach came jogging up, the hint of a smile on his rugged features. 'That back leg is coming down so much faster now.'

'Thanks, Coach.'

'You too, Cody.' He clapped the youngster on his back. 'You're making great progress. It should be a strong season for you – *if you give it your all.*'

Cody's head dropped at the growled final words and Robyn's heart went out to him. As he scuttled away, Robyn dared herself to speak.

'Go easy on Cody, Coach – he's got it tough at home. No mum and a lot of mouths to feed. He's not just working for candy money.'

Coach Tyler tensed at the challenge but Robyn saw his eyes follow Cody as he headed off across the track, and he gave a curt little nod.

'I see. Thanks for telling me, Robyn. I'll, er, do what I can.'

'Great.'

Embarrassed, Robyn turned away, looking for Zak, but he was nowhere to be seen. Then she heard a laugh behind her and spotted him leaning on the railings, his long limbs relaxed and his handsome head thrown back in amusement as he shared a joke with the girl next to him – with Ashleigh.

'Who's that?' Coach asked.

'My sister.'

His eyes widened.

'I didn't know you had a sister.'

'She's visiting from England.'

'Looks like she's enjoying it too – and why not? Zak's a great lad. Always seems such a shame to see him single.'

He threw Robyn what she could swear was a coy look, were this not her gruff old coach.

'What does that mean?' she asked, but he just gave her a grin and sauntered off to tidy up the hurdles. 'Coach! What does that…?'

Deep down, though, she knew what it meant and, as she looked again to Ashleigh and Zak chatting away, she had to acknowledge it for herself. She was jealous. She didn't want Ashleigh to have

Zak because she wanted him herself. He was her training partner, her support, her friend. He was also the man she fancied so much that her legs suddenly felt fifty times weaker than after any damned race. It was time to face up to facts – she liked him. She liked him a lot. But Ashleigh was her sister and she loved her more than anything. She thought about the pain Granny Ginny had suffered over losing her brother and knew she'd never do anything to hurt Ashleigh, but she still cursed herself for being so slow to realise her feelings for Zak.

'Hey,' she called, super-casual.

Zak turned but didn't smile. Her heart flopped.

'Hey, Rob,' he said tightly. 'Great hurdling there.'

'Er, thanks. Fancy grabbing a drink or something?'

She could swear her cheeks were flaring but she willed herself to hold his gaze. To her surprise, however, he looked away.

'Oh, I can't, sorry. Got to, er, get to the labs.'

'On a Sunday?'

'Big deadline. You know how it is.'

'Right. Yes. See you tomorrow then?'

'Course,' he shot back, 'if you've got time.'

'What?' But he was already off, grabbing his bag and following Cody across the track. Robyn looked to Ashleigh. 'What's up with him?'

Her sister shrugged.

'Dunno. He seemed quite happy when we were chatting.'

'What were you talking about?'

'Oh, you know – the treasure hunt, the flight, Malie's amazing house, Connor and his fancy restaurant in the hills.'

'Connor? You told Zak about Connor?'

'Was it a secret?'

Robyn sighed wearily.

'No secret. Shall we get back then?'

'Why don't we grab that drink together? And maybe some lunch? We can read some more of Granny Ginny's letter whilst we're at it.'

Robyn frowned. It wasn't really her sister she'd been hoping to sit down with, but she reminded herself of her vow to try and help Ashleigh find happiness.

'Why not?'

'Great.' Ashleigh looked around the track as she turned in next to Robyn and wheeled herself towards the entrance. 'It's nice here, sis. Zak was right, it does have a great atmosphere.'

Robyn forced herself to nod, but for her the atmosphere had turned distinctly sour and she was beginning to think Ginny had had the right idea, back in 1942, to have nothing to do with love.

Chapter Twenty-One

16 April 1942

'Here we are, ladies – White Waltham!'

Ginny leaned forward in her seat, assuming she'd heard the bus driver wrong. How could they be in the south already? They'd only been on the road for five hours so this had to be some sort of mistake. He did look quite old and was wearing a rough khaki uniform that had to be from the last war, so maybe he was confused?

'We're here already?' she asked him.

'We made good time,' he agreed happily, glancing back at her and Lili, sitting on the front seat to try and prevent poor Lili from being sick. 'I've known it to take nearly six hours on a bad day.'

The women looked at each other, still sure he must be wrong. What sort of country could you cross in five hours? Perhaps this White Waltham airbase wasn't where they'd thought it was.

'Where's London?' Ginny asked him.

'London? 'Bout twenty miles that way.' He pointed straight out of the big windscreen. 'But you don't want to go there. You think Liverpool's been bombed bad, London's something else. Battered it is, the poor old place – battered. Some Kraut even got a bomb right on St Paul's in the Blitz. Blasted a bloody great hole in her roof, bastard.'

Ginny battled to keep up with this barrage of words.

'St Paul's…?'

'Cathedral. Lovely building. Or it was. Cities aren't the place to be, lass, but you stay out here at White Waltham and you'll be safe enough. Office work, is it?'

Ginny bristled.

'Not at all. We're pilots.'

'Pilots?!' He looked in his big mirror and gave a low whistle. 'Well I never. Yank girl pilots. Whatever next?'

'We're very good,' Ginny assured him.

'I don't doubt it, lass. Wouldn't bring you all this way if you weren't, would they?'

'True,' Ginny agreed, mollified. Then she couldn't resist adding, 'You don't think it's mad then?'

'What, women flying? Why should it be? Reckon they hold the controls in the home, so why not in a plane too?'

Ginny let out a splutter of a laugh. She'd been warned about British humour but she reckoned she was going to like it. She looked eagerly out of the window as the driver turned the bus off the road and pulled up rather abruptly at a pair of big gates.

'Yank girls for you,' he told the sentry, who peered curiously at them but cranked open the gates and ushered them inside.

The airfield was a collection of hangars and huts, all looking tired and shabby after the gleaming, sunshine-bright facilities at John Rodgers. Ginny felt Lili's hand sneak into hers, though they both brightened up as the bus turned down a rough track alongside a big runway and they spotted the myriad planes lined up, waiting to fly.

'Tiger Moths,' Ginny breathed, pointing to the smart biplanes.

They looked sturdy but nimble and Ginny itched to fly one. Further along she could see Magisters and Harvards and, if she wasn't much mistaken, two beautiful-looking Spitfires. Excitement bubbled up in her stomach – *this* was why she'd come halfway across the world to this damp, grey country. *These* were the planes she would fly!

'Here we go, ladies – home.'

Ginny was pulled out of her dreams of the skies as the bus juddered to a stop outside a rough-looking hut. She looked uncertainly around.

'Where?'

'There.'

The driver pointed a chubby finger to the hut and, sure enough, a group of women were spilling out of the doors and gathering around the bus. Ginny glanced back but no one, not even Jacqueline, was getting up. It seemed it was down to her, so nervously she pushed herself up and stepped out.

'Mrs Cochran?' a petite older woman asked.

'Me? Lord, no. I'm Virginia Martin, and this is Lilinoe Kamaka.'

'Well, welcome. Let's grab your bags and get you set up with somewhere to sleep. It's all dorms and we've mixed you in with everyone else so we can, you know, get to know each other.'

'Dorms,' Ginny repeated, adding a faint, 'lovely' as the woman stared curiously at her.

She followed them into the hut and found herself in a long, sparse room with rough bunk beds in lines down its length. All were made up with white sheets and khaki blankets, tucked in with military precision. There were tall, metal cupboards beside each bunk, blackout blinds at the windows and bare wooden boards on the floors. An old stove at the far end was belching out smoke but seemingly little heat and, bar a few photos tacked to the walls above most pillows, Ginny could see no homely touches at all.

'It's…' She fought for a polite word. 'Smart,' she found eventually.

One of the girls pulled a face.

'You mean spartan,' she laughed. 'It sure is. They're determined we're to live like "proper military" and seeing as we fought to be let in, we can't really complain, can we? Don't worry – with the lights low and music on the gramophone, we can soon make it cosy. And there are dances and the like over in the mess.'

'Dances?' Lili's eyes lit up. 'With men?'

Their new English friend grinned broadly.

'Definitely with men, and you're in luck – there's one tonight.'

'Tonight?' Ginny yelped. She liked to think of herself as a bit of party girl, but she'd barely slept a wink in Liverpool last night after hideous sirens had squealed out and they'd all been apologetically shoved into a shelter in the bowels of the hotel. That, on top of four nervous nights on the sub-riddled Atlantic, and she was about ready to drop. 'Not for me,' she said firmly. 'I'm done in.'

'But Ginny…'

'Not for me.'

Ginny looked around the heaving dance floor and groaned. How on earth had she let Lili talk her into this? It might have had something to do with her realising how hard her bunk bed was, or how stodgy the food, or how cold it seemed to be in England. Bravely colourful spring flowers were pushing their way out of the grass around the edges of the airfield, but Ginny wanted to rush up to the poor things and tell them to hide away again until the watery sun radiated some actual heat.

She'd eventually agreed to the dance in the hope that some activity, plus a nip or two, might heat her up enough to sleep when it was time to hit the sack and, to be fair, the room was packed with so many bodies that it was lovely and warm. Ginny suddenly felt foolish in her heavy woollen cardigan. Everyone else seemed to have made an effort, and there were pretty dresses and skirts everywhere as the women of the ATA made the most of being out of uniform for a night. The men, too, looked smart in 'mufti' as they seemed to call it, and they outnumbered the women at least two to one.

'They're going to love having us here,' Lili said delightedly.

Now that she'd got over her travel sickness, the Hawaiian was blossoming. Ginny tried to remember the shy girl she'd seen hunched over an engine in too-big overalls when she'd first walked into K-T last year, and smiled at the attractive woman now tugging her into a party somewhere in the middle of the English countryside. As if proving her correct, two young men appeared at their sides almost instantly, asking them to dance. Lili happily let herself be whisked away, but Ginny turned down the offer in favour of a large punchbowl she'd spotted in the corner.

It felt strange, suddenly, to be out at a party without Jack here. Her big brother had always been her escort, and her heart ached to hear his laugh and have him tease her once more. Leaning shakily against the wall as she watched Lilinoe dance, she thought ruefully of Kalani asking her to look after his little girl. It was looking more likely to be the other way round at this rate.

Come on, little sis, Jack's voice said in her head. *This isn't like you. Chin up!*

She smiled tearfully, then pulled her cardigan off, set back her shoulders and made for the punchbowl, chin obligingly high. There was a man standing over it, ladling the orange liquid into a cup, and she edged up to him.

'May I?'

He turned and smiled at her – a smile that seemed to shimmy enticingly across every part of her body. She swallowed.

'Of course. Here.' He held up his already filled cup.

'Oh, I couldn't possibly take yours.'

'As you can see, there's plenty more.' His voice was low and rich, with a cultured English accent that rolled softly off his tongue. He leaned in. 'And, to be honest, it's not that great. I'm really just marking time waiting for Snapdragon to get here with the whisky. Do you like whisky?'

'Whisky?'

He smiled again, amusement twinkling in eyes the colour of Hawaiian seas.

'Scotch. Bourbon.'

'Ah! I do, yes.'

'My sort of girl.'

Again the smile, and to Ginny's horror she realised that she very much wanted to be this man's type of girl. He was pleasingly tall, with hair the colour of meadow honey and strong arms that looked made to wrap themselves around you and—

No way, she said crossly to herself. This was not happening to her. This was not the damned lightning bolt everyone so annoyingly went on and on about. *Better to stand tall and alone*, she reminded herself fiercely.

'I'm Charles,' he said, holding out a hand.

'Virginia,' she offered, taking it and smiling weakly when electricity as fierce as any natural storm shot unavoidably and horribly pleasantly all through her.

'Do you dance, Virginia?' he asked with a little bow of his sandy head.

'That depends on the quality of the whisky.'

'Then the sooner Snapdragon gets here the better.'

'Snapdragon?'

'It's a flower. We once caught him sleeping with one on his finger.'

'Why?'

'Legend has it that if you do that, you'll dream of the girl you're going to marry – though I'm not sure it's the best idea as I'm told they're poisonous.'

'Girls?'

'Snapdragons!' He laughed. 'You're American?'

'Yep,' Ginny agreed, trying desperately to ignore the ridiculous fluttering in her stomach. Was this the damned butterflies everyone always talked about? If so, they were very uncomfortable. She fought to sound sensible. 'I'm new here in England.'

'What do you make of it so far?'

'Grey,' she said succinctly. 'But then, I was out in Hawaii before so most places look grey after that.'

His eyes widened.

'You were at Pearl?' She nodded. 'Was it as awful as they say?'

'Worse.' Instantly images of that terrible morning sprung into her mind. 'We had no warning, you see. No one thought the Japanese could get that far so no one was ready. It was just a normal Sunday morning. My only concern was a hangover.'

He smiled down at her. 'Big night the night before, hey?'

'You could say that. My brother...' The word caught in her throat and she sipped hastily at her punch to try and swallow down her grief, but only succeeded in choking. 'I'm sorry,' she gasped. 'I... That is...'

Heat flooded up across her face and she turned to try and escape before she made a fool of herself, but Charles just reached out and placed two strong, gentle hands on the top of her arms, holding her steady.

'Breathe,' he said quietly. She looked up into his ocean-blue eyes and the tremors began to ease from her body, though her heart was still far, far too full. 'You lost him?' he asked, his voice low and kind. She nodded. 'I'm so, so sorry. I lost my brother too – Dunkirk. Hurts like a bullet in your own heart, doesn't it?'

'That's exactly it,' she whispered.

A tear fell from her eye and he let go of her arm to brush it tenderly away.

'But hearts heal,' he went on. 'Or so I'm told. I wasn't sure I believed it – until now. It seems perhaps I was looking in the wrong place.' The music had dropped to a slower song and he held out his hand to her. 'Dance, Virginia?'

She nodded and let him lead her out onto the crammed dance floor. Somewhere behind she heard a man cry out, 'Snapdragon! You made it!' but she didn't care about whisky any more. She didn't care about anything but the man whose arms were encircling her as if she was the only thing that mattered in the world.

'You'd better not be laughing at me, Jack,' she murmured into Charles's chest, but she knew that, far from it, he would be delighted to see his little sister fall for someone at last and, with a giddy rush of relief, she let herself be held.

Chapter Twenty-Two

Tuesday 12 March

The first thing Robyn heard when she pushed open the door of her flat was singing. She stopped in the corridor, her work bag dangling from her hand, and listened. Ashleigh was belting out what sounded astonishingly like a Miley Cyrus track. Yep – her grumpy sister was in the shower, singing about beaches and birds and Malibu love. Robyn's heart sank. Ashleigh had been very scathing when Robyn had bought a plastic stool to allow her to manage alone in the thankfully large shower, but now listen to her trilling away in there! She'd informed her yesterday that she had a date tonight but Robyn hadn't quite believed it until now. What was going on? First Ginny and now Ashleigh. Was the romance from the past somehow seeping into the present – and if so, why wasn't it reaching her?

The bathroom door swung open and Ashleigh wheeled herself out on a billowing cloud of steam, wrapped in every towel Robyn owned.

'Robyn! Hi. Could I borrow a dress, do you think? I didn't really pack for this warm weather.'

'Sure,' Robyn agreed glumly, pretty certain that Ashleigh would already have helped herself from her wardrobe. She followed her into her own bedroom and spotted one of her favourite sundresses laid out on the bed with, if she wasn't much mistaken, the twisted leather belt Granny Ginny had given her last Christmas and her favourite sparkly pumps. 'You're all set then.'

'Yep,' Ashleigh agreed happily, heading to Robyn's dressing table and helping herself to a squirt of her perfume. Her eyes met Robyn's in the mirror and she paused. 'Is that OK?'

'Of course. Absolutely. Why wouldn't it be?'

'I dunno. You look a bit odd. Well, more odd than usual.'

'Cheers, sis. Not odd at all, just tired.'

'You're always tired. You need to get out more.'

Robyn ground her teeth. 'So, who's this grand date with then?'

'That would be telling,' came the infuriating answer.

'Yes, it would,' she snapped back. 'Which would surely be a good idea if I'm meant to be looking after you.'

Ashleigh rolled her eyes.

'You're meant to be having me to stay, Rob, not "looking after" me. I'm twenty-six, for heaven's sake, I can look after myself.'

Robyn just stopped herself reminding her sister of the number of times she'd come in from work to find her claiming to be incapable even of cooking dinner. To be fair, ever since she'd made it to the labs by herself, Ashleigh had been a lot less needy, but even so, it was a reasonable request to know where she was going.

'He's taking me to Duke's,' Ashleigh supplied happily. 'Apparently I have to have something called Hula pie?'

Robyn nodded glumly. Duke's was a wonderful diner right on Waikiki Beach and the Hula ice cream pie was legendary. It was, in fact, the place she'd met Zak on that horribly awkward date over a year ago. So it *was* him her sister was meeting – and just a day after she'd realised her own feelings. Poor timing or what?

'You'll love it,' she managed. 'Shall I drop you off?'

'Oh no, that's fine. We're meeting just down the road and going there together. Tell you what, Rob, if I'm out, why don't you drop Connor a text? It'd be nice to see him again, right?'

Robyn looked at her through narrowed eyes.

'Are you trying to get me out of the flat, sis?'

'No! I just don't want you feeling lonely.'

The cheek of it, Robyn thought. She was the one who lived in Honolulu, the one who worked here and trained here and had friends here. She'd put her social life on hold for her visitor but now her visitor was going out without her! Well, fine, if Ashleigh was off out with her man – *not yours*, she reminded herself fiercely – then she really ought to find another. Dropping her bag, she pulled out her phone and found Connor's number. *Fancy getting together tonight?* she tapped out, and pressed send before she could lose her nerve.

That would be great came straight back.

'I've already arranged it actually,' she said to Ashleigh with all the dignity she could muster.

'Oh, great. Where are you going?'

How about we meet at…

'We're going…' she said, opening the message up.

Coco's Art Gallery.

'Going…?' Ashleigh prompted.

'To an art gallery,' Robyn finished uncertainly.

Ashleigh laughed like a drain.

'An art gallery. Good one, Rob. Where really?'

Robyn read the rest of the message.

There's an opening of a new exhibition at 7.30 tonight and I've got a couple of paintings in it if you'd like to see? We don't have to stay long if it's boring.

Her heart went out to him. Why should he have to be apologetic about something like that?

Sounds lovely, she typed back. *I'll be there.*

She looked up to see Ashleigh staring at her.

'You really *are* going to an art gallery?'

'Why not?' Robyn demanded, fighting to get pictures of Hula pie out of her head. 'I can do, you know, culture. Connor's got paintings in an exhibition so I said I'd go along.'

'Oooh! Lovely. Lucky you.'

'Yes,' Robyn agreed, 'so I'll need these, thank you very much.'

She swiped her pumps off the floor and retreated to the bathroom, praying Ashleigh had left her some hot water.

She hadn't.

'You hate it, don't you?'

Robyn blinked and looked at Connor. His brown eyes were anxious and she grabbed his hand, hating herself for not knowing the right thing to say. In truth, she'd not really been focusing on the art at all. Pictures of Duke's kept floating across her mind, with Ashleigh and Zak holding hands across a Hula pie, and they were far more vivid than any of the paintings around her. She fought to pull herself back into the gallery.

'I think your paintings are great,' she assured Connor. 'It's just the rest of the stuff I'm not so sure about. What *is* that?'

She pointed to an enormous swirl of pink and brown in the middle of the gallery. It looked, to her, like something a cat had chucked up, but she didn't dare say so. Connor smiled and leaned in close.

'To be honest, I've no idea. It's called *Sexuality* but if that's the way the artist sees it, I pity whoever dates them.'

Robyn giggled.

'Which one is the artist?' Connor indicated a small, nervous-looking man in a brown cardigan, sitting in a corner staring into a glass of bubbly as if it might hold the secrets of the universe. Robyn snorted with laughter. 'Really?'

'Yes, but look.' He pointed to the price tag on the sculpture, then to the small 'sold' sticker next to it. Robyn stared, her eyes physically watering.

'That's more than my annual salary.'

'See – sexuality pays!'

Robyn shook her head in disbelief.

'I only really like art that looks like what it's meant to be,' she confessed. 'I don't think I have the imagination for the other stuff.'

Unbidden, another picture of Duke's flashed through her mind, proving that, on the contrary, her imagination was alive and far too active. Connor was saying something kind about individual tastes but it was hard to concentrate. He was a lovely man and she really did wish him well, but it was clear their worlds were far too far apart for there to be anything between them. She was just a rough-and-ready engineer, far more at home on a sports track than at an art gallery, and she was OK with that. She took Connor's arm.

'I think I'd better go now.'

He gave a little sigh but smiled down at her.

'Fair enough. Thanks for coming, Robyn. It was nice seeing you again.'

'I really hope it goes well for you.'

'And you. Have you finished your treasure hunt yet?'

'Getting there. Close to the tough bit, I fear.'

'Tough bit?' he asked, but she just gave him a little shake of her head.

She wasn't ready to talk about it. Everything felt tipped upside down. Granny Ginny was gone, and Ashleigh was here and out on the very date Robyn herself had got so disastrously wrong a year ago. She, meanwhile, was in an art gallery, surrounded by people she didn't know and paintings she didn't understand, and her main goal in life appeared to be to chase down a dark secret in her grandmother's past that, quite frankly, she'd rather not know about. It all felt about as swirly and unfathomable as the stupid statue in the middle of the room, and a big part of her just wanted to stand up, wave her arms around and demand to get off this roller coaster. Sadly, though, it didn't seem to work that way.

'Are you OK, Robyn?' Connor asked.

'Fine. That is… Yes, of course. I'm fine. Ooh, look – someone's bought one of your paintings.'

She pointed to where the gallery owner was approaching his work with a little 'sold' sticker.

'No way,' he gasped, and Robyn gave his arm a squeeze.

'Well done. You'd better go and see.'

'Yes. Yes, I had. Thanks, Robyn. Stay in touch, yeah?'

'Yeah,' she agreed, but they both knew it was unlikely.

Connor was a lovely guy but he wasn't *her* lovely guy and that was fine. She set her glass down below the *Sexuality* sculpture and edged towards the door. The gallery owner was introducing Connor to a smart-looking couple and she was glad to see his beaming smile as she left.

Out on the street, her eyes strayed right, towards Waikiki and Duke's, but she turned her steps forcibly homeward. She'd grab a pizza and a beer, watch some mindless sport, and forget all about art and sculpture and Hula pie. One of those, however, proved harder to shake than the other two, and as the evening ground on, she found herself looking at her watch more and more often as Ashleigh remained stubbornly out.

She should probably go and check on her, she told herself. After all, she was her sister, she was a stranger to Honolulu and she was in a wheelchair. She might need help. She might need—

'Helloo?'

Robyn jumped out of her skin.

'Ashleigh! You're back.'

'I certainly am,' she agreed, appearing in the living room. 'So are you.'

'Oh, I've been back a while.'

'Art no good?'

'Not really my thing. Turns out Harris girls aren't very good at culture.'

She braced herself for teasing but Ashleigh just placed a hand on her arm and said, 'At least you tried.'

Robyn looked at her sister in confusion. Ashleigh looked soft-eyed, pink-cheeked and suspiciously full-lipped.

'You've been snogging!'

'Snogging, Robyn? What are we, fifteen?'

'What would you call it then?'

Ashleigh went even pinker.

'Nothing,' she tried, but the broad smile gave her away. 'Oh, OK then, maybe a bit of a goodnight kiss at the door.'

Robyn dug her toes into the floorboards to stop herself from jumping up and running to the window, to check if it was Zak who was loping away.

'He's a good kisser is he, er…?'

But Ashleigh wasn't giving anything away.

'Very good, thank you. I may well repeat the experience.'

Robyn's heart sank.

'You're flying home on Saturday,' she pointed out, and felt mean as Ashleigh's face dropped.

Her sister, however, swiftly picked herself up. 'About that. I was thinking I might, you know, extend my stay.'

'Extend it?'

'My lab would like me to do some more work on the spectroscopes, so they said they'd pay the fee for me to change my flight.'

'Right. I see. For, er, how long?'

'Oh, just another week. It would give us more time to finish the treasure hunt, right?'

'Right,' Robyn agreed because, really, what else could she say?

'I know I'm a bit of a pain, and a right grump at times, and I'm using your room and—'

'Ashleigh, it's fine. Lovely. One condition though.'

'What?'

'You have to tell me who you're dating.'

'You should know, Rob. It's thanks to you that I met him.'

So it *was* Zak then. Of course it was. And she had only herself to blame. She'd had a whole year to ask him out and she'd done nothing about it, so there was no reason why Ashleigh shouldn't do so.

'Well,' she said tightly, 'I'm glad you had a lovely time.'

'I did, thank you. And if it's OK with you, I think I'll come down to the track again tomorrow night.'

'Great,' Robyn forced out. Honestly, if she gritted her teeth any tighter she'd grind them away. Then she thought of Ginny and Jack and reminded herself how lucky she was to have a sister at all. 'Well, I'd better get to bed. Work in the morning. Night, Ash.'

She went to duck round her sister but, to her surprise, Ashleigh flung her arms around her and hugged her tight.

'Night, sis. Sleep tight.'

'Will do,' Robyn mumbled, but she already knew it was unlikely.

Ashleigh was as in love as Granny Ginny had been way back in 1942, and it was with a certain masochistic determination that Robyn crawled into bed and grabbed the last section of her latest letter to read herself into the small hours.

Chapter Twenty-Three

25 June 1942

'Surprise!'

Ginny threw back the cockpit of a fragile Hurricane she was bringing in for repairs and stared in astonishment at the man standing on the runway before her. At least, she assumed there was a man behind the vast bunch of flowers.

'Charles?'

'Happy birthday, beautiful!'

Lilinoe, who had landed her own plane ahead, came running across, laughing.

'Go and get them, silly, before the poor man sneezes all the petals off.'

Ginny shook her head at the truth of that. Charles suffered terribly from the effects of pollen, making his romantic gesture all the more special. Feeling ridiculously shy, she climbed out of the cockpit and jumped down onto the tarmac. Charles parted the flowers as she approached so that his handsome face peeked out, like a lion in the jungle, and she laughed and leaned in to kiss him – just before he sneezed.

'Damn! That rather spoiled things, didn't it?'

'Not at all.' She hastily took the flowers to allow him to fetch a handkerchief from his pocket and blow his nose. 'But chocolates would have done, you know?'

'They're not the same. I mean, they're tasty, obviously. In fact…'

He reached behind his back and, after just a little fumbling with

his belt, produced a box of very fine-looking candy. Ginny gaped.
'But they're not as pretty as flowers.'

She smiled up at him.

'You, Charles Harris, are a marvel. Is it safe to kiss you now?'

'I really hope so.'

He gathered her into his arms, drawing her close for a kiss so
prolonged that behind them the little group of engineers let out
a noisy whistle. Ginny simply kissed him harder. She'd been with
this amazing man for nearly three months now, and her feelings
for him seemed to grow stronger and stronger with every day. She
was having to learn to admit that not only was the thunderbolt
element of love true, but all that Will and Eddie and even Jack
had told her about it giving meaning to your life were also true,
unfortunately so.

Being with Charles hadn't changed anything about the day-to-
day running of her life, but he gave it so much more light. As a
flying officer in charge of training he was always around the base,
and her heart skipped for joy in as clichéd a way as any romantic
movie whenever she caught sight of him. But it was more than
that. She didn't just fancy him; she wanted to share everything with
him. An exciting trip in tough weather wasn't complete until she'd
told him about it; a terrible meal in the mess was like the finest
gourmet food if he was across the table; and a dull day trapped
in the barracks by the now all-too-familiar British cloud could be
transformed into the brightest fun just by his tap at the door. It
was all so horribly predictable; and so heart-stoppingly wonderful.

'Are you ready?' he asked, when they eventually prised themselves
apart.

'Ready for what?'

'Your birthday surprise.'

'These aren't it?' she asked, indicating the flowers.

'Of course not. I'm taking you to lunch.'

'Where?'

'My secret. All you need is a pretty dress and a pair of sunglasses. Nice ones.'

Ginny put a defensive hand to the aviator specs Robert Tyce had so kindly lent her that bright dawn before the Japanese had swooped down and taken his life. She would never let them go, though, to be fair, they were a little large and not especially stylish outside a plane, and one of the arms was held together with tape, so perhaps they weren't the best option for a birthday lunch.

'I'll wear my second-best pair,' she told Charles. 'How long have I got?'

He looked at his watch.

'Ten minutes.'

'How's a girl meant to get ready in ten minutes?'

He kissed her again.

'When the girl is already as pretty as you, it should be a doddle. Ten minutes.'

In the event, she took twenty minutes – it didn't do to be too subservient – but it was still a fast turnaround from workaday pilot to birthday girl and Lili had to pull her back at the door to do her lippy, just as Ginny had done hers on their first day in England. She grabbed her in a grateful hug.

'Sorry to rush out on you, doll.'

'Don't be silly. Go and have fun with Charles – we'll be celebrating with you later. I'm off to make a cake with the other girls now.'

Ginny smiled at her friend, delighted she was so happy here. She'd written to Kalani herself to assure him that his daughter had lots of friends and was safely flying around little old Britain. She and Lili had both been over the moon when they'd been allowed up in all manner of planes with only the most basic training and testing.

'Reckon you girls know more about flying than I do,' their instructor had told them on their second day here, and he'd happily passed them fit for duty a week later.

At first they'd stuck to the Tiger Moths and Magisters, but they'd soon moved on to the speedy Hurricanes, which were remarkably nimble, even at low altitudes. Best of all, Ginny had had her first trip up in a Spitfire last week. Lord, that had been magical. The little plane was so light and so agile; it had been almost as if it wasn't there at all. And it went so fast!

'Give it its head if you get a chance,' Charles had said to her the night before. 'It'll knock your socks off!'

Once up and out of sight of base, she'd done as he suggested, checking the skies were clear and then engaging the turbo boost on the magnificent little engine, and, goodness, her socks had been well and truly knocked off. The beautiful plane had shot forward with a confident rush that had thrilled all through her and she could have flown it all day long – if only the damned land hadn't run out.

The first time she and Lili had gone up they'd been unable to believe what they'd seen of England from the air. It was tiny. One of their first assignments had been to take a de Havilland Mosquito from Hatfield to the south coast, ready to be flown on missions over Germany. In under half an hour, the sea had loomed up before them and it had been time to land. Further weeks of flying had taught them that, unless you were sent to Scotland, there was almost no trip from any one base to another that would take more than an hour. The land quite simply ran out. For Ginny, who had been used to flying miles across the plains of Tennessee, it was an endless source of amazement. This tiny country was barely the length of the Hawaiian archipelago, and yet somehow it had single-handedly stood up to the might of the Axis powers for three years.

Mind you, from what she'd seen of the girls she now had the honour to fly with, it was no wonder. They had this fearless, almost careless spirit that they called 'pluck'. Sometimes they talked mysterious nonsense about hockey sticks and 'japes' that all seemed to come down to the same thing – a pull-your-socks-up-and-get-on-with-it approach to life that meant little fazed them. Perhaps, she and Lili had mused over long hours waiting to be allowed to fly, it came from the weather that seemed to be a continual source of frustration on this side of the Atlantic. It was almost impossible to make any decent plans without a raincloud or determined gust putting paid to them; was it any wonder they were all able to 'muddle through' more or less anything, including facing down Hitler?

Jacqueline Cochran, she knew, was keen to get back to America. She was always striding up and down the barracks, muttering about the uselessness of the American military. Precious new planes were backing up in the factories for lack of pilots to fly them to the bases around the US, but they still wouldn't deploy their many talented women. The whole situation drove Jackie mad and Ginny could see where she was coming from, but for herself she was ridiculously happy here in this drizzly little country.

Today, at least, the sun was beating down; not, perhaps, with the ferocity of a Hawaiian midday, but with a pleasant warmth that made the green fields and flower-rich hedgerows around White Waltham look almost idyllic. As Ginny stepped out of the barracks, Charles hooted from a jeep and waved her over.

'At last, Virginia Martin!'

'I was only twenty minutes.'

'That's twice what I told you.'

'Good job I'm worth waiting for then.'

He groaned.

'That you are, Ginny, that you most certainly are.' He kissed her, then let out the clutch on the jeep and jolted her forward. 'Tally ho!'

'Tally what?' Ginny giggled.

He looked at her, his ocean-blue eyes sparkling.

'Tally ho – you know, like at the start of the hunt.'

'Hunt? Like a treasure hunt?'

'No! Treasure hunt indeed. A fox hunt.'

'Oh.' Ginny shivered. 'I think a treasure hunt sounds much more fun.'

Charles considered.

'Actually, I think you might be right. I've always felt rather sad for the poor old fox getting chased down by all those hounds. Not really fair, is it? Not really cricket.'

Ginny squinted at him, more confused than ever.

'Cricket?'

'It means… Oh, never mind. We're here.'

Ginny looked around her. They were barely ten minutes from White Waltham but the busy hangars and buildings of the base had already given way to sweeping meadowlands. Charles pulled up by a gate leading into a field bordered by the prettiest little stream. Ginny could see a pebbly beach where it bent round and leaped eagerly out of the car.

'You said the other day that you missed the beach, my lady, so I found one for you. I mean, it's not very big and not very soft but—'

She stoppered his mouth with a kiss.

'I love it, Charles.'

'Oh. Good. That's good.'

He pushed his fair hair back off his face in the way that she adored. As an officer, he was allowed to keep it a little longer than the enlisted men, and every so often a hint of a curl showed at his temples that made her long to see him freed from the restrictions of the military. His family were from some place called Oxfordshire where his father ran a thriving law practice. Charles had just completed his degree to join him there as a junior partner when war had broken out. He'd enlisted the next day and, with a university education and a pilot's licence, had been swiftly fast-tracked into officer training for the air force. Naturally interested in people, he'd soon been pigeon-holed for training and that was how he'd ended up at White Waltham, apparently arriving just a week before Jacqueline Cochran's girls.

'Fate,' Lili had proclaimed it when she'd heard, and Ginny, self-professedly drowning in a sickly sea of love, had only been able to agree.

Now she skipped happily down to the stream, throwing off her Mary Janes to paddle in the shallows, blissfully cool against the heat of the day. Charles brought the hamper and produced a large rug, delicate sandwiches, a bottle of champagne and even a cherry cake.

'How on earth did you get all this?' Ginny asked him.

Aside from the horrific evidence of the large-scale bombing they'd seen in Liverpool, one of the biggest shocks of wartime life in Britain had been the rationing. They'd had it at home, of course, but nothing like the poor Brits. There was enough food, as long as you liked watery potato and scrawny meat with all the taste cooked out of it, but sweet treats were so hard to come by. Occasionally Ginny's parents sent her a 'mercy package' of chocolate, sugar and candies, and boy, was she popular in the barracks on those days.

Charles tapped the side of his nose – another curious British mannerism.

'I have my ways and means.'

'Black market?'

'*Birthday treat.* Do you want it or not?'

'Yes! Yes, please.'

Charles filled a plate with goodies and handed them over before applying himself to the champagne, popping the cork exuberantly into the stream where it sent up a little splash. Ginny accepted a glassful and looked at the bubbles frothing in the flute.

'Thank you, Charles, this is lovely.'

'It's you who are lovely, Ginny. I can't believe the war brought you to me. I've been raging against it for the last three years but now… Why, if I met Hitler, I might even shake his hand.'

'Charles, no!'

He grimaced.

'I wouldn't, Ginny. The man's pure evil, but if he's done one good thing, it's sending you across the Atlantic and into my arms.' He clinked his glass against hers. 'Happy birthday, Virginia – you're a wonderful woman and I...' He cleared his throat. 'I love you.'

Ginny gasped.

'You do?'

Charles had gone quite pink beneath his smart panama and plucked nervously at his trouser leg.

'Too much? Too soon? It's not very British of me, I know, but I just can't help it because I do, Ginny, I do love you.'

Now his eyes met hers and she threw herself into his arms. Champagne went everywhere but she didn't care, because the words that would have scared the life out of her from any other man sounded like a symphony from Charles.

'I love you too,' she whispered against his chest, then louder, 'I love you too, Charles.'

Oh, Jack, she thought, as he kissed her again. *If you could see me now!*

Her big brother would have been so pleased. He would have been desperate to meet Charles, keen to get him together with Penny and to start forming the family bonds that would have brought them and their children together, and—

She caught herself. Children! Family! Was she getting ahead of herself? And if she and Charles were to, to – she didn't quite dare say the word 'marry', even in her head – would she have to live in England? In this Oxfordshire place? Charles said it was very nice but it wasn't home, was it? Suddenly Ginny's birthday picnic felt as cold as if a habitual English cloud had crossed the sun, and she pulled back from him, confused.

'Are you all right?' he asked tenderly.

'Fine. I'm fine. Just, you know... I mean...'

He steadied her glass and refilled it.

'I know, Ginny,' he said. 'There's a lot to think about, but let's not worry now, shall we? It's a beautiful day, we've got a beautiful lunch, and this pretty stream is enough water to enjoy without thinking about that great big Atlantic – right?'

'Right,' she agreed, grateful he understood.

She reached for the cake, sure everything would seem easier with a slice of it inside her, but barely had she taken the first delicious bite than she heard her voice being called. She turned to see Lili running up the road and jumped to her feet, panicked.

'What is it? What's happened?' Lili burst through the gate and leaned over, her hands on her knees as she drew in breath. Ginny and Charles ran to her. 'Is it bad news?'

Lilinoe shook her dark head and finally stood upright again.

'The reverse. The Americans have attacked the Japanese at Midway and taken the island. It's being hailed as a great victory – maybe a turning point. I thought you'd want to know.'

'I do,' Ginny agreed keenly. 'That's great news.'

'Even better – d'you know what secured the victory?'

'Planes?' Ginny guessed.

Lili frowned.

'Well, yes, planes for sure, but before that – intelligence. Joe and Eddie worked out where the Japanese fleet would be and when. It meant we could surprise the hell out of Admiral Yamamoto, just like he did to us. Joe will be so pleased.'

Ginny smiled, thinking of quiet Joe Rocheford sitting in the jeep next to Eddie that dreadful night last December. *It's all my fault*, he'd said, and now he'd turned that into action.

'There's a long way to go yet,' Charles warned.

Ginny looked at him. 'I know that, but this – this is personal. We were there in Pearl Harbor, remember? We were actually in the skies when the Japanese came. They didn't even declare war, Charles, just snuck up on everyone in their beds. That's not, you know…'

'Cricket?' he suggested.

Ginny frowned.

'You're going to have to introduce me to this cricket thing.'

He laughed and put an arm around her.

'It would be my pleasure, my love.'

Lili raised an eyebrow at the endearment and, behind Charles's back, Ginny stuck a tongue out at her.

'It's wonderful news, doll,' she said out loud. 'And on my birthday too. Come and have some champagne to celebrate.'

But Lili took one look at the little rug and the picnic for two and shook her head.

'No way. I'm not being a – what do you say, Charles? – a gooseberry.' She hugged Ginny tightly. 'I'll leave you to it, *my love*. Have fun.'

She scampered off and Ginny watched her go, delighted at the news but unsettled at the thought of home, of her friends far away in the Pacific, and of America's side of the war. Grief for Jack still dug daily at her heart, and she knew that every day so many other poor families were suffering the same dreadful loss at the hands of this terrible war. Despite that, though, it had somehow brought her more happiness than she'd known possible and, selfishly, she didn't want it to end.

8 September 1942

'You will not believe this!'

Jacqueline Cochran came storming into the barracks, waving a telegram like a vicious weapon. The other girls looked up from their bunks where they were mending clothes, writing letters or reading magazines. September had come in with an unwelcome return of the damp and chill they'd known when they'd first arrived at White Waltham, and those of them not out flying were huddled inside waiting for the dinner bell.

'What's up, Jackie?' Ginny asked.

'Those horrible men in high command have only gone and set up a woman's ferrying corps without me.'

Ginny's heart sank.

'Without any of us,' she said.

'Exactly!' Jacqueline came over to her. 'We're the most accomplished pilots America has – and the most experienced in ferrying thanks to our work over here – and they've just gone and set up a corps under Nancy bloody Love.'

She all but spat out the name and Ginny flinched. She knew Nancy a little as their families were in the same circles and they'd flown out of the same airfields a few times. She was a talented pilot, though without Jacqueline's panache. Critically, she was from an 'old money' family with all the right connections, and now it looked as if she'd been putting her influence to good use.

'How will it work?' she dared to ask.

Jacqueline turned on her, as red in the face as if she'd liberally coated herself in her own signature blusher.

'How would I know?' she shouted. 'I've not been consulted, have I? Oh, no! Despite it being me who wrote to Eleanor Roosevelt about it way back in 1939. Despite it being *me* who chased all the top bods down to explain how it would work. Despite me ferrying a bomber across the Atlantic and telling the whole world that using female pilots was the answer if it came to war. They've just pushed me aside – shipped me out to this backwater of a country and marched on with my ideas without me.'

'Oi!' one of the Brits – a feisty girl called Jean – protested. 'This is not a backwater.'

'To me it is,' Jacqueline snapped, then she saw the girl's face and shook herself. 'Sorry. I didn't mean that. It's not a backwater itself, it's just that when you're used to a country that takes over a day to fly across, it can feel a little… small.'

'Small, perhaps, but not insignificant,' Jean shot back. 'We're keeping Hitler at bay; how can that be insignificant?'

'I didn't say—'

'And what's so bad about flying here anyway? It's the same war, isn't it?'

Ginny looked nervously from Jean to Jacqueline, who seemed to be squaring up to each other.

'Of course it is,' she said, stepping between them. 'And I, for one, love it here. But you must see, Jean, that if our own country wants us, that's hard to resist.'

Jean looked at her and gave a harsh little laugh.

'I do see that,' she agreed. 'But from what Jackie's just said, it sounds as if your own country *doesn't* want you.'

Ginny tried to answer, but was drowned out by Jacqueline's howl of rage and the slam of the door as she stormed out.

'Pack your bags, girls,' she called over her shoulder. 'We're going home whether they want us or not.'

Chapter Twenty-Four

Wednesday 13 March

'So,' Ashleigh said, her voice super-casual, 'I put my ticket back.'

Robyn glanced at her sister, sitting in the passenger seat on the way to the track. Her body, in contrast to her voice, was rigid and she fought to be positive.

'That's great, Ash. Till when?'

'Well, I was going to do a week, but it seemed a bit silly when the lab has plenty of work for me and there's still this treasure hunt to finish.'

Robyn's throat tightened. She'd been poring over the tales of life in England, glad to read about a happy part of Ginny's past after the horrors of the attack and losing Uncle Jack, but from all she'd said it couldn't last. There was still one section left but Ashleigh had been too busy to sit down to it, and Robyn had to confess that she'd been avoiding it. She was horribly afraid that once her grandmother got back to America, away from the love of her life, it was all going to go wrong.

'Things all seem to be going well for Granny in England, don't they?' she said nervously now. 'Where's this terrible secret going to come in, d'you think?'

Ashleigh shook her head. 'No idea, but we've only got two clues left, so it has to be soon. I figure, if we get it done soon then we can relax, and I can enjoy the rest of my time here without chasing around after silly riddles.'

Robyn's throat tightened further.

'Enjoy your time doing what?' she asked, rather more sharply than she'd intended.

Ashleigh looked at her sideways.

'Funny question, sis. This is Hawaii, holiday destination extraordinaire. I've not even been to Waikiki yet.'

'You hate beaches.'

'I hate *bikinis*. There's nothing to stop me sitting on the sand in elegant linen trousers like Granny might have done back in the day, and the weather's so nice here. I've been texting people back home, and apparently it's dead rainy and cold, and you know how damp Granny's house gets. That stupid old heating system just isn't up to the job, is it?'

'Er, no.' Robyn's head was spinning; there suddenly seemed to be so much to take in. 'About the house, Ashleigh...'

'So, I went for two weeks. Is that OK? I can honestly get a hotel if it's too much and—'

'Of course it's OK,' Robyn said on autopilot, though, to be honest, two more weeks on that wretched camp bed was not an enticing prospect.

Perhaps she should just sleep in with Ashleigh, though not if she was going to start inviting people back. Oh God, would she do that? Would she invite Zak back to Robyn's room after a lovely day out on Waikiki Beach, and do things with him in Robyn's bed, whilst she cowered in the box room trying not to listen? It didn't bear thinking about.

'Robyn? Robyn, are you watching the road, because—'

Robyn blinked back into full concentration just in time to slam her foot down at a red light.

'Sorry, Ash. Miles away.'

'So it seems. You'd better sharpen up before you hit the hurdles.'

'I know!'

'OK, OK – just watching out for you.'

'And my loser hurdles race?'

Ashleigh gave an audible sigh.

'I shouldn't have said that, Rob. Your hurdles group is really good.'

'You mean Zak is.'

The light turned green and she jolted angrily forward. The Mini gave a little rev of annoyance.

'I meant all of you, actually,' Ashleigh said with exaggerated patience. 'That young lad's amazing.'

'Cody?' Robyn softened. 'He is. He's got real potential if he gets the chance to show it.'

'If he *takes* the chance to show it,' Ashleigh said crisply as they pulled into the track car park. 'Not back here, Rob. We've got a disabled badge, remember?'

'A *UK* disabled badge,' Robyn pointed out.

'And a bloody great big wheelchair. It's pretty clear I'm not faking it with these pathetic things.'

She gestured scornfully to her lower limbs which had, over years of inactivity, grown wasted and painfully thin. Robyn swallowed and obediently drove down to the big spaces near the door. Another girl had just pulled up and now she pushed open the driver's door, poked out two metal sticks and hoisted herself up to reveal two neat prosthetics.

'Wow,' Ashleigh breathed, then suddenly she was winding the window down and calling a hello. The girl smiled over at them.

'Can you drive with those?' Ashleigh asked.

'What does it look like?' she shot back, eyes narrowing.

'It looks like a miracle,' Ashleigh said calmly. 'I lost my legs seven years ago and didn't think driving would be possible again.'

The girl relaxed straight away.

'Oh, I see. Sure it's possible, with the right prosthetics.'

Ashleigh sighed and pushed open the door, hooking her withered legs out for the other girl to see. Robyn watched with bated breath.

She knew for a fact that Ginny had tried to interest her sister in an adapted car back in England but Ashleigh had refused to engage. She wasn't sure if it was American positivity that was changing her attitude, or just being away from the dark place she'd lurked in since the accident, but changing it was. Ashleigh was usually so defensive about her legs but now here she was offering them openly up for consideration. The girl looked at them, head on one side, and nodded at Ashleigh.

'That's a bit trickier. Ridiculous, right? But with the correct car there's no reason why you shouldn't be able to drive. Here.' She handed a card to Ashleigh. 'I work with a company that does vehicle conversions for all sorts of needs. Give me a call if you want.'

'Thanks,' Ashleigh said, and watched as she went round to the back of her car, opened up the boot and pressed a button to hoist a wheelchair out on a little pulley. Leaning on the car, she unhooked it, unfolded the arms and sank down into it with a wink at Ashleigh.

'I always hated relying on other people,' she said, then grabbed a training bag and was off into the clubhouse.

Ashleigh stared at the card.

'They're good at doing stuff, aren't they, Americans?'

'They often have quite a can-do attitude,' Robyn agreed lightly, choosing not to remind her of the British cars she'd refused to even consider several years ago. 'Now, I need to get to the track. Are you coming?'

Ashleigh looked suddenly self-conscious.

'I'll, er, have a bit of a look around. See what's, you know, going on. I'll be over in a while.'

'No problem.'

Robyn helped her into her chair, locked up the car and left her to it. She could see Zak warming up on the track already and wondered if this was her sister playing it cool. Not that it mattered. She was here to train, not to play romantic games.

'Evening, Robyn.'

Zak's greeting was curt, but Coach Tyler was already calling them to drills and she had to buckle down and concentrate. The session was a short one, so as not to tire them out before the competition at the weekend, but it was fiercely technical and Robyn had to force her tired brain to focus. On one run she clipped a hurdle and went toppling sideways. Zak, standing on the side waiting for his turn, stepped swiftly up and caught her.

'You OK?'

Physically she was fine, but her head was spinning ridiculously with his closeness and she was glad of the excuse to hold on to him.

'Just a little wobbly.'

'Take a moment.'

She was happy to, though it didn't seem to help her catch her breath. He was very close and her whole body was zingingly aware of him.

'I hear you had a nice meal up in the mountains?' he said, his voice strained.

'It was OK. Nice restaurant, not such great company.' She felt horribly guilty being mean about lovely Connor, but for some stupid reason it felt important to tell Zak she wasn't dating.

'Right.'

'How was Duke's?' she demanded.

'What?' He squinted at her, but at that moment Ashleigh came wheeling up. 'Oh, hey, Ashleigh.'

'Hey, Zak, Rob – you look very cosy there.'

Robyn leaped up self-consciously, though Ashleigh seemed more amused than cross. Was she *that* confident?

'I clipped a hurdle,' she said.

'Right. I told you you would.'

'Yes, thank you, guru. It won't happen again.'

Robyn ran back onto the track feeling foolish. She had no idea what was going on here but she did know how to clear a hurdle, and it was time she started proving it. She put her head down and worked flat out, concentrating hard. It paid off and she cleared a full run at top pace.

'Yes!'

Exhilaration ran through her veins and she bounced up and down on the line. She could understand why Granny Ginny had wanted to race cars and fly planes – the buzz of pushing yourself and achieving something was strong in her blood and that had to have come from her grandmother. And if a younger Ginny had taken it a little too far sometimes, then it was surely understandable?

She was horribly aware that clue seven was waiting to be solved. She'd deliberately left it when she'd finished the letter last night, still unsure that she really wanted to get to the end of this damned hunt, but it was probably better to face it sooner rather than later. She spun round, looking for Ashleigh, but couldn't see her anywhere.

'All right, Rob?' Zak asked.

'Have you seen Ashleigh?'

'Not for a while. I think she went that way.'

He pointed round to the finishing straight where the sprinters were training. Robyn scanned the bleachers beyond but there was no sign of a wheelchair.

'You lost something, Robyn?' Cody asked, loping up after a phenomenal run over the high hurdles. Coach had been especially encouraging to him tonight and it had clearly paid off.

'Have you seen my sister?' she asked him.

'The girl in the chair?'

'Er, yes.'

'Sure. She's over there.'

He, too, pointed to the sprint straight but still Robyn couldn't spot her. A race was coming around the bend and she could hear Dylan, the sprints coach, shouting loud encouragement. Several people were coming to the railings, cheering, and Robyn's eyes followed the athletes that were causing such a fuss.

'Oh God, is that...?'

There were four athletes peeling off the bend to hit the finishing straight, all in wheelchairs. Robyn thought she recognised the girl from the car earlier but didn't have time to check because her eyes were inexorably drawn to the one out front – Ashleigh, brow drawn in concentration, arms flying around the wheels, her chair wobbling precariously as she drove it on.

The other three were in light racing chairs, something like the ones the basketball players had used, but Ashleigh was in her own more upright everyday chair, and it clearly wasn't coping with the rigours of racing down a track. Even as Robyn watched, it started to slew dangerously, but her sister, the light of victory in her eyes, paid it no heed.

'Ashleigh!'

Robyn started running, aware of Zak hot on her heels and then overtaking her, but they had the whole infield to cross and were never going to make it in time. As if in a sick slow motion, she watched Ashleigh's chair wobble across the lanes, tip over onto one wheel and then fall sideways, sending her sprawling.

'Ashleigh! Oh God, Ashleigh.'

Her lungs were burning as she sprinted faster than ever before, leaping over the cord alongside the track and flinging herself down next to her sister as the other athletes swerved around them. Ashleigh lay on the track, her right leg helplessly tangled in the chair and her arms splayed out where she'd tried to break her fall. Her head was still down and Robyn cradled it.

'Don't worry, Ashleigh, I've got you. I'll look after you, I…' Ashleigh rolled onto her back and opened her eyes. 'Where does it hurt?'

'Everywhere,' her sister said. Then she gave her a huge grin. 'But so what? I love it!'

Robyn shook her head, laughing in relief. It seems she wasn't the only sister with their grandmother's fiery blood running through her veins, and as she bent over to work out how best to help her sister up, she prayed that Ginny had found the same sort of healthy outlets for her own restless energies. It was time, she feared, to read on.

Chapter Twenty-Five

1 December 1942

Ginny went to the edge of the hangar and peered hopefully out. Nope – still far too foggy to fly. She sighed and turned back in to the other girls with a doleful shake of her head. The weather in Houston, it seemed, was as bad as in England though not, at least, quite as cold. She was here with Jacqueline's first group of recruits to be trained in the ways of the US military but it felt as if obstacles were being constantly put in their way, even by the damned weather.

'It's a blasted pea-souper,' she grumbled.

'A what?' the others shrieked.

Ginny looked over at them.

'It's an English expression – means thick fog. I guess they have pretty odd pea soup over there.'

'*All* the food was odd over there,' Lili said with feeling.

Ginny gave her friend a rueful smile, then went back to glaring at the skies.

'Are you willing it away?' Lili asked, looping an arm through hers.

'Trying to.'

'Well, if anyone can, you can.'

'You think too highly of me, doll. I'm just being impatient as usual.'

'Only because you know your capabilities.'

'Only because I don't like being made to wait for anything. It makes me itch.'

She slid her hands under her bomber jacket, rubbing at her arms as if they did, indeed, physically itch. As always, the feel of the soft lining of the expensive jacket Jack had chosen for her made her heart turn over. God, she missed her brother. Losing him had been the worst thing that had ever happened to her, and now she was haunted with the worry that she might lose someone else who was rapidly becoming just as dear to her.

'Have you heard from Charles recently?' Lili asked, as if she'd heard her thoughts, which she probably had – Lili was the most empathetic person Ginny knew.

'I had a letter yesterday.'

'How is he?'

'Fine. Fed up. He says he wants to fly properly – in combat.'

She swallowed back the bile that rose in her throat every time she heard Charles say that. She understood it, of course she did. Wasn't she here in foggy Houston because she wanted to do her bit for her country? But the thought of the man she loved dogfighting with a German plane, just like those awful scenes over Pearl, made her whole body shake with fear.

'What have you said?' Lili asked carefully.

'I've said that he has to do what he has to do but not to put himself in more danger than he needs to. I've said I... I can't marry a corpse.'

Her voice choked on the last words and Lili hugged her tight. Ginny clutched gratefully at her strong little arms, painfully aware of how much she needed them.

Charles had proposed to her on her last night in England. With Jacqueline in a fury, their departure had all happened very fast, and the girls had been booked on a flight back to Washington within a day of her finding out about Nancy Love's coup. They'd had one last evening on the base and it had been rather embarrassing. Everyone had been very aware that they were letting their new ATA comrades down by fleeing so fast. There had been deliveries scheduled, pilots relying on them, and it had felt wrong to leave them in the lurch just because Jacqueline was cross at being slighted. But they'd been there under her command and had had no choice but to obey her orders.

Their last meal in the White Waltham mess had been awkward until one of the men had produced a contraband bottle of rum and everyone had relaxed. With Jacqueline gone to bed, Susie and Louise had put some music on the gramophone and an impromptu dance had started up. Ginny had almost been enjoying herself again with her too-brief friends, when Charles had taken her hand and whisked her outside.

'I'm sorry,' he'd said, as he'd pulled her away from the entrance and round the side of one of the hangars.

She'd shivered, convinced he was going to tell her that it was over between them, that it had been nothing more than a dalliance and not worth carrying on across the ridiculous miles of ocean that would soon separate them.

'Sorry for what, Charles?'

'Sorry I have to do this, this way. I had something more stylish in mind.'

'Do what?'

'But that's war for you.' He'd given a self-conscious little shrug and then dropped to one knee before her in the dirt of the airfield, with the planes standing shadowy sentinel over them in the moonlight. 'Virginia Martin, will you please do me the very great honour of agreeing to become my wife.'

That had floored her. She'd just stood there, gaping at him, with thoughts swirling around in her mind. *I'm getting married! Lord, Jack, look at me – I'm actually getting married.*

'Ginny?' Charles had said nervously, pulling her back into the glorious here and now.

'Yes! Oh Charles, yes please. Absolutely. I'd love to.'

'Thank God for that!'

He'd leaped up and swept her into his arms, dancing her around the rough scrub as if it were the finest ballroom and, God help her, it had felt that way. When they'd finally danced themselves out, he'd slipped a ring onto her finger with more apologies. It wasn't a fancy diamond, he'd stuttered. He hadn't had time to get into London to buy something worthy of her. She didn't have to wear it if she didn't want to. But she'd just stared down at the dainty antique – dusky rose gold with the prettiest twist of amethysts – and stoppered his apologies with a long kiss.

'It's beautiful, Charles. Where did you get it?'

'It was my mother's. She gave it to me for luck.'

She'd looked at him, horrified.

'Then I can't take it. I can't take your luck away.'

She'd tried to fumble it off and hand it back to him but he'd stopped her.

'Virginia, you're the greatest luck I could ever have, and this ring will protect me far more on your finger than it could ever do around my neck. Please, wear it for me until we're back together and I can take you up the aisle.'

Ginny ran her fingers over the ring now. The poor thing would be worn away, the number of times she caressed it, but it felt as if she could sense a little bit of him in the pretty gems and she needed that. Sometimes she wondered if she and Lili should have stayed with the easy-going, hard-working ATA in England, as Susie and Louise had done, especially when Houston threw fog at them, holding back the training that none of them really needed.

'I just want to fly!' she wailed, pulling away from Lili and striding out onto the airfield.

Her limbs were twitchy and her insides felt as if they might explode with all the hanging around. She needed to do something to justify the sacrifices she'd made to come here, but still the fog hung there, fat and grey and full of its own damned importance, just like everything out here at the Howard R. Hughes Airport in Texas.

Commander Garrett had not been happy at having a group of female pilots thrust on him and had done everything he could to make life uncomfortable at the airfield. He'd refused to find them accommodation on site and when Jacqueline had solved that by billeting them with local families, he'd refused to provide transport out to the base.

Undaunted, Jacqueline had organised it herself, but the only thing she'd been able to find was a vehicle newly retired from transporting a Tyrolean orchestra around the state. With its red-and-white awning and lurid edelweiss painted along both sides, it was about the most conspicuous transport she could have found – and this for a group of women who were meant to be incognito. Jacqueline had ordered them to tell their hosts around Houston that they were part of a women's basketball team, which had been fine for Ginny, but a nonsense for tiny Lili. Their hosts hadn't believed it for a minute but seemed to enjoy the joke and still regularly delighted in asking them about 'basketball practice' when they ate together.

At least life in the billets was pleasant. The only place for the women to eat on the base itself was at the Municipal Terminal, a mile's walk from the training centre, and worse, that was the only place for them to go to the toilet too. Most of them drank barely anything all day to avoid additional walks, but Ginny wasn't having that and had found herself a particularly well-shaded tree. It horrified Lilinoe but she didn't care; if they couldn't provide decent facilities, she'd make her own.

She wasn't the only one bending the rules. This, Jacqueline Cochran's first group of trainees, was made up of proficient pilots who only needed military training to progress into the ferrying corps, and they were a confident bunch. Aside from Lili and Thelma, a feisty farmhand from Mississippi who'd learned in her grandfather's old biplane, they were rich young women, used to getting their own way and not inclined to obey rules they didn't see the point of. They were nominally in the charge of a lovely older lady called Dedie, but the poor woman's only previous experience managing groups of women had been community charities and girl scouts. They were a very different breed to a bunch of high-flying society women, and there'd been a few of what the girls back in White Waltham might have called 'japes'.

Ginny's particular favourite had been the bucket of ice water over the door of Commander Garrett's office. They'd probably heard his shrieks as far away as the ladies' loos, but the women had all been enthusiastically doing their calisthenics class out on the runway at the time, so he'd had no one to punish. The picture of them demurely touching their toes as the commander shot past, drenched from head to foot and purple in the face, had been one of Ginny's best memories of Houston so far.

She sighed. She was glad to be here, really she was, but did it have to be so slow?! From all she'd heard, the planes were still backing up in the factories and she couldn't wait to be out there doing a proper job.

Or even just flying.

'Are you up there, Jack?' she whispered to the lowering skies. 'Are you laughing at me stuck down here? I don't think so. I think you'd be impatient too. Look at you – first into the damned planes at Pearl Harbor.'

Next week it would be a whole year since that fatal day; a whole year without him. That dark dawn of 7 December, she'd dived out of the air as fast as she could and hidden in the hangar. Jack, however had headed right out there to take on the enemy. She was so proud of him and so wanted him to be proud of her too.

'This is ridiculous,' she spat at the fog. 'Who thought this stupid marshland would be a good location for a training field? It's such a waste of all our time stuck here. It'd be fine for racing cars, but planes…'

One of the other girls sauntered up at her side, flicking cigarette ash carelessly from an ivory holder. Marion Florsheim was heiress to the Florsheim shoe empire and not a woman to be trifled with. She'd rented a suite in the very smart Warwick Hotel for herself and her two Afghan hounds, and Ginny had been amazed when she'd wriggled into her shady toilet tree one breaktime with a drawled 'room for another one'? They'd become quite friendly since and now Marion grinned at her.

'Racing cars, you say…'

She raised a perfectly plucked eyebrow towards the run of jeeps parked outside the hangar, keys at the ready. Ginny grinned.

'I'm up for it. Last one to the end of the runway…?'

'Why not? Marylou?'

Marylou Colbert, daughter of a rear admiral and never slow to a challenge, leaped up.

'Count me in. Who else?'

'I can't drive,' her friend Shirley said.

'Can't drive?' Thelma said, hands on hips. 'You can fly a plane but you can't drive?'

Shirley shrugged.

'I've never had to. I always just use Daddy's driver.'

Thelma tossed her ponytail.

'Ridiculous. I'll show you lot how to drive. Ready…'

'Ginny, don't!' Lili grabbed at Ginny's arm but Ginny shook her off. 'Ginny, please, you'll get in terrible trouble.'

'With who? They're airfield vehicles and we're not taking them off the airfield.'

'But racing… What if you crash?'

'Then I'll lose, right, Marion?'

'Too right, girl.'

Lili put herself in front of them, her big brown eyes pleading.

'Don't do it. Jackie won't like it, you know she won't. She'll say it's not ladylike.'

Marion scoffed.

'Jackie Cochran's got no idea about being a proper lady. It's not about beauty products and fancy waves in your hair – it's about standing up to be counted.'

'But not in a stupid jeep,' Lili begged. 'Look, the sun's coming. We'll be able to fly soon.'

'Not soon enough,' Marylou said. 'Stand aside, Lili, or we might knock you over.'

'Ginny!'

Lili turned the full force of her pleading on Ginny, but Ginny had no time for this. She was itching to do something, anything, and if she couldn't get up in the air, why not test her skills on the ground?

'It's just a bit of fun, doll,' she said, taking her by the shoulder and pushing her gently aside. 'Cheer for me, hey?'

Lili folded her arms.

'I will not.'

Ginny's heart twisted but Thelma was calling 'Ready' again, and with her brain as fogged as the stupid air above, she ran to get into line with the others. 'Steady.' The four girls braced. 'Go!'

Ginny was off, racing across the tarmac towards the nearest jeep, her long legs giving her a good start. She felt her lungs fill and her heart start to pound – and she loved it. This was better than pacing around like a fool, better than talking to her dead brother in the clouds. She reached the jeep, jumped in and turned the key. It leaped into life, and she backed it out with a screech of tyres and made off up the runway. The others were into their vehicles too and coming after her, and she pressed her foot to the pedal, willing her steed onwards. She felt Marion coming up on her tail and veered sideways to cut her off.

'Curse you, Martin!' Marion called, and she laughed and pushed on.

Thelma was on the other side and she could just make out Marylou beyond. The four of them were close, but she was still at least half a length ahead and intended to keep it like that. She veered the other way, forcing Thelma to wobble and Marylou to shout in protest. It threw them both but now Marion was gaining on her, and Ginny pushed on. She was vaguely aware of shouts of protest from the side and only now realised the flaw in their plan – if they raced to the end of the tarmac, how did they stop? There was a metal fence about thirty feet away across some scrubland. Was that enough? Only one way to find out.

She pushed her foot down for the line and shot off the end, triumphant, before slamming the brakes on. The jeep juddered and she had to battle to hold it steady as smoke came off the tyres and, with a protesting shriek, it ground to a halt, bonnet kissing the chain-link.

'Yes!'

Ginny turned to claim her victory over the others and saw all three had stopped before the tarmac ran out. Behind them, three heavily decorated and clearly furious men were coming running. She sank back down again and sighed.

'Might have done something a bit stupid, Jack,' she muttered.

Chapter Twenty-Six

Wednesday 13 March

Robyn couldn't sleep. Once she'd got Ashleigh safely home from the track, they'd curled up with takeaway Chinese and the last bit of Granny's letter. It had been nice at the time but now, whenever she began to drift off, her brain would send a swirl of images around her head – Ashleigh pushing her wheelchair down the track, strangely intertwined with a young Ginny racing jeeps across Houston – and she'd find herself wide awake again. It was hopeless. From down the corridor she heard a noise and sat eagerly up.

'Ash? Are you awake?'

'Sure am,' Ashleigh called back. 'Far too pumped to sleep. Come on through.'

Robyn padded down the corridor into her bedroom. Ashleigh patted the side of the big bed and she hopped gladly up next to her. God, she'd forgotten how wonderfully comfy her mattress was! She stretched out luxuriously, pushing her aching limbs into the covers.

'OK there, sis?'

'Very good. You?'

'Best I've been in ages. I can't stop thinking about how it felt to race again.'

'It was madness.'

'I know – glorious madness!'

Robyn shook her head, still haunted by the sight of her sister being tossed from the falling chair. Dylan, the sprints coach, had come running over as she'd been crouched at Ashleigh's side, and Robyn had turned on him.

'How could you let her race in that chair?'

'I didn't. That is, I told her not to, but when I looked around there she was, gaining on the others, even though she'd started from somewhere behind us. I couldn't exactly jump out in front and stop her – that would have been more dangerous.'

'More dangerous than this?'

'No harm done, sis,' Ashleigh had interrupted them from the ground. 'Just help me up, would you? People are trying to train here; the last thing they need is some idiot lolling around on the finishing line.'

'Just *before* the finishing line actually,' Dylan had said, and she'd stuck her tongue out at him.

'This time. I just need the right chair.'

'Very true,' he'd agreed, and before Robyn had known what was happening, they'd been off to talk to Brittany, the girl from the car, about finding some kit.

Ashleigh had been buzzing about it all the way home.

'Dylan says he can get me a chair from the uni tomorrow.

'Dylan says I've got real potential.

'Dylan says there's still time to enter in the race on Saturday.'

Robyn hadn't been able to shut her up. It had been great to see her so enthused, of course, but she couldn't help worrying.

'Are you sure you should race so soon?' she asked now.

'Totally sure.'

'Are you ready though?'

'Ready as I'll ever be. Come on, Rob, you've all been dead keen to get me doing sport again.'

'And you've been totally resistant.'

Ashleigh stuck a cheeky tongue out at her. 'Well I'm not now, so make the most of it. Granny Ginny would have done it, you know she would. Seems she loved a race too.'

She picked up some sheets of paper off the bed and waved them at her.

'You're reading the letter again?' Robyn asked, instantly diverted.

'Yep. Bit of a wild child, wasn't she?'

'When she wanted to be, certainly. Impatient, reckless, competitive – ring any bells?'

Ashleigh grimaced.

'I guess we both have a bit of her in us.'

'Perhaps, but you're cornering the reckless market at the moment.'

'Sorry but, hey, Granny Ginny always said I was…'

'Good with wheels,' they chorused together.

Robyn laughed. 'She was a wily old thing, wasn't she, sending you out here?'

'Maybe. But we still don't know what she did that was so awful. Is it time for clue seven? Shall I read it out?'

Robyn felt her throat tighten but it *was* time. She nodded and Ashleigh rifled through the pages to the last one.

'Queen Emma birthed me so I can safely birth
A nation of babes and keep all in good health.'

She looked at Robyn. 'What on earth? Why is Granny banging on about babies? OMG – she didn't get pregnant, did she? She didn't have a baby and put it up for adoption and it turns out this treasure hunt is going to lead us to a long-lost brother or sister?'

Robyn stared at her. 'Pregnant by whom? She was in love with Charles and he was all the way over in England.'

'True. Good point, bless her. I guess sometimes you have to go a long way to find the right person.' Robyn's stomach churned but Ashleigh was focused on the letter again. 'But, come on, think – what's all this baby stuff? And what on earth has Queen Emma got to do with it, whoever she was?'

Robyn shook her head, trying to concentrate.

'The only Queen Emma I know was married to King Canute.'

'Who?'

'You know – the "turn back the tide" guy in ancient times. Before the Normans and all that.'

Ashleigh frowned.

'You're not making any sense, Rob. What would some medieval queen have to do with a hospital in Hawaii?'

'No idea. Must be a different Queen Emma.'

'You reckon, Sherlock?' Ashleigh was already typing urgently on her phone and now she looked up again. 'Here we go – Queen Emma of Hawaii. Oh wow, she's got a very cool full name – Queen Emma Kalanikaumakaʻamano Kaleleonālani Naʻea Rooke. That's quite the mouthful!'

'Did she have babies?'

'A son – Albert. Doesn't sound significant. Oh, but hang on…' She looked at Robyn. 'It says here that she founded a hospital in Honolulu to improve the medical facilities for the natives.'

Robyn grabbed the letter.

'Queen Emma birthed me so I can safely birth

A nation of babes and keep all in good health. Of course. It's still called the Queen's Medical Center. I drive past it all the time, but I sort of thought it was named after our queen.'

'Because…?'

'Because that's what loads of hospitals back home are called, I suppose. Stupid of me.'

'Very stupid, sis. But you know what this means…?'

Robyn looked at her as it sank in.

'It means that the next treasure chest is in the hospital.'

'And that the next letter is probably *about* the hospital too.'

They stared at each other in the low light of the bedside table. Was this crunch time?

'Do we have to go?' Robyn asked.

Ashleigh considered.

'We don't *have* to.'

'But if we don't, Granny Ginny's seventh chest will sit there unclaimed and eventually go into lost property, and years down the line a total stranger will force it open and find her letter and read it instead of us.'

'Which would be rather sad. Plus, we'd never get to clue eight.'

Robyn groaned. 'I hate hospitals.'

Ashleigh gave a bitter laugh. 'Not half as much as I do, sweetie!'

'Good job you didn't wreck yourself racing in an unsuitable chair then, sis.'

Ashleigh hugged her.

'Good job. Night, Rob.'

'Night, Ash.'

'See you in the morning for a fun trip to the hospital!'

Friday 15 March

The Queen's Medical Center smelled cloyingly crisp and clean. Robyn saw Ashleigh recoil the moment they went through the big main doors and considered the many, many days and nights her poor sister must have spent in similar buildings. It was a horrible thought but so, too, was the anticipation of what Granny Ginny's letter might say. Why else would she send them to the hospital, if they weren't close to whatever accident must, presumably, have befallen poor Lilinoe? She still wasn't sure she wanted to hear it, but here they were all the same – forced on by the pressure of their precious grandmother's last ever treasure hunt.

'Main reception?' she suggested to Ashleigh.

'I guess so, though she's got a cheek, hasn't she? What hospital wants to hold a blinking treasure chest for some bonkers old lady?'

'Ashleigh, shh! Granny Ginny wasn't bonkers.'

'Are you sure?'

Robyn shook her head but she had to admit that, as she approached the desk, she felt utterly ridiculous. There were sick people and worried relatives all around, so she was going to sound ignorant and insensitive asking for a treasure chest. She'd been glad when they'd had to put off this visit last night so that Ashleigh could get to the track again. Dylan had got hold of a racing chair and if she was truly going to race tomorrow – which it seemed she was determined to do – then she badly needed the practice.

Robyn had watched for a while but Ashleigh had snapped at her to 'stop gawping', so she'd given up and gone into the clubhouse to do a stretch session instead. Her sister had been much happier when she'd finally stopped, so Robyn could only assume the race practice had gone well. Certainly, she'd said she didn't need to go again tonight which had left them with the time to come to the Queen's Medical Center. Right now, Robyn wasn't entirely glad.

'Er, hi,' she said to the older man on reception. 'This is going to sound mad, but we've been sent here to ask about a treasure chest.'

The man looked at her sideways.

'A treasure chest? Here?'

'So we were told.'

'By whom?'

Robyn swallowed.

'Our grandmother – Virginia Harris.'

He shook his head.

'Sorry. It means nothing.'

'Right. OK. Well, thank you.' Robyn turned away, not really surprised; this was more the sort of response she'd been expecting all along. But as she reached for the handles of Ashleigh's chair, a woman further along the desk put down the phone and stood up.

'Excuse me, did you say treasure chest?'

Her voice was loud, and several people in the echoing reception area looked curiously over. Robyn wished for a hole to open up in the perfect white tiling but that was never going to happen, so she turned back.

'Do you know something about it?'

She smiled.

'Sure do, honey. You want Dr Tideswell. I'll bleep him for you.'

'Right. Thank you.'

'Take a seat, sugar.'

The woman waved to a bank of seats against the wall and Robyn scurried over to them, turning Ashleigh in next to her and willing all the curious onlookers to lose interest. The receptionist, however, did not seem inclined to let that happen.

'He says he'll be down soon, sugar – and he'll bring the chest.'

'Thank you,' Robyn squeaked out.

'Nightmare,' Ashleigh growled under her breath, then she grinned. 'Still, I guess it beats being stared at for my battered legs. And it means we're in the right place.'

Robyn did not share her optimism. The relentlessly clinical white of the place was getting to her already, and she could see all those waiting nearby nudging each other and talking about them. Ashleigh gave one particularly focused older lady a cheery wave, but Robyn was far too British to enjoy this.

'Well, well, well,' said a booming voice suddenly, 'you must be Ashleigh and Robyn Harris. So glad you made it.'

They turned to see an imposingly large Afro-Caribbean doctor coming bouncing towards them, his considerable belly straining at the buttons of his white coat and a small wooden chest held out before him as if he were one of the Three Wise Men. Everyone in the waiting area perked up. Robyn sought in vain for that hole in the tiles and then forced herself to her feet.

'Dr Tideswell?'

'That's me! And this is your treasure.'

Someone across the way actually clapped. Robyn could feel her cheeks flaming pink as she stepped up and took it from him.

'Thank you so much, doctor.'

'My pleasure. My absolute goddarn pleasure. Now listen, girls, I'm afraid I'm on duty and A&E stops for no man, nor no woman either, not even one like your grandmammy. But how's about I show you to the Peace Garden and you can explore this here chest in – well, in peace?' He beamed. 'Then hopefully I'll be able to join you a bit later?'

There was little to say but 'thank you', and before they knew it Dr Tideswell was ushering them past their gawping audience, down a long corridor and out into a pretty garden full of lush palms and bright hibiscus, with a quietly gurgling fountain in the middle.

'Peace Garden,' Robyn said, looking around the beautiful space in approval.

She wasn't sure that the contents of the small chest in her hands were going to bring either of them much peace, but it was time to dive in anyway. Thanking the doctor, she dropped onto a bench, took out the seventh key and inserted it into the lock.

Chapter Twenty-Seven

*First off, my beautiful girls, a big thank you from your
foolish, ignorant, cowardly grandmother, for getting this far.
I know you must think I'm bonkers going to such lengths to
reveal my past and you're right, but I was going mad with
boredom before I came up with the idea, so at least it's kept
me busy and not just sitting around waiting for the Angel
of Death to come calling.*

*Secondly, an apology. I imagine you've both raged against
me for not being able to talk to you about this face to face.
You're right. It's pathetic, frankly, and goes against everything
I ever taught you about facing up to your challenges and
responsibilities. I'm afraid I epitomise the 'do as I say, not as
I do' adage, but thank heavens you girls learned it so well.*

*And yes, Ashleigh, I know you'll be tutting as you read
this and saying, 'I didn't face up to anything,' but you did,
and you still are, and I know you're going to be a brilliant
woman. As for you, Robyn, having the courage to choose the
priorities in your life and go for them is a huge skill, and
I hope you know how much I admired you for giving your
career a real go. I wish you could have met Lilinoe. She was
a wonderful engineer and you would have got on so well.*

*I should have taken you with me to Hawaii when you
were both young. I kept telling myself I would do it once
you were old enough, but then we lost poor Lili to cancer
and the chance was gone. Or so I told myself. Having since
talked to Malie, I know what a fool I was not to stay in
touch, but of course that would have meant explaining a*

*few things to you and, as established, I was too cowardly
to do that. I still am, really. My hand is shaking as I write
this, girls, but here goes. Try not to think too badly of me…*

18 April 1943

'One week to graduation, Ginny – can you believe it?'

Ginny smiled at Lili as they climbed onto the crazy Tyrolean
bus to take them out to base with the other girls. To be honest, she
couldn't quite believe it. The end date of their training course had
been put back three times already and it was maddening. Over in
Europe, the Russians had defeated the Germans in some frozen
place called Stalingrad and the Nazis were reportedly on the run.
If they didn't get a move on, the war would be over before they'd
served. Plus, for Ginny personally, it had been touch and go whether
they'd let her stay on to the end at all.

She smiled hello to Marion, Marylou and Thelma as they found
a seat, remembering their disciplinary interview after the stunt with
the jeeps. They'd been lined up outside Commander Garrett's office
like schoolgirls – a comparison that had not made them take it as
seriously as they should.

'Do you think he'll rap our knuckles with a ruler?' Marion had
whispered.

'Or make us write lines,' Thelma had suggested. '"I must not
drive army jeeps more skilfully than the idiots who normally drive
them."'

'More recklessly,' Marylou had said with a sigh. 'Dad will kill
me if I'm chucked off.'

'At least you lot stopped at the end of the tarmac,' Ginny had said,
kicking the wall. 'If anyone's going to get chucked off it'll be me.'

It had seemed that Commander Garrett thought so too, for
he'd left Ginny until last and she'd had to listen to him bawling
out the others before dispatching them, tails nominally between

their legs, for punishing hours of latrine duty. Finally, it had been her turn.

She'd done her best to look contrite though it wasn't an attitude that came naturally, especially as she still hadn't really seen what she'd done wrong. The jeeps had been sitting there begging to be driven, and no one had ever specifically told them that they weren't allowed in them, so, technically speaking, she couldn't see what law she'd broken. The army, however, had laws within laws and loved nothing more than catching new recruits out on them.

'Article 12.3c of the Vehicular Section of the Army Training Handbook,' Commander Garrett had rapped at her. 'No cadet is to take a military vehicle for their own use without express permission of their commanding officer.'

'I've not got that far yet, sir,' she'd tried.

'Article 1.0 of the Introductory Section of the Army Training Handbook – no cadet is to operate on base without reading the whole Army Training Handbook.'

'Right.'

'Do you have anything to say for yourself, Martin?'

'Sorry?'

She'd seen a flicker at the edge of his lips but not dared presume it could be a smile.

'Why did you do it?' he'd asked suddenly.

She'd decided there was little to lose in being honest.

'I was fed up with being grounded, sir. I've come from England where I was already ferrying all sorts of planes around the country, so being stuck here "training" gets frustrating.'

He'd leaned forward at that, his eyes suddenly alight.

'Did you fly a Spitfire?'

'I did, sir. She's a beautiful machine.'

He'd nodded slowly.

'Yes, well, in England they do things more off the cuff than out here in the US.'

'Yes, sir.'

'Racing those damned jeeps was reckless, irresponsible and contrary to all the laws of the base. You could have wrecked that vehicle – and yourself. Did you not think of that?'

'Yes, sir. But I wanted to win, sir.'

Again his lip had twitched and he'd raised an eyebrow.

'Well, Martin, you did win and I'll admit that took some skill, not to mention some balls. Damned good driving. Now, dismissed.'

'Sir?'

'Dismissed, Cadet. You'll join the others scrubbing latrines and don't do it again.'

'Yes, sir! I mean, no, sir. Thank you, sir.'

'Get out, Martin!'

The smile had crept onto his face and he'd buried himself in his paperwork as Ginny had scrambled to leave the office, relieved that she was still part of the programme. Lili would have killed her if she'd been thrown off.

After that, she'd been well behaved for weeks. The anniversary of Pearl Harbor had been sobering for everyone, and a quiet Christmas with her folks had reminded her of all that was important – family, home, protecting a respectful, open way of life. Hitler could not be allowed to win this war, nor his Japanese allies, and Ginny had determined to buckle down, but with their training dragging on from winter into spring and now almost to Easter, it had been hard to stay focused. Finally, though, graduation was set for next Saturday and after that, she and Lili were off to Buckingham Field in Florida, flying for gunnery target practice. They couldn't wait.

'We're getting our silver wings!' Lili crowed as the bus bounced towards the base.

'Only thanks to Jackie,' Marion told them. 'D'you know, Garrett refused to order them from stores. Something about not having budgetary authorisation – the git. Jackie's had them made at the local jeweller at her own expense.'

'That's so kind of her,' Lili said. 'I can't wait to see them. Dad will be so proud. Oh, I wish he could see me graduate.'

Ginny had offered to pay for Kalani to get a boat across to the mainland, but the Atlantic was more dangerous than ever with German U-boats prowling. Besides, he'd been taken onto Hickham Field as a military engineer and they couldn't afford to do without him for the month that such a big trip would take.

'We'll send him photos,' Ginny promised. 'And you'll be with my family.'

Her own parents were flying to Texas for the weekend and, even better than that, Charles had permission to come. He'd been promoted to Flight Lieutenant at Christmas and put in charge of all air force training – a role that had, to his frustration and Ginny's unending relief, kept him out of combat. It had also enabled him to wangle a 'consultative visit' to Washington. He should be landing there any moment now for various meetings before coming on to Texas for her graduation and three precious days afterwards. She couldn't wait to see him, and for her parents to meet the man she was going to marry as soon as this damned war was over.

Last week on the phone, he'd suggested they get a special licence to marry in Texas, but Ginny wasn't overly fond of the place that had held her land-bound for so long.

'Would you mind terribly if we waited until we can do it properly?' she'd said. 'Could we, maybe, make it an engagement dinner instead?'

'Done!' he'd agreed instantly. 'That sounds marvellous.'

'You don't mind waiting?'

'I'd wait until the end of days for you, Virginia Martin.'

She'd laughed.

'Goodness, I hope it doesn't have to be that long!'

Right now though, just the week until he arrived felt like forever.

'What are you going to wear for graduation?' Marylou asked, leaning over their seat.

Ginny pulled a face.

'What *can* we wear? There's only so much you can do with tan slacks and a white shirt.'

The military had not yet provided the upcoming graduates with proper uniform, so they'd been ordered to wear their own clothes in vaguely matching colours. The lads on base, horrified at the insult, had offered to lend them their caps to give a semblance of uniform. Whilst the women hadn't been at all sure they wanted to put sweaty male headgear on their carefully washed hair, it was a kind thought and they'd accepted.

'Jackie's coming,' Thelma called from the back. 'She's got all sorts of press lined up and is hoping to use the coverage to push for proper uniforms for the next classes.'

'Nancy Love has been invited too,' Marion said. 'No one thinks she'll come – too much of a climb-down – but so what? Your father's guest of honour, right, Marylou?'

'Right,' Marylou agreed, pink with pride. 'He'll be able to pin my wings on me himself.'

'Thank God you didn't get thrown out then,' Lili said, and they all groaned.

'We've been very good since the jeeps,' Ginny told her.

'So it wasn't you that put that horrible cheese on the radiator the other day so that Commander Garrett thought we had rats?'

'Limburger,' Ginny giggled. 'Effective, wasn't it? But no, actually, it wasn't me – it was Thelma.'

'Can you blame me?' Thelma demanded. 'Garrett was vile about my landing in those hideous winds, despite me doing it ten times better than the four men who wobbled in ahead of me.'

Lili rolled her eyes.

'You lot are so childish that sometimes I actually feel sorry for Commander Garrett. He'll be glad to be rid of this first class.'

'Then he should have got graduation sorted earlier!' Marion retorted. 'Look sharp – we're here!'

The bus bounced onto the base and they all spilled into the hangar laughing noisily, but the sight that met them stopped them dead. Commander Garrett was standing there in full uniform, waiting for them.

'Fall in, ladies,' he snapped.

They looked at each other but, nervous now, arranged themselves into something approaching straight ranks.

'What's wrong?' Marylou asked.

Garrett's eyes narrowed. Cadets were not meant to address the commanding officer, and he stood there icily until it was clear that he was not responding to the foolish question, but offering his own pronouncement. Ginny's legs itched at the ridiculousness of it all. No wonder the top dogs wanted to keep women out of the military – they were worried they'd expose it for the power-farce it was.

Eventually Garrett spoke: 'We have news from the Pacific theatre.'

Ginny gasped. Had there been another big attack? Surely not. Images of that dreadful morning swam across her vision: the evil glare of the pilots as they swarmed around her Piper Cub; the silver bomb dropping onto the ships below; the smoke and the fire and the poor men boiling to death in a harbour full of burning oil. She pictured Robert dying in her arms on the hangar floor and then Jack, her poor, dear Jack, breathing his last in a hospital full of crying men, and blinked back her own tears.

'*Good* news,' Garrett said, with a ghost of a smile. The women stood up straighter and he nodded his approval. 'I am pleased to tell you that today a US army fighter pilot shot down Admiral Isoroku Yamamoto, the man who cruelly, callously and illegally planned the vicious Pearl Harbor attacks on our glorious American forces.'

The women broke into cheers and Garrett did not stop them.

'Our intelligence services intercepted and decoded a Japanese message that included the itinerary for the Admiral's inspection tour of the Solomon Islands, so our planes were in the right place at the right time to bring vengeance for all those killed at Pearl Harbor on December seventh, 1941.'

Ginny looked to Lili.

'Do you think that was Joe?'

'I bet it was. Remember how hard Dagne said he and Eddie were working when she wrote to us last month? They've been on a mission for revenge ever since the attack. Midway and the other battles were part of that, but this – this was personal. This was for Jack.'

Ginny nodded, tears moistening her eyes.

'For Jack and everyone like him.'

All around them women were hugging each other in delight, but still Commander Garrett stood there. Was there more?

'Shh,' Ginny urged the others. 'Settle down.'

Eventually they did. Garrett cleared his throat.

'This is a great step for America, but it does not come without personal cost – something I am sure, as part of the military, you will all understand.'

'We're hardly part of the military,' Marylou muttered, but the commander's face was so solemn that even she did not object further.

'I'm afraid,' Garrett went on, 'that although the assassination of the Japanese Admiral is a great strike for the US, it puts us on high alert for reprisals. That means that all non-essential travel across the States is on hold for at least two weeks, and so...'

But the women already knew what that meant – none of their family would be able to make it to graduation. Uproar broke out in the nominal ranks. Ginny couldn't take it in. This couldn't be happening. Not now. Not after waiting all this time. Charles would be landing in Washington right this moment and Garrett was saying he wouldn't be able to fly down to Texas to see her? Or her parents either? There would be no engagement dinner. It was too, too cruel.

She broke away from the group and ran into the hangar, wanting to be alone. Her emotions seemed to tumble around as if they were on a propeller inside her, and she flung herself down beneath the belly of the nearest plane and folded her head over on her knees.

'Ginny?'

Lili's voice was kind but Ginny didn't want kindness.

'Can't I be upset? Isn't it allowed? Do we just have to put our chins up and take all that this lot keep throwing at us?'

'It isn't their fault Yamamoto's been killed.'

'No. But it *is* their fault we didn't graduate in February when we were meant to. It *is* their fault we don't get proper onsite barracks and have to travel in on a bus covered in bloody edelweiss whilst pretending to be frigging basketball players. It *is* their fault that we don't have uniforms and that Jackie had to pay for our wings and that our graduation isn't counted as "essential". *All* of that is their fault, Lili.

'All we wanted was to stand up and help – to use our skills for our country, like the girls in the ATA over in England. I thought America prided itself on equality and freedom and a chance for all, but that's bullshit when it comes to women, isn't it? At every turn they've put petty obstacles in our way and I, for one, have had enough. Forget their stupid training, forget their poxy graduation, forget going up into the skies and risking our lives to help the men do the "proper job". It's not fair and we shouldn't put up with it.'

Ginny heard a slow clap, growing in volume and enthusiasm, and looked up to see the others standing around.

'Hear, hear, Virginia,' Marion said. 'If they don't value us, why should we put ourselves at risk for them?'

'Let them fly their own planes,' Thelma agreed. 'We'll go back to our pinnies and our kitchens and see if that helps them win this damned war.'

Others threw their anger into the mix and the volume around the plane grew, until Dedie fought her way into the middle.

'Ladies, please. I'm so, so sorry. I feel your anger, really I do. The way you're being treated is wrong but we have to rise above that.'

'Why do we?' Marylou demanded.

'Because we're better than them. I've been so proud of how you've all got on with this. No one else with such advanced skills would be treated in such a shabby fashion and you're right, Virginia, it's not fair. But giving up only lets them win – only tells them that women are as weak as they foolishly imagine. Do you want to give them that satisfaction?'

Ginny groaned.

'Of course not, Dedie, but there's only so much we can be expected to take.'

'And this is the last of it. I'll talk to Jackie. We *will* see you honoured, I promise you. *You* will see yourselves honoured by doing a hard job with all the skill that I know you have.'

The girls were looking at each other and nodding reluctantly, but it was all very well for them. They would see their loved ones at some point in the next few months, but Charles was only here for ten days and then he'd be back over the Atlantic, and her chance to be in his arms would be lost for who knew how long. She wasn't sure she could bear it.

'I want *this* graduation,' she said, but her voice was too small to be heard over the hubbub.

'So, ladies,' Dedie was asking, 'can we put this behind us and get up there and fly?'

It was all any of them really wanted, and one by one the girls peeled off in pairs to get into their airplanes until only Ginny and Lili were left.

'Virginia?' Dedie asked uncertainly.

'Her fiancé is meant to be coming,' Ginny heard Lili say to the kindly older lady. 'From England.'

'Ah. That's hard.' Dedie leaned down and put a hand on Ginny's knee. 'Let me see what we can do. Is he military?'

Ginny looked at her.

'Yes.'

'Then maybe – just maybe – we can sort something out. I'll do my best, I promise.'

'Thank you,' Lili said.

Ginny slowly got up. Already she felt foolish. What had she always said to herself about falling in love? It made you weak, and sure enough here she was now, crying like a baby beneath the wings of the plane she should be flying into the Texan skies. She grabbed at Dedie's arm.

'It doesn't matter. There's no reason why I should get special treatment.'

'But—'

'I'm sure everyone has people they'd like to have here.'

'But England—'

'Is really no different. Lili's father can't come from Hawaii and we don't see her whining about it, do we? Forget it. It's fine. I'm here to do a job, not to show off.'

'Virginia, I really think—'

'Now, if you don't mind, I have a plane to fly. Coming, Lili?'

'Coming, Ginny, but I also think—'

'Now!'

She swung herself out from under the wing and straight up to the cockpit. She had no idea if this AT-6 was her allocated aircraft today but it was as good as any, and she checked wordlessly over the controls as she waited for Lili to climb in front. Her friend's neat back was unusually hunched and her head low as she settled into her seat.

'Ginny, are you sure you're up to this?'

'Why? Because I'm a woman? A weak, emotional woman?'

'No! Because you're a human being who's upset – rightfully upset.'

'I can fly, Lilinoe. If you don't want to come with me, that's up to you.'

Lili spun round and looked at her.

'Of course I'll come with you, Gin. We fly together, remember?'

Ginny closed her eyes a moment, then stood up and reached out a hand to clasp Lili's.

'I remember. Come on – let's go tow a target.'

They taxied out onto the runway. It was a perfect day for flying, with the skies clear, the sun high and barely a breath of wind. The others were heading up, their crafts easing into the air like a flock of birds, and Ginny set her eyes on the tarmac ahead. Two men came to fix the target to the tail – a fabric sleeve on a cable that would trail many feet behind them for the men on the ground to practise shooting at. Once it was firmly secured, they waved her into place and she revved the engine down the runway. Welcome exhilaration shuddered through her body and she pushed the throttle hard, pulling back on the stick to send them soaring upwards at speed.

'Ginny – steady!' Lili called from in front of her, but her words were whipped away on the slipstream.

Ginny pushed the plane out over the Texan plains, circling in behind the others to take her turn at passing the anti-aircraft guns set up at the end of the base.

'Let's see what you've got,' she muttered to the team below – the team of men, in their lovely matching uniforms with their smart mess hall, their onsite toilets, and their grand graduation ceremonies. 'Let's see if you can outsmart me.'

'Shall I take this?' Lili called, as the plane in front of them headed off and Ginny circled them round to get into place for their own turn. 'I could do with the practice.'

Ginny barely heard her and certainly had no intention of handing over the controls. Her blood was pumping hard around her body, her skin was itching, and she had to have something to push all this excess energy into.

'Hold on, Lili,' she shouted, 'we're going low.'

'No! Ginny, no – this isn't a Hurricane. It's not good at low altitudes. Remember what Garrett said the other day about the wing wobble. Go high, Ginny – go high. Please!'

But Ginny wasn't listening. She knew she could handle this plane and she pushed the stick forward, taking it into a dive as they approached the guns. They wouldn't get her. Not here, not today.

'Ginny!' Lili called again, her voice high-pitched with fear, but Ginny was focused on the runway, taking the plane lower and lower.

She could see the men fighting to adjust the gun and smiled at their pathetic manoeuvrings. The plane was starting to judder but she knew she could pull it back, just as she'd pulled back the Cub that time with Will out on Oahu, before the Japanese had come and her world had been looped in on itself. She could feel her own power in the stick and threw everything into it, channelling her anger, frustration and swirling love into the dive.

'Ginny – pull up, now!'

The panic in Lili's voice finally pierced the fog in Ginny's brain. The runway was coming up fast and the AT-6 was a big plane. She shook her head to clear it and pulled back on the stick. The plane didn't budge. Bracing herself against the front plate, she fought it with all she had. The air was rushing past her now, the men scattering as she hurtled towards them.

'Come on,' she said urgently to the plane. 'Work with me.'

She twisted the stick slightly, as they'd been taught, and felt the plane respond at last. It was pulling up just in time and she coaxed it upwards. The belly almost scraped the tarmac and the wings shook but they were climbing. She could feel sweat dripping down her brow and stinging in the corner of her eyes. Through the salty mist she pictured that poor plane spinning downwards into Pearl Harbor a year ago, holes across its tail.

'Ginny, the trees!'

Ginny wiped an arm hastily across her eyes to see, but she was too late. The AT-6 had scraped itself off the runway, but with the target cable trailing helplessly behind them it wasn't gaining height fast enough to clear the clutch of tall cedars just beyond the airfield. Frantically Ginny banked to the left, hoping to dodge to the side of them, but the plane was heavy and her muscles were already on fire, and just as she thought she'd made it, the right wing clipped the uppermost branches and tipped them, at full speed, into the canopy.

All she heard, as she fought with the controls, was Lili's long, terrified scream, and then they upended, crashing through the canopy and hitting the ground with a hideous screech of metal and a violent jerk that sent Ginny flying from her cockpit into the branches. She hung there like a rag doll, caught on her belt, before it snapped and she fell to the ground. Her head bumped but she pulled herself up, and there before her was the crumpled front end of the plane, still holding her dearest friend as the acrid smell of fuel filled the air.

Chapter Twenty-Eight

Friday 15 March

Robyn sat in the Peace Garden at the heart of the Queen's Medical Center and stared at the letter. The words were written in her grandmother's familiar looping hand but formed such hard, sad facts. This, then, was the accident that Granny Ginny had sought to keep from them, and now Robyn could totally see why.

It was all so understandable. Ginny had been through such a lot. She'd clearly still been raw with grief for her brother, and the casual attitude of the American military to those brave women fighting to be allowed to serve was shocking. Even so, to take out a muscular military plane and try to fly stunts with it had been reckless to the point of insanity.

'Do you think Granny Ginny was a bit mad?' she asked Ashleigh in a low voice.

Her sister had also been staring at the letter, but now she looked at Robyn.

'I don't think the explanation is that easy. She wasn't mad, just angry and hurt and horribly impatient.' She kicked a foot against the wheel of her chair. 'Sound familiar?'

Robyn took her hand.

'Yes. It sounds like both of us. You've just had more to be angry about than me over the last few years.'

Ashleigh sighed.

'It was my own fault though, at least in as much as this hideous accident was Granny Ginny's fault.'

'How could it be?'

Ashleigh gave a hoarse laugh.

'I cycled into a stationary car, sis. Stationary, as in not moving.'

'I know what stationary means, thank you, Ashleigh, but the conditions were awful.'

'They were, and maybe we shouldn't have been out in them, but there was a group of five of us and no one else crashed. It was me. I'd mucked up a hill climb not long before – got my pacing wrong and run out of gas, so one of the others overtook me at the top – and I was fuming. It was all I could think about. The fog in the air wasn't a patch on the fog in my mind.'

She kicked off her sandal and reached a toe out to dip it into the fountain before them. She was deep in thought and Robyn sat in silence, willing her on.

'Everything that Granny Ginny says in that letter rings a huge bell with me. That idea of emotions like a propeller inside you – I get that. And not just from recent times, though God knows that propeller has turned pretty often since the accident. I never quite knew how to regulate what I was feeling, save to pound it out on the road. I loved cycling, Robyn. I loved it because I was good at it and because I wanted to do something special with it, but I also loved it because it took me out of myself. Without it these last years, I've had to face up to who I am and it hasn't been pretty.'

'Oh, Ash. You—'

'Don't soft-soap me. I've been a pain in the arse most of the time. Having a life-changing accident like that is meant to make you rethink your priorities, isn't it? It's meant to make you value family and friends and community. It's meant to give you a kick to do charity stuff and support others in a similar situation. That's how *good* people react. Me – it just made me even more selfish.'

Robyn shook her head.

'I don't see why people who are already dealing with tough stuff should have to be kinder and more generous than people who aren't.'

'Me neither, but that's usually the way it is. I've met some amazing people in hospital over the years.' She looked around the little garden and then pointed to a plaque in the middle. 'See – case in point. "This garden was made possible by the generous fundraising of leukaemia sufferer Maisie Thomas. Rest in Peace, Maisie." This is typical. Lovely Maisie spent her last years raising money to create this garden for others to have an escape from the relentless sterile wards when they were stuck in hospital. How wonderful is that?'

Robyn bent to read the plaque and saw the dates below it: 1/7/2005–8/1/2017.

'She was only twelve when she died.'

'Exactly! Only twelve years old and twice as valuable as me at twenty-six.'

'No!' Robyn spun round to her sister. 'That's not true, Ash. You mustn't say that. No one is more valuable than you – not to me at least.'

'Really?'

'Of course, you idiot. It's always been you and me. When Mum and Dad were off saving the world, it was you and me. When Granny Ginny was out socialising, it was you and me. Fighting or giggling, it was always you and me. We've done every damned treasure hunt life threw at us together, and no one could ever replace you. And d'you know what, Ash? I don't want you all virtuous and charitable. That would be weird. We should definitely back charities but there are more ways than just raising cash. Make a good life, make a career – give them your money, your support, your *name*.'

'I don't have a name, Robyn. I gave up the chance to have a name when I pedalled myself into an angry fog and straight into the back of a car.'

'But now you might have a new way. I saw you on the track. You were stupid, yes, but you have something. I saw it in Dylan's eyes – he was so excited. He really thinks there's something special in you.'

'You reckon?'

Ashleigh looked suddenly, ridiculously shy.

'Definitely. Why do you think he's falling over himself to get you a racing chair?'

'Well…'

'And offering you extra training sessions.'

'Robyn…'

'And getting you entered into the competition tomorrow when entries have been officially closed for well over a week.'

'Have they?'

'Yes! They never usually make exceptions so they must be keen to see what you can do. America has an amazing para team, Ashleigh – maybe you could be part of it?'

'America?' They looked at each other. 'What are you saying?'

Robyn flushed.

'I don't know. That is, I'm not sure yet. But you seem good out here, Ash. And really, what is there to go back to England for? Mum and Dad are off building bridges in China, and you can't kick around in Granny's house by yourself working in that backstreet lab.'

'That lab does very good work.'

'I don't doubt it, but you're just a technician and you're worth more than that. Maybe you should think about going back to uni, getting a degree, training…'

'Here? Live with you?'

'Maybe not *that*,' Robyn spluttered, then caught herself. 'That is, not in my current flat. There's definitely not enough room. But if we sell Granny Ginny's house and—'

'Stop!' Ashleigh laughed. 'It's fine. I don't want to live with you either. We'd drive each other nuts. But living close… Maybe that would be nice.'

Robyn hugged her.

'Look at us, almost getting on. Is this what Granny Ginny intended when she sent us on this crazy treasure hunt?'

'Most likely. I was thinking about summers when we were kids the other night, and I reckon the treasure hunts always came after we'd had a big fight. She did them to force us to work as a team again. Amateur psychology or what?'

'It worked though, right? And I guess it's working again.' Robyn looked around the little garden, designed to ease the suffering of so many broken people, and felt regret tug at her heart. 'I'm sorry I went away, Ash.'

'I told you to.'

'I know, but maybe you were wrong. Maybe I shouldn't have listened.'

'Oh, you definitely should. Selfish cow that I am, even I would have hated cutting off your hopes and dreams as well as my own. I wanted you to go. I wanted you to take the scholarship.'

'Which I gave up after the first year.'

Ashleigh stared deep into the fountain's gentle flow.

'I was mad at that,' she said, more to the water than to Robyn. 'I was *really* mad. I couldn't believe you had that chance – the chance I wanted – and you were giving it up.'

'I know. I'm sorry. You were right, Ashleigh. It was cowardly and—'

'God, will you stop beating yourself up! I was *not* right. I hadn't a clue what was going on in your life because – guess what – you might have been avoiding me, but I was sure as hell avoiding you. I never asked you about it once, did I?'

'Well… no.'

'And maybe, like Granny said in the letter, the brave choice was actually giving up – knowing your limits and when you've come to them.'

'You don't really think that, Ash.'

Ashleigh looked up at her and smiled.

'I don't really think that for me, because I'm an idiot who will always push to the limits and, it turns out, beyond. But I'm not saying that's the right way to be. And you know what, Robyn, seeing you here – your life, your work, the track – I've realised what's really brave.'

'You have?'

'I have. What's really brave is carrying on hurdling, not for glory or acclaim, but just because you love it. I was really rude about you and your "loser" group when I first came, and I'm sorry. They're a great lot and I'm… I'm proud of you. What? Don't stare at me like that. I am.'

Robyn flung her arms around her, ignoring her spluttered protests as she hugged her tight.

'Thank you, Ash, that means a lot.'

'Yes, well, good. Now, can you stop gushing – this is meant to be a Peace Garden.'

Robyn giggled.

'You're an idiot, Ashleigh Harris.'

'But you love me.'

''Fraid so. Shall we read the rest of this letter?'

'About the other woman who pushed herself to the limit and beyond?'

Robyn sucked in a deep breath.

'I wish she could have told us.'

Ashleigh patted the seat next to her and rescued the letter from down the side of her chair.

'She's telling us now, sis. Let's read.'

Chapter Twenty-Nine

9 July 1943

Ginny looked down onto the blue water surrounding Oahu and felt her stomach clench. She'd dreamed of being back here when she'd been stuck in the damp of England and the fog of Texas but not like this, never like this.

She looked over to Lilinoe, lying in the seat next to her, a blanket over what had once been her bouncy young legs, and hated herself all over again. Every day, every hour, she felt fresh waves of self-loathing at what her selfish anger had done to the best friend she'd ever had. At times, it had only been having to stay strong enough to get Lilinoe home that had stopped her wanting herself dead. Now she was almost there, but the sight of the beautiful place where she'd first met her friend and carelessly lured her into the skies was not the consolation it should have been.

'Lili.' She gently touched her shoulder to wake her. 'Lili, we're almost here, we're almost home.'

Lilinoe gave a little groan and Ginny looked anxiously to the nurse on her other side, who immediately took out her bag to find the morphine that had got the patient through the gruelling journey. Ginny was paying for her out of her own funds, as well as for the flight and the best possible care once they were back on Oahu, but it was far too little. All the money in the world couldn't give Lili her legs back, and sometimes Ginny feared she was only making things worse.

Her nights were haunted with the image of the plane, its nose crushed into the unforgiving ground and Lili crushed with it. She'd been up from her own fall instantly, trying to pull her friend out of the cockpit before it caught fire. Poor Lili had still been conscious and had cried for her father as Ginny had wrestled to free her legs from the metal clawing at them. Others had been there in moments, dragging pots of sawdust and fire extinguishers, and they'd prised Ginny away so they could get to Lili with giant cutters. They'd got her out with blessed speed, but the minute Ginny had seen the mess of bone and flesh that had once been her lower legs, she'd known that even if poor, dear Lili survived these horrors, she'd never walk again – and that it was all her fault.

If only she'd been the one in the front. If only her foolishness had crushed her own legs. If only she'd listened to Lili and let her take the pass instead of insisting on using the target practice for her own, self-centred frustrations at not being able to see Charles. Love, you see – it ruined everything.

She hadn't seen Charles, hadn't been able to bear it. Someone else – Dedie, she assumed – had told him about the accident, and he'd come to the hospital in Houston where Ginny had spent her days and nights prowling up and down the corridor outside Lili's emergency ward. She'd refused to go down and see him. She'd cried herself to sleep time and again on those hard hospital chairs, longing to feel his arms around her, but there'd been no way she was going to allow herself that luxury and, in the end, he'd gone back to England. Good. When she had time, she'd send him back his beautiful ring. He was better off out of her life; she'd only wreck it, as she'd wrecked Lilinoe's.

The plane was touching down now, with a distinct skew to the left that some part of Ginny's brain registered as a lack of pilot skill. She dismissed the thought instantly; she was not in a position to criticise anyone else's flying. No one had been able to look at her after the accident – not Marion, not Marylou, not even down-to-earth Thelma. They'd all been horrified at how far she'd gone and they'd been right.

She'd never even gone back to the base and had only read about the graduation ceremony in the papers afterwards. It all seemed to have gone well. Jacqueline had made it and most people's families too. The travel ban had been circumventable after all; the ultimate, dark irony. Ginny had looked at the picture of her comrades with their silver wings and felt horribly detached from the women with whom she'd spent so many months. They were all off around the US now, doing their jobs, but for Ginny it was as if those bases didn't exist, as if the war itself didn't exist. Her world had closed down to a hospital bed and one brave woman's fight for survival.

The morphine had at least made Lili too drowsy to truly register the battle to get her off the plane and onto a stretcher for the trip in a private ambulance to the Queen's Hospital in downtown Honolulu. Ginny had booked her a private room in which to rehabilitate, but it would be a slow process.

Lili herself had been amazing. There'd been a lot of tears at first, of course, but never anger. She'd spoken to Ginny calmly and even kindly. Not once had she pushed her away, or yelled at her, or told her she'd been wrong. That almost made it worse, and as they stepped out of the ambulance at the hospital entrance and Ginny saw a small, dark-eyed man come rushing forward, she braced herself to finally receive the anger she knew she deserved.

Kalani, however, did not even register her. His tear-filled eyes were all for his daughter and he ran to hold her hand, saying her name over and over and covering her face in kisses. Ginny caught a ghost of a smile cross Lili's features and then the nurses were pushing her inside, Kalani still attached to her hand, and she was alone in the lobby.

'Can I help you?' someone asked kindly, but Ginny shook her head; no one could help her now.

*

Hours later, she dared to creep up to Lilinoe's room and hovered in the doorway, wanting to see she was as comfortable as possible. Her friend was asleep, her pretty face lit up by a chink of moonlight coming in through the plain hospital curtains, and for a moment she looked so normal that Ginny's breath was taken away. But then she glanced to the empty space where the blanket fell flat at her knees and the sweet moment passed.

'You!' Kalani's voice was harsh. Ginny bowed her head. 'How dare you come here?'

She looked up at him.

'I'm sorry. I just had to see she was comfortable.'

'Comfortable?!' He gave a bitter snort. 'How can she ever, ever be comfortable? She's mutilated. Her poor legs are ruined and her whole life with them.'

Lili stirred in the bed and made a little moan of protest, but Ginny couldn't take her eyes away from Kalani's red-rimmed ones.

'I know. I did it. It was my fault. I was angry and I was impetuous and I overestimated my own skill. Lili told me. She told me not to do it. She told me to let her take the controls but I didn't listen. She's a far, far better pilot than me.'

'Was,' Kalani choked.

'Was,' Ginny agreed.

Again Lili squeaked in protest. Kalani rushed to her.

'What's up, my sweet? Is something hurting?'

'Yes,' Lili gasped. 'You two arguing is hurting.'

They looked at each other, then back to Lili.

'I'm sorry,' Ginny said, 'it's my fault. Your father is angry with me and he's right to be. I'll leave you now. I'll be back. If you want me. I'll be back to see what I can do to help, but if there's nothing then I'll stay away. Whatever you want, Lili, that's what I'll do.'

Lili put out a hand and reached for Ginny's fingers.

'I want you to stop blaming yourself.'

Ginny shook her head.

'That I can never do.' She looked to Kalani. 'I'll find myself somewhere else to live.'

'I think that's best.'

'Father, please…' Lili begged and he turned back to her, leaving Ginny to slink away into the over-generous warmth of an Oahu night.

She crept to Lili's house alone, past Kau Kau Korner, past the Royal Hawaiian, past Pearl Harbor, now back up in full action. She let herself in with the key hidden beneath the steps, gathered the few belongings she'd stored there when they'd gone to England, and made for the door. At the last minute she paused to look back into the little house where she'd been so happy, and her legs buckled. Hawaii had seemed like paradise on earth when she'd first arrived, but now, with Jack dead and Lili broken, it was a ridiculously beautiful hell. Closing the door quietly behind her, she hefted her bags onto her back and made for the dingiest, least comfortable hotel room she could find.

Ginny drifted through the weeks on a fog of misery far thicker than anything the Houston marshes had ever thrown at her. Lili, bless her ever-kind heart, still insisted on seeing her, so she scheduled her visits to cover the times when Kalani had to go to work and tried her best to put on a positive face for her friend. It was hard but at least some progress was being made. Dr Palakiko, an intelligent man with a kind face and a seemingly endless pool of corny jokes, was confident of being able to fit prosthetics, and Ginny had promised she would pay for the very best ones available.

'What about donor legs?' she asked him one day.

He squinted at her.

'Donor legs?'

'*My* legs,' Ginny explained, pointing to her beautifully working limbs. 'Can I give Lili my legs?'

He laughed, then, seeing her face, swiftly stopped himself and put a soft hand on her arm.

'It's kind of you to think of it, Virginia, but no, that's not possible. Sorry.'

'It's not kind. I drove her into the ground and crushed her legs; it's only right she should have mine.'

He nodded slowly.

'Right, perhaps, but not possible.'

She appreciated his honesty but it did little to make her feel any better. Joe, Eddie, Dagne, Will and Helen all came to visit regularly, and Lili opened up like a flower with her old friends around her, chattering away as if they were on a cocktail lawn once more and not stuck in a sterile hospital ward. They were lovely to Ginny too, but she found that almost harder than criticism.

'I don't deserve all this kindness,' she said to Joe and Eddie one night, when they dropped by on their way home from the naval offices to find Lili already asleep.

Joe took her hand.

'Remember Pearl Harbor?'

'Joe! How could I ever forget? It was the worst day of my life – until the crash, at least.'

'And it was preventable. If I'd done my job better, we would have known they were coming.'

'It was an impossibly hard job.'

'As is flying a plane.'

'Not really, it—'

He cut firmly across her.

'If I'd done my job better,' he repeated, nudging his glasses up his nose, 'we would have known they were coming. It's the same. I'll beat myself up about it until the day I die, but that doesn't help anyone. Tracking the Japs to Midway, that helped. Locating Admiral Yamamoto on the Solomon Islands, that helped too. It's not about what happened, it's about what you do next.'

He had a point, and Ginny battled to pull herself out of her stupid fog and get on with something positive. With Dr Palakiko's help, she researched the prosthetics available, seeking out the ones with the most pliable wood and the softest leather to cushion the still-raw scars below Lili's knees. Lili was full of how brilliant they were going to be and, sitting at the foot of her bed one afternoon, watching her sleep, Ginny just prayed she was right.

'She's got her hopes up so high,' she said to Dr Palakiko when he came in to check on her.

He looked down on her with a soft smile.

'She's an amazing woman. So positive.'

'She's always been like that.'

'But still, to stay that way after such a horrible accident is remarkable.'

'It wasn't an accident, doctor.'

He turned to Ginny.

'Did you mean to do it?'

'No, of course not.'

'Then it was an accident.'

She gripped her clutch bag tightly in her lap, wishing she could somehow use it to turn back time.

'A preventable one,' she growled.

'Most are. There will always be fifty if-onlys for every bad outcome. And OK, you misjudged the dive but you have to get over it, for Lili's sake. The last thing she needs is to be looking back. It's the future that matters now.'

Ginny looked at him and nodded.

'You're right but, doctor, what sort of a future can she have?'

He laughed at that.

'They're only legs, Virginia. It's not her mind, it's not the rest of her body, it's not her heart. She can still love, and isn't that the most important thing of all?'

'No,' Ginny said shortly, then spotted the way Dr Palakiko was looking at her friend and gaped. 'Do you mean…?'

'I don't mean anything,' he said hastily, colouring in a way that made Ginny smile for the first time since she'd got off that stupid Tyrolean bus back in April to Garret's dreadful announcement that the girls' families would be unable to travel to their graduation. 'Oh, look, you have a visitor.'

The relief in his voice was still amusing her as she turned and saw the neat, smart, glamorous woman tapping down the corridor towards them. Her stomach turned over.

'Jackie?'

Jacqueline Cochran came up and stuck out her hand in a way that brooked no refusal.

'Virginia Martin, good to see you.'

'Is it?'

'Of course. I'm always pleased to see my pilots.'

'I'm not—'

'And where is Lilinoe?' Ginny stood aside and Jackie went straight up to the bed. 'Poor girl. I'm told she's making very good progress.'

'Considering.'

'Yes.' Jacqueline spun round and eyeballed Ginny. 'We all make mistakes, Virginia.'

'We don't usually break our friends, though.'

'Cut the self-pity. It's helping no one, right, doctor?'

'I was just saying something similar,' Dr Palakiko managed.

Ginny felt something dangerously familiar prickle at her skin. Was that anger? She fought it with all she had.

'It's not self-pity, Jackie, it's responsibility.'

'And I see you're stepping up to that admirably. You're here, aren't you, caring for her? Watching out for her?'

'Of course.'

'Good.' Lili's eyelids fluttered and Jacqueline was straight back to her. 'Lilinoe, my dear, how are you?'

Lilinoe looked at Jacqueline, blinked three times, then cleared her throat.

'Not too bad, thank you, Mrs Cochran.'

'Jackie, dear, please. We're all equals here. I came to bring you something very special.'

Lili tried to shuffle herself up on her pillows and Ginny rushed to help. They both looked curiously at Jacqueline, who opened a very smart handbag and took out a small box. She clicked it open to reveal two pairs of beautiful silver wings with 'W-1' engraved in the centre, marking them out as part of the first ever women's class.

'Our wings,' Lili gasped.

'Very well deserved, too. May I?'

Jacqueline gestured to the lapel of Lili's striped cotton pyjamas and she nodded keenly. Ginny watched as the great aviatrix bent over and tenderly fastened them on. Lili beamed and touched her fingers wonderingly to the smart brooch but all Ginny could see was the propeller of the tow-plane, spinning manically as she battled to lift it up over the cedars.

'Virginia?' Jacqueline asked, turning to her with the second brooch, but Ginny put up her hands to ward it off.

'No! No way. I don't deserve those. I'm not a pilot any more.'

'Rubbish,' Jacqueline said crisply. 'Commander Garrett says you're one of the finest pilots he's ever had train beneath him and, as I'm sure you know, he's not a man to offer praise readily.'

Ginny sucked in her breath, stunned.

'He said that?'

'Not a word of lie. He said it to me direct. Passed on his good wishes to you both.'

Ginny felt a little nudge in her back and turned to see Lili nodding at her.

'See, Ginny. I told you. One little mistake doesn't change things.'

'It wasn't a *little* mistake!'

Lili put up her hands.

'OK, smart-arse, one huge mistake doesn't change things.'

Ginny felt tears spring to her eyes. It was so kind of her to say that, so kind of them both to reach out to her, but it didn't make any difference. What would Jack have said, she'd asked herself time and again over these last dark months, and she knew the answer. She could remember it from his own lips. That day when she'd taken Will Dauth out to impress his wife with stunts and nearly killed them both, he'd leaned in and said, *I told you not to do anything stupid.* But she had – she'd done something very, very stupid and she shouldn't be allowed to risk it ever again.

'Thank you, Jackie,' she said as calmly as she could manage. 'It's very kind of you to come all this way. I will treasure these wings but I don't want to wear them.'

Jacqueline looked at her for a long minute, then reached out and pressed them into her hand. Ginny turned them in her fingers for a moment or two, loving the tempting feel of them, then set them down on the table by Lili's bed.

'I can't fly again,' she said firmly.

'You can, you—'

'I can't fly again because, you see, Lili and I, we fly together. Now Lili can't fly, so I won't fly either.'

Jacqueline gave a sad nod but at her side, Lili reached out a hand for Dr Palakiko and said quietly, 'We'll see about that.'

Chapter Thirty

Friday 15 March

Robyn and Ashleigh looked at each other in the increasingly dim light of the Peace Garden.

'Poor Granny Ginny,' Robyn said. 'How much she hated herself.'

Ashleigh nodded.

'I can see why. At least I only wrecked my own life, not someone else's. That would definitely have been worse.'

The door to the garden suddenly clicked open and Dr Tideswell came tumbling through.

'So glad you're still here, ladies. Apologies I've been so long.'

They looked up at him, dazed.

'Have you?' Robyn asked.

He chuckled.

'You've had some good reading to keep you busy.'

'Not *good* as such.'

'Perhaps not, but striking.' He sank onto the bench opposite. 'I knew Dr Frank Palakiko. He was my mentor when I was a young houseman. A wonderful doctor – calm, kind and so knowledgeable. He became quite the expert in prosthetics, and his clinics were cutting edge in the seventies when new plastics were making so much difference. Working with him was thrilling, I can tell you. And with Lilinoe too.'

'You knew her?'

'Oh yes. She was in the hospital all the time. She qualified as a nurse after the war and worked as Dr Palakiko's assistant right up until he retired.'

'His assistant?' Ashleigh asked, disappointed.

Dr Tideswell smiled.

'His much-valued assistant and his wife. Such a team they were. There's a lab dedicated to them here in the hospital – the Palakiko Prosthetics Research laboratory. I can show you, if you'd like?'

'Please,' Ashleigh agreed eagerly.

He smiled at her.

'We're doing some very interesting work at the moment on prosthetic attachments to help non-functioning limbs.'

Ashleigh stared.

'You are? Need any guinea pigs?'

He smiled even more broadly.

'Always. Let me tell you a little more…'

He sat down next to Ashleigh, already gabbling away about straps and sensory implants. Robyn tried to concentrate but it was clear they didn't need her in this conversation, and her eyes drifted back to the final part of the letter. She read on eagerly until, letter finished, she sat back and stared into the fountain, trying to take everything in.

She thought of the way Granny Ginny had described her emotions as being like a propeller. Ashleigh had said she understood that, and right now Robyn knew exactly what she meant too. It was as if everything that had happened over the last month was swirling round and round inside her: seeing Granny Ginny so frail; her telling them about the crazy treasure hunt and the secret at its heart; getting Ashleigh out here to Oahu; tracking down the past; and facing up to a few issues in the present as well.

She and Ashleigh were, at least, in a good place together, but Lord knew what the future would bring. It would be lovely to have her sister closer, living with her on this beautiful island, but what if she and Zak got serious? Could Robyn bear that? She'd be like that sweet but unbearably tragic man in *Love Actually* who's in love with his best friend's wife. She pictured Zak as Keira Knightley to lighten herself up a little, but the handsome reality of him kept intruding. It wasn't just his athletic body – though that was pretty damned attractive – but his warm smile that reached right up into his lovely brown eyes and made you feel as if you were lighting up his world, as if… Not for the first time, she cursed herself for not coming to this realisation sooner.

'Robyn? Robyn!' She snapped out of her daze to see Ashleigh looking furiously at her. 'Dr Tideswell is offering us dinner.'

'Oh. How kind. Sorry. I was just… thinking.'

'I imagine there's been rather a lot of this with your grandmother's mad treasure hunt,' the doctor said kindly. 'Are you hungry?'

Was she? Robyn wasn't sure but thankfully Ashleigh took charge.

'Would you mind very much, Dr Tideswell, if we took you up on that another day? You see, we're racing tomorrow so we probably ought to get home and rest up.'

'Racing?' he said. 'Both of you?'

'Both of us,' Ashleigh confirmed proudly.

'Your grandmother would be delighted, and of course we can postpone. Good luck to you both. I'm sure she'll be with you in spirit.'

Robyn looked at him and managed a small smile.

'God, I hope so,' she said, the propeller churning harder in her stomach. 'I, for one, am going to need all the help I can get.'

Saturday 16 March

Robyn stood at the entrance to the athletics stadium feeling as if her feet were rooted to the tarmac. Another dream-ridden night's sleep had not improved her nerves, and she clutched tighter at the handles of Ashleigh's wheelchair as she took in the bustle of the competition, and sought for inner strength.

'Ready for this, Ash?'

'Nope!'

Robyn went round to face her sister and saw she looked as white as Robyn herself felt. She squeezed her hand.

'You should read the last bit of Granny's letter,' she suggested, taking it out of her bag and handing it over. Ashleigh shoved it back at her as if she'd just put a spitting cat in her lap.

'Why on earth would I do that now?'

'It might help.'

Ashleigh snorted.

'Doesn't look as if it's helped you.'

There was no comeback on that one, but now Zak was running over. Robyn's heart skipped a beat but he was totally focused on her sister.

'Hey, Ashleigh, all set for your big debut?'

'Nervous, to be honest, Zak,' Ashleigh said, smiling up at him in a way Robyn couldn't bear right now.

She could see Dylan approaching with an empty race chair, so she knew Ashleigh would be well looked after and, shoving the letter back in her bag, she made off on a warm-up run. Her job was to focus on herself right now. It might be dangerous for Ashleigh to race unprepared, but it was even more so for her with ten hurdles to clear. She thought she heard Zak call for her to 'wait up' but he didn't need her now, and she made for the rest of the group at speed.

'Hey, guys, all set?' she chirped.

She heard herself, all bouncy and positive, and hoped that no one could see through the act.

'Hey, Rob,' Cody said tightly.

He was warming up with his usual fluid grace, but he looked tense and kept glancing over to a man standing at the side, tapping impatiently on the railings with his fingertips.

'That your dad?' Robyn asked.

He nodded.

'I'm meant to be starting my shift at Maccies in an hour, so he's here to get me there as fast as possible.'

'And to watch you race, right?'

'Guess he'll have to.'

'I'm sure he wants to, Cody.'

'Glad *you* are,' the teen shot back.

Robyn looked across to his dad and, feeling reckless, marched up to him, hand outstretched.

'Good morning. I'm Robyn Harris. I train with your son.' The man looked confused but shook her hand. 'He's very talented, you know.' She got little more than a grunt in return, but pushed on. 'Coach Tyler says he reckons he's the best kid he's ever coached.'

'What?' The man looked up, surprised out of his surliness. 'Nonsense.'

'No, it isn't. He's a natural over the barriers and his basic speed is amazing. He could be a star, sir.'

'Robyn!' Cody sidled up and tugged on her hoodie. 'Come away.'

'No. I won't. Your father deserves to know how good you are. Watch him race, sir – and then watch the scouts come calling.'

'Scouts?' the man asked, looking even more confused.

'College scouts. They'll all want him.'

'Cody can't go to college. We can't afford it.'

Robyn smiled.

'That's the point – you won't need to. It would be a sports scholarship. Your son races well and it could be the key to his future. To *all* your futures. How cool would that be?'

Cody's father blinked at her, then looked at Cody.

'Is that true, son? Could you get a scholarship?'

'Only if I'm really good.'

'Which he is,' Coach Tyler said, coming up and putting an arm around Cody's shoulders. 'But he still needs to warm up properly, so let's give him some space, shall we?'

Robyn nodded and jogged off, but not before she saw Cody's dad grab him and give him a quick hug.

'Don't worry about Maccies,' she heard him say. 'They'll wait just this once.'

Cody nodded and when he came back to join them, he was smiling. Robyn prayed it gave him the confidence he needed to perform at his best, because if he did that, the sky was the limit. The silly phrase made her think of her grandmother again, and she almost tripped over a hurdle in the first run of warm-up skips.

'Whoa there!' Zak reached out and caught her. 'You're meant to go over them.'

She laughed, then felt awkward and pulled away.

'I'm nervous.'

'Same as your sister, hey?'

She jumped.

'Does that matter?'

'What?'

'Ashleigh can look after herself, you know.'

'I know. I'm sorry, I…'

But she'd gone, taking herself off where she could stop snapping at everyone for no reason. Getting angry hadn't done Granny Ginny any good and that was a lesson she should learn too. Zak looked hurt, but so what? Let Ashleigh deal with him now. She focused hard on her warm-up, letting the familiar routines take her into a carefully controlled space. Right at this moment, nothing mattered but clearing ten hurdles as fast and as cleanly as possible, and suddenly she was itching to get on the start line.

'Robyn! Did I make it on time?'

Malie was coming running towards her, a handsome, silver-haired man just behind.

'To see me?' she asked incredulously.

'Of course. I love hurdles.'

'You do?'

'Oh, not competing in them – I'd be hopeless – but watching them, yes. This is Trey, my husband. He wanted to come and meet you too, but there's time for that later. Are you all set?'

Was she? Robyn had no idea, but they were calling Cody's race to the start, and she drew Malie and Trey to the railings and pointed out her protégé. She was used to him looking relatively small next to the older hurdlers in their group and it was good to see him against others of his own age looking far stronger. If she was a betting woman, she'd bet on him for sure – and she'd be right to.

From the moment the gun sounded, Cody was off like a whippet. He cleared the first hurdle out front and extended his lead with every one. Robyn saw Coach roaring him on from the finish line and his father, just along the railings, screaming like a banshee, his face purple with pride. She shouted out her own support as Cody cleared the last barrier and sprinted for the line to the cheers of the whole crowd. Spotting something astonishing, she looked around for Zak and saw him leaping up and down just a few people away.

'Look, Zak!'

The big finishing clock had stopped at a startling time. If it was correct, it would be an age-group record. Robyn saw Cody notice it and stand, staring, before his father rushed onto the track and, totally against regulations, grab him in a huge hug.

'Dad!' she heard him protest, but he was grinning widely and no one seemed to care. The time was ratified and called out over the tannoy as a record, and suddenly a photographer was hustling Cody up next to the clock to take his picture, and several men and women in university tracksuits were pushing their way to the gates. Scouts!

'That's amazing,' Zak said.

'Isn't it?' She hugged him, carried away by the moment, then remembered herself. 'Oh, er, sorry.'

'For what?' he asked. 'Have I done something wrong, Robyn?'

'No.'

She stepped back and he sighed.

'There you go again, pulling away from me. I *must* have done something wrong.'

'Not wrong, no. I just don't think it's appropriate, me hugging you if…'

'If what? Robyn, will you…'

Embarrassed, Robyn looked around for Ashleigh and spotted her up at the far side with the other chair racers.

'If you're with…' she started to say, but as she watched, a tall, strong, athletic young man bent over and dropped a long, slow kiss on her sister's lips. Robyn stared. She turned slowly and there was Zak, still at her side.

'What's up?' he asked.

'You're… you're here,' she stuttered.

'Where else would I be?' Dumbly, she pointed over to Ashleigh. Zak followed her finger and frowned. 'Why would I be over there?'

Robyn watched as Ashleigh's kisser reluctantly untangled himself and stood up.

'Dylan!' She looked to Zak. 'Ashleigh's with Dylan.'

'Well, yes,' he agreed. 'Didn't you know?'

'No. I thought… That is…' She drew in a deep breath and looked up into Zak's gorgeous brown eyes. 'I thought she was with you.'

'Me?!' Zak spluttered. 'Why would you think that?'

'You were always there being so nice to her.'

'Because I thought you wanted me to. I thought that it might make you, you know, like me more.'

Robyn stared up at him. How had she been so monumentally stupid? She glanced at the track, remembering how coy Ashleigh had been about Dylan the other night and how eager she'd been to train with him. It had been right there in front of her eyes but she'd been too blind to see it! Now, though, it was as clear as day. Zak was looking down at her, his gorgeous brown eyes so wonderfully uncertain, and she knew what she had to do. She'd just watched Cody go for what he wanted and now it was her turn. She squared her shoulders.

'That,' she told Zak, 'would be impossible.'

He frowned.

'What would?'

'For me to like you more. I'm mad about you already.'

'You are?'

His eyes lit up and he took a step forward, but at that moment the tannoy rang out above them: 'All senior hurdlers to the starting area, please. All senior hurdlers.'

Zak rolled his eyes. 'Looks like we're up. Perhaps we can, erm, revisit this later, but for now, shall we…?'

He held out his hand and, heart pounding with a joyous propeller of nerves, happiness and anticipation, Robyn took it and let him lead her forward.

Her race was first and as she stepped up to the start line, she worried that the sudden rush of happiness would ruin her concentration. In fact, it seemed to fizz down her legs as she settled herself in her blocks. She saw Ashleigh whizzing across to watch, Dylan at her side. She saw Cody near the finish line with his father, Malie and Trey on the railings, and Coach Tyler shouting, 'Back leg down!' Her heart thudded in her chest and she looked down the run of hurdles, steadying herself, going over her stride pattern, feeling her muscles twitch in anticipation.

'On your marks.'

She drew in a deep breath and positioned her fingers carefully behind the white line.

'Get set!'

Pushing herself up in her blocks, she tensed her legs ready and then, *bang*, the gun fired and she leaped forward, rising up into her sprint and pushing for the first barrier. Clear. Her limbs sang as she stretched out, curling over each hurdle and bringing her back leg down as fast as possible to make the push for the next one. She could sense the other racers either side of her but no one was going clear and she drove on, her muscles starting to burn, until she was safely over the last barrier and could put her head down and sprint for the line.

There was one girl ahead and pulling away. She didn't have the speed to quite catch her, but she went over the line barely a step behind and a glance at the clock told her she was bound to have done a PB. Her muscles screamed, her breath heaved out of her lungs, but her blood sang. She'd done it and done it well!

'Yay, Robyn!' she heard a voice whoop, and looked back down the track to see Ashleigh punching the air.

She put her thumbs up and saw her start to make her way down the outside of the track. The officials dismissed them and she turned to leave, but now Zak's race was being called and she hovered just outside the gate to watch. It was almost more nerve-racking than her own. The win was unlikely as there were a couple of National Squad hopefuls here, but if he could run well, he would be happy and suddenly Zak's happiness meant a lot to her – a painful lot. She thought of Granny Ginny's letters. Their grandmother had thought that love made her weak, but she'd been wrong. Love made you vulnerable, perhaps, but never weak.

Come on, Zak, she willed him as he settled into his blocks, and then the gun was sounding out and they were all pounding towards her, the hurdles clattering and the crowd roaring them on. From her position at the end, it was impossible to see how Zak was doing and she just let herself be mesmerised by the flow of his long legs and lean, muscular body over the barriers.

'Go on, Zak!'

The racers were nearly upon her now and she could see him battling it out for third place as they came off the final hurdle. His handsome face was creased in concentration and she willed him on as he dived for the line. Third!

'Yes!'

The other athletes pulled up and turned obediently towards the officials to have their numbers checked, but Zak was still running, across the track and straight into her arms.

'Sir!' she heard the official call. 'Sir, you need to come here, please.'

But Zak was lifting her into his arms and his lips were on hers, and for a long, blissful moment, she was aware of nothing but the heady joy of his kiss.

'Sir! You'll forfeit your medal if you don't come back.'

The official was most persistent and, laughing, Robyn pushed Zak back onto the track as Cody and the others from their group swamped her.

'You and Zak! We knew it! We always knew it.'

'Glad someone did,' Robyn said ruefully, and now Malie was hugging her and telling her how proud she was, and for a moment it was as if Granny Ginny were here too, watching and smiling. *Just a tiny bit more, girl, and you'd have won*, she could hear her saying, but she didn't care. Today she *had* won and nothing could mar her joy.

Nothing, that is, save the girl wheeling herself rapidly towards her.

'Well done, Rob,' Ashleigh said, but her words were hollow and her eyes dark with sudden shadows.

'What is it?' Robyn asked, grabbing her arms. 'What's wrong?'

'Nothing.'

'Rubbish. I'm your sister, you idiot – you can't fool me. What's wrong?'

Ashleigh swallowed.

'I can't do this. I can't race.'

Robyn kneeled down before her.

'When's your event?'

'Not for about an hour. But I can't—'

'Shh.' Robyn put a gentle finger on her lips. 'Come on – let's find a quiet corner.'

'Now?'

'Definitely now.'

Zak, released at last, was jogging back over, and it was one of the hardest things she'd done not to just throw herself into his arms and kiss him for the rest of the morning. Even before he reached them, however, Zak clocked that Ashleigh was troubled and waved her on, making her love him even more. What on earth had she been doing turning down the chance to be with this wonderful man? For the sake of a stupid bit of shyness, she'd wasted a whole year with him and she wasn't going to waste any more time. Right now, though, her sister needed her.

'Come on, Ash,' she said. 'You've got a letter to read.'

Chapter Thirty-One

10 September 1943

Ginny sat on a bench outside the hospital, looking up at the relentlessly cheerful palms and wishing for just one or two leaves to drop. Two years ago, in her first happy fall on Hawaii, she'd loved the fact that the only indication of the seasons had been a slight chill in the evening air, but now the changelessness of the island was grating on her. The days were relentlessly long and sunny, Lili was still in hospital, and Ginny was stuck in an endless loop of nothingness. Her skin physically itched with the frustration of doing so little. She took it as punishment for her innate impatience and tried to bear it as best she could but, oh, it was hard.

Lili, at least, was due out next week. Kalani was desperate to get her home, and there was little doubt that Dr Palakiko could be relied upon to continue his care even once it was no longer his official job. The pair were forever mooning over each other.

'I'd give up my legs time and again if they brought me Frank,' Lilinoe had said to Ginny the other day.

'Lili! You can't say that!'

'Yes, I can, because it's true. I'd never have found him if I hadn't come to the hospital.'

'You'd have found someone else.'

'I don't want someone else.'

It was all so simple in Lili's wonderfully positive world and Ginny envied her that. Frank had proposed two weeks ago, sneaking her out into the hospital grounds to get down on one knee beneath a full moon. They were getting married as soon as she was confident she could walk down the aisle on her prosthetics, and it was the one thing driving her on as she battled to get used to them. Ginny couldn't wait. On that day, she could see Lili safely into the arms of her handsome doctor. Then it would be time to kiss her goodbye and go back home to Tennessee. Her parents were worried about her, she knew. They wrote to her all the time and paid a fortune to call her when they could.

'What good are you doing there?' her mum had dared to ask her recently.

'I've no idea,' she'd told her wearily, but Lili still liked to see her and whilst that was the case, there was no way she was leaving.

Of course, once Lili got back into Kalani's house, Ginny wouldn't even be able to visit. He still hated her and she understood that; she still hated herself too. All she could do was pray that Lili would master her prosthetics, hide them beneath a beautiful white dress and release her from this paradise of a hell.

Someone else wrote to her too.

Charles's letters came even more often than her parents' and were sitting in a basket beneath her saggy bed in her dank hotel room. She refused to open them, sure that if she waited it out he would grow weary and stop writing, but she hadn't the strength to throw them away and every night they taunted her with the tantalising chance that they contained the threads of love that might just hold her together. What would Jack have told her to do, she'd asked herself so many times, but she'd lost her brother's voice along with everything else and the answers never came.

The hospital clock struck a cheery nine and Ginny looked up at it. Kalani would be off to work at Hickham Field by now so the coast would be clear to go in and see Lili, but still she sat there, watching the world go carelessly by. Even the war was progressing. Just two days ago General Eisenhower had announced that the Italians had surrendered to the Allies, and that, on top of the continued news of the German retreat from Russia, was fuelling cautious optimism. Out here in the Pacific, too, the Allies were close to recapturing New Guinea and were slowly but surely pushing the Japanese back.

It turned out that the Pearl Harbor attacks had not wreaked nearly enough damage on the mighty US to give the Japanese the chance they'd needed, and having wakened the giant, they were starting to truly feel its fury. Enough airplanes were getting to enough places to win this war without Ginny, and although her body still ached with longing whenever she heard a plane overhead, she wasn't going up there again. Her feet were firmly on the hard, dull ground.

With a sigh, she heaved herself up and made for the hospital doors, desperately trying to summon up a smile for Lili. She spotted a couple of broken-stemmed flowers in the nearest bed and bent over to pick them for her friend. They were roses and reminded Ginny overwhelmingly of the ridiculously large bouquet Charles had bought for her on her birthday back in England last year.

So vivid was the picture that for a moment she thought she heard his voice calling her name, and it was all she could do not to turn round and look for him. It came again. She frowned. Was she actually going mad? Shaking her head to try and clear it, she took the first of the steps up to the main entrance, but at that moment someone grabbed her arm and she shrieked.

'Ginny, it's me. It's Charles.'

'Charles?' Ginny stopped fighting, drew in a deep breath and looked up into the kindest, most amazingly familiar and unbelievably gorgeous eyes. 'Charles!'

Instinctively she crushed herself against him. His arms went around her, holding her so close that she felt almost as if she had stepped right into him. The passing world faded into nothingness, the white hospital seemed to cast a glow down on them, and the palm trees waved their beautifully evergreen leaves. Slowly he reached down and cupped a hand beneath her chin, tilting it so that he could place the gentlest of kisses on her lips. She responded instantly and as his kiss deepened, she groaned in too-long-forgotten pleasure, then remembered herself. She yanked away.

'What are you doing here?'

'What do you think? I came to see you, Ginny. I came to tell you that I love you and I want to be with you. I came to marry you.'

She gasped.

'You can't.'

'Why?'

'I'm not worth marrying.'

He looked deep into her eyes and gave a small shake of his head.

'That, my beautiful Virginia, is the most ridiculous nonsense I've ever heard. You made a mistake. We all do it. You can't spend the rest of your life making reparation.'

'I can.'

'You can't, darling, because it's not what anyone will want.'

Ginny thought of Lili, so happy with Frank and determined to walk on her fancy new prosthetics down the aisle to her new life with him. She thought of the rest of the women from her Houston class, now flying airplanes around America to aid the amazing progress of the Allies against the forces of evil. She thought of her parents sending her their love day after day, and of Joe and Eddie battling to fathom the enemy plans and avenge Pearl Harbor, and of Charles, somehow, miraculously, standing before her.

'How did you get here?'

He smiled.

'I've got a job in Washington. They've seconded me to the war office to help coordinate army and naval pilots and form an independent US air force, just like we have in England.'

'A job? In Washington?'

Her brain didn't seem to be working properly this morning, and she was struggling to take this all in.

'Yes, darling. An American job, in an American department. All I need now is an American wife, so will you please, Virginia Martin, do me the very great honour – again – of agreeing to marry me?'

He dropped onto one knee and she looked down at him there in front of the hospital, with all the arriving visitors staring curiously their way, and felt something strange flooding through her. If she wasn't much mistaken it was happiness, seeping back into her like warmth returning to frozen toes. Charles still loved her. He still wanted her. He was here, halfway across the world, for her. The tears spilled out of her eyes as she dropped to her own knees and grabbed his hands.

'I'm not a good person, Charles. I'm impatient and impetuous. I'm aggressive and competitive and reckless and foolish.'

He smiled.

'I know.'

'What?'

'I know you are. You're all that and so, so much more. You're brave and fierce and exciting. You're generous and spontaneous and lively and fun. You set my heart alight, Ginny, and I don't want it to ever have to be cold again. Please, please say you'll marry me.'

Ginny couldn't believe it. Charles knew who she was and he wanted her anyway – had there ever been a greater miracle?

'Yes,' she gasped. 'Yes, I'll marry you. I'd love to. Oh God, Charles, I would so, so love to.'

And then they were kissing again, clutching at each other and laughing as the elderly porter came out and asked them to 'please desist from this lewdness'.

'He's come from England,' Ginny said to him. 'He's come all the way from England.'

'Then he should know how to behave with more decorum,' came the tight reply that had them laughing even harder.

'Will you come and see Lili?' Ginny asked, suddenly shy again.

'I'd love to,' Charles said and, taking her hand firmly in his, led her up the steps past the pursed-lip porter and into the hospital.

The walls were still glaringly white, the smell still cloyingly clinical and the corridors to Lili's room still long and blank, but somehow, with Charles at her side they felt less daunting. Ginny swung into Lili's ward, then paused at the door to her room.

'She's very injured, Charles.'

'I know that, darling.'

'She's got no legs below the knee. She can't walk, she—'

'Ginny!' a voice called from inside the room. 'Stay right there.'

'Lili?'

Ginny stared as the door swung open to reveal her friend standing before her, both prosthetics fitted. She was leaning heavily on two sticks and had Frank hovering solicitously at her side, but as Ginny watched she began to walk towards her, unsteady at first but growing in confidence.

'Lili! You're doing it! You're walking!'

'I am. Get that white dress ordered.'

Ginny smiled at her.

'Make that two.'

'What?' For the first time Lili registered the man at Ginny's side. 'Charles!' She wobbled precariously but Frank was there to catch her and they took the final few steps together. 'Thank God you came,' Lili said, leaning in to kiss his cheek. 'I'm sick to death of this one moping around like she's at a permanent funeral.'

'Lili!'

Her friend shot her a cheeky grin.

'What? It's true. The last thing I need is you all sad. It's boring and it's weird and it's just not *you*.'

Ginny hugged her tight.

'I don't like me very much, doll.'

'Well try, please, because I like you, and Frank would like you given a chance, and quite clearly Charles likes you. Look!' She waved to the prosthetics strapped to her knees. 'I've got my legs back, and now I want Ginny back as well.'

'Your dad…'

'Misses you too.'

Ginny gasped as Kalani stepped out from behind the door.

'You're not at work,' she said stupidly.

'Day off. Wanted to see Lili give these new legs a try.' He looked awkwardly at Ginny. 'Thank you for paying for them, for all this.'

'Kalani, it's the very least I could do.'

He shook his head.

'Not true. A lot of people would have walked away. You could have done that. You could have run home, or gone off to fly with the others in your class. You could have turned your back on Lili and what you did to her.'

'Dad!' Lili protested, but he put up a hand.

'Virginia understands me. She doesn't want excuses.'

'I don't,' Ginny agreed. 'I really don't.'

'And I admire that. You didn't run away, you didn't hide. You've been here, supporting Lilinoe and helping her get better. I admire that and I… I'm sorry I shouted at you. Can we be friends again?'

Ginny's eyes filled with tears and she leaped forward, hugging the little Hawaiian so tightly that he squeaked in protest.

'I'd love that. Oh my God, what a day! Why are you all being so nice to me?'

Lili laughed.

'Because we love you, Gin, you idiot. So, please – can I have my crazy, fun pilot of a friend back?'

At that, though, Ginny shook her head.

'Not the pilot, Lili. Never the pilot.'

Lili looked back to Frank and then, leaning against him, put her hands on her hips.

'Well, that's a shame because you see, Ginny, it's the pilot I need.'

'What?'

'I've been talking to Jackie Cochran. Her force and Nancy Love's force have been combined now into the WASP – Women Airforce Service Pilots – and there's a place for both of us if we want it.'

'Which we don't.'

'Which we *do*. If Douglas Bader can fly without legs, then why can't I? Jackie agrees. She says she's happy to have me and I'm happy to fly – on one condition.'

Ginny stared at her.

'No. Lili, no.'

'Yes, Gin – you and me, we fly together, so if I'm going to fly again, you have to fly with me.'

Ginny's mind whirled. Jacqueline Cochran trusted her to fly and, even more importantly, so did Lilinoe. Her skin itched with a fierce longing but did she dare allow herself to take the risk? Charles leaned in, his hand tight in hers and his voice warm in her ear.

'You won't do it again, Ginny. I know you won't. You may be fierce and determined and competitive but you're no fool.'

She wanted to believe him, really she did, but could she? Dare she? Lili was walking once more, making for the cabinet beside her bed.

'Come here please, Ginny,' she instructed, and Ginny hurried forward.

Her friend was taking something from the cabinet, and Ginny gasped as she saw what it was.

'No, I can't—'

Lili placed a finger on her lips to silence her and reached gently for her lapel. Carefully, she pinned the silver wings onto it, and Ginny looked down in amazement as they glinted in the Hawaiian sun pouring through the hospital window. Right on cue, a naval plane flew past, and Ginny touched her fingers to her badge of honour and went to the window to watch its painful, beautiful path.

Her eyes filled with tears at the tantalising possibility of taking to the skies again, and then suddenly she could hear Jack's voice again, clear and kind: *You won't do anything stupid, Ginny, I know you won't.*

'I won't,' she whispered to him, and then more loudly, 'I won't.'

It would be terrifying, but if Lili could fly again so could she.

Chapter Thirty-Two

Saturday 16 March

'How did Lili do that?' Ashleigh said to Robyn, reading the last lines of the letter again. 'How did she dare fly again? It must have been so scary.'

Robyn thought about it.

'I guess, at the end of the day, *not* flying again was even scarier.'

Ashleigh looked out at the track where a four hundred-metre race was in progress. In the infield, a young man was curving himself gracefully over a high-jump bar, and further away a girl was lining up a javelin. The two sisters watched as she ran down the runway and released it to soar up into the sky and land, point first, in the green grass. The girl jumped excitedly and turned to beam at a waving mother. Another PB, it seemed.

'It's certainly hard not doing what you love,' Ashleigh said quietly.

'How long till you race?'

Her sister looked at her watch.

'Twenty minutes.'

'Shall we get you to the start then?'

Ashleigh stared down at the letter for what felt like forever, then suddenly gave a sharp nod.

'If Granny could get back up in an aeroplane, then I can manage two hundred metres of an athletics track. Let's do it!'

She spun her fancy chair round and pointed it determinedly at the top of the track. Robyn jumped up to walk alongside her.

'There's going to be lots of time to get this right, Ash, so don't feel you have to do it all immediately. Take it easy today.'

Ashleigh looked up at her and laughed.

'Take it easy? Yeah, right!'

Then she was off, spinning the wheels expertly as she shot onto the track and made her way towards the warm-up area at the far side. Robyn groaned and headed back towards Zak.

'All OK?' he asked, slotting an arm around her waist in a way that felt wonderfully natural.

'It is now. I just hope she doesn't try and do too much.'

'Oh, she will,' he said cheerfully. 'All we can do is cheer her on, right, Malie?'

'Right,' Malie agreed from his other side. 'Mum hated it if we tried to do things for her. I knew from an early age to stand back and let her go for it her own way. If she wanted help, she'd ask for it. The rest of the time, she just stumbled on through, much like the rest of us.'

Robyn smiled. She'd certainly done her fair share of stumbling recently and she nestled into Zak, daring to reach up and kiss him. His response set her body flaring but this was hardly the place.

'Can I buy you dinner later?' she asked him.

He kissed her again.

'Sounds wonderful to me.'

She could hardly wait, but now the announcer was calling the para events and nerves for her sister cut through her giddy anticipation. She looked at the track, remembering Ashleigh tumbling out of her chair only the other night. What had she been doing talking her into this race? She surely wasn't ready for it. She'd had no training or practice, learned no technique. She hadn't even been in a racing chair until yesterday, so taking part in a two hundred-metre sprint was surely madness.

'Ashleigh!' she started to shout, but Zak silenced her with another kiss and when she surfaced, her sister was on the line, her eyes focused on the track and her mouth set in a grim determination that Robyn knew all too well. 'I can't watch,' she gulped.

'Fine,' Zak said, squeezing her tight. 'I'll watch for you.'

Robyn heard the starter call them and closed her eyes. She wished with all her heart that Granny Ginny were here to see this, and then realised the ridiculousness of that when she wasn't even watching herself. The gun went and the crowd began to shout.

'Go, Ashleigh!' she heard Zak call in her ear, echoed by Malie and Trey. They sounded excited.

'Steady round the bend, Ashleigh,' came another voice behind her. Dylan. 'That's it – now go. Go, go, go!'

It was too much. Robyn forced her eyes open in time to see her sister come off the bend ahead, picking up pace all the time. Her arms were pushing madly at the little handles on the wheels and she was crouched forward in the chair, driving herself on. The others were close behind but Robyn saw the light in Ashleigh's eyes and knew, with seventy metres still to go, that none of them stood a chance of catching her sister. She just wouldn't allow it. It was how she'd been with her cycling and how, miraculously, she was again now.

'Go, Ashleigh!' she screamed. 'Go!'

There was no way her sister could hear her, but still she thrust her chair over the line to victory and the man on the tannoy excitedly announced another track record.

'Looks like today is seeing the birth of a few stars of the future, folks,' he called out. 'Just remember, you saw them here on Oahu first!'

Then Robyn was running onto the track to hug Ashleigh and it was less about winning or records, and more about doing something that made you feel so very wonderfully, happily alive.

The next day, Robyn felt considerably less alive. She woke to a pounding head and a desperate thirst, and reached blindly for the water glass she always kept on her bedside table. Her hand, however, connected with something far warmer, softer and altogether more exciting.

'Zak,' she whispered, feeling instantly better.

He was there, sleeping at her side, his arms wrapped around her, and, OK, so they were both flopped out on her sofa, still in their athletics kit and surrounded by the pizza boxes and beer bottles of last night's impromptu party, but he was here and the world felt like a wonderful place whatever the mess. It hadn't quite been the romantic meal for two they'd both envisaged at the trackside, but there was plenty of time for that. Last night had been about celebrating success for all of them – and far more besides.

'Thank God you two got together at last,' Coach Tyler had teased Robyn and Zak with rare humour. 'It was driving me mad.'

'I thought you *were* together,' Cody had said, already looking dazed after three scouts had asked him to come and talk to them about university scholarships.

'We are now,' Zak had said firmly, and that had been enough for Robyn.

Cody wasn't the only one looking at university study. Dylan had joined them, fresh from a meeting with the university athletics committee, and had offered Ashleigh a position with the para team, effect immediate. He'd also arranged a meeting with the chemistry department about picking up her studies come September, and she'd been full of it last night, firing off emails to various Oxfordshire estate agents to start the process of selling Granny Ginny's house and releasing the cash for them both to buy apartments here in Honolulu.

'Separate apartments,' Robyn had said.

'Separate,' Ashleigh had agreed.

'But close,' they'd added together.

If she remembered rightly, they'd opened the bubbly after that and the evening had really kicked off. Now, she slid out of Zak's delicious embrace and padded to the kitchen for water. Filling a glass, she stepped to the window to peek out across the roofs of the pretty city to the tantalising stretch of sand and water beyond. After being taken on a tour of what this island had meant to Granny Ginny, it meant even more to Robyn and she was excited to make it her permanent home.

She wouldn't want to say goodbye to England totally, but they had plenty of friends and relatives back there, and their mum and dad were talking about buying a flat that could be a base for them all. They'd had an embarrassingly tearful FaceTime call with them to share both their successes in the present and their plans for the future, and they were already talking about coming to visit.

'After all,' their dad had said, 'it's only a short hop round from China.'

Robyn had had to fight hard to picture the map without England in the middle, but then she'd realised how right they were. Hadn't it, after all, been the Japanese advancing down China that had threatened US territories in the Pacific back in 1941 and started off the whole chain of events?

'Water,' someone gasped, and Robyn turned from the window to see Ashleigh wheeling her way into the little kitchen looking very sorry for herself. She hastily refilled the glass and handed it to her sister, who drank it down in one. 'That's better. What did we drink last night?'

'Too much,' Robyn said ruefully. 'It was fun though.'

'Fantastic.' Ashleigh smiled, already apparently restored. 'I'm happy, Robyn. Isn't that amazing? Grumpy, miserable old me is actually happy.'

Robyn flung her arms round her.

'I'm so glad, Ash. I am too.'

'Good to see you got your act together with Zak, though you took your time!'

'I thought he was with *you*.'

Ashleigh grinned.

'I know you did. It was hilarious.'

'No?!' Robyn batted furiously at her sister's arm. 'You made me think that on purpose? You cow!'

'Yep,' Ashleigh agreed happily. 'Did the trick though, didn't it? You'd never have realised how you felt until you thought you were losing him.'

Robyn shook her head ruefully. 'I'm sure I would eventually, but I admit I'd wasted enough time already.'

'Like Granny did. I can't believe that she and Grandpa Charles nearly didn't get married.'

'Grandpa wasn't going to let that happen, thank God. They were so happy together for so long.'

Robyn thought of her grandparents who had always been such a solid, settled couple, despite their clear differences in personality. Grandpa Charles had been a calm, clever, logical man, always interested in everything anyone had to say and the perfect foil to his wife's more impetuous, explosive approach to life. Granny had been heartbroken when he'd died ten years ago. So had Robyn. Reading about their romance had been one of the biggest gifts of this strange fortnight chasing around Hawaii – and it seemed to have found them both lovely men of their own.

'It looks like Granny Ginny's wily treasure hunt has sorted us both out,' she said, and Ashleigh grinned.

'I guess so, bless her. We've not quite finished it though, have we?'

That much was true. Clue eight was still to be solved and Robyn looked around for the last letter. It was sitting on the table, half hidden beneath a pizza box and with a circular drink stain blurring some of the letters.

'Granny Ginny would approve,' Robyn said. 'Even if it's not quite a Mai Tai.'

'We'll have them tonight,' Ashleigh replied.

'Tonight?' Robyn gasped, her head pulsing at the mere thought.

'Oh, come on, sis, you'll be fine by then. You'll have to toughen up if you're going to be partying with me from now on.'

Robyn groaned and took the letter from her.

'We'll see, Ash. But for now – here's the clue:

'You were here at the start, so I'm taking you full circle.

Your grandmother, I'm afraid, was a very flawed mortal,

but I was saved by love, by friendship, and by the force

of silver-winged angels and sisters of great worth.'

'Sweet,' Ashleigh said. 'But also quite annoying. Is Granny Ginny saying that our eighth and final box is in the same place as the very first one?'

Robyn stared at her.

'At the airport with Mikala? I'll kill him!'

'Not if I get there first. Hey, Zak!' Ashleigh turned back into the living area and gave poor sleeping Zak a vigorous nudge with her foot. 'Wake up – we've got a treasure chest to find.'

'Now?' he asked, rubbing his eyes.

'After a quick cuppa,' was Ashleigh's answer.

He looked pleadingly to Robyn. 'What's a cuppa?'

'Tea,' she told him, laughing.

'I'm allowed one cup of that weird drink of yours and then we're going out?'

'Looks like it.'

He shook his head.

'You English girls are rock hard.'

'Some of us are,' Ashleigh agreed smugly. 'You put the kettle on, Rob. I'll get Dylan up.'

Dylan was no keener than Zak on a hasty exit, and in the end Robyn had to make a run for pastries to give the boys the energy to join their English girlfriends in her little Mini. She turned onto the familiar road to the airport, unable to believe it was only two weeks since she and Ashleigh had landed here and started out on the treasure hunt that they would hopefully, this morning, complete.

'Granny Ginny would be proud of us,' Ashleigh said from the passenger seat.

'And us,' Dylan said drily from the rear, where he and Zak had their long limbs crammed awkwardly into the tiny space.

Ashleigh looked back at him. 'I wish she could have met you.'

'Me too,' Dylan agreed. 'She sounds like an amazing woman. But hey, I'll take Mark Two if that's all that's on offer.'

Ashleigh stuck her tongue out at him and Robyn didn't even bother hiding her smile. It seemed that her feisty sister had met her match in Dylan and she was delighted to see it. Her eyes met Zak's in the rear-view mirror and he smiled warmly at her. He knew how much Granny Ginny had meant and how much this hunt had cost her, but it seemed, in the end, it had gained her even more. Now she was keen to get to its conclusion.

She parked up in a staff space and led the others into Departures. She'd checked the shift spreadsheet and knew Micky would be on, so was surprised to see his desk empty.

'Micky?'

'I'm not here,' a deep voice said from behind the desk.

Robyn shook her head and levered herself up on her arms to look over the desk. There, crouching down like a toddler, was Micky.

'What are you doing?'

'Hiding. I saw you come in and you looked a bit cross.'

'And you know exactly why.'

He looked up at her, a big grin on his neat little face.

'Sure do, honey.'

'You've got the last box, haven't you?'

His grin widened and he unfolded his arms to show, cradled in his lap, a small but perfectly formed treasure chest.

'Had it all along.'

'Can I have it then?'

'Only if you're still with your sister. That's what your grand-mammy said. You weren't to have it unless you were with your sister. So are you? Is Ashleigh here?'

'She certainly is,' Ashleigh called. 'And if you think Robyn is cross, you should see me!'

Micky gave a deep chuckle and uncurled, standing up and placing the chest on the desk, though he kept one hand tight upon it.

'Just doing what your grandmammy ordered, girls. Seriously though, I'm glad you've made it together – and with some fine-looking escorts too. That would have pleased her no end.'

'How do you know?' Robyn asked.

'Oh, I had a good few chats with Virginia. These shifts can be long, you know, especially at night, and she was a dab hand on FaceTime. She said I reminded her of a Hawaiian she knew a long time back – Kalani.'

Robyn nodded.

'Lilinoe's father. He was an engineer at John Rodgers and later at Hickham Field.'

'That's right. None too pleased about what she did to his daughter either.'

'She told you about that?' both girls gasped.

'She did,' Micky agreed solemnly. 'Not at first, but in time, yes. She said I was like a priest she could confess to. I was quite chuffed at that actually. Wish my old mammy could have heard her; she'd have been dead proud.'

'But she and Kalani made up,' Robyn said, feeling a strange need to prove that she knew about Ginny's past too.

'Oh, they did, yes. She told me she always understood his anger, but even more so once she'd got kids of her own, once she saw that you'd tear every last part of your own world apart if it meant you could keep theirs intact.' He looked at Ashleigh suddenly. 'She told me that if she wanted to give Lilinoe her legs after the plane crash, she wanted to do so fifty times more for you.'

'She did?'

'Yep. She also told me that the war, with all its trials and sufferings, taught her that the most important thing to keep safe was your heart. If that's beating in the right rhythm, she said, then everything else will eventually fall into place.'

Ashleigh looked to Robyn, her eyes shining.

'She was right,' she said, reaching for her hand and squeezing it. 'She was so right.'

Micky wiped at his own eyes, then grinned again.

'Oh, and she also said she'd learned that most things could be fixed with the perfect Mai Tai.'

Ashleigh grinned back.

'She was indeed a wise woman. I guess that means there's only one place to open this last chest.'

'The Royal Hawaiian?' Robyn suggested.

'The very same. Come on, lads, Mai Tais are on us.'

'Mai Tais?' Zak went a little green. 'Now?'

'Hair of the dog,' they told him together.

He groaned and looked to Dylan.

'What have we got ourselves into?'

Dylan shook his head.

'I've got no idea, but I'm sure as hell looking forward to finding out.'

They settled themselves at the perfect table, right by the golden sands of Waikiki, and ordered Mai Tais and a large jug of water.

'To Granny Ginny!' Robyn proposed, and the others took up her toast with alacrity, though only Ashleigh, she noted, actually drank her cocktail. She smiled at her.

'And to us.'

'To us, sis! May we both fly, as Granny Ginny flew. And now – the last letter?'

Robyn nodded, but as she took out the final key to open the little box, she felt tears threaten and fumbled with the lock. She'd been keen to get to the end of the hunt, but now they were here she felt a sudden aching reluctance. Inside was Granny Ginny's final letter. Once they'd read it, she would truly be gone.

'We'll have them all to pore over whenever we want,' Ashleigh said, reading her mind. 'And our own memories of her too.'

Robyn smiled at her.

'When did you get so wise?'

'When I got close to you again? Now, open the damned chest, will you. The suspense is killing me!'

Robyn drew in a deep breath, turned the key and reached inside. There, as expected, was the last white envelope, and when she lifted it out, she saw something that made her laugh aloud. She raised the chest so that Ashleigh could see and she, too, burst out laughing.

'Peacock-blue mascara!'

'There's only one,' Robyn said.

'Then it's a good job we're going to be living nearby. Pass it!'

Ashleigh took the tube and, to the boys' amazement, lifted up her Mai Tai glass as a makeshift mirror and applied a slick of glimmering blue to her lashes. She handed it to Robyn who, feeling like a giddy teen again, did the same. Then together, eyes sparkling like the ocean before them, they unfolded their grandmother's last letter and began to read.

Chapter Thirty-Three

You made it to the end then, girls. Bet that Micky laughed and laughed. Quite a character, he is. Helped me a lot in some of the darker parts of the night, when this whole thing looked like madness and I nearly just jacked it in and went to my grave with your memories of me unsullied. But I didn't, so now you know. I hope you don't think less of me. I doubt you will, not because I don't deserve it, but because you're intelligent, kind-hearted women (yes, even you, Ashleigh) and because, I hope, you loved me. I certainly loved you with all my heart. I was a fool to ever think that love was a myth and an even bigger fool to think it was a pain – because it is, but the happiest, most joyous pain anyone will ever know.

I went through hell after the attack on Pearl Harbor. I think, perhaps, it shook all of us up more than we realised and cut hard into our swaggering American confidence. It certainly did for mine, but I was brought out of it by love. The love of Charles, of my friends, and of my wonderful, brave, positive Lilinoe. She was my sister on the ground and ultimately in the skies, and I'm so, so glad we flew together again – as I know you two will fly too.

20 November 1943

Ginny eased herself into the cockpit and looked cautiously around, but already the nerves that had been pounding through her veins all morning were settling as she considered the world through the glorious curve of the plane's glass cover.

'OK there, Pilot Palakiko?'

Lili looked over her shoulder and beamed.

'Fabulous, Pilot Harris.' She giggled. 'Oh, Ginny, it's so good to be back.'

Ginny drew in a deep breath and touched her fingers to the stick.

'It is,' she agreed. 'It really is. I could never have done it without you, doll.'

'Of course not,' came back the jaunty reply. 'Nor I you. We fly together, remember?'

'I remember.'

Ginny thought back to that first time she'd seen Lili walking again and looked gratefully over to where Frank was standing, ready to cheer them into the air. He was leaning in to say something to Charles, and now the pair of them roared with laughter. Ginny smiled to see it. Next week she and Lili were off to the mainland to join the ferrying corps as the Allies ramped up the pressure on Germany, and Charles was going back to Washington, leaving only Frank here to keep treating the poor men and women maimed by this terrible war. Who knew where they'd all end up once it was finally over?

Charles would, she was sure, want to return to his precious Oxfordshire, and the other day she'd had a very interesting letter from one of the ATA leaders, asking her if she'd ever consider flying in England again. The RAF were talking about taking women into their ranks full time and would be open to considering their cross-Atlantic cousins for roles. It was an exciting possibility but a scary one too, and for today she was happy just to be here on her favourite island with her best friends.

It had been wonderful being with the Oahu gang again and last month, they'd all turned out for her and Lili's double wedding, right here in Honolulu, with a ceremony in the pretty Kawaiahao Church and a wonderful reception in the Royal Hawaiian Hotel. If Ginny closed her eyes, she could still picture Joe, Eddie, Dagne, Will and Helen lined up outside the church, airplane propeller blades held up in an arch for them to walk beneath. To Ginny's great surprise and joy, on the end, a little red-eyed but standing tall and proud, had been Penny, holding a blade of her own.

'This one's from Jack,' she'd said as Ginny had emerged beneath it, and Ginny had clasped her tight and wished with all her heart that there could have been three brides there that day. But life, as she'd learned the hard way, had to go on whatever tragedy cut up its path – that's why she was here now.

'Come on, dreamy,' Lili called into her thoughts. 'If we don't get onto the runway, we'll miss our slot and we can't have that on our first official flight, can we?'

'No, ma'am. Buckle up!'

Ginny started the engine and felt the hum of it throb through her like her own blood. She'd loved planes from the very first time she'd ever been near one and she loved them still, though now she perhaps respected them more. It had been a long road to here from Lili's hospital room, with interviews and retraining and hours on the simulators before they'd been allowed up. Today, at last, they were in a real plane, just the two of them, and it felt marvellous.

If this flight went well, they were heading to Seattle to join a squadron of other WASP ferrying B-17s down to California to be shipped across the Pacific for a huge assault on New Guinea, and they would both be proud to finally do their bit for the US war effort. The Axis forces were crumbling and a push would surely see the Allies heading for victory. It was all hands on deck, and even more so in the air.

Ginny turned the plane onto the runway and watched as the one in front of them accelerated down the tarmac and lifted lightly into the air. For a terrible moment, her heart quailed and her hand shook on the stick.

'You do it, Lili,' she said, but her friend shook her dark head.

'No. We agreed – you take the first turn around the island, I'll take the second.'

Ginny swallowed.

'I'm not sure I can do it,' she admitted, but Lili just looked back and smiled.

'Of course you can, Gin. Of course you can and if you struggle, I'm here. We fly this together.'

'We fly this together,' Ginny echoed, and then she set her eyes on the runway ahead, pulled back on the stick and sent them soaring upwards into the ocean-blue skies.

A Letter from Anna

Dear reader,

I want to say a huge thank you for choosing to read *A Letter from Pearl Harbor*. From the moment I discovered that there had been female pilots up in the air on the terrible morning that the Japanese bombed Pearl Harbor, I knew I had a story to tell and I really hope you enjoyed it. If you want to keep up to date with all my latest releases, just sign up at the following link. Your email address will never be shared and you can unsubscribe at any time.

www.bookouture.com/anna-stuart

As a Brit, I really only knew about Pearl Harbor as the disaster that brought the United States into the war but when I started to dive into not just the awful events of the day itself, but the months leading up to it, I became fascinated. Politically I found it really interesting but, more importantly for me, the lives of the individuals out on the beautiful island of Oahu were captivating – especially those of the female pilots.

The 1930s were the age of the aviatrix. In America, airshows became a hugely popular family entertainment, with stunt pilots drawing much admiration and the country going especially mad for glamorous females like Amelia Earhart. These darlings of the air performed feats of great skill and daring and the press loved them (google some of the wonderful pictures if you get a minute) but when it came to war, the American government was hugely reticent about allowing them into the forces. Theirs was a fight to be allowed to fight and I hope that *A Letter from Pearl Harbor* brings that struggle to life.

The modern-day story in this novel is also an important one to me. Ashleigh's horrible cycling accident is based on one that really happened to an amazing young man I knew a long time ago and who went on to play wheelchair tennis at a high level. The resilience and determination of so many people battling with disabilities is inspiring and I hope Ashleigh's story goes some way to demonstrating my admiration of their courage.

If you enjoyed this novel, I'd be very grateful if you could write a review. I'd love to hear what you think, and it makes such a difference helping new readers to discover one of my books for the first time. I also love hearing from my readers – you can get in touch on my Facebook page, through Twitter, Goodreads or my website.

Thanks for reading,
Anna

annastuartauthor

@annastuartbooks

www.annastuartbooks.com

Acknowledgements

This is the third of my World War II novels for Bookouture and I must credit my clever editor, Natasha Harding, for coming up with the idea of writing about Pearl Harbor. At first, I was sceptical of writing about what was essentially a horrible failure, but as I slowly unearthed the personal stories in the months leading up to the attack, I began to be truly inspired by both the island of Oahu and its varied inhabitants. It was when I came across Cornelia Fort and realised that a female pilot had been the very first person to be shot at by the invading Japanese that I knew I had my story. I didn't want to tell her life direct, so took the liberty of using her as a starting point for the character of Ginny, but truly the inspiration first started with Natasha, so thank you.

I also want to give a huge shout-out to the rest of the amazing team at Bookouture who have helped bring this book to the virtual shelves. Thank you so much to Alex in editorial, Alba in audio, to Sarah, Kim and Noelle in publicity, and to everyone in this wonderfully forward-thinking, proactive publishing house. Your belief, support and hard work is so much appreciated.

Talking of which, a big thank you, as always, to my agent Kate Shaw. I signed to Kate back in 2010 and in the last eleven years she has nurtured my hopes and dreams, talked me out of my (many) insecurities, and always been the voice of common sense and commercial know-how in this strange authorial path through life. Thank you, Kate xxx

On a more personal note, I couldn't do this without my husband, Stuart, who is very patient about the vagaries of life with a novelist. One of the problems with this otherwise wonderful job is that there is no one else in the 'office' to chew over your plans and your problems, so Stuart is the one who often has to stand as my sounding board. He's rarely expected to do anything more than listen as I talk myself around things, but he's often expected to do that for longer than I suspect is reasonable. He is ever-patient and I hope he knows how much it means to me.

This novel is dedicated to Barbie Short, my auntie, my god-mother and a great supporter of my writing, having stood as a brave and very helpful beta reader of almost all of my books. Her support was especially vital in the early years when sending my work out of the house into the scary big wide world felt even more daunting than it does now, but it's still hugely valued and appreciated today. Thank you, Barbie, and this one's for you!

Historical Notes

When I set about researching Pearl Harbor (about which, like Robyn and Ashleigh, I knew shockingly little), I was astonished to find that although the attack was a total surprise, there had also – with the wonders of hindsight – been many signs that it was a possibility. I really wanted to include some of these in the novel for verisimilitude and luckily it was highly likely that Ginny, as a pilot, would have been of the moneyed set (flying lessons were expensive!) so of the right social class to be mixing with the officers at Pearl. Although Jack, Ginny, Lilinoe and Kalani are all fictitious, many of the characters in the 1940s thread of this novel are real people who played an intrinsic part in the events of the terrible attack on Pearl Harbor.

Notable Real-Life Characters

Cornelia Fort was the first name that came up when I started researching female pilots and with good reason. She was in the air above Pearl Harbor when the Japanese swooped in on that fateful morning in December 1941 and I used her as the inspiration for Ginny in the novel. Born to a wealthy family from Nashville, she was the second woman in Tennessee to get her commercial pilot's licence and the first to get an instructor's licence.

Sadly, her story ends in tragedy. On 21 March 1943, as part of Nancy Love's ferrying squadron, she was flying in close formation with six male pilots in BT-13 Valiants when one of them accidentally flew into her plane, sending her into a spin and plummeting to earth. The plane hit the ground vertically and with such force that the engine was buried two feet in the ground, killing her instantly.

It's possible the tragedy was in part her own fault because flying in close formation wasn't permitted and it was this that gave me the idea for Ginny's own terrible accident.

Cornelia's funeral was held four days later. The coffin was draped with an American flag, but because WAFS were civilians, the army didn't pay for her funeral expenses and her widowed mother only got a $200 Civil Service Commission death benefit, rather than the $10,000 she'd have received if her daughter had been recognised as a military pilot like her male counterparts. It was one of many great injustices doled out to the brave women who just wanted to serve their country.

Jacqueline Cochran was a genuinely remarkable woman and deserves a book all of her own, but these brief notes will have to suffice. Forceful, brash and opinionated, she did not always make friends but she certainly got things done. She came from a very poor family of millworkers in the Florida Panhandle and dropped out of school for good aged eight to join the mill. She showed her fire immediately and was promoted to supervisor by the age of nine!

In 1920, aged fourteen, she got pregnant by Robert Cochran, married him and gave birth to a son. The marriage did not last long and, sadly, her son did not either, dying in May 1925. She buried him under a heart-shaped headstone then went off to start a new life as a beautician, eventually using her style, skill and undoubted panache to secure a job in the prestigious Saks salon on Fifth Avenue in New York, and working hard all her life to obscure her poor origins.

Jacqueline – Jackie to her friends - learned to fly as part of a bet with Floyd Bostwick Odlum, a self-made businessman reputed to be one of the ten richest men in America. He said that if she learned in six weeks, he'd pay for it; she did it in three weeks and three days. Floyd paid up and then married her! He backed her line of cosmetics, Wings to Beauty, which she promoted from her own aircraft. But her flying ambitions were far greater and she won the prestigious Bendix race in 1938, set records in both speed and altitude, and won her first of five Harmon trophies, a prize awarded to outstanding pilots.

Jacqueline met Eleanor Roosevelt in 1938 when the president's wife presented her with that first Harmon trophy, and again after Jacqueline flew a Lockheed bomber across the Atlantic in June 1941, as shown in the novel. Eleanor backed her proposal to use qualified female pilots for ferrying duties in August 1941 but, even so, Lieutenant General 'Hap' Arnold turned it down.

He proposed that Jacqueline take a group of women to fly with the ATA in England instead and promised that he would make no decisions regarding women flying until she returned. He then, however, gave in to the better-connected Nancy Love (see below), authorising the formation of the Women's Auxiliary Ferrying Squadron (WAFS) under her command. Needless to say, Jacqueline was furious and returned almost immediately to confront him. Arnold caved and formed the Women's Flying Training Detachment (WFTD) under her. In August 1943, the WAFS and the WFTD merged to create the Women Airforce Service Pilots (WASP) with Jacqueline as director and Nancy as head of the ferrying division.

Jacqueline's exploits in the air did not stop with the war. She was the first woman to break the sound barrier, the first woman to land and take off from an aircraft carrier, the first woman to make a blind (instrument) landing, the only woman ever to be president of the Fédération Aéronautique Internationale, and the first pilot to fly above 20,000 feet (6,096 m) with an oxygen mask. Sometimes known as the Speed Queen, at the time of her death in 1980, no other pilot held more speed, distance or altitude records in aviation history than the remarkable Jackie Cochran.

Nancy Love was also an impressive woman, though I give her little space and, perhaps unfairly, little credit in the novel. Totally oppo-

site to Jacqueline, she was from old money and got the flying bug
at a young age, gaining her pilot's licence at sixteen. She celebrated
by flying her brother dangerously close over her school, and only
avoided expulsion because they had a policy banning girls from
driving cars but not planes!

In 1932, she got her commercial licence, one of only fifty-six
women in the US to do so, and was offered a job at Inter-City
Aviation demonstrating planes to customers, to show they were
so easy to fly that even a woman could do it! The company was
owned by Robert Love. They were instantly attracted and married
in January 1936. Nancy worked as a commercial test pilot
throughout the 1930s, and in May 1940 she started talking to
the military top brass about female pilots – with greater success
than poor Jackie.

Writing this novel from the perspective of the girls in Jacqueline
Cochran's group, it is hard not to make Nancy Love seem in some
way an 'enemy'. In truth, she was a passionate and brilliant pilot
who was fighting, not exactly alongside Jacqueline Cochran but
certainly not against her, to allow women to fly for their country.

Marguerite Gambo was a young Hawaiian who was taught to fly
by Robert Tyce, achieved her commercial pilot's licence in 1937,
and established the Gambo Flying Service. Like Cornelia Fort
and my invented Ginny, she was in the air on the morning of 7
December 1941, taking a student on a cross-country trip. Luckily
that put her out of the immediate path of the incoming Japanese,
and she managed to navigate her little plane through a seldom-used
mountain pass and land safely.

Robert Tyce ran K-T Flying Service and snapped up the chance to
join the government's Civilian Pilot Training Program in the late

1930s, increasing his fleet to ten planes – all Piper Cubs – and taking on new instructors, such as the fictitious Ginny in the novel. Tyce was killed by a Japanese bullet on 7 December, the first recorded civilian death on that sad day.

Lieutenant Commander Edwin Thomas Layton – a thirty-eight-year-old fleet intelligence officer who liaised between the naval intelligence department and Admiral Kimmel. Handsome and something of a ladies' man (Dagne was his second wife of three), he had a brilliant mind and, like his best friend Joe Rochefort, was wounded by the intelligence failures at Pearl Harbor and worked tirelessly throughout the rest of the war to repair that damage.

Commander Joseph John Rochefort – a forty-one-year-old 'mustang' (an enlistee in the Great War who'd made it as an officer without a diploma from the Naval Academy) who ran the Combat Intelligence Unit out of a cellar room known as the Dungeon. A talented cryptanalyst, it was his skills that led to the Americans surprising the Japanese at Midway and to the assassination of Admiral Yamamoto.

Admiral Patrick Bellinger – a hero of the Great War and a renowned pilot. He was made a Rear Admiral in December 1940 and sent to Pearl Harbor where, in March 1941, he prepared a report that warned of precisely how a Japanese attack might come – getting it eerily spot on (see below).

Lieutenant William (Billy) W. Outerbridge – a junior officer, given command of the *Ward* destroyer just two days before the attack.

He apparently missed his wife, Grace, and three little boys, but was so wrapped up in the excitement of his role on 7 December that it took five days before he thought to let her know that he was alive! A cheerful soul, he later wrote to her more fully describing his promotion thus: 'Joined the ship Friday, got under way Saturday morning, and started the war on Sunday.'

William Dauth – nephew-in-law to Admiral Kimmel via his wife, Helen, who came out to Hawaii a week before the attack.

Admiral Husband E. Kimmel – the fit and apparently youthful fifty-nine-year-old commander of the navy at Pearl Harbor.

Major General Walter C. Short – commander of the army on Oahu.

One of the most ridiculous aspects of the military situation at Pearl Harbor was that the navy and army ran alongside one another with no overall commander. Kimmel had made big leaps forward in communicating with Short (they were due to play golf on the morning of 7 December!) but it wasn't enough. Short was obsessed with sabotage from the native Japanese (little evidence of any was ever found) and it was he who lined all his planes up in the middle of the runway, thus making them easy targets.

An overall commander on Oahu, whilst he would still have been victim of the poor communication from Washington and the general complacency about the location of Pearl Harbor, could quite possibly have set up the whole area in a more efficient and coordinated way and helped repel the terrible attack more effectively.

Timeline of Events

I hope I have given a good indication of the critical events before and on the fateful day of the Pearl Harbor attack, but for those who are interested in precise detail, here is a timeline:

29 April 1940: Roosevelt moves the entire fleet to Pearl Harbor, despite concerns that it will look aggressive to Japan.

27 September 1940: Japan enters into military alliance with the Germans and Italians.

1 February 1941: Admiral Husband Kimmel is placed in command of the navy at Pearl Harbor.

31 March 1941: Rear Admiral Bellinger and Major General Martin present a document detailing how the Japanese could execute a surprise attack on Pearl Harbor. They note that:

- Japan has never preceded hostile acts with a declaration of war.
- The most likely form of attack will be by air.
- It will be launched from one or more carriers, probably inside 300 miles of Oahu.
- They will attack at dawn so they can fly in close under cover of darkness.

Their conclusion, chillingly, is: 'That Orange submarines and/ or an Orange fast raiding force might arrive in Hawaiian waters with no prior warning from our intelligence service' – exactly what happened!

July 1941: Japan takes Southern Indochina, giving them a launchpad to attack the Malay peninsula, British Singapore, Thailand, Burma and India.

August 1941: The US impose an embargo on oil and gas exports to Japan until they withdraw.

26 November 1941: Washington delivers an ultimatum to Japan, outlining their 'Ten Points' to peace, but the Japanese fleet has already sailed for Pearl Harbor, 3,150 miles away.

27 November: The passenger ships *Lurline* and *Matsonia* sail into Honolulu from California to a party-like reception. One arrival is Helen Dauth, niece of Husband Kimmel. In Washington, Admiral Harold Stark, Chief of Naval Operations, sends a dispatch to all commanders in the Pacific which opens: 'This dispatch is to be considered a war warning.' It goes on to say that 'an aggressive move by Japan is expected within the next few days' but suggests that Japanese troop movement 'indicates an amphibious expedition against either the Philippines, Thai or Kra Peninsula or possibly Borneo.' Those areas named go on high alert; Pearl Harbor does not.

28 November: The *Enterprise* aircraft carrier leaves for Wake Island. Major General Short puts soldiers on guard all over Hawaii, fearing sabotage from the local Japanese population. He orders his six mobile radar units to operate 4 a.m.–7 a.m., though still as a training exercise rather than on high alert.

30 November: The Japanese change their codes only a month after last doing so, instead of the usual six.

2 December: Kimmel asks for an estimation of all Japanese fleet positions. Layton delivers what he can, including four missing carriers, but they are presumed to be in port.

3 December: The Americans' 'Magic' decoding machine picks up a message to the Japanese embassy in Washington telling them to destroy one of two code machines and all documents, strongly suggesting war is imminent.

5 December: The second big aircraft carrier, the *Lexington*, leaves Pearl Harbor for Midway, meaning there are no carriers left in port. However, the battleships *Arizona*, *Nevada* and *Oklahoma* return from a week of exercises, so all eight battleships are in the harbour for the weekend. Billy Outerbridge is assigned as captain of the destroyer *Ward*.

6 December: Billy is ordered to take the *Ward* out of Pearl Harbor to 'carve lazy laps' on watch for subs. Kimmel receives intelligence from Manila saying that thirty-six Japanese transports and twenty-eight warships are rounding the tip of Indochina, assumed to be heading for the Philippines.

7 December: Overnight listeners pick up the final Magic intercept of the Japanese response to the peace demands, which says 'all hope of peace has finally been lost'. Messages are also picked up to the Japanese embassy, telling the ambassador to officially present this message at 1 p.m. (7 a.m. Hawaiian time) and to destroy the last code machine and all remaining documents. It is clear an attack is coming, though not yet where. Bets are still on the Philippines. A message is passed to the army dispatch centre to send to Hawaii as an alert, but the radio signal is disrupted by atmospheric interference so they have to send a telegram which doesn't make it in time.

Meanwhile, in Hawaii:

4 a.m.: A navy minesweeper reports a periscope off the harbour entrance. The *Ward* goes to inspect but finds nothing.

6.37 a.m.: Billy Outerbridge is called urgently to the bridge of the *Ward* and now he does see a periscope, heading into harbour just behind the *Antares* cargo ship. They fire on it and take it out. At 6.54 he radios an urgent message about the enemy sub but it does not get passed on to Kimmel, at home, until 7.30 a.m. He is not unduly worried and issues no orders.

7.02 a.m.: At the radar unit at Opana, George Elliot and Joseph Lockard pick up a massive blob of unknown, inbound aircraft. They report it to the command post but it is assumed that this is twelve B-17s coming in from California, and they are told to turn off the machine and go for breakfast!

Around 7.30 a.m.: Cornelia Fort takes off in her flimsy Interstate plane with a pupil. Also in the air are Marguerite Gambo and five other light aircraft. Only five of the seven will make it back.

7.48 a.m.: The attack commences with a first wave of 183 planes, led by Commander Mitsuo Fuchida. They fly past Cornelia Fort and she has to make a hasty landing under fire. The first torpedoes hit the *Nevada*, the *California*, the *West Virginia* and the *Oklahoma*, which overturns in minutes, trapping hundreds of men inside.

8 a.m.: Kimmel leaves his house to find Japanese planes everywhere. As he drives down, a bomb hits the forward magazine of the *Arizona*, and she explodes with a huge bang and disappears in a mass of smoke that reaches a thousand feet.

8.12 a.m.: Kimmel's office radios to the fleet still at sea and to Main Navy in Washington: 'Hostilities with Japan commenced with air raid on Pearl Harbor.' Admiral Bellinger sends a further message to Washington: 'Air Raid Pearl Harbor. This is no drill.' The next wave of Japanese planes sweeps in, hitting many more ships. Oil spreads across the water, catching fire and burning men trying to escape the sinking ships. The smoke dims the tropical light and the noise is thunderous. Kimmel can only watch from the submarine building's second deck as the fleet is destroyed. At one point, his window is broken by a bullet, striking him just above the heart and tumbling him to the floor. He reportedly says: 'It would have been merciful had it killed me.'

8.17 a.m.: Kimmel radios Bellinger to order the patrol planes to 'locate enemy force', but the Japanese have already taken out many planes, including almost all of the army's, clumped together on the runway. A few make it into the air but most are destroyed.

9.18 a.m.: Ninety minutes after it began, the attack is over. 2,008 sailors have been killed and 710 wounded. Eighteen ships have sunk or run aground, including five battleships.

8 December: Roosevelt speaks to a joint session of Congress, describing 7 December, famously, as 'a date which will live in infamy' (a change he made to his original draft; 'a date which will live in world history'). Within an hour of the speech, Congress

passes a formal declaration of war against Japan and officially brings the US into World War II.

Air Transport Auxiliary

The Air Transport Auxiliary (ATA) was set up across Britain to ferry new, repaired and damaged military aircraft between factories, assembly plants, repair depots and airfields. The aim was to use pilots unfit for active service, and from 14 November 1939, Commander Pauline Gower was tasked with organising a women's section. The first eight female pilots were accepted into service on 1 January 1940. At first they only flew Tiger Moths, but they soon moved on to flying virtually every type used by the RAF, including the heavy bombers. Hurricanes were first flown by women pilots in July 1941, and the coveted Spitfires a month later.

As the war progressed, one in eight ATA pilots were female and 166 women flew in total, including volunteers from Canada, Australia, New Zealand, South Africa, the United States, the Netherlands, Poland, Argentina and Chile. One of their more notable achievements is that, under a ruling of 1943, they were the first to receive equal pay to men of equal rank. Overall, they were treated far more fairly and honourably than their American counterparts, who were given as little as 65 per cent of the pay of their male equivalents and no military honours or benefits.

Training at Houston

The first class of Jackie Cochran's training programme was, as shown in the novel, set up at the Howard R. Hughes Airport in Houston, and everything described about the ridiculous set-up there was true.

Lili and Ginny are fictious, as is Thelma, but Marion Florsheim was real and truly did take a suite for herself and her two Afghan hounds in the very smart Warwick Hotel for the duration of her training. Marylou Colbert was the daughter of Rear Admiral Leo Otis Colbert, who did pin her wings onto her lapel at graduation. What is also true is that the women were mainly rich girls not used to *any* discipline, let alone army discipline, and far from the most cooperative cadets!

The poor woman with that job was thirty-nine-year-old Leni Leoti 'Dedie' Deaton, a housewife, mother, scout leader and general community volunteer who was more or less railroaded into the job by Jackie. She was helped by a sympathetic army lieutenant, Alfred Fleishman, but the commanding officer Captain Paul C. Garrett and his adjutant captain, Jessie L. Simon, were apparently openly hostile to having women on their base.

The first recruits really were asked to keep their jobs a secret and were encouraged to state that they were part of a girls' basketball team, which was very tricky for those women, like Lilinoe, who were barely above five feet tall! Their only canteen or toilets really were at the Houston Municipal Airport Terminal, a mile away. And the final, unbelievable truth is that the bus Dedie found to transport the girls to the airfield had previously been used to transport a Tyrolean orchestra, so was white with red-and-white striped awning and decorated all over with edelweiss! These highly skilled volunteer women were only trying to serve their country and were treated very poorly, especially in this first class.

Honolulu Landmarks

The Royal Hawaiian Hotel was opened in 1927 by the Matson Navigation Company to house the richer of the passengers on their luxury liners coming in from California. It was designed in an elaborate Moorish style, exaggerated with pink paint, which was very popular in the period and remains today.

The Mai Tai has a disputed history. Its invention is claimed by 'Trader Vic', who served it in his tiki bar in California, and it was probably brought to Hawaii via the Matson liners after the war. However, 'Don the Beachcomber' had a Mai Tai swizzle on his Hollywood bar menu back in 1933, so it seems that versions of the drink were around earlier and, most likely, enjoyed by both men on their travels. At the Royal Hawaiian, orange and pineapple were added to what had originally been a simpler – and stronger – cocktail of rum, orange Curaçao, syrup and mint, creating the Royal Hawaiian Mai Tai that purists will tell you is not the 'true' cocktail, but is usually the most popular one. This version wasn't recorded until the 1950s, but I hope readers will forgive me the poetic licence that allows Ginny to enjoy the iconic Hawaiian cocktail in the hotel that eventually became famous for it.

Kau Kau Korner opened as a twenty-four-hour drive-in restaurant in 1935 and was hugely popular with the young people of Honolulu. As described in the novel, you could drive into the parking lot in your car, and order fried chicken and soft drinks from carhop waitresses in short skirts and soda hats. Music would be played and sometimes a live DJ operated out of a glass enclosure in the parking lot.

On the far side of the lot was the Crossroads of the Pacific sign, made famous by numerous photos taken beneath it (well worth a google). This sign shows the distance to various cities around the world and demonstrates how very central the Hawaiian archipelago is to the Pacific – and how very far away it was from anywhere else. No wonder the people stationed there felt safe from Japanese attack…